To Rosie
with fond and

Bob Muscutt

Robert Muscutt

A Life For A Life
The Real Story of Mary Ball

EUGEP
Röthlein und Karlowski GbRmbH
www.eugep.com

A Life For A Life
The Real Story Of Mary Ball

EUGEP
Röthlein und Karlowski GbRmbH
www.eugep.com

Hardcover
First Edition 2006

published by
EUGEP Röthlein und Karlowski GbRmbH

Cover:
Lars Kirkow

ISBN 3-933570-14-X

Dear Reader

This book dramatises a real event: the execution, and the events leading up to it, of my great, great grandmother, Mary Ball, in Coventry, shortly after 10 o'clock on Thursday, 9th of August 1849 for the murder of her husband, Thomas Ball. She was the last woman to be publicly hanged in Warwickshire.

The trial and the hanging are extensively described in contemporary documents kept by the Coventry and Nuneaton municipal Libraries. I have made use of these and other authentic sources in my research. Nevertheless, I ask you to read the novel, apart from the stark fact of the execution, as if it were purely fiction. Even when real names and places are seemingly mentioned, they still serve the single purpose of making the story as good as I can tell it.

The web site: http://www.eugep.com/maryball awaits those interested in unravelling fact from fiction, as well as other issues connected with Mary's story.

My express thanks go to:

The Nuneaton and North Warwickshire Family History Society, especially its Chairman, Peter Lee; individual members of the NNWFHS for their generosity in sharing the results of their research, in particular Kate Keens; The Coventry Police Museum in Little Park Street passionately cared for by Tony Rose; Keith Cook of Manor Park, East London for initial and sustained advice; my sister Linda Mayne, for her enthusiasm and logistical support.

Both myself and the publishers acknowledge with thanks the permission granted by the Nuneaton Public Library for the use of a lithograph in their possession which provides the background on the cover of this book. The picture depicts Nuneaton's Trent Valley Railway Station in the mid-nineteenth century. We also thank Marc Platte (Solingen, Germany) for supplying the original picture for the cover's image of the female face.

Dedication

To the memory of my parents Frank Arthur and Grace Edith Muscutt (born Farnell), especially my mother whose paternal grandmother was Mary Ball's only child of six to survive infancy.

This is the point I aim at: I do not wish (women) to have power over men: but over themselves.

Mary Wollstonecraft, in A VINDICATION OF THE RIGHTS OF WOMAN

Prologue

Despite the hot August weather John Astley had decided to dress formally for the unannounced visit he was making. His starched white collar scratched irritatingly at his neck as he nervously lifted the brass knocker on the front door of the newly-built terraced house. He held the polished sliver of metal, ran his thumb over its smooth surface and hesitated. He still had the chance to lower it gently, silently and return to his shop, leaving no trace, not even a ripple of curiosity to record his presence. Duty, commitment to the truth, responsibility to preserve the past, the promised fulfilment of someone's dying wish; these were the phrases his rational self had used to justify his impulsive decision. But this dapper, silvery-haired man knew himself well enough to acknowledge that the real motivation was emotional, a kind of love that spread almost physically through his body like a muscular vine whenever his thoughts dwelled on the events of twenty years before. His neck was itching and he would have liked to loosen his collar but, with the door knocker in one hand and the large, thick parcel in the other, he was forced to wait uncomfortably aggravated. Whatever apologies he construed for delivering the parcel, they would seem expedient, even self-indulgent against the upheaval he might cause Lizzie when she read its contents. His eyes closed as if he were fatigued by the swirling tensions inside him and he settled them by abruptly rapping the brass knob more sharply and more times than he intended. Almost immediately he saw through the door's narrow opaque glass panels, a vague figure slowly approaching on the inside and his indecision dissipated like water drowning in sand. As the door opened he recognised the woman he had hoped would be at home, Lizzie Farnell, and noticed that her initial look of surprise quickly relaxed into a slight smile of understanding.

"Mr Astley! Of all people you're the last I expected."

Of course, they knew each other by sight. Astley still kept the general stores in the market place, now much modernised with bright gas lighting and an expansive eye-catching street front window, the shop which his father had started in the times when the flames of the French Revolution were still unnerving most of Britain with their ominous if distant glow and which had quickly become the town's centre of Jacobin debate and reformist agitation. As the recently appointed official Inspector of Public Nuisances, a kind of roaming ombudsman, John Astley was to be seen wherever a drain stank or a gas light didn't combust. A local celebrity in the town with a reputation for outspoken criticism of what most regarded reverently as the march of progress, he dedicated his talents and his time to investigating and reporting with informed persistence the complaints of the town's poorest inhabitants. Undoubtedly things had changed since the turn of the century but especially so in the last twenty years. New industries like quarries and brickworks, attracted by the excellent transport links by rail and canal for their bulky goods, as well as traditional coal-mining, rejuvenated by an influx of capital and technology, found a ready supply of experienced labour due to the long decline, almost demise of the weaving trade. The town's streets were now almost all gas lit and the High Street boasted a bright diversity of shops on either side of its hard, all-weather macadamised surface. Always a Radical, Astley welcomed improvement and innovation such as the sewers, the hospital and the efficient municipal administration, especially when they benefited the mass of the population still living in poverty and insecurity.

But his intellectual concern as well as his emotional obsession was also with the past, with ensuring that whatever was of value was not swept away in the purblind enthusiasm of social reformation and this had motivated his visit to the young woman who now greeted him, framed in the doorway of her new home. The difference in their ages and the fact he had known her since her mother had brought her along into his shop as a baby in arms, entitled him to call this married woman, now only a few weeks before the birth of her first child, by her first name. Partly out of impatience and partly out of a polite eagerness to explain the reason for his appearance, he wasted no time with formalities.

"Lizzie, you know what today marks."

Of course she knew. Not a single anniversary of this day, of her mother's execution, had gone unmentioned by her Aunt Jane when they had still lived together in one house. In fact, in those twenty years her Aunt Jane had taken every opportunity to demand gratitude for adopting and caring for her, which her niece granted. But she also required proof that Lizzie supported her unappeasable condemnation of the child's own mother. Here, Jane bit on granite and Lizzie steadfastly and calmly refused to render her this tribute.

"The twentieth anniversary," was all she said, apparently without feeling, though she'd been thinking about it constantly all day, and he followed her through the dim passageway into the kitchen at the back of the house.

His consciously brisk and matter-of-fact manner had relaxed involuntarily when she spoke. She signalled to him to sit down and she placed the kettle on the hob of the meticulously clean stove. She was barefoot and wore a loose-fitting coarse dress and, despite her heavy pregnancy, looked and felt at ease even in the hot weather. Though her long black hair was unpinned, she had pushed it back behind her head and fastened it with a simple ribbon so that he could see her face with its strong, bold features.

"You're so like her. When you were a baby, a child, you resembled your father more. But not now," he said in a softer, less tense voice.

She didn't resent Astley's familiar remarks but she was still slightly uncomfortable with this older man who knew so much about her mother and about herself, an unease with the advantage he had over her. As if sensing this he changed the subject and nodded towards her belly, with its almost spherical boast of pregnancy.

"Soon?"

"I hope so."

"And the name?"

"If it's a boy, William. William Arthur."

It was the usual choice for a first born son – the names of the father and the paternal grandfather.

"And if it's a girl?"

She knew Astley was hoping she'd say Mary and she didn't want to disappoint him.

"I wanted to call her Mary Jane, or even Jane Mary, out of gratitude to my aunt. She has brought me up as she promised, after all. But she said she won't share the name with my mother, with *that woman* as she calls her. She's making me choose. I haven't decided yet."

"I hope it's a girl, Lizzie. And I hope you choose Mary."

He paused, ridiculously having to force back tears for which there was no evident reason, and placed the big envelope, tied both longwise and across with thick ribbon, onto the table between them.

"That's why I'm here. I wanted to give you this."

She noticed for the first time how thick the packet was, at least four inches deep. He recognised the genuine consternation on her face as she tried in vain to imagine what could be wrapped in the paper. Her fingers moved without much energy, picking at the knotted ribbon bow.

"You needn't open it now. I can tell you what's in it. It's everything I know about your mother, more than anybody else knows. Even more than Jane. Perhaps more than she knew herself. Documents. Letters. Some bits of my diary. Pages from, let's say, somebody else's diary. And the newspaper reports. Read them last, Lizzie. Read the rest first. Try not to judge."

"I won't judge my mother, Mr Astley."

"Well, I don't just mean Mary. Others too."

Noticing the softness in his voice when he spoke her mother's name, it occurred to her that this sharp-eyed, compassionate man, a bachelor well-known for his philandering and flagrant disregard for the middle-classes' prudish morality, may have known her mother even more closely than she had assumed.

"Were you friends, you and my mother? I mean, real friends?"

"We weren't lovers." He used the word without embarrassment or innuendo and she suspected neither. "But real friends."

They drank tea without speaking at the rough wooden table in the centre of the room, the door onto the backyard wide open to let whatever fresh air there was into the stiflingly warm kitchen.

"There were the three of us really. Me, Mary and Lizzie."

He added quickly in answer to her inquisitive look.

"Yes. She named you after her. And the ones that died. All called Lizzie. They'd come into the shop, Lizzie and Mary, or Polly as we called her then. Always laughing and happy. That was a long time before she'd even met your father though."

He leaned forward and laid his hand briefly on the back of her hand.

"I've never told anyone this before, but it was Lizzie I loved. If she'd have taken me, there was nothing that could have stopped me marrying her. Nothing. Not her past or the way she lived. But even then when she was 16 or so, before she left, she knew what life she wanted and it didn't include me."

She sensed that he was drifting away from her into memories he couldn't share with her, she asked hastily:

"And my mother?"

Searching for the right words, he looked around the small, neat room with its simple but sturdy furniture, its own pump over the deep butler's sink, the small but definitely increasing number of brass, decorative objects around the stove – nothing luxurious or superfluous but everything just slightly better and more abundant than necessity dictated.

"I know you're life's not easy, Lizzie. But you probably can't imagine what it was like then, twenty, thirty, forty years ago. To me when I was young the world seemed to be made of, of mud."

She laughed spontaneously, warming to this pert middle-aged man, whose accurate words and decent manner created such a reassuring intimacy between them.

"I used to walk over the coal fields sometimes. Fields we called them! The mines were tiny compared with today and they were surrounded by these fields, meadows, flats, I don't know what to call them. Coal-pit fields or black banks they call them in the mining villages. No grass, not even weeds, just slack, shale, slate. Sometimes flat, sometimes drifting into steep banks and hillocks I'd have to climb over. It was dusty and soft and its surface gave way so that my feet sank into it up to my knees in places. That's another thing I think of when I try to remember what life was like then. And the incessant rattling and shaking of the looms. For your mother, life was work. Either in the house, in your grand-parents' pub, then at Muscat's mill, or at the loom at home. But her brain was busier than her hands and feet. To look at her you'd think she was just like the other girls of her age. Better-looking than most, but normal. She wasn't though. There was something different about Mary. Everybody who knew her noticed it. Some frowned on it, some hated it, others were even afraid of it."

He paused and looked at the daughter but spoke as if to the mother who had been dead for twenty years.

"In spite of everything it led to, I think it was something good. I'm glad I knew her."

He patted the envelope.

"You'll find it all in here."

*

As soon as Astley had gone, she opened the packet and began to read. William, her husband, arrived home in the early evening when the light was still good and only laughed in his permanently good-humoured way when she admitted she'd forgotten to get him something to eat. He went to bed soon after darkness fell, kissing her on the forehead before he left her reading. For the next few days she went to bed long after dark and rose before first light almost every day, reading through everything in the envelope. Some parts she read several times. Without stopping to wonder how Astley had got hold of all the documents – pages removed carefully from William Bacon's diary, Home Office reports on Chartist activities, his own diary included notes of long conversations with Charles Hardcastle, and Hetty Cameron, a fellow-inmate of her mother's in Coventry's prison – she read every page, every sentence, every word, convinced of their authenticity by the way everything fell into place and fitted without the least friction into what her instincts told her was a cohesive pattern of truth. Stopping only for necessary breaks, she read for as long as she could stay awake for several days and nights. William, who had heard that pregnancy could also affect a woman's mind almost as much as her body, became worried and, without chiding, asked if her almost unbroken concentration on the papers might be harmful to her and the child. All she could do was to acknowledge his concern by gently stroking his face, knowing that she couldn't yet explain her preoccupation. She knew she wouldn't be able to stop and hardly even interrupt her reading until she had scrutinised and understood every single word of the mass of documents.

By the time she had finished, she felt she knew her mother as well as she knew anybody – even better perhaps than she had until then known her Aunt Jane. But, despite the sense of discovery, of revelation, she still felt an unremitting restlessness which occupied her during the day and woke her at night, a sense that something essential but indefinable was still missing. Sitting in the cool darkness of the kitchen in the early hours of the morning, her unseeing eyes transfixed on the indifferent blackness outside the window, she decided on impulse to travel the next day to the place where her mother had been hanged. She told William, but his protests were of course short-lived and he had quickly busied himself making her something to eat for the journey. He'd loved her ever since his senses had been able to register her presence and, though the strength of her determination, once she'd decided on what she believed was right, sometimes disconcerted him, he'd always support her rather than try in vain to dissuade her. On his way to work he considered dropping by at the station to ask the Master, a friend of his and Lizzie's, to watch out for her, but knew she'd resent it if she found out and so he resigned himself to a day of probably groundless worrying.

*

For the other passengers in the second class carriage, the sight of a robustly handsome young woman making no effort to conceal her advanced pregnancy was slightly unnerving, for others simply indecent. Comfortable and relaxed in the light cotton dress, perfect for both the hot weather and her own condition, she ignored the looks, the haughty sniffs and even subdued comments she attracted and gripped the small bag on her lap, now thinking for the first time about what she would do when she arrived at the prison. She'd reassured William when he left the house, knowing full well the effect what Aunt Jane called her headstrong vanity and stubbornness had on him. However, after several stops, as the train pulled out of Bedworth station for the last few miles to Coventry, she began to wonder if it really had been wise to make this journey without any preparation and she began to feel some apprehension. But before she really began to regret the journey the train was pulling into the station in the centre of Coventry.

As soon as she got off the train in the busy railway station, all her doubts evaporated and she made her way purposefully forwards, following the instructions her Uncle John had given her, only after making her swear never to tell his wife he'd been in any way a party to her reckless venture. Past the cathedral, she turned into Pepper Lane and at once saw the prison's massive, flat-fronted brick wall. Instantly and without conscious premeditation, her body stopped moving as if her mind had deserted it. From Astley's documents, especially from the drawing on the penny broadsheet which had been sold in the streets of Coventry on the day of the execution, she knew she was gazing at the exact spot where the scaffold had been erected and where her mother had dropped to her death. To the left of the twenty-foot wall was a flat-topped tower with an arched wooden gate, which she assumed would take her inside. Before she moved towards it, a policeman approached her.

"You feeling alright Missus?"

She pointed at the gate.

"Is that the entrance to the prison?"

"Well, it was the entrance, yes. Place closed a few years ago though. It's in Warwick now."

It was almost as if she had been expecting this nevertheless brutal confirmation that the journey had after all been a silly idea. The constable must have mistaken her visible disappointment for pain.

"Look, are you sure you're alright? I think you'd better come with me, love."

Suddenly too tired and indifferent to resist, she let him lead her a few hundred yards to a small, obviously new police station.

"Take a seat here, dear and I'll get you some water. Or any tea going, Henry?"

The Constable behind the desk brought a mug of tea, a jug of water and a glass to the small table where Lizzie was sitting.

"Look, I have to be getting back on the beat. Constable Robinson here will get you back on your feet again."

He exchanged a few muffled words with the duty Constable and left.

"Are you lost, Missus? Or were you wanting to visit somebody in the old prison? I can find out for you if they're in Warwick if you like. If you just give me a name."

The tea and the coolness of the station had brought Lizzie back to her senses and she answered the attentive policeman.

"My name? Lizzie Farnell." She paused, realising how involved an explanation of why she was there was going to be so she simply said: "My mother was Mary Ball."

He looked at her intently, trying to guess her age and compare it with the time of her mother's death.

"So you must have been a baby then?"

"You've heard of her?"

"Who hasn't? Especially us in the force."

He hesitated.

"I saw it all. About ten I was then. Must have been getting on for thirty thousand people here, only for the … Only to watch."

Again he tried to assess her reaction to what he was saying, not wishing to upset a woman so near to giving birth. No knowing what it might bring on. That would be an inconvenient turn up – Mary Ball's grandchild, born in a police station almost within sight of where she herself had been hanged and that almost twenty years ago to the day! But his experienced eye concluded that she was a strong woman who had probably made a bit of a journey to be there. Now he was restless to speak out, but before he came out with what he really wanted to say, he probed more.

"Strange I've never seen you here before, though."

"I came from Nuneaton. By train."

He waited and she continued.

"Don't ask me why I came today of all days. It was a mad idea. Apart from the heat, I'm close to my time."

She patted her belly.

"I thought I might be able to talk to someone who knew her. The Governor perhaps."

She drank the rest of a glass of water and was on the point of leaving.

"You'd better wait a minute or two, Mrs Farnell. It's a goodish way back. There's a clean new privy out the back."

He nodded towards a side door, as if trying to shake away the practical indelicacy of his remark. He paused again and fidgeted with the long quill on the desk in front of him as she left. When she returned, he said:

"Look, Mrs Farnell, Warwick's too far for you to travel today. In this heat and everything. But I don't like to see you come all this way for nothing. Just wait a minute, would you?"

He took a key from a hook on the wall and disappeared through a door behind him. Although he had closed the door she could hear the rattle of a key in a metal lock, a heavy door creaking open, then closing, and the Constable re-appeared holding something wrapped in thick, waxed paper. He sat down at the table, opposite her, laid the small parcel on the wooden surface and unwrapped it meticulously. As soon as she saw it, Lizzie knew what it was. Cast in plaster twenty years before, it had acquired a sombre bronze colour, and now it lay there on the table, her mother's death mask. The full, smooth solidity of the material blended faultlessly with the strong, rounded features. Even closed, the large, slightly bulging eyes demanded attention. The overall impression was one of contentment, even serenity. The policeman spoke Lizzie's thoughts exactly when he said:

"She seems to be almost smiling, doesn't she? I wonder why. Everyone who sees it does."

Lizzie ran her fingers over the eyelids and her fingertips felt the broad nose with its tiny bump, something she had inherited from her mother, and then the full lips of the confident, broad mouth. She closed her own eyes and lay the open palm of her hand gently over the whole face, as if trying to absorb its physical entirety. It was only when she realised that tears were flowing down her cheeks that she opened and began to wipe her eyes. He watched her with dispassionate fascination. In an effort to regain her composure she asked:

"It's her, isn't it?"

He nodded superfluously.

"We don't show it to people generally. Perhaps we'd have to take entrance money if we did!"

She squinted questioningly.

"Hardly a month or week goes by that we don't notice some woman standing where the constable found you. Just gazing at the wall. Some of them are crying, a few praying. We don't know why. They never speak to us and if they did, I daresay they couldn't tell us why they come. Pilgrimage of evil, the

Reverend at St. Michael's Church calls it. I don't agree though. I can't explain it. She just seems to touch their lives somehow. I don't suppose we'll ever know why. Forgive me for being so blunt, Mrs Farnell, but that's all that's left of her now. Not even a photograph. Just this death mask. That doesn't tell us much, does it?"

She felt the warm contours again, this time her eyes wide open, noticing that there was no reflection from the matt, polished surface, as if behind the glow of the deep golden and black static veneer there was an interior where something was stored. Impetuously, crazily, she turned the mask over, as if expecting to find a legible record of all the knowledge and experience the inscrutable facial exterior implied. Constable Robinson saw the gesture and spoke with spontaneous sympathy.

"You won't find her there, love. There's nothing behind the face any more. It's just a mask."

Chapter 1

Nuneaton, 1832. For its muddy streets and slightly raised
stone pavements to be swarming with people on a mid-
December morning was probably unique in the history of the
small market town. Every year in May, the flat meadows they
called the Pingles would be covered by the stalls, side-shows
and livestock for the three days of the Wakes and, occasionally,
a boxing contest would have the land alongside the canal,
bordering the Earl of Newdigate's estate, thronging with a
chaotic cross section of the local population. When the
aeronaut Green landed his hot-air balloon just outside the
town to start the celebrations to mark the passing of the Great
Reform Bill in the summer that year, most people could not
imagine anything like the extravagance of the following week
ever being repeated. Beer and beef, paid for willingly by
subscriptions from the local Independent manufacturers and
grudgingly by the town's fewer members of the lower gentry,
were distributed free to all adults. Processions, entertainments
and festivities lasted till well after dark every night of the week.
And the Waxworks Exhibition caused a sensation in the town,
its four caravans parked end to end and decorated to look like
a great ship, the entrance being through the stern. All the
scenes were perfectly presented and subtly illuminated to
provide a spectacle long-remembered in the town; the horrors
of the French Revolution culminating in the ascendancy of the
arch-enemy Napoleon; Nelson and Wellington in heroic

postures and full uniform; an ostensibly morally indignant but, for most spectators, titivating portrayal of a slave market featuring a beautiful, scantily-clad nubile female slave. As an additional subject of marvel, the complete and perfectly reconstructed skeleton of a whale had been fitted out with tables and chairs, providing an exotic dining room for a couple of dozen of the local dignitaries.

But however spectacular and memorable these events were, they had all been carefully planned and organised attractions, craftily designed to induce celebration and entertainment. But now, on the blustery, damp winter morning, no persuasion had been needed to fetch the folks out of the innumerable public houses, the small mills and workshops, the damp mines and coal-fired warmth of their own homes. Today, they were neither observers nor even participants but the pageant itself, and the whole town was like a raked fire, throwing up a fountain of sparks in a rare burst of vivacity. The two adolescent girls walking briskly towards the Market Square were no different to most others in that they didn't really know what to expect from the coming day but were determined not to miss any of it. The younger of the two, Mary, short, sturdy, dark-haired and already on the verge of becoming an attractive young woman, had sneaked away from her family's public house to meet her slightly older friend, Lizzie. In comparison with others of her age, Lizzie already led an unusual, adventurous life and shared a lot of its excitement with Mary. Wrapped up, almost swaddled as she was against the drizzly winter weather, Lizzie still attracted looks from almost all the men, and some women, who passed near her. Golden brown curls spilled out from under the shawl she'd draped untidily over her face. Her skirts were hitched up only a few inches below her knees to keep them out of the mud, showing off the naked ankles and calves to anyone who cared to look. Mary herself was a good-looking girl of fourteen and already had to deal with enough advances when she helped out in the family pub, but Lizzie was something different - staggeringly handsome, vibrant, with something candid and challenging in her movements, and in addition to all that, she was known to be *wicked*, the friends' favourite word to describe her and her bold way of life. Elisabeth Johnson, Lizzie's mother, had run away from her home in Bath with an officer who had been killed in the Napoleonic Wars only a few years after their marriage. Left with a small legacy but accustomed to a comfortable, fashionable almost extravagant life-style, she cut her cloth to suit her circumstances, rented inexpensive rooms in profoundly provincial Nuneaton which she knew only because it was near a large military barracks, and opened a house of ill repute. Still an attractive woman, at first she tended to a few customers herself and in a rare moment of carelessness she conceived her daughter, who never knew who her father was. So Lizzie grew up in the lively and matriarchal atmosphere of the well-run and financially successful brothel, fascinated and spoilt by the whores, mainly good-natured country girls escaping the poverty and boredom of rural life, sometimes missing their own brothers and sisters they'd left behind and lavishing their affectionate attention on Lizzie instead. Madam Elisabeth, as her mother was known, had rushed headlong into her early marriage, motivated by both love and lust, but had learned well from her initial impetuousness. Her plan was to earn and save enough money from which both she and her daughter could one day live in modest, independent comfort in a town large enough to afford the anonymity required for a new start in life. For her, it would be a gracious, respectable retirement, as she expected to have to ply her trade for around twenty years, until about 1836, when her daughter would, at twenty, still be at the very best marriageable age and she herself would be in her fifties.

For some years it seemed that nothing would come between Madam Elisabeth and her meticulously planned ambitions. The business thrived thanks to its perfect suitability both in size and location. With six scrupulously selected girls, she was able to cater for the range of demands and tastes her customers required and Nuneaton, within easy reach of several military and ecclesiastical establishments, was the ideal place for discrete but unfettered and lucrative indulgence. Though Lizzie lived in the house, she was never allowed to enter the part of the premises used for trade during business hours. She sometimes caught a glimpse of the clients as they were leaving in the morning after a whole night of expensive debauchery but her mother made sure she was never seen by them. By the time she was twelve, it was clear that she was going to be an exceptionally beautiful young woman, which was all the more reason for her mother to isolate her from the officers, clergymen, businessmen and sundry gentlemen who frequented the premises. At the same time, Lizzie was brought up in many ways like a typical middle-class girl, going to church on Sundays, accompanied by her heavily veiled mother, and attending a local day school where she learned to read and write perfectly, and acquired the social skills of drawing, music and some French. The other girls at the school were being prepared either to marry or to work as governesses, depending on their physical attractiveness and the financial situation of their parents. For them, Lizzie was exotic, as unreal as a fictional heroine. Her cleverness, outstanding looks, good clothes and irreverent verbal skills ensured that no-one, not even the instructresses or the school's owner, let alone the girls, dared to tease or goad her about her background. In fact she was revered as a celebrity but, like something essentially unknowable and alien, she was never integrated, never invited to their homes and made no friends there. While after school, even in winter, most of the girls walked home, usually no more than a mile or so, Lizzie was collected by a huge, cheerful, friendly but terrifyingly ugly man, his nose almost flattened across his bristly red face, his ears deformed into the shape of cauliflower leaves by years of fighting bare-knuckled as a professional pugilist. As well as his main job of making sure that no rowdiness occurred at Madam Elisabeth's, he also drove the establishment's small but well-constructed carriage, and six days a week he'd bring Lizzie to and from school in it. Despite his intimidating appearance, Growler shared his two rooms in the top floor of the house with Percy, a younger man, who was physically his opposite, slender and effeminate, whom he loved and cherished as an older man might dote on a younger, beautiful wife. Knowing that neither Growler, whose official title was *the butler*, nor Percy, who cooked, cleaned and sewed for the household, bathed and generally pampered the girls, presented any kind of sexual threat, all the females loved and trusted them both, respecting their mutual adoration of each other as an amusing, even enviable freak of nature. Lizzie knew, everyone knew, that the friendships between the girls sometimes became love affairs but, given the business they were in and Madam Elisabeth's severe but inconsistent moral values, this was restricted to clandestine or tacitly tolerated meetings. The two men, on the other hand, enjoyed a freedom and acceptance, like eunuchs in an Arabian harem, which Lizzie had grown up with and never thought to question. So when her school mates tried to envisage what her life was like after school, whatever they felt, whether pity, revulsion, contempt or just blank amazement, they all imagined somehow that, when she returned to the Red Lantern, as the house was known, she was descending into some kind of moral vacuum, a vicious sewer from which she was privileged to emerge the next morning. In fact, for Lizzie, the exact opposite was true. For her, her home and extended family were reality and the school, though she enjoyed and

22

utilised her time there, was a kind of fiction, just one of many artificially fabricated settings in the illusory world of respectable provincial town life. Though most of the fathers of the girls at the day school usually struggled to pay even those moderate fees, occasionally one of them would treat himself to an evening at Madam Elisabeth's and while he could rely on his visit remaining a secret from the world in general, the girls invariably chatted about their clients amongst themselves. And so it did sometimes happen that Lizzie got to hear about the escapades of some of her class-mates' fathers. It was at such moments that this bright young woman would try to compare the two environments in which she spent her parallel lives. Educated according to the prevailing morality and mixing everyday with its female products but brought up in a milieu of an honest if unconventional crucible of experience and unfettered personalities, she stepped from one to the other as if they were adjacent houses, being equally familiar with each and feeling comfortable in both, though really at home in only one of them. It was the world her school friends believed to be so materially orderly and serious that she found so amusingly full of contradictions, so hypocritical and false. Imbued from earliest childhood with the strict code of total confidentiality, she never revealed any of the goings-on in her mother's premises but she enjoyed with immense pleasure listening to Rosamund Jermyn, for example, extolling the virtues of her father, the lawyer Jermyn. She would listen without comment to an encomium on his refined taste in wine, and his knowledge of music and the fine arts, and then compare the eulogy to the way Dolly, his favourite whore, mimicked him in the indulgence and culmination of his various other tastes.

Though she herself had different, secret plans of her own which she shared with no-one, Lizzie always knew those of her mother and for the time being co-operated towards their fulfilment. At fourteen she was a startlingly beautiful young woman, accomplished in all the graces and skills the wife of an affluent gentleman would need. In 1830 Mrs Johnson was in the process of making arrangements for her daughter to tour Europe, in appropriate company of course, in order to complete her education and perhaps to make the acquaintance of a future husband when their lives were changed by a radical turn of fortune. Over the previous five years, the social life of the town had become increasingly influenced by the various low churches, chapels and meeting houses and due to the direct intervention of Brother Muscat, mill owner and a leading light in the Independent Church, the brothel became the object of their joint moral vilification. After only a few weeks of intense observation, during which time only the military clientele dared visit, the Red Lantern was closed down and Mrs Johnson was sent to prison. Despite the relatively lenient sentence of one year's imprisonment, her plans for herself and her daughter were in tatters and her spirit was broken, more by the harsh, public declamation than by the punishment itself. After six months, during which her savings somehow disappeared, she died, leaving Lizzie penniless and friendless, equipped only with the social accomplishments she had acquired at the day school and the life experience garnered in the isolated but complex little world of her mother's business. It was seemingly the former but in reality the latter that provided her with the chance of more than mere survival. As everyone employed at the Red Lantern had either been imprisoned or had fled when it was closed, Lizzie was alone in the large house. Though the business had prospered and her mother had husbanded her income wisely, the landlord took money for rent and repairs. In addition, legal costs and the usual bribes and expenses of prison life soon meant that Lizzie was destitute and about to become homeless. When Muscat offered her accommodation with him and his wife, she at first believed that he really did want to make amends for the grief he had inadvertently caused her by hounding her mother into the grave. After all, he assured her, the actions he had taken against that house of sin were directed against the sinners not against her, an innocent victim. Perhaps his motives really had been genuine at first. But then came closeness to her, to her forthright but cultivated behaviour, to something licentious flaring within her decent, cool demeanour. The hybrid product of her two existences inflamed him, at first with infatuation then with a sexual desire he had never previously known existed. He searched the Gospels, Revelations and Corinthians, for guidance but could find none that suited him, and so he willingly convinced himself his passion was not sinful on his part. It was her power over him that must have derived from something wicked as it led him to such thoughts and eventually, after some months, deeds. Lizzie had recognised what was happening long before he had, and, after considering it coolly and deliberately, decided a controlled assent, more accession than submission, served her interest better than rebuttal. After all, without Growler's protection and with no money to her name, she was dependent on him both physically and financially. And so she gave him what he craved; indeed she had picked up from the girls so much about the techniques of sex that she was able to give far more than he even dreamed of while at the same time withholding the promise of even more. As soon as his lust was satiated it began to rekindle, and from this she derived the illusion of control. Of course, he could have ravished her and thrown her out onto the streets without redress. No-one would have taken her word, the daughter of a convicted brothel keeper, against his, a pillar of society and of Christian philanthropy. She was in no doubt about her reliance on him for shelter and sustenance. But his need for her was also great and gave her enough strength to elicit from him an oath that he would never use violence against her and he even agreed to pay her a small weekly allowance which she could dispose of as she wished. The arrangement satisfied her as she concluded that she had derived some profit from apparently barren circumstances.

Lizzie's friendship with Mary occurred because, at about the same time as the Red Lantern was shut down, a law was passed in far away London which disrupted both town life in general and that of Mary's father, Isaac Wright, his wife, Hanna, and her three younger sisters in particular. The Ministerial Acts of 1830 liberalised the granting of licences to sell alcohol and also abolished the duty on beer, thus throwing trade open in arguably England's most popular commodity. Isaac, whose experience as a malt house worker had provided him with a good knowledge of that trade, immediately decided to open a public house of his own. Backed by loans from a local brewery and his former employer, he became landlord of one of the twenty completely new public houses to open in Nuneaton as a result of the change in the law. The town with a resident population of around six thousand now had fifty public houses. For Mary, the eldest daughter, this meant leaving the free school which, due to her early duties of helping to care for her younger sisters, she had only been able to attend for two years anyway, two short years which had given her a keen appetite for literacy but only an imperfect grounding. Regretfully but without resentment, the twelve-year-old began helping out in the day-time pub business, doing family chores and spending any spare time weaving on the loom in the pub's attic. The one duty that gave her any pleasure was buying any food and items that weren't delivered by tradesmen, especially as this gave her precious opportunities to get away from the pub with its blue pipe smoke, its stench of beer, the sullen broodiness and latent violence of many of its customers. Most of all she valued her visits to Astley's General Store where young Johnnie helped his legendary father, the radical John Astley, who, despite his atheistic irreverence for any kind of authority, exerted a fascination on all segments of Nuneaton's population, regardless of their social standing. Anarchic and iconoclastic in politics, in business he was equally revolutionary, allowing the weavers unlimited credit when the ribbon trade was slack or middling, which it usually was, but insisting on prompt payment from the better situated customers, who in turn accepted his terms because he supplied the best quality merchandise, for much of which only he seemed to enjoy the arcane knowledge necessary for its procurement. Even those who detested his political or religious convictions, which he flaunted at every opportunity, bought regularly and paid punctually at his shop, and these included Mrs Muscat, the wife of the mill owner and Lizzie's self-appointed guardian. After a few chaperoned excursions, Lizzie was quick to manipulate her way free of the older woman's companionship and, like Mary, soon delighted in any excuse to spend time as often as possible in the store. In an indefinable but unmistakable way, the mixture of people, many of whom dropped by to exchange gossip with the older Astley but increasingly often with his son, their discrete conversations and their voluble discussions all created an almost constant vibration of excitement that was otherwise sparse in the provincial town. Partly to help satisfy his own insatiable appetite for news, however trivial, and partly for the comfort of his customers, Astley reserved an area about four yards square in one corner for where small groups, usually but not always men, could sit down at a couple of tables and drink tea and wag their chins. The General Store was the place most people made a bee-line for when they'd been told about or witnessed something scandalous, incriminating, hilarious or indelicate. Equally, anyone wanting to discuss issues of significance, whether they be civic, religious or political, would also loiter at the tables in Astley's corner until an exchange of views fermented. For Mary and Lizzie though, the main attraction was Johnnie, a couple of years older than Lizzie, always good tempered, witty, garrulous and full of delicious morsels of scandal, usually scurrilous and often downright salacious. As the three young people got to know each other a deep, tacit trust developed between them. Though Lizzie shared with both of them information she wouldn't reveal to anyone else so that Johnnie knew about the real arrangement that existed between her and Muscat, she also revealed her inmost thoughts and aspirations only to Mary. Before that eventful year was over, Lizzie and Mary were intimate friends and Johnnie was head over heels in love with Lizzie.

*

Bustled off the paved causeway into the mud of the broad street, Lizzie pulled her skirts up higher just as a cartload of bedraggled navvies, towed through the slush by an equally dripping but sober nag, drew level with them. Hoots of appreciation mingled with their obscene offers, which merely increased when they noticed that the well-formed young woman's only response was a cheeky smile as she hitched the dress up tantalisingly above the knee, pretending to shake the mud of her shoe. The two girls laughed and waved dismissively at the men's reaction and pushed their way back off the road and let the cart move steadily away from them. Mary, still smirking at the effect her friend had on men and her uninhibited way of dealing with it, kept as close to her as possible. It was already too crowded for them to link arms as usual as they jostled and dodged between the other pedestrians, exchanging looks and remarks as often as they could. Names, what other people called them, what they wanted to be called; that was their favourite topic. At least, it was when they thought there was not the slightest chance of them being overheard. Lizzie's experiences with men and what the two girls made of it all, fascinated, puzzled and also amused them most. But now they had to shout to be heard even when their heads came close, so they bantered their way harmlessly towards the town. As they passed the open door of Astley's General Stores someone called out:

"Lizzie! Poll! Wait!"

They exchanged *Should we hear him?* glances, and Mary weakened, although the young Johnnie Astley had used the name she rejected most vehemently. *Poll*, indeed! Not even *Polly*, which was bad enough. Without a word, they both turned and went into the shop, throwing the shawls off their heads and tossing the damp out of their hair, to where Johnnie was alone and looking busy by sweeping the floor with a twig broom, which he quickly laid to one side so he could hastily drag two stools towards the counter. Nimble and with the natural coordination of a born actor, his movements were graceful and at the same time just a little exaggerated, theatrical without being ridiculous.

"Take yours seats, my good ladies. What about a bowl of lovely warming soup on this miserable drizzly day? Please allow me to take your shawl, Madame."

Lizzie allowed him to lay a hand on each of her lovely shoulders and remove one of the several shawls draped over them.

The girls grinned, despite their initial resolve to play the haughty, unimpressed damsels. Incorrigible, predictable and blatantly infatuated with Lizzie as he was, Johnnie's company always cheered them up and having spent almost every working day of the last six years in his father's shop, the most frequented in the town, he was by far and away their best source of gossip and, for them, entertainment. At nineteen he already knew and was known by everyone who ever purchased or ordered goods locally. He had even met the local gentry, the Earl of Newdigate and the Baronet, Dugdale, though not in the shop of course, and the aristocrat's land agent, Evans, was, together with his bright and chatty daughter Mary Anne, a frequent customer.

Johnnie hung up Lizzie's shawl, pressing it first to his face and pretending to swoon, then disappeared into an adjoining room.

"What about *my* shawl, Johnnie?" Mary called after him. "Am I to sit around here in these wet rags and catch my death?" She lowered her voice a little but made sure it was loud enough for Johnnie to hear. "Lizzie, sweetheart, you'll have to put your arms around me to warm me from the cold and damp!" As Johnnie returned with two bowls of soup, Lizzie flung her arms dramatically around Mary and pulled her against her, stroking her face and kissing her cheeks. "Oh, let me protect and warm you, my little angel!"

The young man placed the bowls on the counter, threw up his arms histrionically in despair and slumped onto a chair, his arm held in front of his eyes as though to shield himself from the sight of the two girls.

"Have I no chance of winning the affections of the fair Elisabeth?"

"Oh, Elisabeth is it! And for me plain Poll will do! And not even a piece of bread to go with the soup!"

As Lizzie and Mary tucked into the bowls of gruel, Johnnie accepted they had let the curtain fall on his dramatics and fetched them their bits of bread. He stood on the other side of the counter watching them, or rather watching Lizzie, until she spoke.

"No tittle-tattle today, Johnnie?"

"You've heard about Pope?"

"We're not interested in religion. You know the kind of stories we like."

"Not the Pope. I mean Mr Pope in Abbey Street."

He saw from their eager attention that they hadn't heard about it yet and was glad because it was bound to be the most chewed piece of gossip within the next few days.

"Well, I've just written it in my diary. The ink's not dry on yet!"

He disappeared into the back room and returned with a large, thick bound block of writing paper he used as his diary. He flitted through the pages then, after making sure no-one else was in hearing distance he read his latest entry in a low, conspiratorial and at the same time theatrical voice:

> *A report in circulation, which has obtained some degree of credibility, claims that Mr Thomas Pope of the Engine, Abbey Street had committed the atrocious crime of sodomy upon a boy lodging at the said premises. The following lines were posted on the Engine door:*
>
> *"Friends and dear neighbours I hope*
> *You'll all beware of the Pope!*
> *For should you be ever so kind*
> *Set traps and spring guns*
> *On each of your buns,*
> *Or else he'll be in your behind!"*

The shocking content and Johnnie's delivery ensured a burst of laughter from both of the girls, though Mary wasn't quite sure she'd understood exactly what Mr Pope was supposed to have done and Lizzie's reaction was tinged slightly with a fleeting, affectionate memory of Growler and his darling Percy, so that Johnnie was a little disappointed that their amusement dissipated so quickly. Instead of trying to revive the frivolous mood, he watched them eating, becoming serious and obviously preoccupied with something despite his efforts to be jocular. Finally he asked:

"And how are they treating you, Lizzie? At Brother Muscat's?"

The girls exchanged sideways looks, their faces bent down over the soup, invisible for Johnnie, before Lizzie answered.

"Oh, they're nice to me." She paused, stopping the spoon on its way to her mouth. "As long as I'm nice to him, of course!"

Mary spluttered a little. But, looking up, she saw that Johnnie really was affected by Lizzie's answer. She couldn't tell if he was hurt or annoyed but she saw him chewing on the inside of his lip, which she knew he always did when he was agitated. In Lizzie's company he was often agitated. She nudged Lizzie gently and she also noticed that Johnnie had suddenly become a bit morose.

"Don't sulk, Johnnie. What would you prefer me to do? You know as well as I do the choices I've got. I'm better off where I am. That's the main thing, isn't it?"

She looked Johnnie full in the face and saw how sombre he had become. He leaned forward onto his folded arms and all at once looked 10 years older, frowning and making chewing movements with his tightly closed mouth. She placed a hand gently on his cheek and his face relaxed as he gazed back at her with unashamed adoration into her eyes. He spoke falteringly:

"I know Lizzie. It's easy for me to talk. But it's the thought of that sanctimonious hypocrite. I've heard him in here, boasting of how him and his wife care for you. *Poor orphaned child! Another sinner saved!*"

"That what he calls me? A sinner? Well, he has saved me I suppose. For himself."

Mary looked on and listened. This feeling she often had for Lizzie flowed through her; admiration, love, respect? She couldn't name it but she sensed the strength and honesty in this friend of hers, hardly more than a child but talking with such confidence and knowledge about herself. Johnnie perceived it too, but he was a man and had other emotions to contend with.

"But you let him …" he sought the right word, "… use you, Lizzie."

His voice betrayed that for all his antics just a few minutes previously, he was disconsolate, close to tears.

"Have you been thinking about this too much again, Johnnie? Don't feel sorry for me. Feel sorry for all the respectable wives and daughters who come into your shop everyday. And for others too, the not so respectable ones."

"You mean like Janet Buchanan?"

Both girls immediately looked up at him, curious to hear what he had to tell about this beautiful, charismatic woman, the wife of one the town's leading businessmen, the Lawyer Buchanan. Wherever she went and whoever accompanied her, it was invariably Janet Buchanan who attracted the most interest. Whether the weekly church attendance, or one of the town's social events, or simply in the streets and shops of daily life, her looks, her clothing but above all her haughty, almost arrogant manner made her the town's most remarkable female. Weeks before, her body, covered only by a cotton night gown, had been found in the freezing putrid water of the town's River Anker. Suicides were not uncommon but usually easily explainable by either mental disorder or bankruptcy. But unaccountable mystery surrounded the death of this woman who, though for all intents and purposes was an exemplary pillar of respectable society but still strangely isolated by a disconcerting independence, had exerted fascination, wonder but also evoked subdued disapproval since she had married into this affluent and influential but widely detested family. Now it seemed that Johnnie had at last received some information about the death from perhaps either the newly-appointed Constable Haddon or, more likely, from the

Buchanans' domestic servants. He savoured their hungry attention before speaking.

"He threw her out. In the middle of the night. One of the maids heard him call her and she heard her go downstairs. There was some shouting, the maid said, about her drinking and her disobedience and then the door slammed. After he'd gone to bed, the maid who told me all this, went down and into the street to look for her mistress but she'd gone. She thought she'd gone to her mother or even to the Reverend Tryan's house. She was," he paused for effect, "*friendly* with him. The next morning they found her in the river."

Lizzie, though captivated by the revelation, remained emotionally unaffected, as if she'd listened to an anecdote that merely confirmed her existing knowledge. She spoke as if she had already formed an opinion on a familiar topic.

"And that's what's left of her. A frozen corpse in a dirty river. And he struts about town in his black suit letting everybody tell him how much they pity and feel for him in his tragic loss! That's the way with respectable people!"

The amused, superior tone of Lizzie's voice provoked Mary, who was usually absorbed by Lizzie's and Johnnie's more serious conversations and thought long and hard about them when she was alone. She asked:

"But won't Constable Haddon do something? He just threw her out. That's why she died. She must have frozen to death. Did she just lie there and die? The Anker's not deep enough to drown in. That's not right. A husband can't do that to his wife!"

Lizzie sensed that if she spoke, a gulf would open between herself and her only friend so she didn't speak. Johnnie just said:

"It's not right, Polly, love. But he can do it. He did it. And it's none of Haddon's business. Janet was Buchanan's wife."

They watched the younger girl grappling with the stark, unambiguous clarity of what Johnnie had said. Then Lizzie spoke with a serious, muffled voice.

"No man will ever do that to me."

As if anticipating what she would say, Johnnie blurted out before she had hardly finished her sentence:

"And isn't what Brother Muscat does to you almost as bad?"

She took his face in both of her hands again so that their eyes were only ten inches or so apart and at the same level. Choosing her words carefully, she spoke with a flat, emphatic voice, intent on putting the matter to rest and beyond further discussion.

"He doesn't use me any more than I use him. It's a kind of bargain. Business. Just like when you sell your things here. Your father gets something for what he sells."

She let him go and began eating the rest of her soup. Johnnie was calm now and thinking with her, learning from her.

"But he makes sure he takes more than what he spends, Lizzie."

She mopped the rest of the soup up with a piece of bread, finished eating and pushed the bowl towards Johnnie as if she were playing a trump card.

"And that's exactly what I've learned to do as well."

She turned to Mary but before she could speak they all three noticed that someone had entered the shop. Two men, one tall and powerfully-built, the other thick-set and poorly-dressed, stood just inside the doorway looking and pointing at a barrel of apples. Johnnie spoke to them in his cheerful shopkeeper voice.

"Good morning gentlemen. There are better ones over here. Those are windfall, bruised and soft."

Ignoring the faintly ironical tone that was an almost permanent feature of Johnnie's voice, the taller man looked at his companion and smiled slightly.

"These will do fine. Put twenty or so in a sack. Make it thirty."

He gave the other man a few coins and waited at the door while his scruffy friend wandered over towards the counter and placed himself to get a good look at Lizzie. He jingled the coins in his palm and winked at her, twisting his face into something between a grin and a drool.

Lizzie turned and spoke loudly in the unadulterated local slang to Johnnie who was filling the sack from the barrel.

"Have you got a bucket of water, Johnnie? It stinks over here! Has your dog been in this morning?" She turned to face the man leering at her and spoke to him directly. "Or have you trod in something?"

It was only when he noticed Mary smiling that the scruff, who did in fact smell quite strongly, caught on. He raised his hand threateningly but immediately, almost as if he knew what was coming, his boss at the door called not loudly but clearly.

"Leave that, Green! Just put the coins on the counter and come over here and carry the sack."

"Six pence, Johnnie. Is that enough?," she called across the shop.

"Enough for thirty soggy apples. Yes, that's plenty. Thank you Sir. Good day to you Sir."

Mary sensed that Lizzie was about to throw another taunt at Green so she put her hand on her arm and shook her head.

Lizzie fetched her scarf from where Johnnie had hung it up.

"So there is somebody in Nuneaton you don't know by name, Johnnie."

"The tall one's called Hardcastle. He's here for the election. Working for one of the candidates."

"And the other one's called Green and he stinks!" Mary chimed in. "Thanks for the soup, Johnnie."

36

Lizzie looked at him for a second or two without speaking, glanced at the closed door then pulled his head down towards hers and kissed him hard on the lips.

"That's for the soup. Cheer up!"

He watched them walk out and then ran to the door and called after them.

"Come in on your way home and tell me about the hustings!"

They waved back to show they'd heard but were soon lost from sight in the mass of people. Although the market square was still filling up when they arrived they decided not to go across it but to stay on the perimeter, making their way along the top edge towards the river where the voting booths, for the first time in the town's history, had been set up a hundred yards or so from where they entered the square. The fact that the vast majority of those present had no vote didn't discourage a boisterous, rowdy debate among the crowd where groups with different coloured ribbons and cockades waded into each other with raucous abuse usually followed by inane honking noises intended to drown out any reply. There were also speakers with more sophisticated powers of propaganda and, after watching several groups haranguing and mocking each other, the two girls noticed a tall, bearded man with long, flowing hair and dressed in a long, black coat, posing on an improvised platform about a foot high, addressing and discussing with an attentive crowd of about fifty listeners. Attracted more by his exotic appearance than by anything he was saying, they weren't listening closely but Mary, more observant and naturally curious than Lizzie, noticed he was wearing no party's colours and caught snatches of his speech, which reminded her of some of the trade unionists who sometimes drank in her father's pub and tried to agitate the navvies, colliers and stone-workers and who mistook their mindless, silent indifference for attentiveness and conversion.

"A man's share!" she heard him say several times. *"Not a pig's share, not the share of a machine fed with oil to make it work and nothing else."* Then she only registered some individual words *Monopolists ... Inspectors.* And then a full sentence:

"To bring up your families, the ignorant sons of ignorant fathers! That's a slave's share!"

His voice faded as they moved a few yards further to where a fat, red-faced man, constantly dabbing the sweat from his forehead despite the cold weather, was spouting insults against the Radical candidate, Hemmings.

"... calls himself a Radical. A democrat! A believer in freedom! And where has he made the wealth he flaunts so brashly in the faces of decent folks? I'll tell you where. The same place he found his Negro concubine! Why, from the slaves on his plantations in the West Indies! That's what he owes his money to! And that's where he bought his so-called housekeeper! Who ever saw a housekeeper travel into town in her own carriage of four? And is it part of a housekeeper's duties to provide her master with a dusky-skinned son?"

Mary and Lizzie enjoyed the unveiled allusions to Hemmings' scandalous past, many details of which Johnnie had already told them. Although the speaker's supporters derided and jeered loyally at every mention of the upstart's immorality, there was a tinge of envy and even respect for him that blunted the polemics. Especially those who had seen the proudly beautiful black woman, over six feet tall and perfectly proportioned, couldn't really bring themselves to disdain or scorn the man fortunate to share a bed with her, whether she was his mistress or, as some maintained, his wife. Though extremely unconventional, aberrant, and, in the eyes of some, godless, his commercial and sexual acquisitions were tacitly seen by most men as conquests which commanded either secret or open admiration. For the two girls such extravagant beings were rare chinks in the gloom of provincial life and they listened patiently, hoping for new revelations about Hemmings and his wife, to the obese, perspiring orator whose efforts to defame only incited interest and envy.

As they approached the voting booths they could hear two bands playing. They could just make out the tunes – the musicians decked out in Tory colours were playing *Auld Lang Syne* and the others tried to outplay them with *O Whistle and I will come to thee, my lad!* Both melodies were standard repertoire of the bands that played at the Wakes so the girls whistled and hummed along as best they could, each choosing a different tune. Mary was happier and more elated than she could ever remember but she had sense enough to indicate to Lizzie that they ought to make a diversion away from the pub doors a few yards ahead of them. Groups of inebriated men, heavy-set, loud and ill-tempered and scowling, their shirt fronts unbuttoned oblivious to the cold, spilled out of both doors onto the street and, recognising each others' colours, immediately began to goad and scuffle with each other. There was no real outright fighting but, as the girls moved ten yards or so into the square, they noticed that the mood was more aggressive the closer they got to the actual voting stations. Buffeting, pushing, wrestling, everything short of out-and-out assault broke out sporadically all around them, flaring up and subsiding when the special constables appeared whirling their sticks. As soon as they were past the pub exits they got out of the crowd and back to the edge of the square, where narrow allies ran every few yards between the buildings. Lizzie nudged Mary to glance down one where two gaudily clad prostitutes were negotiating with a group of burly navvies. The girls stopped and watched unnoticed till one of the men opened a side door and the two women went inside followed by two of the labourers. The men waiting their turn spotted the two girls and intended to make some remark but they stepped quickly away towards the row of booths.

Now the whole square was so crowded that they linked arms again for fear of being separated. Both of them were bright-eyed, eager to experience more, hardly noticing the fine but driving rain. Apart from the density of the crowds and the voting booths, there was nothing there that Mary had never seen before. But it was as if the sights, sensations, emotions and incidents of her whole past life were being staged all at one moment in time, in one place. Wherever she looked there was action, sound, colour and though some of it was violent, brutish and ugly, she felt intensely entertained, boosted to a higher level of experience.

On the opposite side of the square there were the tallest, most substantial buildings the town had - the Castle Hotel, the town hall and other four-storey houses and offices. Away from that far edge the ground sloped gradually down towards the river which was divided from the road where they were standing by a strip of rough grass. The booths had been set in a row backing right up to the grass so the river was hidden from the road. The small footbridge crossing the river, barely visible, was so crammed that the people on it could hardly move one way or the other. Mary and Lizzie knew little and cared less about the politics of the day but they did know that Hemming, the Radical was *our* man, the people's man, that his colours were yellow for Liberal and that, given the new voting rights, he was bound to score a big victory over the Tory, Dugdale whose supporters with their blue ribbons were almost submerged by the sea of yellow. Loud, raucous, beery shouting filled the air but the mood was still on the whole good-humoured. One of the bands was blaring out distorted sound again near the bridge so that with all the noise the two girls could only signal and mouth whatever they wanted to tell each other. They had been wandering around, bewildered by the sounds and sights, tugged and buffeted in various direction, when Mary yanked heftily on Lizzie's sleeve to get her attention. She pointed towards the footbridge which was suddenly empty except for one tall man.

"That's him who bought the apples at Johnnie's," she shouted into Lizzie's ear.

Hardcastle waved his hand as a kind of signal and the band instantly stopped playing and then he was gone from sight. The sudden cessation of the music caused most of the crowd within hearing distance to turn and look towards where the din had ceased so inexplicably. They saw a group of four men sporting yards of yellow ribbon, shoving and pulling a man covered in blue ribbons onto the bridge and then, when the indignant shouts of protest from much of the crowd had drawn even more attention in that direction, they heaved him over the low railings and a dull, washy splash could be heard in the shocked pocket of silence near the river. The four men left the bridge as fast as they could and disappeared in the crowd. The bridge re-filled up with spectators who could see the man thrashing about wildly in the river. Those in the crowd could only watch the people on the bridge and infer what the victim was doing from their reaction. After some expectant moments it became clear that the blue ribbon man had come to no serious harm. The people on the bridge were pointing, laughing, some slapping their sides in glee, and generally catcalling. As they all gradually turned towards the square it was obvious that the victim must have been dragging himself out of the filthy water on the river bank directly behind the booths. By this time the mood had lost its edge, and merriment greeted the drenched gentleman draped with blue ribbons and dark slimy plants as he made his way between the booths towards the edge of the crowd.

Mary turned to look at Lizzie and noticed Hardcastle standing only a few yards away from them. Again he made some kind of signal with his hand and the girls immediately heard the sounds of scuffling and cries of fear. As the crowd opened up, they caught brief but vivid and horrifying glimpses of the four men thumping and kicking their drenched and helpless victim . This was different kind of violence to the clumsy brawling they'd seen up till then and instantly, a change came over the crowd. Especially the yellow-ribboned supporters gasped appalled at the gratuitous brutality of what they had seen done by their own supporters. Before anyone could intervene, the four men had already slipped away into the mass so there was no specific target for their outrage. Now scuffles were breaking out all over the square. Occasionally spaces opened up in the crowd and the girls caught glimpses of fists and feet jabbing out, people shouting in pain and anger and then the Specials rushing in, blowing their whistles and aiming their stout wooden sticks at the limbs and bodies of the rowdies. And then the gap was closed and all they could see above the heads of the people next to them were men on horseback, lashing out with whips and clubs at anyone who refused to disperse and make way. Indignation and anger became audible as the crowd turned and wheeled around on itself, like a caged animal taking on a collective will of its own. Gradually, most heads had turned into the direction of the Castle Hotel where several men had assembled on the second-storey balcony. Two uniformed constables flanked a tall, very well-dressed man holding a kind of staff of office. Another man came onto the balcony and conversed with the tall gentleman.

Lizzie felt her sleeve being tugged at frantically again. Mary nodded to their right and again Hardcastle was there, moving easily and quickly through the mass of bodies. With a shove, Mary urged her friend to follow him. They did so partly out of curiosity, as this stranger had appeared at several critical moments in such a short space of time, and also because they wanted to get out of the centre of a crowd that was becoming increasingly aggressive. Keeping just a few yards behind him, it was easy to move right across the square and by the time the policeman began to demand that the crowd be quiet and listen to an important announcement, they were on the edge of the gathering but still only twenty yards or so from the hotel façade, Hardcastle about five yards ahead of them.

Slowly but perceptibly the crowd became more subdued and the voices from those on the balcony could be heard across the square. Mary heard some words being repeatedly murmured by people close to her. *Newdigate, Magistrate, Riot Act* and then the voice of the Earl of Newdigate:

"Our Sovereign Lord the King chargeth and commandeth all persons being assembled immediately to disperse themselves, and peaceably to depart to their habitations or to their lawful business, upon the pains contained in the act made in the first year of King George for preventing tumultuous and riotous assemblies. God save the King."

One of the constable whispered something to him and he spoke again:

"Citizens of Nuneaton, you have an hour to disperse peacefully. If you fail to do so, I will exercise my right, my duty as magistrate and call for help from the military. I advise you to go home immediately. Voting will continue tomorrow."

It was late morning and many of the franchised voters who had come in a long way from outlying areas had not yet voted. Now they would have to make the long journey home and back the next day. A resentful, disgruntled, confused collective muttering slowly swelled up but within a few minutes individuals began to drift away. Despite the unpleasantness, the shocking violence, Mary and Lizzie were enjoying it. Excitement like they had never known before and somehow this mysterious, good-looking man who so smoothly cut a swathe through the dense crowd were beginning to fascinate them. They scoured the area around them for the sight of him. He was easy to spot. Standing on a low wall to the right of the hotel, he was clearly visible both to Mary and to the group of four men, Green and three others, who had positioned themselves directly in front of the balcony, where the two constables and Newdigate had been joined by a man in military uniform.

Green stooped out of sight and the other three bent slightly to take something from him. He then made his way off from the square to the left, the opposite side to where Mary, Lizzie and Hardcastle stood. Mary watched all this but only understood what was happening when the remaining three men began throwing the mushy apples at the balcony. Some fell short. Some looped over the heads of Newdigate and his bodyguards and splattered against the hotel wall. One of them hit Newdigate's shoulders and, already reduced almost to pulp by the rain and being dragged about in the moist sack, virtually disintegrated, leaving a smear on his fine cloth. Mary laughed, it seemed so comic and trivial. But the officer next to Newdigate drew his sword, raised it as high as he could and waved it from side to side. Half a minute later Mary heard a kind of dull bang resonate from somewhere in the distance.

A man standing next to them spoke rapidly as he began to moved away:

"Get off home you girls, as fast as your legs will carry. Get off! Now. The army's coming."

Others heard him, and others repeated more less what he had said. *The army's coming!* For the first time in her life, Mary heard panic and terror in people's voices and saw it in their faces. She stood still, frozen more by indecision than fear. Most of the people were trying to flee in the opposite direction, from where the shot seemed to have been fired, the main street out of the square where Lizzie and Mary had come from that morning. But there were still people arriving from that direction so after the crowd had progressed about thirty yards the street was virtually blocked, the two deep rows of people crashing against each other like waves and making the way impassable in both directions. Pressed from both sides, some on the fringe turned around and made for the narrow footbridge across the river, others jumped into and half-waded and half-swam through the sludgy mixture of slush and sewage. Mary and Lizzie still stood there, as if marooned on a tiny island, their arms still interlocked, glancing frantically around them and at each other.

"Hey! You two! Follow me!"

They looked at each other for a split second, long enough to recognise agreement, and moved off towards where Hardcastle was standing. Although he seemed to be walking towards a high, closed wall they followed him. When it seemed he could go no further, he rapped on a narrow, heavy gate and held it open long enough for the two girls to get through it. As it slammed closed behind them the instant silence made them realise how deafening it had been in the square. The sounds from the other side of the wall were no louder now than gently lapping water but, still close to the gate, they could just make out a kind of low rumbling, like very quiet thunder, from outside.

They were in the sudden quietness of the hotel courtyard, a rectangle about fifty yards across and thirty yards deep. Stables and sheds lined both sides and at the back there was a high wall with narrow gates set into each corner right and left. The main gate onto the square was on the other side of the hotel front. In the centre of the yard there was a small garden with seats and stone features. Clusters of uniformed soldiers were lounging about, calmly smoking pipes, drinking beer and joking with a few over-dressed women with pink cheeks and ostentatiously low cut dresses, in defiance of the weather.

It had stopped raining. Lizzie looked around very slowly, seeming to take everything in. She removed a shawl or two and rearranged her clothes so that her figure could be appreciated. Mary was about four paces behind her as they strolled without any haste into the yard. Hardcastle spoke with the man who had opened and locked the gate and he approached them.

"Come with me, you two."

He walked briskly ahead of them, making for the gate in the right-hand corner and at first Mary tried to catch up with him but slowed down when she was alongside Lizzie, who seemed to be in no hurry at all.

"Come on, Lizzie. That gate will let us out into Wash Lane and we can get back without going anywhere near the trouble."

"You can go if you want, Polly. But I think I like it here. I'd like to stay a bit."

"Do you think they'll let you stay?"

Lizzie stopped and looked across the yard at a group of soldiers who had their eyes fixed on her. Mary saw the same and they both chuckled.

"I think they'll let me stay! But you go. Try to get away tomorrow morning and we'll meet at Johnnie's."

They both paused, not quite wanting to let each other go until Mary finally spoke for both of them.

"It was incredible, wasn't it? I mean, exciting. Horrible but exciting." Mary paused again. "What are you going to do here, Lizzie?"

"Psst! Call me Elisabeth here, not Lizzie!"

"You call me Marianne then, not Polly!"

They laughed.

"Mary. Not Marianne. You're not that far yet. So now you'd better go. Mary. Wish me luck."

For some reason both felt sure something momentous was about to happen, something even more momentous than that they had already witnessed. They hugged each other, cheek pressed hard against cheek.

"Go. Or they'll think I give it away. See you tomorrow!"

As Mary hurried off towards the corner of the yard where the soldier was waiting with a large key, she noticed that a shawl had slipped off Lizzie's shoulder but she let it lie on the paved ground. When she reached the gate she turned, looked back and saw that a soldier was handing Lizzie her shawl. As he did so his arm slipped around her waist but Lizzie pushed him gently away and her gaze went up slowly to the brilliantly-lit second-storey window where older men in splendid uniforms adorned with braid and medals could be seen drinking brandy and smoking cigars. Two of them were looking down closely at the young woman in the court yard, raising their glasses invitingly and smiling. And Elisabeth smiled back.

Chapter 2

In the evening the rain returned but Mary's mother had made a pot of gruel for a neighbour and sent Mary to take it to her. Arriving at her neighbour's house, she didn't want to go through the dark entry and into the filthy yard, so she stopped in the street. To avoid waking the baby, she knocked hardly audibly on the window. The pot was beginning to feel quite heavy when Polly Button finally opened the door directly onto the muddy sidewalk where Mary was waiting. A small, scrawny, ugly woman almost dragged Mary in and took the pot off her straight away, put it down and pressed Mary's face between her two hands, kissing her repeatedly on the forehead, nose and cheeks. Mary was expecting this greeting and accepted it without resistance and she was also braced for the effusive verbal welcome.

"Oh. Poll, me love! You are so good to me, to a miserable old cow who don't deserve nowt better than the workhouse. Some says worse. Tell your Mam she's too good to me. This pot'll last me the week out and that Danks hasn't paid a penny again so it comes just right. And it'll do the babbie no end of good an all. These dried up udders couldn't produce much at the best of times but without you lot looking after me, the poor beggar would have snuffed it long ago. It'd a bin the first of them to go. The first of five. You know, there's good uns snuffin' it like one a minute, rich and poor. But mainly poor. And mine, me a sinner like. All mine make it. The oldest already started courting strong herself. You see her out there with her fancy bloke? I know they're at it. But what can I say? What we got, Poll me love? What we got? The Church. Gin. And men. That's all. Teck yer pick. I ain't bin to church since I was christened and gin costs money I ain't got. So it's only men for me. Me mother said that all men are pigs. Sooner do it with a bloke than with a pig though. Poll, you're so quiet. Are you alright? Come here you little smasher you, let me give you a kiss."

She finally stopped talking long enough to hug Mary, who returned the embrace but did, in spite of her real affection for Polly, turn her face slightly so that the repeated kisses missed her mouth, their intended target, and landed on her cheeks.

"My Mam says she needs the pot Polly, so if you could ladle the gruel into one of yours? And here's some bread."

"I'll warm the pot first though, love. Come over here. Have a look. Ain't she lovely?"

"She is. Can I hold her?"

"Course you can. Careful mind. Keep the blanket round her. Blanket I says. Bit of rag really. But none of mine died. I don't know what it is comes out my dugs but it must be good stuff. Not much on it though."

Polly spooned all the gruel into one of her own heavy saucepans and swilled out the one Mary brought.

"She's smiling. She's smiling at me Polly!"

"Guts-ache more like."

Then, to spare Mary's feelings:

"Might be smiling though. She's three months to the day."

"I want a daughter one day."

"A daughter! You got a fancy man already? How old are you?"

"Not now. Not soon. But one day. Look at her Polly. She's smiling at me again."

The older woman didn't correct her, but repeated the question.

"Fifteen?"

"Fourteen, coming on fifteen. But mine won't be like me. Things'll be different then."

"Some things never change, Mary, my love. They never will."

"Why have you got so many, Polly?"

Polly looked disturbed, almost hurt, and asked suspiciously.

"You started going to chapel?"

"I mean, you can do it without having kids. Lizzie explained it to me."

"Danks'd never pull it out before he spills. Sometimes he's so quick, it's out before it's in."

"No, you can use a sponge. Lizzie told me how."

"Suppose she learnt a trick or two in her mother's business. Won't be needing them living with that holy-Joe family."

Mary said nothing and Polly continued.

"A sponge? What do you mean, use a sponge?" She tried to imagine what the girl meant. "A sponge is soft, Poll my love. Even an innocent lamb like you ought to know that's no good."

Mary laughed at the older, vastly more experienced older woman's naivety. "Not for that, Polly. I can explain it, if you like, but I must get going now. It's getting really dark and there was a lot of trouble today."

She moved towards the door but Polly's agitated muttering started off on a different topic, one that the child had reminded her of.

"A shilling a week is what he's supposed to pay, that Danks. The elders said if he don't cough up now they'll deport him. Send him off. He's had enough chances they say and enough's enough. That's what I'll tell him when he comes round tonight. Pay up or you're off."

The girl felt for the older woman but knew that this subject, if Polly once really got into it, could delay her departure so she gave her a surprise embrace, and planted a light kiss on the child's head. "Has she got a name yet?"

"On the certificate it's Mary. But they all are. We just call her babbie though."

"I'm going to call my first daughter Lizzie."

"Elisabeth?"

"But I'll call her Lizzie. I like it better."

The only light was from the houses, dim, spluttering, tallow candlelight, as Mary made her way through the few streets back home. As she left Polly's alley off Abbey Street, she glanced back over her shoulder and thought she caught a glimpse of a man at Polly's door. That would be Danks and she wondered briefly if Polly would at last be able to persuade or force him to pay the shilling a week. Mary thought about the baby and smiled to herself. She felt pleased with how she'd been able to talk with the older woman and she was already beginning to think of a way she could help Polly deal with Danks.

*

The next morning Mary was so anxious to meet Lizzie that she got away early without either of her parents seeing her. Expecting the streets to be packed again, she was amazed to find them as good as deserted. And the weather had changed. A clear, pale blue sky, crisp dry air and cold. Very cold. Partly because of the freezing temperature, bearable, in fact almost pleasant because of the windless aridity, and partly because she didn't want to waste any time, she started to run. No need to mind the mud as the street was frozen in rock-hard ruts and shallow, bony crevasses.

The shop-door was closed and curtained against the cold and, once she was inside, she quickly shut it behind her.

Though Mary probably visited Astley's store at least three time a week, now it seemed strange to her. She noticed that heavy drapes had been hung across the expansive windows and though there were a few candles lit, it was dim, subdued, almost mournful in the usually bright and lively shop. Johnnie was behind the counter and raised his eyebrows and nodded when he saw Mary, but said nothing. In an almost dark corner, two men were sitting on stools at a tiny table, drinking tea and talking in murmurs. Johnnie's father, John Astley, and a workman Mary didn't know looked up briefly as she crossed the shop towards the counter and then returned to their brooding.

"Where is everybody, Johnnie? Have you seen Lizzie?"

She noticed at once how strange and agitated he looked, his eyes darting out of control in all directions.

"You must know what happened, Poll. You were both at the hustings. You don't think anybody'll be venturing out today do you?"

He paused and could see from her bewildered expression that she really didn't know what he was talking about. Steadying his voice and trying to look calmer, he spoke deliberately, though Mary could hear the effort he needed to control his voice. "The Greys came in. On horseback. They killed three people. Almost hacked an arms off two others. To stop the rioting and protect life and property they're saying."

She remembered the low, thunder-like rumbling from behind the heavy gate after it had been slammed, locked and bolted noisily; the soldiers lounging nonchalantly around the quiet hotel courtyard; how relaxed and safe they had both suddenly felt there. And was it true? On the other side of the wall, hardly audible and blocked from her sight, people, maybe some of them she knew, were being attacked by mounted soldiers? Here in Nuneaton? She looked hard at Johnnie, as if searching for some explanation for the blatant but almost unimaginable truth. He understood. He had felt exactly the same himself when his father had told him what he had witnessed. "It's true, Polly. I was worried sick about you and Liz but then I heard all the casualties were men. But why didn't you see it? It was only an hour or so after you left here."

Before Mary could answer the door opened and closed quickly with a crash. A tall, bearded man in a heavy overcoat that almost reached the ground strode across to where old Astley and his companion were sitting and they threw their arms around each other, silently, more in comfort than greeting.

The sudden movement, the door banging open and shut, the grating of chairs on the rough wooden boards, had suddenly shattered the gloomy quietness that had hung over the room and the three men spoke now so loudly that Mary and Johnnie could hear them clearly.

"Bring some more tea over, Johnnie. And bring Felix something to eat. Polly, you are Polly Wright, aren't you? Isaac and Hannah's girl."

Mary nodded.

"Unless you need something important, you'd better be running along."

Mary didn't move. "I'm waiting for somebody, Mr Astley. And I want to get warm again before I go out there." And then for no reason that she was aware of, she added: "My name's Mary, by the way. Not Polly."

But Astley's attention was now fixed on Felix who was rummaging in his overcoat pockets.

"Here it is," he said at last, brandishing a largish piece of paper. He laid it on the small table and brushed it flat. "God knows how they managed to get it printed and posted all over the town already. Especially with the election going on. But here it is anyway. Puts the blame fair and square on the Radical supporters for provoking a riot and attacking the Magistrate. Here:

> ... *repeatedly beseeched the mob to disperse and return to their homes peacefully when he was hit by a large, solid missile, well-aimed by a group of individuals who had positioned themselves in advance to ensure the success of their evil intentions. The yards of yellow ribbon with which they had adorned themselves left their political allegiances in no doubt. Sir Robert Dugdale, who thanks the military for their prompt and retrained action which saved the town from a riot of unforeseeable proportions, pointed out that this was exactly what the opponents of the so-called Reform Bill had constantly warned of: that the forces of Jacobinism and anarchy would be unleashed on our unwitting nation. We all thank God that the life Sir Robert Frances, the Earl of Newdigate and our protecting Magistrate is no longer in danger as a result of the cowardly and treacherous attack.*

The three men were silent again, mulling over one single shared thought: Someone from their own ranks had been so stupid, so violent as to risk the success of what they had been planning for half a year – the return of the Radical candidate Hemmings against the Tory Dugdale. Felix walked over to the window and carefully removed the thick cloth, letting in a sharp beam of dusty light. "At least there are a few people getting out and about again. There'll be little or no voting today though. Hardcastle might try to get some of the Tory voters in from the country but I daresay Hemmings will call for a boycott. Protest against the army being called in."

He was talking more to himself, articulating his thoughts but both Mary and Johnnie could hear him and exchanged looks when Hardcastle's name was mentioned. She asked quietly, hoping that only her friend would hear her. "Johnnie, is Hardcastle the man who bought the apples here yesterday?" Johnnie nodded.

"Tell me again. What are the colours? Blue for Tory and yellow for the Radicals?"

But now the three men were listening to Mary, suddenly amused by the interest this pleasantly attractive girl was showing in such weighty matters which were no concern of hers. Before she could continue, the tall man came over to her.

"Here, Miss Nosey, read it all for yourself." Felix held the handbill out for Mary to fetch.

"I can't read. Not good enough for something as hard as that, anyway."

The two other men, but not Johnnie and his father, laughed loudly. "She can't read but she wants to interfere in politics!"

After the men had sat down again and were no longer staring at her, Mary left without a word. On the short way home she wondered about Lizzie. And she wondered about Polly's baby. You needed more than piles of rags to keep warm in weather like this. Coal was cheap in the town which was surrounded by shallow mines but perhaps not so cheap that Polly would have enough for a good fire. She'd ask her mother to spare Polly a bucketful.

Chapter 3

Although almost all the mines around Nuneaton were on his land, Newdigate didn't like coal fires. The servants were of course allowed to use coal in their quarters and they were supplied with it for free. But he himself insisted on wood. Oak or beech branches, chopped, split and then dry-stacked for at least two years. His agent, Evans, was the best man for wood in the county and he made sure that only perfect logs were burned in the massive fireplaces of Arbury Hall. Good man, Evans. Newdigate mused and let his thoughts wander as he sat in front of the blazing fire in the suite reserved for him at the Castle Hotel, one hand resting on his walking stick and the other dangling over the enormous dog lying at his feet so that he could stretch his fingers slightly and tickle her behind the ears.

A hardly audible knock at the door and a male servant came in and whispered something to the Earl, whose eyelashes flickered assent. The servant left and Sir Robert Dugdale entered through the still open door. After they had greeted each other with fleeting eye contact, Dugdale took a seat at the hearth, the dog's bulging eyes acknowledging the visitor's familiar presence.

Before the two men heard Jermyn's and Hardcastle's footsteps in the corridor, the dog had raised her head and looked expectantly at her master, begging for some indication of how she should behave when the intruders appeared. Both

Newdigate and Dugdale recognised the dog's signal and stood up to greet their guests, the Earl reducing the muscular animal at his feet to a heavily breathing rug with a brief wave of his hand and a few very quiet words.

Seated at the highly polished table and each with a glass of brandy in front of him, the four men had exchanged pleasantries when Newdigate took control of the conversation.

"I, or rather we," nodding slightly towards Dugdale, "have asked you all" - he expressly acknowledged Hardcastle's presence with a nod - "to meet here because the situation is so, let us say, critical. I don't mean to say that it is unfavourable. On the contrary, events have gone exceedingly well until now." He looked pointedly at both Jermyn and Hardcastle. "No. But it is indeed critical. The battle, so to speak, is in its decisive phase."

Hardcastle showed no emotion whatsoever but inwardly he scoffed at the choice of phrase. The only fighting this lord had ever seen was at a boxing match or in a day's hunting. But his lordship continued.

"And let us make no mistake. This is not only a battle. It is a war. If my good friend Dugdale is not elected to this parliament, then our constituency will never again in the future be adequately represented."

You mean, your dandified, pink-fisted puppet here will never get into parliament, thought Hardcastle contemptuously, but with a bland expression that those present, had they bothered to spare him a glance, might have taken for stoical obedience.

Newdigate continued: "If you ever entertained even the slightest doubts as to our determination to ensure a successful outcome to our campaign, then yesterday's events will have put paid to them." He paused, reached into his side pocket and took out a slip of paper which he passed on to Jermyn. "Five hundred guineas, Mr Hardcastle. For your efforts so far. Jermyn will be so good as to pay it out to you today."

Hardcastle realised that even a *thank you* would be inappropriate and said nothing.

"A further five hundred will be paid on my friend's election to the House of Commons. On Monday."

Both Jermyn and Hardcastle indicated the surprise they knew they were expected to feel.

"Yes, gentlemen. There will be a third day's voting on Monday to compensate for the lack of activity due to the riots and its lawful suppression. Of course the Radicals will protest but arrangements have already been made." He turned towards the sleek, corpulent lawyer seated to his right. "Perhaps, Jermyn would be so good as to describe the situation and our immediate plans."

Hardcastle sat motionless and made a determined, conscious effort to avoid betraying his loathing and contempt for this pompous lawyer who, after clearing his throat, adjusting his cravat and stretching his fingers several times like a pianist preparing to perform, finally began:

"As his lordship has pointed out, voting was curtailed yesterday due to the riots, but even so the Radicals have a clear lead. Hemmings has about two hundred votes to our Sir Robert's eighty or so. Our influence in other parts of the borough will of course partly counterbalance this, but Coventry is, so to speak, beyond our sphere of influence and the new Bill has granted many new franchises there which will probably be used in favour of the Radical candidate. It is, as you know, an unfortunate consequence of the Reform Act that …"

Newdigate coughed very quietly and tapped the floor with the point of his stick and the lawyer took his hint immediately.

"I will come to the point. What happens here, in Nuneaton, will probably decide whether Hemmings or Sir Robert is elected or not. That is the one fact. The second is: left to, er, chance, we can expect, also as a consequence of the Reform Bill, that the Radicals would carry the day here as in most similar boroughs throughout the land. Which is why the course of things cannot be left to chance. If events can be so, er, guided so that Sir Robert has a small majority here in Nuneaton, then he will be elected. If not, Hemmings and the Radicals will, as I said, carry the day."

He assured himself that Newdigate was satisfied with the concision and content of his speech and continued.

"Today, not many votes will be cast. The Radicals are staying away in protest at yesterday's events. Many of our supporters are afraid to come into the town for fear of further riots. So, our course of action is clear: Mr Hardcastle, you must see to it that on Monday - there will of course be no voting on the Sabbath - our supporters get into town and vote. And that Hemming's men don't! You have the Lord's Day at your disposal to ensure the work is done on Monday! Sufficient resources will be made available."

That's what Hardcastle liked. A target you can set your sights on, a defined, achievable target. Get the right result in this small section and the whole borough will fall to Dugdale. It was what he was good at and he had no doubt that he would do it. Though expected to take his leave, he paused and looked at Jermyn, who understood the tacit question.

"The resources? Financially, as far as you are concerned, there is no limit. So far our expenses," he looked at Newdigate for permission to proceed and got it, "are in the region of ten thousand guineas. We expect to invest at least that amount again for, er, entertainments and other services. The problem of course is that these Dissenters mostly have enough money of their own and care little for the kind of entertainment we can offer. It will be difficult to sway them."

Despite his awareness of his lordship's impatience, he couldn't resist pausing to ensure maximum effect for his following remark.

"We have, however, received some intelligence from one of the ladies, er, downstairs which might at least, let's say, neutralise enough of them intending to …"

Newdigate coughed and tapped the floor with his cane. Jermyn stopped in full flow, resigning himself to the fact that their business was done and the meeting was over.

Hardcastle was the first to leave and as he walked slowly down the broad staircase he asked himself what that well-oiled lawyer had meant by *the ladies downstairs*. Why Newdigate was prepared to invest a colossal sum to secure his candidate's election didn't interest him. A good soldier never asks *Why*. He had learnt that lesson from the Iron Duke. But he couldn't rest without knowing all the factual details of the part of the campaign he was directly involved in.

He tried the door on the second-floor landing. It opened silently. A thickly carpeted corridor stretched the length of the whole floor and there were four five doors, some open, to the rooms and suites on either side of it. He could hear the animated voices and laughter of young women coming from the rooms. Were they the families of the soldiers? Or servants preparing the rooms? He walked ten yards or so along the corridor till he reached the first open door and looked in. Warm, heavily and sweetly perfumed air floated towards him and one of the two young women in the room turned to face him. Although she was only half-dressed, she walked without embarrassment towards the door.

"Business starts after dinner and not before. Even for a handsome fellow like you!"

Hearing this, the other woman turned to get a look at him and he caught a brief but clear glimpse of the elder of the two girls he had seen in the shop and whom he had led into the hotel courtyard away from the riots. She was lounging contentedly in a plush armchair, one bare leg stretched out and the other rested over the arm of the seat, her cheeks flushed pink from both the warmth of the room and from the champagne she was sipping. As she turned her head, her brown, curly hair fell onto her naked shoulders. Her petticoats were pulled up almost to her waist and her bodice was unhooked so that her breasts were partly exposed but she made no attempt to cover herself. There was a long instant of mutual recognition before the door closed silently in his face.

Chapter 4

The Independent Chapel was full as usual on that Sunday evening but the atmosphere surrounding the congregation was exceptionally tense, as every person present was gnawed by the need to hear what their elders' comments on the events of the day before would be. Every word from the Minister's sermon, even the short quotation from Revelations, had seemed to have a direct relevance to the horror when fifty cavalrymen of the Scots Grey regiment had ridden through the town centre on horses whose withers stood higher than a man's head. Great, snorting powerful drays, foaming, sweating and their heads tossing, drove straight as a furrow through the mud, sending it flying ten feet in the air in big, soft clods. The horsemen stood in the stirrups and struck out with the flats of their swords at anything and anyone in their reach, their bright red uniforms and the glinting metal forming enormous blotches of colour in the grey drizzle. Except for one group of men, either too drunk, too stupid or even too brave to move, the crowd scattered in all directions. About a dozen men tried to stay on one side of the charge and some threw stones that had been churned up out of the street surface. The column rode past them and turned suddenly, veering at the last moment into a curve, returning and forming a revolving circle so that the cluster of resistance had no chance to escape. A few of the men threw themselves flat onto the ground when they saw the soldiers had turned their blades to strike down those who had remained standing with the cutting edge of their swords. Then they rode away in the direction they had come from. Three of the men were dead on the spot and two others lay screaming and writhing in the mud, blood gushing from their gaping wounds.

It was all over within two minutes. And the shock still gripped the body and minds of the many members of the congregation who had witnessed it. It had been as sudden and as punitive as the wrath of God. None of the dead or maimed were worshippers at this or any church. They were truculent miners or weavers who had no vote anyway, their latent defiance turned to recklessness by drink. But here, the soberly but expensively dressed brethren were almost all voters, newly franchised by the Reform Bill. Now guilt tainted their new-found right. As though their loss of political innocence had been purchased with the terrible violence and terrifying force of those fifty men on horseback, as well as by the blood, limbs and lives of the few who had foolishly dared resist them. Rationally, the guilt was undeserved. But there was hardly a man present who could shrug it off completely. They expected Brother Muscat to refer to it when he spoke to the gathering after the formal end of the service. He stood on the floor of the chapel, as suited his ambiguous position as neither simply one of the elders nor a minister of the church. It was well lit and he could see the door at the end of the middle aisle and most of the people on the benches to the right and left of it. He clutched a Bible to his chest and looked down at the newly paved floor. As he raised his head to speak there was total silence and so some heads turned irritably as the door opened at the back and a tall, well-built man, unknown to all except Brother Muscat, entered, took off his hat and sat down at the seat nearest the door. The arrival of the stranger seemed to have distracted the speaker because he paused as if needing time to recollect his thoughts before he spoke:

"Brothers and Sisters. What I have to say is brief. I have thought long and very hard. I have prayed for guidance. I have read the scriptures and I have looked deep into my own heart."

He raised his head so that his gaze was directed over the heads of his audience. Hardcastle thought with whimsical amusement that he looked as if he were about to start singing but Muscat spoke with the faintest trace of nervousness in his voice:

"My conscience tells me it would be wrong for us to cast our votes tomorrow."

Amazement hissed round the gathering like a sudden gust of cold air. He waited for the murmuring to subside before he resumed:

"Mr Hemmings has lodged a protest, which his legal advisors assure him has every chance of success, against the polling. His case is that the events, the riots, the disorders, call them what we will, have so disturbed the due process of this election, this historic election, that it should be declared void and new elections arranged immediately."

He paused again and, unwillingly detecting the faintest suggestion of an approving nod from the stranger, directed his eyes again over and beyond the heads of the congregation.

"As the great majority, if not all of our community would, I dare to assume, be voting for Mr Hemmings, our participation in the voting would weaken the protest and lend validity to any polling that takes place. My advice, my earnest exhortation to those men who have the franchise is: do not exercise it tomorrow. Stay away and let law and justice take their due course. In the calm of re-arranged polling days – the lawyers agree they can take place within two weeks – we can be of sure of the victory that is rightly ours."

Few people noticed Hardcastle leave in the commotion that followed. Muscat took his seat on the bench reserved for elders. He had done what he could. But Hardcastle had made

Dugdale's election the condition of Lizzie's silence. And so the slut could still ruin him. He closed his eyes and asked himself: Why did I do it? And his imagination provided him with the answer instantly and vividly in his mind's eye. Lizzie sitting naked from the waist up on her bed, waiting for him, leaning towards him expectantly, unfastening his trousers and doing things to him that would shame a whore. Wicked things and it was the wickedness that excited him beyond control, her wickedness not his. All he could do now was wait and hope and pray that Dugdale would be returned.

On the following Wednesday, two days after the polls had closed, Hemmings' protest was rejected and Dugdale was officially returned as Member of Parliament for Warwickshire, Northern Division. As expected Newdigate's candidate had won a big majority in the rural area and Hemmings had prevailed in the urban areas of Coventry and parts of Birmingham. Due to the abstention of numerous Radical supporters, Dugdale gained a slight majority in Nuneaton which tipped the overall balance in his favour.

Hardcastle was glad that only one more piece of business remained for him to finalise before he could at last leave this town for good. As arranged, Muscat arrived punctually at an isolated spot on Newdigate's estate, the same place they had met on the Sunday, a few hours before the evening service. He was visibly relieved and spoke directly.

"I hope you are here to inform me that this episode of blackmail is now over and done with."

Hardcastle held out an envelope towards him with the carefully practised words:

"Here is the avadavat, Sir. Without this any accusations against your good name are simply slander. You can be sure no-one would take a whore's word against yours."

Muscat took the envelope, sealed with a generous patch of hard wax, bearing Jermyn's stamp.

"Why did she do this to me? I was never unkind to her."

"For the five hundred guineas I dare say! And a complete wardrobe. Not to mention rent-free rooms in Manchester. She is a business woman, Mr Muscat. And a damned good one."

Muscat looked at Hardcastle blankly, as if the word *damned* was completely unknown to him. Sensing the other man was anxious to leave, Hardcastle spoke quickly.

"There is one other thing I am supposed to tell you, Sir. This has not been a way of doing business the Earl prefers. It was done purely according to the dictates of necessity. I'm to give you this as proof of his Lordship's sincere regret about how circumstances have created unpleasantness between you and himself." He handed Muscat a large envelope. "He hopes that you will come to understand the constraints that forced him to take the steps he did and that some time in the future, should the situation arise, that you may even join him in ventures of mutual interest."

Muscat was dumbfounded. He fumbled with the second envelope Hardcastle had handed to him, this one containing banknotes for one thousand guineas.

"Ventures of mutual interest? What on earth can he mean?"

Again Hardcastle sounded almost as if he had rehearsed the sentence when he said:

"He anticipated that question, Sir, and instructed me to reply to it with one word: *Railways*."

Chapter 5

That same morning Johnnie took the daily supplies to the Castle Hotel with the faint hope of seeing Lizzie but she had gone, had taken the North-bound coach, inside seat, at 6 o'clock. Her last act before leaving had been to insist, in front of several servants, the coachman and other passengers, that the officer who bade her goodbye call her Elisabeth! When Johnnie told Mary about it that evening, he cried. He had always dreamed she would marry him one day, that she would get into such a mess that she'd have no alternative but to take him. He was too intelligent to believe she'd marry him out of choice.

When he told Mary, she didn't cry. She was saddened but many other things. Above all she wanted to know: Was Lizzie free? Was she happy? She knew that men wanted her too. She wasn't as beautiful as her friend but she was an attractive girl. She thought about what Lizzie had said to Johnnie the last time they were together. Something like: *Don't feel sorry for me. Feel sorry for the respectable women who come in here!* Did she mean it was bad to be a respectable woman, like Mary's mother for example, who was not well-off but who was respectable? Or was she? She'd like to ask her: *Mother, are you respectable?* But she knew she couldn't. Perhaps she could ask Polly Button. Her father wasn't respectable. He worked hard but he was no better than the men who came into the public house to drink. He often tried to watch her when she was washing herself and sometimes he'd creep up on her and try to fondle her. What would her mother say if she told her? Maybe she knew. Mary had heard her, beside herself with rage, screaming at her father once. Lizzie was sure that Mrs Muscat had known about her husband and Lizzie. Why did she keep quiet, accept? Was that being respectable? Keeping bad things secret. If so she could understand why Lizzie thought respectable women were to be pitied. But to be pitied more than a whore? Is it so bad to be respectable? Or perhaps being a whore is not as bad as people say.

*

It was still very cold and Mary had wrapped rags around her hands which made it hard for her to grip the heavy bucket of coal she was taking to Polly. Although it was only a few hundred yards she had to stop and rest her arms so often that it took her almost ten minutes to reach the yard where Polly had her tiny house. In the dark, the broken slabs made the going more difficult, but when she tapped carefully on the window she received the usual rapturous welcome from the gnarled, vivacious woman.

Warming her hands on the mug of tea, she watched Polly on her knees transferring the coal from the bucket to a scuttle. Polly wasn't as talkative as usual so she had time to think about the question she wanted to ask but it still came out blunt and awkward.

"What's worse for a woman, Polly, being respectable or being a whore?"

Polly had five daughters, all illegitimate from three different fathers, and she had heard a lot of questions in her time. But this one stopped her in her tracks. She was about to drop a lump of coal into the scuttle, lowered her head a little and looked at Mary from under her outstretched arm. Finally she let the piece of coal fall.

"I ain't neither dear. So how would I know?"

"But if you could choose. You'd be respectable wouldn't you?"

"Choose? What's that? We're women, Poll. We don't choose. We just accept what happens to us."

She stood up and wiped her hands on some rags.

"Men can choose. Like Danks. He can pay me the shilling a week the Elders told him to cough up for Babbie here. Or he can let it be."

"And you can't do anything to make him pay?"

"Oh yes. I can shop him. Then they'll send him off to 'Stralia. You know. Transport him. Fat lot of good that'd do me though. No chance of getting the money. And not even a bit of widow's comfort now and then. Not until somebody else came along anyway."

Much as she liked Polly, Mary had always wondered how this scrawny, wrinkled woman, at forty already worn out by childbirth, poverty and work, always seemed to have a man. Now it was Danks, a large, gangly farm labourer, married to a much older woman who tyrannised him and whom he feared more than he feared the town Elders.

"I suppose somebody'd turn up sooner or later. Men'll do it with anybody. Even me. When they're poking the fire they don't bother about what's on the mantelpiece. But I'm used to Danks. Another might be even worse. He'll be round again soon I expect. Now I'm over the birth. If he can get away from that wife of his. Don't know why he risks coming to me when he's got it at home anyway. She begrudges it him I expect. And I'm grateful for it."

She was rumbling on more to herself, but Mary was hanging on to every word.

"Does she know?"

"Course she don't. He's scared stiff she'll find out. Apart from her tongue, she'd have her brother kick his ribs in if she got wind of us."

In the dim yellowy candlelight Mary noticed that Polly's face was smudged with coal dust so she went over to her, dipped some clean rag in a bowl of water and began wiping the woman's face clean.

"Why don't you say you'll tell her."

"That'd be worse for him than being sent to 'Stralia."

For the second time within a few days Mary found herself giving advice and she suddenly became slightly impatient with the older woman, whose apparent charity for the man willing to let his bastard child starve seemed to be blocking her suggestion. She almost shouted:

"Don't really tell her. But threaten to. If he don't give you the money for Lizzie."

"Lizzie? The babbie! Just threaten him, you mean? Put the fear of her up him. He'll shit himself." She looked at the girl with a slow recognition of how shrewd her idea was. "You mean scare him into doing what I want him to do?" For as along as she could remember this scrawny but resilient woman had been involved with scavenging men in a tacit trade of her body in return for scraps of pleasure and the hope of affection. Now a girl hardly out of puberty was suggesting how she might intimidate a man and manipulate his behaviour. She spoke quietly, almost to herself:

"I'd put the boot on the other foot, that's for sure." Then she looked at Mary with a cagey, almost respectful curiosity:

"You know, that's a bold notion for a chicken like you."

Chapter 6

Almost exactly two years later, shortly before Christmas 1834, there was a short boom in the town for the production of new ribbon and Mary started work at Muscat's mill. At home she'd been using a loom since she was twelve as well as helping in the public house so that she was used to hard work. She left home before six and got back twelve hours later and soon after was helping in the pub which meant her younger sister was now doing the shopping at Astley's store. So she gradually lost contact with Johnnie and his limitless supply of gossip but even he had no news about Lizzie anyway. She thought about Lizzie and about Polly and her mother. Without being really conscious of it she had always somehow assumed that she would become one of the three - that her life as a grown woman would be similar to that of one of these three women. But at the factory, where about fifty women, twenty men and a few children worked, her world suddenly became much bigger. The first factory in the area to have steam power, there was something pioneering, a sense of being at the forefront which made the men proud and the women cocky despite the long tedious working hours. In fact, the advanced technology of the Jacquard looms, with their punch-card controlled pattern-making operation, capable of producing intricate patterns at high speed and a minimum of labour, had only progressed as far as nearby Coventry, where the first ones had been destroyed by weavers who feared their hunger would become starvation should they not halt the general introduction of machinery. The fear was far from being without foundation. Mary had been to a meeting where Joseph Gutteridge, a skilled Coventry weaver forced to accept menial work in a newly-opened factory, had informed his fellows in Nuneaton about his own experience with the effects of the most modern production methods combined with the depression in the weaving trade. She could recall the gist of his words as he had spoken about the effect progress had had on his family:

> *In the dead of winter we thought we would lose our youngest child and we broke up our last pieces of furniture to make a fire and warm him back to life. For two days we had eaten nothing and, had it not been for my thought of my wife and children, I would have been maddened to suicide. I remember one morning standing in front of a baker's shop, the loaves of fresh bread were for a few moments left unattended. Never in my life had I been so close to becoming a thief. Whether from cowardice, conscience or rational fear of punishment I do not know, but I walked away, honest in act if not in thought.*

There was similar suffering amongst her neighbours too, but still Mary and most of the hands found something like exhilaration in their work, which, though exacting and unhealthy, had given up much of its manual exertion to the great steam-driven wheel driving shaft that stretched the length of the workshop. The shaft moved the shuttles and threw the battens backwards and forwards by means of a system of cranks. The various threads of the warp were raised and lowered to create simple but exact patterns by a rod or bar, which gave the machines the name of a-la-bar looms, and which connected the great wheel with the mechanism over each loom. Mary's work involved watching out for flaws or grouts in the fabric, picking up broken threads and ensuring that the exhausted shuttles were refilled. At home she still used the old engine or Dutch loom to be found in most of the town's homes but that work was far more tiring, both physically and mentally. She had to sit leaning forward against a rest and activated the treadles with her feet to raise and lower the threads of the warp. At the same time she would swiftly throw the shuttle with the lateral weft from hand to hand with a precision that required both concentration and dexterity. The vertical warp was unwound by a simple weight, many home-based weavers used a brick but Mary used a bottle so that she could vary the speed at which the warp was released by the amount of water she filled it with. In the mill she was deprived of this autonomy and had to adapt to the dictates of the machinery but, gruelling and relentless as the work was, there was a cheerfulness and companionship that was as novel as the technology itself.

Most of the women were slightly older than Mary, only a few of them married, so their meagre earnings enhanced them with a definite if limited amount of extra income. The six shillings a week Mary was taking home made a big impact on her family's income and some of the older girls were getting as much as 10 shillings a week, when there was enough work. And now there was plenty.

Muscat was one of the new breed of manufacturers, proud of his use of the latest manufacturing technology. He had moved from Birmingham, where he had worked and been well trained at the factory belonging to Mathew Boulton and James Watt, to set up his own business. With his sound technical understanding and ability to raise and invest capital wisely, he had already made a lot of money in an otherwise struggling area of manufacturing. And he had brought more than just knowledge with him from Boulton's works. A stubborn, vital residue of the old paternalism occupied a strong position in his mentality, despite his allegiance to functional utilitarianism. The two handsome and much-loved horses, for example, that had been used for power before the steam engines had been installed and were now redundant, had not been knackered as purely commercial business sense dictated. They had a comfortable paddock adjacent to the mill and they'd come lumbering up to the fence as the first workers arrived, sure of some tit-bits to supplement their already adequate fodder.

Mary's favourite was Caroline – a dappled mare who would often stand back from most of the visitors but always ambled up purposefully to greet Mary. Perhaps it was because Mary often mixed some oats into the small sack of stale bread she fed Caroline from, but they'd stand with their heads close together even when the fodder was long gone, Mary cooing and humming softly to the magnificent animal. Occasionally the horses, both still in their prime, would be hitched up to the mill's ornately decorated wagon used for festivities and very special deliveries. Once, Mary had been in town with her two younger sisters when they had spotted Caroline yoked alongside her companion, waiting patiently for their wagoner. The girls looked lost in admiration and envy of their big sister as she reached up to stroke the muzzle of her special friend who looked especially regal in the spotless leather reins, adorned with brass ornaments, and the brightly polished bit. The combination of leather, wood and metal enhanced the superb animal's natural dignity and her presence soon attracted a crowd of people and children, all trying to get close to this celebrity.

From then on Mary would sometimes take her sisters along with her when she went to Caroline on Sundays, though she most liked to enjoy the mare's strength and serenity alone. The latent power of the dray, though transformed into quiescence, was perceptible not so much in her size and proportions but in the almost tangible aura of harmony and health that surrounded her. There was a subdued completeness about her and Mary allowed it to imbue her with contentment, as if the horse's satisfaction were also her own.

She was alone the first time that Muscat's nephew, Henry, had already been standing near the paddock apparently by chance when she arrived. She knew him by sight as he worked as bookkeeper at the mill, in his own small room next to his uncle's office. He seemed to have a soft spot for one of the girls, Nancy, who he often chatted with when his uncle was out and who was also Mary's closest friend. A few days before, Mary had noticed them talking earnestly together about something that obviously amused and interested them intensely. For a second they returned her glance but it didn't occur to Mary, observant as she was, that they were talking about her.

In the breaks the girls sat in small groups and chatted about their families, about snippets of gossip that relatives working as servants in the houses of the better-off had picked up. Most of all though, they talked about men. The men they liked; the men they disliked or hated or feared; the men they wanted to marry or who wanted to marry them; and sometimes about the men they loved. Mary began to understand that only two things, if anything, kept the girls chaste; lack of opportunity and fear of pregnancy.

Mary's friend, Nancy, was extrovert and experienced, and Mary was both amused and fascinated by her explicit, unfettered talk.

"My mother told me not to do it before I'm engaged. But I tell you, once you've had it you'll not want to wait! You needn't look so bashful, Poll. I can remember when I was your age. I used to think about it all the time." She tickled Mary under the chin. "My thinking days are over now though! And you? I've seen enough chaps giving you the eye. When are you going to start?"

The question didn't surprise or embarrass Mary. In fact it was something she asked herself often enough. Polly had told her that she had had her first experience when she was fourteen and at Mary's age, 17, already had a daughter of her own, so Mary didn't feel she was too young. She wasn't afraid either. Lizzie had taught her quite a bit about sex, even explained to her in detail how a woman could, with a high level of certainty, avoid getting pregnant. So she answered Nancy's question truthfully.

"Soon. But I don't know who with."

"What about …" But she stopped suddenly when she noticed the mill-owner, Mr Muscat, walking over to them. Nancy nodded towards him as she spoke and they both looked down to avoid his glance in their direction. A staidly but well-dressed, slightly corpulent man, Muscat did his rounds at least once a day through his factory, though seldom during break time. Inevitably he found something to quibble about or pick fault with, or even sometimes to admonish, always with a view to saving costs and increasing profit, albeit to a miniscule degree. He also found time to chat with a few employees, usually female, young and attractive ones.

"Oh no! He's coming over!"

"No, no young ladies, please stay seated. Recuperate your strength in your breaks. That's why we have them."

He greeted Nancy by her first name and then looked carefully at Mary.

"I don't think I know your name."

"Wright, Sir. Mary Wright. I only started here not long ago."

"But your face is familiar, Miss Wright. Have I seen you perhaps at the Chapel?"

"No, Sir. My father keeps the Malter's Arms public house. I help out there. Perhaps … "

He raised his hands.

"Perish the thought child that I should enter such a place."

Mary could have bitten off her lip for being so stupid but remained silent for fear of making things worse. But then she realised where Muscat had in fact seen her, spoken to her in fact.

"Excuse me, Sir. But I think we met briefly in Astley's shop. You said Good-day to me."

He looked at her, now even more confused. Why should he greet a strange girl of sixteen or so? She recognised his look.

"I was with Lizzie Johnson. Your … lodger she was then."

It was her uncertainty, the slight pause and then the choice of the word *lodger* that made him think that she perhaps knew all about him and Lizzie. His face became very serious; he clasped his hands together, then placed them on the table Mary and Nancy were sitting at, and leaned forward.

"Are you trying to vex me, child?"

Her astonished reaction to the accusation was so sincere that Muscat relaxed inwardly. *No, she knows nothing. She was just genuinely looking for the right word. How could she know? The Jezebel would never have divulged such a valuable secret for nothing. She had proved that later.* His thoughts calmed him and he straightened himself.

"Of course you didn't mean to vex me. It was only the word lodger. You know, a lodger pays for his board but my good wife and I took in that poor orphan without asking an earthly reward. The mere suggestion that it might be so annoyed me for a second. Please forget all about it."

Despite herself, Mary couldn't help acknowledging, even admiring the composure and ease with which Muscat slipped into his lie, into his assumed identity. Strange. All the women Mary knew seemed to be only one person. Polly was always

Polly, her mother was as constant as the North Star. Even Lizzie had never kept up any pretence, not towards her friend at least. When the time came she changed one way of life for another, just as she had changed her few simple clothes for an abundant wardrobe. She had always been, and hopefully still was, just what she seemed. But the men could somehow be two people at one and the same time and it didn't appear to bother them nor anyone else. Even her own father, if he caught her alone in the rooms where his daughters washed themselves, would try to touch her, and then, a few minutes later in the crowded bar of the pub would behave as if nothing had happened. And it was, in fact, almost as if nothing had happened. If Mary had decided to forget it or never to think about it, then who was to say it had ever happened? Of course she would never even think of telling anyone but equally she was determined not to forget it. Mary was alert. She noticed things. Everyone who knew her well commented on that. What they couldn't know was that she thought about things constantly, turned them over in her mind, trying to make sense of them; things like her father's behaviour and now Muscat's ability to belie with total accomplishment one dimension of his life and character as if each of them could step in and out of who they were at will.

Mary looked at the mill-owner as he stood there in front of her in flesh and blood and tried to imagine at the same time some of the things Lizzie had told her about him. How, when they were alone in the house, he would read parts of the Bible to her, about wickedness, lewdness, fornication and sin. Sometimes he would prove to her that the devil was at large in the world by reading from French novels and when he was excited beyond control would demand that she enact on him some of the most outrageous scenes. Lizzie didn't mind it. He was clean, had no disease and was never violent to her. All he required was that she would pray with him together after it was over and ask for her sins to be forgiven, for her wickedness to be atoned. It was a bargain, she said. Not a bad bargain for her, though he had the advantage, his forbidden, ecstatic pleasures against her free board and lodging, plus a tiny cash allowance.

She suddenly became aware of Henry approaching, and dreaded for a second that he wanted to speak to her but he only touched his uncle's arm gently to get his attention, whispering something into his ear. The mill owner took his leave with a nod towards Mary and Nancy and left hurriedly in the direction of his office. Henry scurried after him but still managed to throw a glance back at the girls. When the two men had disappeared Nancy looked at Mary with a big inquisitive grin on her face.

"Well? Will he do?"

Mary smiled back faintly and the slight movement of her eyes showed that if she didn't actually assent, she didn't reject the suggestion outright either.

*

In the months that followed Henry often found an excuse to talk and joke with Mary and as soon as that winter had gone, and the days became warmer, dryer and longer and she freed herself, layer by layer, from the shapeless mass of clothing that only half protected her from the incessant cold that had chilled her body, she decided that the time had come for her to make love with him. On a warm Sunday evening in early May, Mary slipped away from the family's public house and met Henry, who was dressed in his Sunday best for the meeting house assembly he had just left, and they hurried the mile or so to the place she had chosen. They walked a hundred yards along the canal tow path then crossed a narrow bridge and went down into a meadow lower than the level of the canal. She led him, hand in hand, through a dense thicket of hawthorns alongside the waterside, moving her bare legs carefully between the briars until they reached a small hollow hidden from sight from the open field by a row of bushes and behind them by the raised canal bank. Honeysuckle and deadly nightshade wove and tangled themselves between the brambles and the lower branches of the hawthorn bushes and in the long dry grass she could see cowslips, daisies, dandelions and wild violet. In the quiet seclusion she savoured the balmy fragrance from the spring flowers and blossoms surrounding them, lying on her back on the grassy slope which raised her slightly so that when she looked at Henry, kneeling and unfastening his clothes like the young but experienced lover he was, their heads were at the same level. He looked back at her, and was surprised when she pulled her skirts up around her waist. She had taken something out of her dress pocket. Seeing the direction of his gaze and his look of surprise, she laughed as if reading his thoughts.

"It'll stop anything happening. You don't want to have to marry me, do you Henry?"

Having removed some of his clothes and laid them neatly to one side and discretely unbuttoned others, he was now ready and lay close beside her, touching her face and loosening the upper part of her dress. "You said it was the first time." His hand felt the thin thread between the top of her legs. "How do you know about this?"

"From Lizzie. She taught me a lot of things."

He wanted to ask her who Lizzie was but his curiosity soon gave way to pleasure and excitement.

By the time they were dressed again the sun was low. They left their bower to make their way into town before darkness fell but just as they were crossing the bridge they heard a dog yapping from a canal barge, towed silently by a hefty dray horse. They looked down over the wall of the bridge, his arm affectionately around her waist, until the boat, laden with coal and sitting low in the placid brown water, had passed under them. Despite the calmness around them, the unease he had felt momentarily before they made love returned and he asked her:

"This Lizzie you talk about. Who is she?"

There were many answers she could have given him and they all flashed through her agile mind. She took a piece of loose stone from the wall and threw it into the water, where it plopped and disappeared without a ripple. For some reason the sound amused her and she threw in a larger stone which made a splash somehow at odds with the comforting harmony of the moment. He needn't know that her friend Lizzie was the same orphaned girl who had lived with his pious uncle and had suddenly left the town when the regiment of Scots Greys had withdrawn. That was almost four years ago now and perhaps he hadn't even heard about it or had forgotten. Whatever, there was no reason to complicate their simple relationship which, for both of them, rested on some affection and much pleasure.

"Someone, an older woman who used to come into my father's pub. I think she's dead now."

The lie came so easily she shocked herself but when Henry took her hand she felt confident and slightly proud as they walked towards the town, already planning their next meeting.

Chapter 7

*J*ohn Astley's Diary

1836. June.

> *Ribbon trade very flat. Only power mill still in full employment. Meeting of weavers to put a stop to practice of home weavers accepting prices below those on list as this will have ruinous consequences for all involved in this trade.*
>
> *During this week the town has been the scene of riotous tumult. Several outrages were committed on persons by placing them on an ass face to tail and conveying them through the streets for having taken wages at low prices. Windows were also broken and a general strike for wages ensued. On Saturday the magistrates assembled in the Town Hall and recommended the distribution of twenty pounds to the poor. However, a meeting of weavers held a few hours later decided to discontinue working for a few days further hoping to force some masters to accept list prices.*
>
> *For almost two months weather has been dry and warm. Vegetation and crops in great need of some rain.*

Rain fell, doing great good to French beans, potatoes and shoots of corn.

A strong degree of excitement produced by the Reverend Tryan of Stockingford Church obtaining a licence from the Bishop to deliver evening lectures.

Ribbon trade in ruinous state.

Many weavers from Nuneaton and Coton have left for Derby to be employed in steam power looms there, where a disagreement between masters and men has left some looms vacant. About fifty went off in a boat provided by employers for that purpose.

Inhabitants amused by gossip of love affair which occurred at Attleborough. The hero, a baker, made his visits to the idol of his heart, a married woman, by means of a ladder placed for convenient access to her chamber window. To signal her availability the heroine let a silk cord hang down from the said window. This not having gone unnoticed by some women neighbours, they waited their chance and removed the ladder, thus forcing the fair one's visitor to effect his retreat through the house and onto the street where he was pursued by outraged husband.

Stone thrown through window of Attleborough Church. Rev. Tryan continues undeterred with evening lectures nonetheless.

July
The Gas and Coke Company reports making good

progress on gas works. First brick laid by Mr Craddock.

Your humble Diarist received long visit from bosom female friend, M, who revealed inmost thoughts and secrets mainly of an amorous nature to him. Recorded on separate paper to ensure discretion.

Match at Cricket with Hinckley Cricket Club (11 each side) in G. Taylor's Field. Prize 5 pounds 10 shillings per side. Nuneaton first Innings 25, second 37. Hinckley first innings 91 thus beating N. in one innings.

Prices back to normal: best beef 5d, mutton 6d, pork 7d, cheese 5 – 7d, candles 7d per doz.

August
The drought continues, having had but few falls of rain which from the excessive heat are soon drawn up again. Grassland brown. Cattle eat interior fodder (as if winter) with avidity. Boughs cut from trees for them. Received very small delivery of vegetables to shop. Potatoes selling here at 8d per stone, at Birmingham 12d to 16d. A turnip is a rarity.

September
The pipes for gas being laid in streets. 80 streets lamps intended in time for winter.

October
Extraordinary case of alleged murder of infant child by servant girl of Mr Nayson, surgeon. Verdict of wilful murder against girl. Though facing hanging,

girl refuses to reveal identity of child's father and he has not come forward, suggesting he has much to lose.

Tempestuous weather.

The Board of Guardians ordered soup to be made for the poor of Nuneaton and Coton. A charitable subscription started on initiative of Tories to be doled out to poor in the form of coal, soup, clothing. Town Crier announced to inhabitants that a list was lying at Mr Short's bookseller and that subscriptions would be thankfully received there.

December
Heavy falls of snow which drifted considerably in strong wind causing great obstructions to roads and coaches. Town without usual bag of London letters for three days.

A soup shop opened with bread for poor. Soup sold at 1d per quart and having about 1lb of meat to the gallon of soup. Ball at Town Hall was attended by 169 persons at 5 and 6 shillings per ticket and netted for the soup shop about 30 pounds. Several persons subscribed in addition for same cause:

Bracebridge		*10.*	*0.*	*0.*
Buchanan		*20.*	*0.*	*0.*
Hood	*5.*	*0.*	*0.*	
Dugdale	*20.*	*0.*	*0.*	

And numerous others making about 130 pounds in all.

Overseers of the Poor renewed order on John Danks to pay Mary Green, known generally as Polly Button, 1s per week per child for upkeep of 2 illegitimate offspring by said woman. Final warning. Woe betide Danks if his wife finds out he's taken up again with Polly!

1837 January

Plans for sections of railway deposited with Parish Clerk, Mr S. Deeming. Protest of more than two hundred owners and occupiers of property of intended line of Tamworth and Rugby against obtaining Bill.

February
First day of introduction of gas into the town and on following day the town was lit generally. Bells ringing, music playing through streets.

Chapter 8

The barn Mary and Henry had used throughout the winter was only a few hundred yards from the main street, just behind Polly Button's house. They met as usual at dusk at the end of the road where the houses finished and walked for less than five minutes along the muddy path without any light to where they wanted to make love. They had been meeting several times a month for about nine months and were totally at ease with each other by now so when he slipped his arm round her in the darkness as they went the last few steps she turned towards him so that he could kiss her on the mouth. Intense and pleasurable as it was, their relationship was for each of them an unreal retreat from their daily lives, in which it had no presence, like a bridge over a road on which they travelled separately. They never mentioned the word *love* to each other nor ever tried to involve each other in their individual lives. He chatted and joked with her at the mill but no more than with other girls. He could have easily and without arousing suspicion shared time with her at her family's pub or she could have pretended faith and attended the Meeting House. But this dislocation of their time together from their usual lives gave each of them a kind of freedom they both enjoyed but which neither of them tried to find words for. It was so unlike anything either of them had ever observed or heard about, as if they had stumbled by chance on a unique, precious place and that merely to mention it might make it disappear. For him, brought up in the constraints and obligations of a family of dissenters, it was the separation of pleasure from guilt, of choice from duty that induced his feelings of release. He already knew enough of religious faith and commercial book-keeping to realise that the pious brethren who divided their lives between profit and prayer, instead of transferring Charity to their businesses, were more adept at grafting the principles of good trade onto their dealings with God, tallying evil and virtue against each other in a moral balance sheet which was inevitably credited in their favour. His unemotional, conscientious dedication to his uncle's accounts strengthened his natural inclination towards disbelief, but this never confused or diluted his determination that when his life's ledger was audited, be it locally in the small community of the Meeting House or domestically before the eyes and ears of his own devout family, or even on Judgement Day, if there were ever to be such an event, then he would be sure that the time and deeds he had invested in the appearance of faith would yield their dividends. To identify an advantage in all, even in adverse situations, was, his uncle often told him, the essence of good business sense. And so it was natural that at first he had dreaded that Mary would sooner or later mention marriage, as if her unrestrained favours were a kind of debt he would some day have to redeem, his unfettered indulgence a bond that she would one day call due. However, as the long hot summer months went by, he came to understand that there was no transaction taking place between himself and her. She demanded nothing of him, neither commitment nor gratitude, and she feigned no sacrifice. The hours she spent with him offered her escape from the dreary, parochial terrain of her everyday life, without the destructive addictions of alcohol or the mental bondage to the Church, an entertainment devoid of consequence or expense. Each meeting gave them unconnected periods of independence from the stagnant murkiness of the small world they returned to inhabit day in day out.

Close to him in the heat of the Sabbath evenings, she felt self-contained, secure, fulfilled, but she never attributed this to an exclusive love for him. She assumed intuitively that their bliss was due to the convergence of favourable circumstances. Some were fortuitous, like her sensual nature and handsome body. Some were the products of design, such as the choice of their first meeting-place, an almost poetic arbour immune to detection, allowing them involvement with each other free from distraction. But most of all, and he knew this because he had so much experience with women, her total lack of guilt and her ability to minimise the risk of pregnancy released them from the ballast of anxiety that had cloyed all his other relationships with an element of deceit. Tacitly allowing servant girls to believe he might reward their compliance with marriage; exploiting the promiscuity of some of the mill girls to thwart any paternity claim that might occur; parrying the women's protestations of sacrificed honour in the hope of him making some concession in the form of engagement or, if the woman was married, of gifts and professions of fidelity; there was none of this with Mary.

She was even more uninhibited and eager now than she had been in the early summer and an hour later they both lay, as so often before, relaxed, satisfied and glad in the dry straw at the back of the barn. They had climbed up into the loft and Henry had pulled up the short ladder and laid it beside them. Mary felt strange security, not complacency but a feeling of being in control of what she had done with Henry. Enclosed in the temporary, comforting isolation of the nest they had arranged in the loft, both of them wanting the same, both giving and taking equally from each other, she knew it was a moment she'd want to recall and think about. Whether it was due to her life in the small world of her family's public house or the unusually close friendships with Lizzie and Johnnie, or if it was something inherent, purely accidental in her character, whatever the cause was, if there indeed was a cause, she had both the ability to observe and the driving determination to understand what went on around her. And now, lying caressed in an event she had created, trying to find words to clarify and describe her feelings, a sudden realisation came to her: she wished she could read. Or write. Which would be more valuable? To write down what she felt or to search for it in what others had written? Without consideration she asked impulsively:

"Can you read Henry?" And then before he could answer: "Of course you can. A clerk has to read. And write."

He propped his head on his hand and looked down at her. Most of the servant girls he had made love with fled as soon as it was over. Either through fear of discovery or shame, he didn't know. The factory girls were different. Some of them would just chatter about people they both knew or about things that had happened at the mill; others became moody, almost sullen and he knew they were thinking about courting, even about getting engaged. Though the girl in question was still too young to approach formally, Henry already knew that he intended one day to marry one of the lawyer Jermyn's daughters. He had always steered adamantly clear of any commitment that might get in the way of this plan. But Mary was like none of the other girls, neither trivialising what they had done nor trying to escalate him into obligation. She looked him in the eye and ran her fingers through his hair while she was thinking.

"Are there books about things like this? About what we're doing?"

"The Bible."

"I mean about people like me and you?"

He thought about the few books he knew. The Waverly novels of Sir Walter Scott were his favourite reading.

"I don't think anybody writes books about people like us, Mary. Why should they?"

"I'll have to find my own words then."

"The Bible calls it fornication. That's what my uncle calls it too."

Mary thought briefly about telling Henry about his uncle and Lizzie. *Wickedness* had been his word for it then but finally she only asked:

"Do you think I'm wicked? Because we - what did you call it - fornicate?"

Henry thought before he spoke, like a bookkeeper checking his addition before committing himself to a final sum.

"I wouldn't call it that. And Nancy wouldn't either. But most of the people I know would."

"And you? What would the people you know say about you?"

He checked his figures even more carefully before he answered:

"The men would say I'm lucky."

"And the women?"

"They'd pretend they didn't know!"

They laughed and Henry felt himself, as so often, warming towards her more than he intended. She pulled his face down to hers and he was pushing his hands along her thighs again when they both heard the barn door creak open. They stopped and Henry rolled quietly onto the hay at Mary's side. They could hear two voices, a muffled male voice and a woman's slightly louder but they couldn't make out what either was saying. Luckily the ladder was in the loft with them so even if the couple stayed, they'd be below and out of sight. Mary was most worried that she might laugh out loud and give their presence away but then she recognised the woman's voice. She pulled Henry's head close to her mouth.

"It's Polly! Polly Button! I think the man is Danks."

She moved forwards as if to admit their presence but Henry held her back.

"Wait till they've gone!"

She was in two minds. She didn't want to eavesdrop on Polly and her lover but what harm would it do if they just kept quiet as Henry advised? She would tell Polly the next day anyway and they'd have a good laugh about it. She lay back on the shallow layer of hay. In the stillness she heard the man's gruff, low voice but couldn't make out what he was saying. Then Polly laughed. Not as Mary knew her vulgar but good-natured laugh but harshly, mockingly, tauntingly. Then the speaking became shouting.

"You think I've come here for that? You fool! I told you. You pay me something tonight or I'm telling tomorrow."

Again there were the muffled tones of the man's voice, followed by Polly screeching at him now, shrill and without restraint.

"No, John Danks. It won't be the town Elders I'll be telling about the payments you haven't made. It's your good lady wife who'll be hearing about us! About how you've been humping me even though you promised her it was over. And now that I'm up to it again, you pressing me to start all over again."

There was a long silence. Mary, though tense, was enjoying the drama of the situation and felt pleased with herself that Polly had listened to her at last, happy that it was her idea that would perhaps force Danks to pay Polly at least some of the money due to her. There was the sound of sudden, hectic movements. Polly's voice, still loud, had changed. There was fear and panic in it.

"Don't be a fool, John!"

Polly screamed at him to let her go and Danks was shouting at her to be quiet. The terror in Polly's voice jolted Mary. She felt her own body become rigid, and her eyes opened wide in the near darkness in an involuntary effort to perceive more of what was happening. All that she could hear was Polly gurgling and heaving frantically for breath. Her senses strained by the tension, she heard the faint rustling of clothes and a light thud. Mary sat up, supporting the upper part of her body on her elbows and just made out Danks' head as he hurried out, leaving the door wide open. Then she fell onto her back again, gazing without seeing at the roof of the hovel, instinctively convinced that Polly was beyond help.

They lay there for seconds, motionless, until Mary tried to place the ladder against the edge of the loft but it was only when Henry came to his senses and helped her that they could descend the few feet to the ground where Polly's body lay.

She wasn't quite dead. Danks had left the pale tallow candle burning where Polly had placed it on the floor. In its grisly yellow light they could see Polly. Her bulging, panic-stricken eyes were still rolling out of control, and her head hung limply to one side. Although blood was still gushing from jagged wounds on each side of her neck, she seemed to be trying to speak. Then she stopped moving and Mary knew she was dead. Henry was first to say anything:

"I'll fetch Constable Haddon!"

Despite the shock, she grabbed his arm and spoke with authority:

"Wait a minute. Let Danks get away first. He's got a knife."

Henry turned towards Mary and watched her slowly fastening her open bodice with exaggerated, unnatural calmness, her eyes fixed in the direction of Polly's blood-drenched body, hardly more than a heap of old clothes. Then he spoke again, with hesitant tact, as if preparing her for bad news:

"Mary, what are we going to say when Haddon comes?"

"Tell him what we heard of course. What else?"

"Not about ..." he paused, then pointed at the twisted wreath of cloth, hair, starkly white skin and crimson blood at his feet. "…not about this. About us. About what we were doing here."

In her look there was incredulity and confusion but also dread, the swelling fear that the young man she had just made love with had suddenly become someone else, a stranger. He mistook the look for a request for an explanation.

"What if my uncle gets to hear of it? He doesn't care what the factory girls and the hands do but he expects us in the office, especially me, to be, well, respectable, like him."

Numbed, emotionally paralysed as she was, she realised with horror that all these months she had been sharing something she cherished with someone she had already inexorably begun to despise. She dropped onto her knee and lifted one of Polly's hands, pressing it against her cheek.

"Tell him what you like. Tell him you were teaching me to pray! But go and get him. Now!"

*

Constable Haddon instructed his younger assistant, Vernon, to run to the barn and he arrived only fifty yards or so ahead of the small crowd of neighbours who had already got wind of the fact that something terrible had occurred. The young policeman put one arm around Mary's shoulder and a hand under her elbow and raised her gently from where she was still kneeling close to her friend's corpse. She was cold now and her body shuddered every few seconds, shaken by incontrollable sobbing. He waited a few minutes before he asked:

"You saw what happened, Mary?"

"Heard it. Heard them talking, then Polly screamed. *Let me loose! Let me loose!* I saw Danks walk out of the door. Henry was here as well."

Vernon covered Polly's body as best he could with his own cape and then ushered the group standing in the doorway further away. Without turning her eyes away from where Polly lay, Mary asked, deliberately and loudly so he would be sure to hear:

"Have they got Danks, Constable?"

"I don't know. Constable Haddon was on his way to his house. But you go home now. Someone might be round to talk to you tomorrow morning."

A woman came into the barn and took Mary's arm in hers and they walked unsteadily along the narrow, muddy path towards the nearest street.

*

Henry followed a few paces behind Haddon. When they reached the door of Danks' house the policeman signalled to him to stand back, drew the stout truncheon from the leather loop and walked confidently without knocking to the kitchen where Danks was slumped over the table. His eyes darted around the dimly lit room.

"You alone, Danks?"

He nodded.

Haddon moved to the table, where the blood-stained knife lay, wrapped it in some cloth and put it in his pocket.

"Are you ready?"

Again he nodded gratefully, as if the policeman was his rescuer who had thankfully arrived before his wife had.

*

The police station consisted of a room and the cell, where Danks lay manacled on the rough plank that served as a bed. In the ample light of several oil lamps Constable Haddon and Henry sat either side of the desk, paper and a pot of ink between them while the policeman wrote his report with a long, scratchy quill. Henry was still hoping that Danks would confess or that there would be so much evidence against him he wouldn't have to appear as a witness. After all, he could at best only corroborate what Mary would say. She had been the one who sat up cautiously when Polly stopped screaming. She must have seen Danks. And she could recognise him whereas he had never seen the killer before Haddon arrested him. The experienced, stolid Peeler listened patiently to the agitated young man. He knew what the pleading was really about and in fact had some sympathy for his concern. Positions like his, assistant to the head book-keeper at the town's most successful business, were hard to come by. It wasn't just blind panic or exaggerated self-interest that made the young fellow so anxious. The case would be reported in the Coventry Herald and the presence of two key witnesses at the scene of the crime, lovers in a hay loft, was bound to feature prominently in the reports. And there was no doubt as to how Muscat would react. One of his most trusted employees, a young relative he had given the opportunity of a lifetime to and who he was grooming to be his chief financial advisor at some time in the not too distant future, this person had repaid him by seducing a factory girl. And, to compound the error, had allowed their lewdness to become public knowledge. A pretty girl, attractive many would say who had gone along willingly for the pleasure. That was true. But that would not mitigate Muscat's judgement. Henry would certainly lose his position if the facts about him and Mary became widely known. Muscat would make no exception, not even for his own nephew. That would be harsh. Haddon belonged to the same congregation as the Muscat family but he was not naturally a judgemental man. If things had really been as Henry described, which the older man was inclined to believe, then he could hardly bring himself to condemn Henry as a sinner, as Muscat would. Imprudent, foolish, reckless even, but he'd done nothing to merit a punishment that would determine the whole future course of his life, hurling him from a deserved position of trust and relative security into an existence, poised precariously on the edge between little more than subsistence and destitution. The hard-headed, in many ways intransigent but basically humane policeman saw no purpose to be served in that. The indiscretion couldn't be undone but if somehow it could be prevented from becoming a local scandal then perhaps Muscat could be won over to turning a blind eye.

The inquest would probably be the next day in the afternoon and Danks would certainly be committed to trial for murder just as his conviction and execution were forgone conclusions, with or without the boy's testimony. Haddon leaned back in his heavy wooden chair and thought carefully. After the inquest it would be too late because then he would have to inform any witnesses of their legal obligation to appear in court. But if Henry were to disappear before the inquest, that night or early the following morning, then he could be called as a witness but his failure to appear would have no consequences. And with luck on his side, his name might never be mentioned.

And so it was that at the crack of dawn the following day Henry boarded the Birmingham coach. After making sure he had really gone, Constable Haddon went to speak with his fellow member of the congregational, Brother Muscat, and convinced him that as long as Henry's indiscretion didn't become widely known it would be unwise to dismiss the lad as this would draw unnecessary attention to the affair. Better for all concerned if he were to lie low for the few weeks until Danks had been disposed of.

"And the girl?"

Muscat asked the question when Haddon was on the point of leaving.

"Mr Vernon instructed her to stay home today. I'm on my way there now. She won't make trouble. Mary's maybe too headstrong for her own good on occasions but she's a sensible lass."

Mary did accede to Haddon's persuasion but not because she was sensible. A weariness, a physical fatigue had overwhelmed her as soon as she had arrived home the night before. Emotionally drained, she simply wanted to forget what she had seen, at least until she had regained enough strength to think about it. Her sobbing had stopped but she couldn't stop her body heaving, emptying her stomach of everything as if in an attempt to jettison the experience of the last twelve or so hours. Haddon convinced her that even if Danks didn't confess, and if his experience was anything to go by he would do so, there was ample evidence to guarantee both his conviction and proper punishment three times over. He looked at the young woman slumped opposite him who had matured so much since he last saw her as a girl a few months before. Though now her face was haggard, sallow and there were ugly dark rings around her eyes, he noticed her full, well-proportioned figure, thick, long black hair and her handsome face with its full lips and slightly bumpy nose.

"And time passes fast, Mary. You'll be old enough to be thinking about marriage soon. There's no sense in ruining the prospects of the chap you might be sharing your life with one day, is there?"

Events followed the course Haddon predicted. Within ten days Danks was standing in the dock waiting to hear the judge pronounce his sentence. After Haddon had read out his report in the noisy courtroom, including Danks' confession, the defence counsel had signalled his disinterest in wasting time pleading his client's innocence. His meagre fee, paid for out of the town's Poor Relief fund, hardly induced him to make a fool of himself by trying to defend the pitiful specimen who stood, head bowed meekly, blubbering a few yards away from him. The judge was about to give the customary guidance to the jury, but he hesitated, reviewing swiftly in his mind the key points of the short trial. The victim had been a loose woman, not a whore but, in Haddon's words, *almost indiscriminately promiscuous with five illegitimate offspring from as many men, and this had undoubtedly played a part in the events that led to her death.* So she in fact, albeit to a small degree, shared the guilt. And as for the motive, didn't her attempt to blackmail Danks also increase her own involvement and perhaps even mitigate Danks' guilt? He pondered the wording of the labourer's confession.

> *She said she'd tell my wife about the child. Now I'd swored to my missus I'd finished with the cow. And I had an' all, 'cept she dragged me back into sin with her shameless ways. But then she said she'd tell if I finished with her for good. And I don't mind admitting, my wife has a vicious tongue. Hurts more than twenty lashes. I go in fear of her, I don't deny it. And so I did for Green, for Polly. I grabbed her by the hair and slapped her a few times, just to scare her. But she wouldn't shut her mouth. Kept on screaming- Loose! Loose! Let loose! So I did for her. I slit her throat. Twice, from ear to ear. Two good uns, deep and long. Her 'ead almost come off.*

So, again, the victim had provoked the violence committed against her. She had seduced Danks to the barn where she intended to fornicate with him like a cat in heat. Fearing she might lose his carnal services she threatened to reveal their debauchery to his wife, whose venomous tongue he dreaded even more than the law. She had refused to retract her threats even when he beat her. He looked again at Danks. A pitiful, abject broken, snivelling figure, without resistance or even the will-power to raise his eyes and look the judge in the face. He had repented to the priest, confessed to Haddon and, despite the formality of the not guilty plea his counsel had entered, had submitted himself totally to the will of God, the law and now to their representative, the Judge, who at last began his summing up.

Haddon, like Astley, who was sitting as near the front of the public space as possible, listened with satisfaction as the judge, in his opening remarks, pointed out the heinous nature of the crime and the apparently incontrovertible force of the evidence against the accused. But then he hesitated and the policeman and shopkeeper exchanged nervous glances as they heard the next sentence:

"It requires the most deliberate consideration before you, gentlemen of the jury, to consign the prisoner to an ignominious death. It is your solemn duty to consider all the circumstances of the case and if, in the course of the investigation of these circumstances there arises any reasonable doubt in your minds as to the guilt of the defendant then, …"

He paused again, looking at the members of the jury one by one before continuing:

"… you are duty-bound to reach a verdict of Not Guilty."

Many had only caught the last utterance in isolation from the preceding condition and cheering and cat-calling broke out in the improvised courtroom and the judged banged his pulpit and bellowed angrily for silence.

Numbskull as he was, Danks slowly grasped that his life might be spared yet and he sluggishly lifted his head, gazing moronically first at the judge and then around the almost riotous court room. As his eyes met Haddon's an imbecilic grin gradually spread across his face. A shock jolted the policeman's body. He closed his eyes and pursed his lips, aghast at the thought of what he might have done. Astley, who had attended many trials, though none for murder, was confused by the judge's apparent but inexplicable benevolence towards Danks. Now both he and the policeman were scrutinising the jurymen's brief consultation, their exchange of questioning looks, the nodding of heads, until, without leaving the court, the foreman of the jury stood up and the courtroom din subsided.

"We have reached a verdict, Your Honour. We find the defendant, John Danks, guilty of wilful murder!"

Chapter 9

She became fully aware of the fact that her contact with Henry was over just as she had heard Danks had been hanged in Warwick. But it meant anything to her. Neither did the news of the execution. In the mill it was as if she became an extension of her loom. Now driven in unison by a long shaft that extended the length of the workshop, the looms still demanded concentration, dexterity from the operators, as well as their constant presence and Mary willingly let the machinery dictate the hours and days of her existence. Not even Nancy could stimulate her into conversation let alone laughter and after a while the other hands began to neglect her then finally left her alone. No more acute than a hardly perceived ache, her recollections of the two men, Danks and Henry, were swamped and cloyed into an unrecognisable shapelessness, like stumps of trees in overgrown, stagnant pools. It was the constant vision of Polly's death that annihilated her efforts to forget and repress that moment when she had knelt alone over the mutilated body, its memory flashing incisively into her consciousness like suddenly dazzling sunlight bursting between swiftly drawn curtains. She only knew this alternation between two sources of suffering, either the searing pain of confronting the memory or the debilitating burden of avoiding it. When she was working at the great clattering machines in Muscat's mill, or treading the loom in the attic of her home, or moving, cleaning, wiping and carrying in the din and smoky gloom of the public house, then it was easy to exist. But whenever her thoughts were freed from their attention on some immediate task, they returned to the scene of the murder. She tried to eat but whatever she forced inside her, she ejected. At night she lay exhausted until the longed-for void enveloped her and smothered her in a fretful sleep for at least a few hours.

Those who noticed the change in Mary attributed it simply to the loss of her friend Polly. Even Astley, the only person she had confided in about herself and Henry, suspected that a compound of reasons, a bundle of sad passions were at the heart of her loss of vitality. Though she still came into the shop occasionally, she never spoke more than necessary and her friend observed things about her that others didn't, especially the contrast between her apparent remoteness from her surroundings and at the same time a concentrated focus on something intangible, out of sight to others. Eventually he began to fear that Mary was going mad. There had been enough people in the town who had suddenly begun to gibber incessant nonsense, to point at and run away from beings no-one else could see. Although Mary was taciturn, Astley could see that her body was tense, her mouth was tightly pursed and her eyes darted not vacuously and at random but with a controlled intensity, as if some turbulence was writhing around inside her and she was struggling to dominate it.

As the months went by, Astley concluded she wasn't insane but, scientifically curious as he was, wondered if there were some condition of the mind that could displace a person's previous character, a kind of substitute soul which entered a healthy person and either banished that body's previous inmate or fought and contended with it for domination of that mortal space. He asked Dr Prouse, a man who tried his best to keep abreast of medical developments in France and Germany, though the provincial sphere of his work would never allow him scope to practise what he read. He disappointed Astley and said that, if such a condition did indeed exist, then it would simply be another word for madness and so the shopkeeper let the subject drop. As time passed, he concluded she wasn't demented but he also knew she had changed, was not the self she had been before the murder. And so he watched her, talked to her as much as he could and she answered him without returning his look, her head bowed and her now spindly body slightly hunched. His one abiding fear was that she would, sooner or later, seek some kind of comfort in gin or even release in suicide. And perhaps she would have done so had her mother not suddenly died.

The day of her mother's burial was so cold that two men had to break the cemetery ground open with picks. She noticed that the sides of the grave didn't crumble on contact with the rough wooden coffin as it was lowered unsteadily, swaying from side to side. Mary could hear it scratch and grate against protruding stones and, when it finally lay deep down on the base of the grave, she heard a few loosened pebbles clatter down onto it, bouncing a few inches then rolling off the gently sloping lid to finally come to a halt, lodged between the edge of the box and the vertical soil wall. In that static, suspended moment before any of the mourners moved, looking down on the oblong, tapered lid that protected the corpse from the hard dirt the two men were shovelling onto it, she recovered from her melancholy as suddenly as the first day of spring shakes off the grip of winter. For the first time since her trauma began, she became sharply conscious of her immediate vicinity, her eyes relaxing and settling their gaze on what really was before them, not scurrying away from the inward image of Polly's wretched corpse which this manic force in her brain had tried constantly to impose on them. She felt the cold, biting wind, aggressive but harmless like a yapping dog, and, for the first time since Polly's death, she responded to the squeeze of her younger sister's hand in hers. Raising her head she noticed the tears of others and then her own, stinging and trapped in the corners of her eyes, unable to flow. She realised for the first time that day that Johnnie Astley was also there, standing decently a few yards behind her father, wishing to register his sympathy with the family without intruding. Mary nodded in his direction and her lips moved gently in a kind of restrained kiss, a greeting he returned with a wide, but tight-lipped smile. It was a reawakening, an emergence from a disturbed state of consciousness that had separated her from the immediacy of life. Looking down again at the coffin, she thought of her mother calmly without the furious invasion of Polly's image scratching at her mind like the tenacious, thorny tentacles of bramble bushes. Around the grave were all the people who had a distinct identity in her life. Her younger sisters, her father and Johnnie Astley. But Lizzie, Polly and her mother had gone forever, and now Mary, confronted by a moment of blatant clarity, felt the emptiness they had left her. For the first time in two years, she was fully aware of where she was, as though she had bridged the chasm, the hiatus that the shock of Polly's murder had caused in her life and at last she stood on something firm again.

*

She still worked every night in the family's pub which was where, some weeks after the funeral, she met Thomas Ball, a wiry, lively young miner who at that time drank somewhat less than his cronies. He had mistaken her apathy for a challenging aloofness that he tried to overcome it by playful teasing and clumsy flattery. When at last she began to respond to his attention, he invited her to meet him outside the town and walk with him. Still emotionally indifferent, she agreed. When he kissed her she didn't object, though her response didn't encourage him. And so as she regained the conscious knowledge of her own presence in her surroundings, she let herself drift towards a socially definable bonding with this man who wooed and courted her with clumsy energy. Their engagement was an uncomplicated result of the time they spent together. Despite the total lack of any real enthusiasm on her part, there was nothing to inhibit his attraction for her now and they made love often without any precautions. Thomas knew nothing of such possibilities anyway. Mary had recovered her health and good figure since she had been able to eat and to digest what she ate, and he was besotted by her shapely body and her albeit passive willingness to let him enjoy it without restraint. Pregnancy and marriage, in as far he thought about the future at all, seemed pretty much inevitable, neither causing him alarm or even apprehension.

As her thoughts about the past lost their fear and grew stronger and more confident, she could look back and remember without pain. And gradually her feelings changed. Polly's children recurred with increasing fondness in her memories as she struggled to reconstruct some of the past, as if after some crippling illness she was re-learning the basic competence of life. At first, though lacking the resolve to prevent it, she had sometimes been troubled by the thought of conceiving. When she discovered she was pregnant, she decided it was time to marry and the thought of having a child, a daughter she already hoped for, hitched a kind of future to her life. After the simple wedding in that spring, he came to share the room in the pub with her. After his day's work either at the pit or navvying on the small railway sidings on the Newdigate estate, he'd help out in the pub, serving beer and gin, throwing out customers who couldn't drink or pay any more and, after only a few weeks of marriage, pouncing on any sexual favours tossed his way by women drinkers. The rambling, haphazard building they worked and lived in had enough crannies, alcoves and chambers to hide the brief adventures.

A few years before Mary and Thomas married, Thomas' elder sister, Jane, at thirty a pious, arid woman, had married John Bacon, a newcomer to the town who had invested his modest income in the formation of a small business providing gangs of labourers for railway construction. With the backing of the town's businessmen John's shrewdness and industry were already bringing handsome rewards so that, when the marriage of his wife's younger brother was fixed, he bought two small adjoining terraced houses in Back Lane, a crescent just off the main street, and offered Thomas and Mary the rent of one of them. In addition he persuaded his future brother-in-law to leave the pits and work for him, first as a labourer and then, who knows, in a few years time perhaps as a ganger himself. Of course John could have afforded a larger house, even a servant perhaps. But Jane hated excess and barely tolerated comfort. She saw many real advantages, not just the virtue of thrift, in inhabiting the small house next door to her younger brother and his young wife. She knew Mary's family, the Wrights and knew they kept a public house and attended neither church nor chapel. The pregnancy was no secret either and Jane learnt of it well before the marriage, suspecting that it was due to the woman's scheming that this bond had come about. It would be a fine life for her sister-in-law to be at home, doing no more work than a little weaving, or so she supposed. As a navvy, her husband, as well she knew, would spend a lot of time away from home. This, she perhaps imagined, might allow scope for her lewdness. But she, Jane, next door and vigilant, would forestall any lasciviousness. She would ensure the baby would feel the force of a Christian influence even if its mother denied it a Christian upbringing.

*

The baby was not yet born when Thomas and Mary, after a short time in Abbey Street, moved into the small, decent house in Back Lane and when it came, it was the good-natured John Bacon who made sure a christening took place the very next day because the child was already ailing, and at the end of its first week the child was dead. The following years were strange repetitions of each other, as cyclical as the seasons. Mary conceived, struggled through the days, weeks and months. In the first three years of marriage, she gave birth to a boy she named John, and two girls, each briefly called Lizzie. Each child died within weeks of the birth

Mary seemed to need no comfort, grew cold and hard but did not shrivel back into the depression she had been shaken out of by her mother's death. All the time her sister-in-law watched and judged her. Jane wouldn't envy her, though she longed for a child herself, longed at least to be able to conceive. Mary's almost constant state of pregnancy, Jane believed, must have something to do with the rabid wantonness of her nature so that, joyless and resigned as she seemed, it must have been the concealed lust inside her that warmed and coaxed her husband's seeds to infect her with fertility. Neither would Jane admire, nor mistake the stubbornness she showed when the babies died for strength. Only lack of feeling could bear that sorrow, only carelessness could overcome that loss. That was nothing Jane could admire. She could barely endure to watch it even, especially as her own great, lumbering husband was unable to see through Mary, to recognise how she could manipulate him and other men without saying a word. He'd put his arm around her and pat her cheek, mumbling a few quiet words to console her. And she'd say nothing, apparently making an effort to smile but Jane was inwardly convinced, rejoicing over the pain she was causing decent women who could only watch, perceive and suffer.

But each time a child was buried, the two women went together, unaccompanied by anyone else, to the cemetery. Despite the tacit enmity Jane felt for Mary and the icy void that separated both of them, at the short services, made at John's insistence and paid for by him, there was a bond between them, a bond neither of them wanted but which neither could prevent. Each knew what the other was thinking as they watched every shovel-full of earth slap down onto the tiny wooden box. Mary sensed Jane's hope for another child rested on her. Jane somehow knew she herself would never conceive. If it had been meant to be, it would have happened by now. The closest she would get to having a child would be to somehow obtain a share in one of Mary's, if one were ever to survive. Mary witnessed the genuine bitterness of Jane's disappointment at each child's death and knew it was not grief but defeat. Mary realised Jane had no compassion for her, that it was a despondency only for the children they had in different ways both lost.

So, like the town itself, Mary was dragged through the years, surviving the cycles of weather, trade and harvests, dependent on events she hardly noticed and on causes she didn't even suspect for the direction the sluggish current took her, and it was the deaths of her children, rather than hours, months or years, that marked the divisions of time. Her husband was able to work as a weaver, a miner and a navvy so he had a more or less regular income even when the ribbon trade was slack or the pits were closed. Sometimes he travelled out with John and a gang of labourers to where tracks were being laid, either staying overnight in tents, occasionally in rough lodgings. It made little difference to Mary whether he was there or not. Though she had freed herself from the clutches of depression, her outward behaviour hardly changed. What was before a compulsive listlessness became a conscious, almost rational detachment from everything and everyone around her. As

Thomas became addled and septic from a combination of drink and the natural brutality of something fierce and angry inside him, her feelings towards him also changed from a passive indifference to silent contempt and hatred.

*

The first time the smouldering resentment between them flared into open confrontation was on one late afternoon when he returned home earlier than usual. Torrential rain had made work on the cutting impossible and when Mary got home just after darkness fell, he was sitting at the kitchen table with the assortment of stones he had been collecting since he had started labouring on the railways. He caressed and gazed at them, as if mesmerised by their solemnity. As she entered quietly he was holding one of them, cupped tenderly in both hands, but as soon as he noticed her, he slammed it down against the table-top, pushed the chair back noisily and grabbed his jacket, as a sign that he was about to go out. She was soaked and shivering from the cold rain, threw off her shawl and looked for clean rags to dry her hair. There was an empty bowl and bits of bread on the table so Jane must have been in to light the stove and warm up some gruel for him. Angry at her and ashamed of himself for being discovered at his intensely private preoccupation, he shouted at her as he made his way to the door, though as she bent forward to let her hair hang down while she rubbed it in strands with the cloth, he could see nothing of her face so didn't know if she was paying him attention.

"… and get those rocks away. Under the bed. I might be bringing somebody back!"

As she heard his footsteps banging in the alley at the side of the house, she sat down with her back to the stove and threw her hair back, letting it hang in the warmth. He'd be drenched by the time he reached the pub and the thought made her feel sheltered. The rain was still pelting down, flapping noisily in wind-driven sheets against the pitch black kitchen window, which shuddered and trembled under the onslaught. Without turning the chair round, she got up and sat down again with her face towards the stove, her legs wide open with the chair back between them, her skirts pushed up around the tops of her naked thighs. She began to enjoy the warmth and seclusion of the room. Now she was calm but her legs were so close to the fire that her skin began to sting. Taking the candle from the table she walked over to the window. All light from the outside was obliterated as if blown away by the wind or doused by the downpour. She could hear the willow, swaying and swirling in the wind but all she could see clearly in the window were her own reflection and the candle. Her black hair merged almost into invisibility in the blackness of the window pane so that the candle's pale, yellowish flame and her own vapid image were all she could see. Almost as if she were seeing herself for the first time, the childish thought occurred to her:

Is that me?

With her nose only inches from the glass, she stared into her own dark eyes. Placing the candle back on the table she noticed the stones and recalled his growled instructions. There was also a half-full bottle of cheap gin on the table which he'd forgotten in his haste. She often drank, not enough to make her drunk but whenever she felt her hackles of defiance rising, she'd drink to dull and soothe them. Now, however, the gin didn't dim her perceptions, but made her resolve not to obey the orders he had given her. With a sudden determination, she cleared the table except for the stones, laid her forearm on the table top carefully and with a deliberate, bold sweep of her arm, sent all the stones off the table clattering onto the slabbed floor. Then she went upstairs, changed into a heavy night gown, got into bed and waited for him to return. She heard every sound inside and from outside the house, every dog bark, every door open and shut. Then she recognised the hasty, almost running footsteps instantly, the sound of feet thudding down the alley and finally the kitchen door slamming shut. There were at least two voices, his and another, possibly a woman's, at first confused then only his, clearly, bellowing from the bottom of the stairs.

"Woman! Bitch! Come down here!"

She got out of bed, went to the top of the stairs and listened, able to make out some words.

"… make me look a fool! The last time …!"

Tense and expectant but unafraid of his violence she went slowly down the stairs, stopping as she got to the bottom step. He was on his hands and knees, trying to collect the stones, holding four or five in the crook of one arm. As he stood up with them, they fell out of his arms onto the floor again and he kicked out against one in fury. There was a fat, poorly dressed woman, looking the worse for drink, supporting herself with her broad backside half on, half against the table. He bent down again and picked up a few chips that had broken off the stones when they fell.

"I'll kill her for this when she gets down here!"

The fat woman nodded in Mary's direction and he turned to face her. Perhaps if she had flinched or tried to flee, he would have attacked her but, though it was too dark in the corner where she stood for him to see her face clearly, her posture and the slight tilt of her head told him she was standing her ground. He knew, even after years of her routine compliance, that she had this stubborn, unyielding capacity to resist and that if he wanted to make her submit now he'd have to put the fear of death into her. He leaned forward slightly like a snarling dog stretches its neck to increase its ferocity, and pointed his fist at the floor:

"I told you to clear them up!"

She had no intention of provoking him and didn't relish his violence, especially with the rocks lying around within his reach. He was livid, insulted, drunk and she knew what he was capable of. But her resolve not to obey him had clenched around her now. In the far corner of the kitchen she could see the box he kept his stones in and without a word she walked slowly over to it, past the woman, who stood up straight as she passed her in an act of involuntary respect or admiration, picked up the box and threw it as calmly as she could towards him and it landed just in front of his feet. She gestured towards the woman.

"She can help you. I'm going to bed."

The fat woman gasped, sensing this would provoke him into attacking his wife, but he just stared blankly, then he pushed the box out of the way with his foot and moved a few steps forwards so she would have to go very close to him as she crossed the kitchen towards the stairs. Or she would have to make the obvious effort to go round him and he might be satisfied with this implicit submission. But she walked towards the stairs, apparently ignoring his presence now, although he stood directly in her path. When she was level with him they stood for a moment stationary, face-to-face, then, with a calmness that looked like disdain, she moved past him. He grabbed her arms from behind, swivelling her round to face him again. The fat woman screamed in shock.

"Let her go, Tommy! I'll help you clear up. Let her go!"

He held her, hesitating and confused, trying to decide what to do with her limp, unresisting body, then impulsively he spun her round and pushed her hard towards the door which he opened with one hand and shoved her outside with the other, slamming the door behind her.

Suddenly finding herself away from the stifling warmth, the smell of tobacco and alcohol and rid of the confrontation, she savoured the cold air and the rain lashing into her, relaxed and exhilarated at once. But then she gradually became conscious of the reality of her situation. The invigorating, almost intoxicating briskness had turned into vicious cold and her nightgown was already sodden, water was streaming down her face and her hair was drenched again. Without much hope she tried the door but he'd bolted it. Pressing her back hard up against the house wall to get as much shelter as possible, she edged her way towards the cover of the alley which would at least keep the rain off her. As she passed the window she glanced over her shoulder into the kitchen, expecting to see them watching her. She remembered how she'd peered into the window from the inside a few hours before and had seen her own reflection suspended like a lantern in the darkness that engulfed her. Now outside and exposed she felt stronger and more determined than in the formless, blurring warmth of the house. In the flickering light of the kitchen she could see his back, the woman's arms around him and the blubber of her fleshy legs. They hadn't picked the stones up. At first she laughed grimly at the grotesque love-making but then she thought clearly. If she stayed out in the rain she'd catch her death. She could wake up Jane and John but what then? Nothing could force Thomas to let her back into the house, not even Constable Haddon. The only refuge guaranteed her was the workhouse. Or death. Indeed. Why not just stand in the rain until she couldn't stand any longer? Then collapse and lie in the almost freezing cold water until she became so numb she would feel nothing, until even her thoughts would stop and she would drift into painless unconsciousness and then death? She remembered the story of the local lawyer and his wife, Janet Buchanan. They'd had guests and she'd done something to annoy him, something trivial but which he felt humiliated him in the eyes of his friends. After they'd left, he'd dragged her out of her bed, beaten her and locked her out. Neighbours had heard screams and the door bang, then they'd seen her standing in the darkness dressed in only her sodden nightgown. Then, they said, she was suddenly not there and they assumed he'd let her back into the house. But the next day her body had been found in the river. Mary wasn't yet ready to end like that. She'd sometimes thought of suicide and believed she could do it, take her own life. But not just lie down and never stand up again. That would be capitulation and that was beyond her. She glanced over her shoulder again and, despite the clumsy debauchery going on, she recalled how she'd felt a few hours before and she knew she wanted to live, although she had no evident reason for wanting to do so. Ignoring the rain, she crossed the narrow yard to the rough plot of garden and even in the darkness she quickly found a lump of brick which she wrapped in the loose skirts of her nightgown and, with a few short blows, knocked out a window pane, stretched her hand through and opened the window from the inside. Somehow she managed to clamber up onto the narrow window sill, through the window and let herself down into the kitchen, where Thomas and the woman stood watching her in amazement. Without acknowledging them, she held her hand over the stove to test its warmth, then opened the small hatch and threw several large lumps of coal onto the smouldering ashes and cinders. All she said, without looking at them, was:

"I need the stove."

She made a clothes line by fastening a piece of string to the hooks at each side of the mantle piece and tugged at the shoulders of her gown so that the saturated cloth came away from the skin of her thighs and buttocks where it had stuck like wet paper. Water was still dripping profusely from the hem and when she shook her head water sprayed from her hair making them move back a few paces.

"Don't you understand? I must dry myself."

They finally realised that she was going to take off the nightdress and the confrontation dissipated. Hitching and adjusting her clothes hastily, the woman took a last swig of gin and lurched off, mumbling and cursing, into the rainy night. As if he weren't there, Mary unfastened the buttons of her nightgown and let it drop to the floor, shook it and hung it over the line. For a brief moment she had stood naked in front of him, the man who had a few minutes before been on the verge of assaulting her and who had thrown her out of the house, oblivious of what might happen to her. It was a moment of vulnerability but not of weakness. Without haste, she turned and looked into the lurid gloom behind the window and could just make out the nebulous image of her own body, of herself. Her disregard for him, for the violence he and his bits of rock might do to her, made him, for a short but unforgettable period of time, abject and powerless. Covering herself as best she could with a few clothes and rags that lay in a basket beside the stove, she huddled herself as close to the grate as possible, while he began to gather up the stones, placing each one almost tenderly in the wooden box.

Chapter 10

1845. John Astley couldn't remember the last time his father had closed the shop so early. When Victoria had acceded to the throne some eight years before, he had stayed demonstratively open to signify his indifference, just as he'd refused to close whenever a monarch died. And now, on the apparently trivial occasion of a public meeting he'd told his son to tidy up both the shop and his own appearance because he was going along too.

The dining hall of the Castle Hotel had been carefully prepared for the meeting. At the far end, a platform about two feet high with a few steps at each side had been erected, and on it was a long, polished table with twelve high-backed chairs behind it for the organisers stretching almost the whole width of the improvised podium. On the wall behind the stage, large and prominent, hung a portrait of Queen Victoria. The table itself was decked generously with glasses, jugs and decanters. Two long rows of tables with seats on both sides provided space for about 60 people while allowing waiters to move easily between them with beer and plates of cold meat and bread.

The shopkeeper and his son were amongst the first to arrive so Johnnie had time to study the handbill announcing the meeting in the brightly lit room. A glance at the names of the subscribers told him that something very important was going on: Bull, Craddock and Bulstrode, the banker, the men of law Buchanan, Jermyn, and the town's most prominent manufacturers, Muscat, Green, Hood and Robinson. In the chair was J. Newdigate Chetwood, the Earl's nephew, and as they all took their seats, he was flanked by Dugdale, the Tory MP and Craddock junior, who ran the trading side of his family's local but lucrative business empire.

The hall was, despite the obvious import of the gathering, little more than half full and as he glanced round at the audience he found there was no-one he didn't know by face and name: churchmen, doctors, shopkeepers, small traders, one of his father's Radical friends – Felix Holt, who sat between the only women present, his *companion* Esther Lyon, the Independent minister's daughter, on his left, and on his right Mary Anne Evans, next to her father, Newdigate's land agent. Johnnie couldn't help smiling to himself, wondering if the aging Robert Evans knew he was sitting within a yard of a Chartist, in his eyes the same as a godless Jacobin. Certainly Marianne knew who he was but was unlikely to risk provoking her father into a fit of rage by telling him. Though they only met infrequently since she had moved to Coventry, Mary Anne recognised Johnnie and acknowledged him discretely.

A signal was given to the waiters to leave the room, to close the doors behind them and the meeting began by the Chairman calling everyone to order with a few curt taps of a spoon against his brandy glass.

"Gentlemen, as you see from the handbill…"

He stopped in surprise at the first interruption which came from Felix Holt.

"Sir, should my good lady here and also the lady on my left take this address as a deliberate snub or has their presence escaped you?"

With obviously no idea what the fellow was talking about, the Chairman fidgeted with a pair of spectacles until they perched on his nose and peered in the Felix's direction, eventually recognising the speaker and grasping the reason for his interjection.

"Ah, Mr Holt, Sir. My apologies to your, er, to the good lady on your right and to Miss Evans. Allow me to welcome you, ladies, especially warmly to our meeting to compensate for my inexcusable though not intended exclusion."

Laconically but charmingly delivered the apology was taken in good humour by everyone present, except Robert Evans who, at the mention of the name Holt, sat bolt upright in shock at sharing a table with an insurgent. Mary Anne exchanged the briefest of glances with Johnnie, who, though instantly appreciating the irony of her position between her revered, conservative yeoman father and the glowering, bearded reformer, suppressed a smile for her sake.

"Gentlemen, all of you, welcome. Ladies, both of you, welcome!"

Before he could proceed he was interrupted again by the door opening and the entrance of the large figure of John Bacon, who blustered in, hat in hand, intensely embarrassed, muttering apologies and awkwardly sitting down on the first available chair at the end of the row where Johnnie and his father were also sitting. John was liked by all who knew him and, apart from the frosty stares he received from one or two of the committee on the stage, he was consoled by smiles and winks from several members of the audience. Chetwode struck the spoon against the brandy glass again with the precision of a piano tuner and waited for silence before he spoke.

"If anyone has the intention of interrupting me, would he have the goodness to do so before I begin?"

Chetwode's unexpected humour appealed rather more to those who had come in relishing the prospect of a good argument than to the serious company he shared the table with, so that he could at last set the meeting into motion.

"As many of you know, mainly due to the effort of our Member of Parliament, the Trent Valley Bill came before the House of Commons last year. I am delighted to be able to confirm the many unofficial reports that the Bill was passed by Parliament last week, on the 21st of July and that the construction of the Trent Valley Railway line, connecting Rugby with Stafford, will commence before the end of this year!"

Cheering broke out in the hall and the gentlemen on the podium sat back in their well-upholstered seats, basking in the applause regardless of whether or not they had personally deserved any of it. The group around Astley also clapped their approval without conceding any of the rapturous praise of the more enthusiastic participants. After a minute or so, Chetwode only needed to waver his spoon around his glass threateningly and order was restored.

"As well as being an opportunity to congratulate those most responsible for our town's advancement, this meeting has also a practical purpose."

He paused to allow the mood adjust accordingly.

"Ladies and gentlemen, we stand on the threshold of a new age. A great wave of progress is about to surge throughout our country, bringing with it great change, both political and social. And, not least, prosperity. It is our duty this evening to ensure that our community is prepared for these tremendous upheavals, is able to withstand their impact and channel them in a beneficial direction. One of the driving forces behind recent change has undoubtedly been the introduction of steam power. The evidence is, even in our modest, provincial economy, plain to see. The pumps at the local collieries, allowing us to extract coal from ever deeper seams; the steam powered looms at several locals mills, producing high-quality ribbon in quantities unimaginable twenty years ago; and now, the greatest achievement of steam stamps impatiently at our doorstep, eagerly waiting to be released: the railways. Not just a devourer of coal, but also its conveyor, the Trent Valley railway will connect this town directly with London and Manchester, opening up vast new markets for the goods manufactured here: the coal, the ribbon, but also the bricks and stones from our kilns and our quarries. It is a rare, a historic opportunity. Let us all cooperate, amalgamate all possibilities at our disposal, be they in natural resources, in finance, in manufacture or in construction, to ensure the greatest benefit for the greatest number of our citizens!"

The assembly rose with an explosive burst of applause and cheering that could be heard on the street. When it had died down, the practical business of the meeting got underway and various resolutions were passed by a unanimous show of hands, the main one being to support an exerted effort to secure the building of a first-class station at a site already purchased at a price of 500 guineas an acre. Of course, both Astley and Felix knew that even the least arable land, if it lay on the route designated for the line, would now fetch the price for prime building land, adding to the already enormous wealth of the Newdigates, Craddock and one or two other families. A strip of land a mile long and twenty-two yards wide made eights acres, now worth four thousand guineas and between them the Earl and the banker owned ten miles of such land, the perfect synchrony of interests of the gentry and the classes immediately below them. And so, after the meeting had broken up and small groups stood around the hall, sipping the last of their drinks and discussing the evening's events, Chetwode made a point, of getting into conversation with the radical contingent.

"Mr Astley, Mr Holt, I want to thank you for your sincere support during the meeting. But, please let me be frank, it did surprise me. It is not often that we have opinions, let alone actions in common."

The two men were both involved through trade unionism and Chartism with the key political issues of the day, both with a reputation for ideologies many regarded as subversive, Astley more from a theoretician's but Felix from activist's point of view. They exchanged glances before the tall, bearded Holt answered Chetwode's implicit question.

"We agree with you, Mr Chetwode, that great change is afoot. But there are two routes it can take. You spoke of goods and manufactures. That's true enough. The railways will move them and make even a small town like this into part of a market covering the whole country, even foreign countries. And we welcome that. But the railways will also move people, will connect them and, we hope, open their eyes to all kinds of possibilities. Some that may not be to your or to your uncle's, the Earl's taste."

Astley, though addicted to a ruthless intellectual clash of ideas, shunned confrontation at a personal level and attempted to lessen the aristocrat's obvious discomfort at the slight but unmistakable hint of a threat in Felix's tone.

"Mr Chetwode, Sir, you know the recent volume of poems by Mr Tennyson?"

Chetwode nodded without commitment.

"You know the lines?"

> *Forward, forward let us range,*
> *Let the great world spin for ever down the ringing*
> *grooves of change.*

The *grooves of change!* Not much of an engineer, the poet, but he's talking about the railways, you know. Like Felix, my friend here. And what they're both saying is that we don't really know where this change will take us, Sir. At the moment, it's men like yourself and your uncle, Mr Craddock, and Mr Muscat who decide the course of events. But in future, who knows where change will take us? It's both a risk and an opportunity. For all of us."

Chapter 11

November 1847. Looking down from the first-floor window of the dingy terraced house onto the dark street below, William Bacon now felt absolutely sure that it was time for him to leave Manchester. With his face pressed against the cold glass of the window, he stared down into the almost impenetrably black street but he could hardly make out the shapes of the houses opposite let alone a human figure. He listened hard but could hear nothing. He opened the window but could still discern nothing except the light wind and the fine drizzle it blew into his face. He felt sure, though, Hardcastle and his men would be looking for him and would find him, if not today then very soon.

It wasn't merely fear of imprisonment that made him decide to leave. It was as much the disappointment about how, at the Chartist meeting, the rival parties had almost come to blows over their different views and that one of the most militant of them had turned out to be a government informer. He had revealed the whereabouts of the printing press to Hardcastle and his agents smashed it to bits. Now they'd probably be out searching for the men whose names the spy had given them.

William wouldn't be at the top of this list. He knew there were men who had openly called for armed revolution and were determined to see it through. They were the ones that the police most wanted. But he played his part in the movement, was involved if not committed. Maybe they'd just try to extort information from him, even try to win him as an informer, too.

He heard the bed creak and Betty moan sleepily.

"William, come back to bed. It's not even light yet. Why are you dressed?"

Betty, drowsy, naked and snug, was perhaps the only reason he might have stayed but she was, when all was said and done, one woman amongst many and, although her affection for him was probably genuine, he still had to pay her something for it. Not that he minded that. From a small family inheritance, he had money to live on the way he did, with a little over for indulgences. He wondered for a brief moment which of her few options she would choose after he left.

He picked up his bag, looked at it and then at Betty.

"I'm sorry."

She sat up in bed, her knees pulled up to her chest, the blanket under her chin, now suddenly wide awake. "There's some money next to you. "She spread out the coins on the small table beside the bed so she could count them. She didn't seem disappointed. "You've still got a bit of credit, William."

"I've got to be away before it gets light. You'll be alright, won't you Betty?"

"Course I will. You were always nice and generous to me. Maybe the next one will be just as good."

She leaned back on her elbows, letting the blanket fall so that it only covered her to just below the waist, and stretched out her legs. Tilting her head back slightly, her long, fair hair fell down straight.

"Come here."

He shouldn't have done but he did, and when, a few minutes later, the door burst open, Hardcastle and his two men saw William sitting on the side of the bed facing the door and they saw Betty's slender, bare back, as she knelt on the floor, her head moving rhythmically in his lap.

*

Two hours later William was on the train, about to leave for Birmingham. He sat facing the station entrance so that he would spot Hardcastle and his men if they followed him.

There was a certain logic, almost justice in the fact that it was Betty who had saved him, winning him time to get out before they could beat him up or arrest him. After all she had invited him to stay longer than need be when he was on the point of leaving. When she made them the offer, he'd said nothing, just fastened his clothing, picked up his bag and moved cautiously towards the door. On Hardcastle's signal, the two toughs didn't try to stop him. He was, after all, small fry.

Maybe she might have made an even better deal with Hardcastle by now. They'd maybe even pay her. There'd certainly be no rape or violence. Betty so obviously had her wits about her that Hardcastle, a paid Home Office agent, wouldn't have risked that. And, looked at objectively, he, William, was a man with a mission; he was about to achieve things of significance for society at large. He was working for a better future, not just for himself but for his fellow men. Betty, when all was said and done, lived for the day and for herself. Maybe she'd even be able to boast one day, when he had become a person of importance, that she'd secured his liberty and thus made possible all the changes his future would bring. That alone would make her sacrifice worthwhile.

He scoured the length of the crowded platform and he could just still glimpse the street outside the station. He began to relax and to think of how his brother, John Bacon, would react to him turning up. He didn't know yet exactly how he would get from Birmingham to Nuneaton but he'd make his way there somehow. Things had always worked out for him before.

People seemed to like him, he had enough if not plenty of money. Why should his luck change now?

His brother was in Nuneaton because of the railways, a ganger working on a new stretch of rail with sixty men and earning more money than their father had ever done with his small printing business. They hadn't had any contact for almost three years now but William was sure his older brother would give him a warm welcome.

The train lurched into motion and William was now certain he hadn't been followed. He took one more relieved look back into the station and then moved across the small first-class compartment so that he could face in the direction the train was travelling. Within minutes the train was picking up speed noisily, leaving the town behind, and his relief turned slowly into a slight elation. He thought once more of Betty, her slightly crooked mouth when she smiled, her lovely broad accent spiced with the slang and the idioms of the mills. Pity that Hardcastle and his men hadn't arrived just a bit later.

The carriage door opened and a good looking woman in her early thirties, well-dressed with slightly too much rouge on her cheeks stood in the open doorway, one eyebrow cocked questioningly. Not Betty, but sufficiently like her.

"Would a lady travelling alone be welcome in here, Sir?"

William let a few sovereigns chink through his fingers. Why not? She was here of her own free will and he was in need of diversion.

"Yes, indeed. Please, take a seat, madam. There's room enough on both sides of the carriage."

She smiled, turned and spoke softly to the guard standing near her, gave him a coin and entered the compartment, closing the door and pulling down the blinds behind her.

They shared the carriage all the way to Birmingham, where William left it to search out his brother John and his wife Jane. The whore spent some of the money William had paid her on food and drink and then returned to Manchester on the next train, bribing the guard and hoping to find another client as clean and generous as William.

*

Mary Ball had tried, for the second night in succession, to stay awake at the side of her baby's bed. She sat on a simple wooden chair but despite her deliberate discomfort and her anxiety which she hoped would keep her awake, she had fallen asleep again and again, though never for more than a few minutes at a time. When she woke up this time she knew without looking or listening that her child was dead. The fifth born and the fifth to die before its first birthday. And when the others had died Mary had also been asleep. This time she had tried to believe that if she could only stay awake the child would survive, although Doctor Prouse had told her it was hopeless. She hadn't really believed in her own superstition and now she felt almost nothing, just a relentless numbness as she lifted the child from its bed.

She thought of waking Thomas and telling him their daughter was dead but what was the point? He'd probably curse her for waking him up before daybreak and what would it change anyway? She'd tell her sister-in-law, who'd go and fetch the doctor. Thomas would resent the shilling fee, which was what the doctor took for such a call in that neighbourhood. But she knew through bitter experience that it was now her legal duty to have a doctor come to certify any death.

It was more than grief or resignation she felt as she carried the tiny bundle down the dark staircase towards the pitch black yard. She felt as dead as the child. Before she reached the bottom of the stairs, she paused and leaned wearily against the coarse brickwork of the staircase wall, closed her eyes and breathed in deeply. She would have liked to have some comfort now. She had wrapped some rags around her waist and between her legs and she hitched them up as best she could with one hand. In that dark stillness, and in a kind of delirium, her face rested gently on the cool cheek of her dead child.

She stood motionless, her mind devoid of feeling and as she gradually became conscious of her real surroundings again she felt the harsh surface of the wall scratching the flesh of her upper arm. She was clutching the child hard against her and she relaxed her grip slightly, as if afraid she would crush the fragile bundle.

She forced herself to walk down the few remaining steps, across the yard and on to Jane's door. She was already up and making tea. Without them exchanging a word she knew what had happened.

"I'll do this and then I'll fetch the Doctor."

There was no charity in Jane's help, only duty. Mary seldom sought out Jane's company but she couldn't walk twenty minutes in the unlit street to Dr Prouse's home with a dead child in her arms. And she was not ready yet to lay the child down for the last time and confront herself with the finality of its death.

Jane threw her shawl over her shoulders and left, occupied with her own usual thoughts in the darkness. Was this all she'd ever see of God's commandment to multiply – arranging the disposal of other people's dead infants? She made her way by the light of a covered candle and with her hand on the house wall, up the entry and along the street towards the surgeon's house.

By the time the doctor arrived it was getting light and Jane had poured tea and cut bread for her husband, who came down the stairs, yawning and stretching his arms. Without seeing Mary or the doctor he went out onto the yard noisily, expelling gas or liquid from every natural outlet.

As he came in Jane hissed at him:

"Why don't you use the privy?"

"You wouldn't want a rat jumping up out of that hole and biting it off now, would you?"

"Shut your filthy mouth," nodding in the direction of the table.

It was only then he saw Mary sitting at one side of the table, the doctor at the other and a bundle between them, next to the tea and bread.

"Why didn't you tell me they're here, woman?"

He ambled across the room towards them and spoke as clumsily as he moved.

"Morning doctor, Mary. The child, is it?"

But they ignored him.

"Here's the death certificate Mary." Dr Prouse looked again at the shrivelled, dehydrated body.

"Get the funeral done as soon as possible. We don't know much about cholera but no point taking risks"

"Why do they get it, doctor?" John butted in.

"We don't know. Most say it's from stench. It forms a miasma. Where there's sewage, things rotting."

Jane gave Mary a sharp look and almost, even in such a moment, said something about her house cleaning, though she could see that Mary was all but oblivious to her surroundings.

Then a loud, male voice with a strange accent coming from the direction of the doorway startled all of them.

"So what you mean is that the poor are dirty and cause their own calamities, doctor."

Apart from Mary they all looked up and saw William standing in the open doorway.

"That's the argument that will at least save the masters from having to provide the people who create their wealth with decent drains and clean water! Aren't you going to invite me in, brother?"

"William? Come here, nipper! You're welcome now and at any time but you've chosen a bad moment to arrive."

John nodded towards the corpse and William raised his eyebrows questioningly, looking at his brother then his sister-in-law for an answer.

"Your child?"

"No, we've not had children," - a sentence John could never speak without glancing at his wife. "Not yet anyway. It's Mary's."

The doctor stood up.

"I'll be leaving you now. Mary, can you hear me?"

She nodded almost imperceptibly.

"Get some sleep. The weaker you are the more prone you are to illness yourself. Pleased to make your acquaintance, Mr Bacon, Sir. I did understand rightly that you are John's brother?"

"You did, doctor. I'm pleased to meet you too and I hope we can continue our discussion about the causes of cholera at some other time."

"Well, perhaps. Now is certainly not the time to do so."

The men all looked again at Mary sitting impassive and haggard in the yellow light of the tallow candle. Jane didn't need to look. She already had her own mental picture, fraught with negative emotion, of Mary, her fecundity, her wantonness and her dead children. Even her great hulking husband, who managed sixty navvies, would cower when his wife reared up on him. But whatever she invoked, she could never loom over Mary and control her. It was what she hated and sometimes feared in her.

As soon as the doctor had left Jane spoke loudly without addressing anyone in particular.

"It's almost light and my brother's still in bed. Someone ought to wake him if he's to get off to work in time."

John relayed the message in a lower, more sympathetic voice.

"Jane's right, Mary. Better go and wake him. We must be getting off. I'll see he has time off for the funeral. If he wants it."

Jane spoke again to no-one in particular.

"He doesn't even know his child's dead yet!"

"Jane, you can see the state she's in," said John, turning again to Mary. "But he does have a right to know, love, that's true enough."

Mary's sudden clarity and quiet but biting voice surprised them.

"He has a lot of rights, hasn't he? But I don't suppose he'll care any more for her now she's dead than he did when she was alive."

She lifted the remains of her fifth child and when she got to the door she turned to Jane, speaking directly at her to avoid using her name.

"I thank you for your help. You'll be coming with me when she's buried?"

Without looking at Mary, Jane nodded assent. William watched the two women, sensed the subdued antagonism between them, smelled and almost touched Mary as she went past him with the child.

Chapter 12

It was in late February that Will began to realise his feelings for Mary were obstinately becoming stronger by the day even without the nourishment of encouragement or much contact. Glimpses of her as she crossed the yard or fetched water from the pump were enough to bother him for hours. Despite his many experiences with women, he couldn't remember a precedent for what he felt for this woman who was so close to him physically but emotionally so remote. Had he tried, he could have found a word to characterise all the relationships he'd had before. People's daughters, the sisters, the wives and the mothers, the whores and the simple lovers – all the women he had been with were identifiable, and his relationships with them, even the strong and complex attachment he had felt for Betty, could be encapsulated within a few words or crucial memories. But with Mary it was not so. Both her real and her imagined presence swarmed around his head like the intangible, persistent chaos of summer flies. His erratic attempts to disperse them only seemed to incense them into a maddening agitation. At night he lay awake, knowing she was just yards away from him, separated only by the house wall. He tried to connect the random sounds he heard into a coherent statement of what she was doing. He knew she often went to bed long before her husband got home from his drinking. Sometimes there'd be fierce, almost savage shouting. Then sometimes came indefinable noises of restless movement but, even with his ear pressed hard against the rough brickwork, he could only perceive enough to tantalise and confuse him, scattering his thoughts again into turmoil. One morning, as he crossed the yard, he saw her in her kitchen with her naked back towards him, washing herself. There was a bowl and a heavy jug on the table beside her and he noticed that the small sturdy door of the crude stove was open so he glimpsed the red glow of the coal fire. Knowing his brother's wife, Jane, would probably be lurking at one of the windows, he was afraid to stop and stare, even linger in the hope she might turn round to face him, and so this fleeting but vivid image, in time a momentary fragment but visually perfect, remained intact for days. In his many hours of solitude he cherished and nurtured it, conscious of its brittle transience, but it faded and the more he tried to restore it the less it resembled that original moment and he knew that only physical love with the woman would give his emotions a real, durable existence. And so instead of brooding, moping and despairing, he began to hope and even to plan. His hopes were never without foundation. Though most of his affairs had simply occurred, had been the sudden product of chance circumstances crystallising into an opportunity he had seized, there had been times when Will had deliberately pursued a woman he found desirable. And, as far as he could remember, he had never failed. Perhaps it was due to his looks, his fastidious cleanliness and his gentle but determined manner; perhaps he only really sought women who his instincts told him were available and willing. Whatever the reasons, every woman he had ever really wanted had invariably surrendered to him. Why should it be different with Mary?

On one of the first fine days of the year, still in the cold dryness of late winter, Will overcame his nervousness and decided to walk into the town. Perhaps he was exaggerating, even imagining the danger of being identified and even arrested, an attempt to titillate himself with inflated illusions about his own importance. After the first uneventful venture, his excursions soon became habitual. As his only reliable diversions from the company of his hearty, but unimaginative brother and his taught-lipped wife were a few books he had already read several times, even the dreary, muddy town, with its sparse selection of shops but dense profusion of public houses, provided a measure of entertainment. Without being told, he soon realised that Astley's store was the hub of what political undercurrents there were in the town. John Astley the elder still kept as ever a few tables reserved in the same corner of the shop for anyone who wanted to impart or acquire information about local occurrences, or to discuss national politics. Although or perhaps because he had gone to great lengths to behave unobtrusively, Will was surprised when, as he was paying for a newspaper, the son murmured to him:

"My father would be happy if you'd drink a glass of beer with him, Mr Bacon."

He nodded in the direction of the older man, who was sitting alone at the table deepest in the corner of the shop. Taken aback by the use of his name, Will's first impulse was to leave without a word but, Johnnie's mild, relaxed and unconcerned manner, his direct understanding look as he handed Will a newspaper, defused his irritation, and feigning indifference as best he could, he ambled to where the old man was sitting.

"Take a seat, Mr Bacon. No, not there. You won't be able to see anything but this broom cupboard from that angle. Here, alongside me. You have a view of the whole shop from here."

"That's a mightily fascinating perspective, indeed, Mr Astley," Will replied, allowing his voice to carry slightly more sarcasm than the elderly gentleman's hospitality deserved. Astley chuckled.

"And what's your perspective, if I may ask? On life?"

Dumbfounded by the directness of the question, Will mumbled a few broken sentences hesitantly, taking short pecks at his beer. The older man interrupted him.

"Now, if your opinions were of the, let's say, average or public sort, you know what I mean, Tory or Liberal or even the new parliamentary Radical hue and colour, then you'd have no problems with my question."

He took a deep draught from his glass and continued.

"And if you were a young man here on average private or professional business, then you wouldn't be keeping yourself to yourself and slinking furtively about the town as if you weren't really there. Would you now?"

He cocked his head to one side with a kind of conspiratorial curiosity. The sheer impudence of the shopkeeper's remarks but also their uncanny accuracy were too much for Will and his face broke into a broad grin. From the counter the son could see both his father and Will and he shook his head slightly in silent acknowledgement that this stranger had already been disarmed by his father's irresistible charm which Will felt enclosing him like a woman's embrace.

"Let me put it like this," the older man said. He lowered his voice just a little. "I'd say you are a Chartist." He raised his glass but replaced it on the table dramatically without taking a sip. "Am I right?"

The fact that Will remained seated and didn't speak was answer enough for the wily old armchair philosopher who enjoyed such a privileged status in everyone's, including his own estimation, that he was exempt from repercussions to his frankness and, even if he had been wrong and Will had taken offence, he would have been immune to any feelings of regret. He had thought carefully before approaching Will, observing him and garnering a few snippets of information about him and then forming his rational conclusion. Why shouldn't he confront Will with this conclusion? If it had been incorrect then no real harm apart from a few ruffled feathers would have been done. And now it was clearly true, Will only stood to benefit from the rationalist's honesty and he already sensed this. He watched the old man sip his beer in silent triumph. At last Astley spoke again, even more quietly than before so that Will had to move his head closer to him. The older man seemed to register this as a further tribute and submission to the magnetic properties of his speech.

"You'll have a hard time of it here if you've come to agitate. The miners and weavers here are a desperate lot. Rowdy, uncouth and disrespectful. But not capable of political activity. Nothing organised at any rate." He paused and appeared to lose his train of thought. "Unlike the mill workers in Manchester. Or so I'm told."

He lifted his glass as if symbolically withdrawing, for the first time, from the conversation, leaving an empty space and Will leapt into it without thinking and blurted out:

"That's something I can tell you a thing or two about. It's where I've just come from. We had strikes planned, not just for wages but for the Charter. But the Home Office and their agents are everywhere. I had to leave, you understand."

Will stopped abruptly and glanced at the man, just catching the hint of a smile which immediately disappeared, as if it had never been there at all, like a drop of water on a hot stove. He cursed himself inwardly for allowing himself to be drawn out, lured into exposing himself by this old fox. In ten seconds, he'd revealed enough about himself to earn him almost as many years imprisonment if Astley had been inclined to betray him. But, annoyed as he was with his own indiscretion, Will knew there wasn't a dram of malice or self-interest in this finely intelligent old man. Before either of them could continue a young woman, plainly but well-dressed, approached the table and Astley stood up to greet her.

"Miss Evans! An increasingly infrequent visitor. But nonetheless increasingly welcome!"

It was clear to Will that the woman, about Mary's age but, though well-proportioned, far less attractive, was there to do more than merely pass the time of day, and so he waited for a chance to take his leave while the two exchanged pleasantries. Though the woman, Miss Evans Astley had called her, sported a pugnaciously hooked nose which dominated her face, Will couldn't help but notice the vibrancy and intelligence which exuded from her movements and her speech. The old shopkeeper obviously rejoiced in her unexpected company and almost forced her to take a seat, took hold of Will's elbow gently and walked a few steps with him towards the door.

"My young friend, do forgive me interrupting our conversation. The lady's visits are few and far between now she has moved to Coventry and I cherish every second of her valuable company. But please let us resume our discourse soon. I'm sure it will be of great mutual benefit. I have never been to Manchester and would appreciate the chance to hear about our common struggle there. And, I may be able to furnish you with something interesting very soon."

Enlivened by his encounter with old Astley, Will, instead of returning directly to Back Lane, decided to walk a bit further away from the town to where some buildings adjoining the new Trent Valley Railway Station were being completed. In spite of the still inclement weather, dozens of workers were busy on the largest building project on the town's living memory. All the construction was now above ground so he had a good view of the masons, carpenters, metal workers and their labourers using ladders, scaffolds, hoists, pulleys and wheelbarrows as well as their tools, their hammers, chisels, planes, saws and winches, to raise the walls, install the windows and the doors and mount the pre-formed Gothic ornamentation of this monument to progress. He wiped a large stone and sat down on it, as close as he could get to the site. He could smell the horses and the great traction machinery and felt the vibrations and sound of its massive chugging that underscored the banging, clanging, whining and grating of the construction work. For the first time he had the sense that something really was happening in this soporific town. He drew in a deep breath and felt a kind of strength he had almost forgotten. In Manchester it had been familiar to him almost constantly. The small acts he had performed there, writing, printing and distributing pamphlets, arguing with his fellow Chartists and defining the next short practical steps, were all relatively insignificant when viewed in isolation. But it was as if somewhere, looming in the background, invisible but dominant, there was a gigantic machine, a colossal engine whose cogs and belts, crankshafts, pistons, valves and wheels could not rotate, drive and convey without the multitude of tiny efforts of men like him. Now here in this murky backwater of a town he had stumbled across the Astleys, men who, he instinctively felt, shared his vision and contributed to the same universal cause. There had been many times recently when he had longed for something to displace his obsessive preoccupation with Mary; a practical task, political agitation or even another, more easily accessible woman. Now something had re-entered his life and was surging through his body. He acknowledged and relished it as he sat there watching the orchestrated power of the building work. But it didn't, as he had expected it would, compete with his passion for her. Instead, the two driving forces bonded like confluent rivers. He thought of her in this heady moment of taught exhilaration. Galvanised by his conviction that he was able to influence the world around him, just as, a hundred yards away from him, muscles and brains were transforming a few acres of barely arable land into a dynamic, potent hub of social evolution, he realised that he wanted to share all this with her, with a woman he was constantly near but seldom with. He wanted to know her and to find out if he could love her. She seemed to mean as much to him already as his desire for social progress and only if he could entwine these two strands into one strong thread could he be really happy.

Chapter 13

It was several weeks before the ground behind the houses was really dry enough for William to break open the yard with the pick and shovel John had brought home from work. There had never been any buildings on this land before the houses were built so once he had removed the heavy slabs, the work was easy and by mid afternoon he had located the blue-stone drains and dug out the soil around them.

Mary watched him from the kitchen for some time before she went out and spoke to him for the first time.

"Are you making something new? Is that what you've come here for?"

William laughed. He was in a good mood, liking this physical labour although he was not used to it. Not like his older, bigger brother John.

"New? In a way, Mrs Ball. I want to find out if the drain from the privy has anything to do with the water from this pump here."

"You said something about that to Dr Prouse, didn't you? The morning the baby died."

"You heard that? You remember it? I thought you weren't aware of anything that morning."

At the time Mary had thought the same but later everything she had seen, heard and felt from when the child died to when she buried her had come back to her, far more vividly than when she had experienced it.

"Call me Mary. Not Mrs Ball. We're related, aren't we? Well, almost."

"And I'm William. Will."

He suddenly realised that he had taken off his shirt in the late winter sunshine. He reached for it but then decided to remain naked from the waist up. After all, they were related. Almost.

"If the filth from this privy was getting into your water I think this might have something to do with the cholera."

"No other houses on the street have had it. John had it mild, but got over it. Then the baby. They say it takes the weakest first. How do you know about the drains and cholera? Are you a doctor?"

He smiled, slightly flattered in spite of himself: "I don't know about the cholera and I'm not a doctor, but a doctor I know of believes that when all this filth floods into the drinking water it causes cholera."

She thought carefully before she spoke again: "The cholera always came after heavy rain, that's right. But why should we be the only ones on the street to get it?"

His voice became enthusiastic, almost excited: "Exactly what I want to know. That's why I'm digging up the yard. That overflow from the privy might be getting to this water on its way to the cess pit. If so, then we probably know why these two houses are the only ones on the street affected by the outbreaks. That can't happen with the other houses. I've had a look at them."

She answered in a flat, matter-of-fact tone: "Knowing that won't bring Lizzie and the others back, will it?"

"But the drains could be re-laid and your next child won't, well, maybe you'll be spared the cholera in future."

"My next child? She was my last one. I'll make sure there'll be no more children born in this house."

They both looked at the house and a slight movement attracted their attention to the house next door where Jane was standing at the kitchen window watching them.

"And there'll be no children at all in the house next to it." She moved her head slightly in Jane's direction as she spoke: "More chance of growing flowers on these slabs than getting her pregnant. Let me have a look at that drain."

Mary stepped down the eighteen inches or so into the shallow trench, placing her hand on William's naked shoulder to steady herself. She didn't notice he was half naked, not at that moment. William got out of the trench to give her room. He glanced back at where his sister-in-law was still standing at the kitchen window. Mary was kneeling over the brick barrel pipe, pulling the loose dirt clear of it with her hands.

"It's perhaps better if I do that, Mary."

She ignored his offer of help and asked: "This brick pipe is coming from the privy? And this?"

"It's just what I expected. That's a lead water pipe. If the tank under the pump overflows, the water runs into the brick pipe and then down there into the cess pit. With the sewage."

"Just before Lizzie and John got sick the yard flooded. It came up through the slabs. And the water stank. The slabs still stink a bit though Jane scrubbed them."

"So either the cess pit was overfull or this pipe is blocked somewhere. And some of that floodwater must have come back up this pipe into the tank. It's exactly what Snow found in London. He's the doctor I know. Let me help you out of there." He stretched out his hand and they gripped each others' wrists. As she stepped out of the trench she was more aware of his part nakedness, but it didn't disturb her.

"Come in. I'll make tea." She noticed that William glanced guardedly towards Jane's kitchen window. "She'll think the worst anyway. You can pump some water into the jug while we're waiting. Put your shirt on though."

After they had both swilled the worst of the grime from their hands, Mary poured the tea. William had watched her, enjoying the sight of her broad, shapely figure and her thick black hair.

"Are you going to tell me now? Why you came here."

He thought about how he could best answer. It was a shade more pride than honesty that made him tell the truth.

"I'm hiding. From the police."

"Well, you chose a clever place to do that. Constable Haddon only lives fifty yards down the street!"

She sat down, one forearm on the table and her chin rested in the cup of her other hand, supported by her elbow, looking him straight in the eye. He returned the look, then said:

"Not that police. The political police."

"So, honest John Bacon's brother is a criminal?"

"The police think so. At least they pretend to."

"And what have you done?"

In spite of himself William became restless, agitated, moving and gesticulating as Mary sat impassive opposite him. He felt conscious of trying to use language he thought this handsome, probably uneducated woman would understand.

"They call me a radical. I try to change things in a way the government doesn't like. But I don't see that's a crime. Was it a crime, for instance, that I tried to mend your drains just now? Or is it a crime to talk to men about their right to strike?"

Mary was unimpressed.

"There have been enough strikes here. The ribbon workers. They didn't have to run away and hide though. There must be more to it than that."

"We're after the right to vote as well. For everybody."

"For women?"

"Not at first. But when we've got the right for working men, they'll vote for their parliament. And they'll pass a law to give women the vote, too. Once we've got a majority in parliament we can pass laws to change everything else. Once the working men have got the right to vote they can free themselves and everyone else."

Neither of them spoke for a minute or so until she asked: "How old are you? Twenty-five? Twenty-six?"

He nodded.

"So in the year of the riots you were what? Ten? At any rate you wouldn't remember that year would you? I remember it here in Nuneaton. That's what they called them. Riots."

"You mean the Reform elections? You saw that?"

"I was there with Lizzie. She was my friend then. My daughters were all named after her. She still is my friend, or would be if she hadn't left us." She noticed his questioning look. "No, not dead. People like Jane say she'd be better off dead, though. The Scots Greys came in and killed people. Stopped the voting for that day. There wasn't a riot though."

She sensed she was losing him with her random memories and stopped. But she wanted to go on, to talk to him, to know him. Now he was looking intently at her, listening to every word.

"Perhaps it's wrong to dwell on the past. We can't change it, can we?" she said.

"But we can change the future, shape it."

There was something about the weight and authority of her memories, though she was not much older than he was, that stopped him using his eloquence to impress or influence her, so he waited quietly until she spoke again.

"Then. Now. Nothing changes. We might just as well sit here till we die. If things do change they only change for the worse anyway."

"Do you really believe that?"

"I don't believe anything. I don't know and I don't care. You'd better go. He'll be home soon. You know, Thomas, my husband. One of the men who is going to give me freedom when he has the right to vote. I hope he doesn't fall into the ditch round the drains. It would only make him even more bad tempered. It's not deep enough for him to break his neck and it's as dry as a bone so he can't drown in it."

*

He arrived so soon after William had left that he asked Mary:

"What's he been doing here? God knows why John lets him scrounge a bed in his house. Did he dig up those drains? I almost fell in."

"Go back and try again when it's dark. You might have better luck."

"Don't start a quarrel with me. I'm in no mood for it."

He took a large, smooth stone out of his pocket and placed it on the table. He often brought home stones he had found at work. He would leave each of them around the kitchen for some days, looking at it, picking it up, feeling it, almost as if he thought these stones contained some message. Then, reconciled to the intransigent muteness, he would take the stone and place it into the box he kept under the bed and never look at it again. This stone was the size of a swan's egg and almost the same shape, amazingly smooth, with only a few shallow pitted freckles. He picked it up almost reverently, tossed it up a few inches into the air and caught it in his cupped palm as if trying to gauge its weight. He ran the tip of his finger gently over the slight pock marks which hardly flawed the stone's surface.

Mary placed a bowl of gruel and some bread on the table.

She watched him caressing the small lump of rock. Now that the child was dead what kept her here, with him? Perhaps the fact that she had nowhere better to go. If she'd have had any life left in her, she'd have gone anyway. But what would that change? Her deadness was inside her. She'd take it with her wherever she went. Different surroundings wouldn't make any difference to that. The only other person she could go to was Lizzie, her childhood friend. But there was no knowing where she was, even if she'd wanted to find her.

He raised the stone to his face and, just as Mary thought he was going to kiss it, he noticed her gaze fixed on him.

"What are you staring at?" he snapped at her.

She blinked hard to break her stare and said the first thing that came into her head.

"He said he would fill the trench in when somebody or other has seen the drains."

"He needn't bother. I've done it. "

He put the stone down next to his bowl and began to eat noisily. He considered whether or not to break this stone open. Why shouldn't it, like the egg it resembled, contain something? At first he had always split the stones, hoping to make some kind of discovery. The continuous disappointments stopped him after a time. But this one was so perfect. Perhaps this perfection was a trick to dissuade him from cracking it open. Just as the superficial beauty of the inanimate, motionless piece of rock fascinated him, its relentless impenetrability provoked, disturbed him. It was a strange obsession – wanting to see inside the stone without damaging it.

He pushed his bowl away from him and went outside. Mary could hear the urine splattering onto the yard. As she picked up the plate, she too was struck by the sheer surface and the shape of the stone and held it tenderly, almost as she would support a baby's head in her open hand.

"What are you doing with that? It's mine."

Before he could reach her and snatch it away she laid the stone back on the table and moved away with the plate, her back towards him. He stared hard at her black hair, her broad, sloping shoulders and the curves of her body.

"Put that down and come here."

"What for?"

"You'll find out soon enough!"

"I don't want."

He spun her round and the bowl smashed on the slabbed floor.

"You don't have to want. Just do."

He shoved his hand under her dress and tried to feel her between the legs and push them apart. This was the first time he'd tried to take her since the last child had died. Before then, she didn't normally resist him but would try to separate herself from him emotionally. At the same time she'd remain motionless and rigid, killing any sensation of either disgust or pleasure. Now, spontaneously but definitively, she decided she didn't want it and tried to push him away. He seemed excited by this resistance, preferring it to her normal frigid compliance and he began to fight her for her body. The thought that she could conceive again made her more determined to defy him. She supported herself with one hand against the table and pushed his face away with the other. Still trying to force her legs apart, he slapped her with his free hand but she didn't give way. Unable to force his head back she dropped her hand where he was trying to force himself into her and pushed with the flat of her palm against his body, away from her own. Sensing it would soon be too late if he couldn't overcome her soon, he raised his hand in front of her face and clenched his fist.

"Do you want this first?"

Mary, determined, unafraid and fiercely unwilling, saw the broad, knuckled fist and began to brace herself for the blow just as her hand on the table came into contact with the stone. Her fingers closed around it and, without even thinking, she clubbed the side of his head, behind the temple where the skull was thick and matted with his filthy hair. A split second before the stone thudded satisfyingly against his head, she felt something sticking on her other wrist. In one motion she moved away from him and struck him again on the same spot. He dropped to his knees and, as she pulled herself completely free from him, he lurched forward and hit his head on the rim of the table before sinking lifelessly onto the floor.

She looked at the stone in her hand, laid it on the table. He lay very still on the floor, his head at a strange angle against a table leg. Looking again at the stone, she saw the blood and hair on it. Without going any closer to him, she left and hurried to John and Jane's back door. As she made the few steps across the yard, treading carefully over the puddle he had made, she was aware that the trench had been filled in as Thomas had said.

In the kitchen William was holding a book and had been reading to John from it by the light of an oil lamp. Jane was standing with her back to them at the sink. Mary spoke flatly, not needing to suppress emotion because she didn't feel any.

"I think I've killed Thomas."

Despite the matter-of-fact tone of Mary's voice, Jane didn't doubt that she might be telling the truth. She pushed her way past Mary, glancing with a look of distaste at her hand as she went by. She was the first to reach the kitchen. She was standing motionless and silent just inside the door when John shoved her aside, looked inside and bellowed a short explosive laugh. Thomas was just rising to his feet, feeling his head with one hand and supporting himself on the table with the other. By now John was laughing uncontrollably and William arrived in time to see Jane, scowling, move across the room to arrange his clothes to save him from further ridicule and indecency. Thomas had recovered enough to glance down at his trousers and he covered himself with one hand. Then he sat down at the table, picked up the stone and stupidly, almost apologetically, started to clean off the hair and blood from the unresponsive surface.

Chapter 14

When Constable Haddon knocked at Mary's door two days later, she was neither surprised nor alarmed. She had hardly thought again about the incident with Thomas and anyway Haddon often dropped by. He had become a policeman soon after the force had been introduced and, though in the small market town there was little chance of significant advancement, he was now reasonably well-off and well respected. He needed the information he garnered from visits to his neighbours, amongst whom were Mary and Jane, who trusted him and spoke freely about the gossip their husbands brought home from work.

They'd chatted for several minutes, Haddon slurping noisily at his tea, before he asked:

"Well, what was it all about then Mary, the other night?"

At first she didn't understand what he meant and it crossed her mind for an instant that he was asking about something to do with William. Then she realised what he meant.

"You mean me and Thomas? The fight?"

"Fight? It takes two to make a fight."

"Yes. Me and Thomas."

"But by all accounts he wasn't fighting, Mary. Quite the opposite."

"You mean punching a woman in the face isn't fighting?"

"Nobody said anything about that to me."

"He held his fist up and asked me if I wanted it. I expected him to hit me. Wouldn't have been the first time."

"Well, Mary, according to what I've been told he was holding something up. But it wasn't his fist."

Mary had known Haddon for a long time and had no reason to dislike him. But in that instant she felt the tacit bond between him and Thomas, a bond based simply but inexorably on the fact that they were both male. She wondered fleetingly if William belonged to this fraternity, too.

"He threatened to hit me if I didn't give in to him."

"Give in? He's your husband. He has his rights. And every wife has her duties, Mary."

The fatigue and resignation she had felt since Lizzie's death was still dragging her down but something made her resist Haddon's insistent moral pressure.

"So my will has nothing to do with it. He can have me whenever he likes. If I refuse he can thump me. Is that what you're saying?"

Haddon paused a long time. He took time to slurp again at his tea. He'd seen enough violence between husband and wife and he knew the law well, even if he didn't always like it. He put the cup down and, with both elbows on the table between them, clasped his hands into a kind of praying position and looked steadily at this woman.

"Being struck in the face hurts. I know that. But you're not going to tell me you were in fear of your life? There are some, Mary, who would say you tried to kill Thomas when you hit him with that stone. For whatever reason."

Suddenly alert, she flashed a genuinely worried glance at him. He spoke slowly, as if giving evidence or explaining some matter of principle.

"No, I'm not going to arrest you Mary. Nobody wants that. I've talked to Thomas, and to John. I don't approve of what he tried to do to you. Or what you say he tried to do. His version is a bit different. That's not my job, to approve or disapprove. But he didn't break the law. Even if he had managed to have intercourse with you, as you say, against your will, to violate you, he would still have been within his rights."

He rested his chin on his clasped hands and waited, hoping she would answer. He tried to rouse her out of her indifference, to find out what she was thinking.

"You understand me, Mary?"

"Oh, yes. You mean my body is his and he can do what he wants with it. As long as he doesn't try to kill me."

Haddon ignored the bitter irony in her voice and answered in a matter-of-fact way.

"That's right. He can't take away your right to live."

"To live? To exist, you mean. My children die before they know who I am. I live with an animal, a pig and when he wants to mount me I have to let him. Is that living, Constable Haddon?"

He had got the response he hoped for, provoked her into opening up and saying what she thought without premeditation.

"You know I've always admired your spirit, Mary. But you can take it too far. So far it might cause you grief. You don't want that; nobody does. There are things you can't change; things nobody can change. They're in the scriptures, they're laid down by law. Accept them. Like everybody else does." He paused, then added uncomfortably: "And look for something you can live for." He paused again, then said: "That's what my wife asked me to tell you, Mary. It's not my job to give advice of that kind."

"Something to live for? You mean the Church?"

"You're young enough Mary. You can still have children."

"Do you know, I never saw any of mine smile. Not one of them. Not even once. Disease and pain, and then death. I'm not going through that again, not if I can stop it. And I can stop it."

Haddon sensed the granite resolution behind what Mary said. He'd sought this confrontation to help clarify things for her, to help her foresee where being over-headstrong might lead. To avoid having to hear her words escalate from defiance to recklessness, he prepared to leave.

"Thanks for the tea, Mary. Think about what I've said."

Before he could go, she asked:

"Constable Haddon, what did you mean just then? His version was different? What did he say happened?"

Haddon was annoyed with himself again for underestimating her acuteness. He took a few steps towards the door, his long cylindrical hat in his hand, before he answered in his naturally pedestrian tone.

"Let it rest now, Mary. Good day to you."

Chapter 15

Two weeks after his first conversation with the older Astley, Will had decided that Constable Haddon had more than enough to do to deal with the gangs of navvies that invaded the town centre every few weeks and that he regarded him, if he took notice of him at all, simply as a young man visiting his relatives, one of the more respectable families in the neighbourhood. So he had been going to Astley's store several times a week, participated in discussions in the shop's Conspirators' Corner, as he had christened it to himself, and even dared to take a pamphlet or two home with him, which he read in the privacy of his own bedroom. What in Manchester had been real commitment, involving activities the state saw as seditious and which could have brought him imprisonment and even transportation, was here developing into a kind of luxury, a hobby. He recognised this and both enjoyed and regretted it. He had always despised the desk-bound propagandists in the movement who had written about and preached social change but had never risked their own comfort and liberty for the cause. Now he watched himself drifting towards this role. The German he had met and had become friends with in Manchester had told him.

"It is up to us not simply to understand the world, my friend, but we also have to change it!"

He'd confided this to the younger Astley, Johnnie, who was by now in his thirties so a few years older than Will but they had become good friends within the last few intense weeks. But as usual he was thinking of Mary when he entered the shop and at first didn't notice Johnnie beckoning to him discretely to follow him into the small room behind the counter. It was little more than a cupboard with a small high window which allowed just enough light for him to see that the shopkeeper was holding a hand-written note.

"It's an address in Hinckley," he explained hastily. "There's a meeting, planning something important. Think hard about it before you decide to go. If you do go, be careful."

They returned to the shop and Will sat down alone in the dimly lit corner. Holding the slip of paper close to the open flame of the candle he read and memorised the address and time of the meeting and then let it burn in the yellow flame, blowing the crumbled black ash onto the floor.

*

To find the town he simply followed the Hinckley Road at the end of Back Lane, walking the five miles or so in less than two hours. It was a decent road, crossing the Roman road, the Watling Street about mid-way between the two towns, and he had no worries about making his way back in the dark after the meeting. Until he got within a mile of the town he had only encountered a few farm labourers on carts or on foot, then an Irish family walking with all their worldly possessions, the man with one child on his back and two others perched on top of the bag of belongings balanced on the wheel barrow he was pushing. The pregnant wife was struggling to control a fat pig she had tethered to a long piece of rope and which was dragging her faster than she could walk, while she cursed and swore at it to slow down. When they saw Will, an unusually well-dressed man, they immediately stopped talking and lowered the heads, hoping he was not from the Poor Relief and would have them taken to the workhouse. Though he didn't know the reason for it, he noticed their deferential fear and gave them some coins, for which they thanked him so profusely that he hurried away, leaving them behind to pelt him with shouts of gratitude. Before he reached the first houses he could hear the tremendous clatter of the stocking weaving frames which seemed to emanate from every single house. Approaching the town, he noticed there was something strange, incongruous about what he saw but couldn't decide exactly what it was. Some minutes passed before he realised that there was no smoke coming from the chimneys of the huddled groups of tiny, decrepit dwellings .There were no mines in this town and the coal that people in Nuneaton either bought for little money or scavenged from the slag heaps for nothing was here an often unaffordable luxury.

He didn't approach the house until near the time the meeting was to begin and it was already dark when he tapped on the door. His clothes, his manners and his accent obviously provoked a great deal of distrust among the eight people who stood leaning against the walls of the bare, unheated room. Finally they agreed to let him stay for the first two points of the meeting but he would have to leave then as there were sensitive matters to discuss. The next time he came he was to bring a letter from old John Astley vouching for his genuine interest in their cause and confirming he wasn't, to the best of the revered shopkeeper's knowledge, a government agent. Amused as he was at the thought that they could take him of all people for an informer, he was also reassured by their caution and settled down on the dirty floor to listen to the proceedings. A skinny man of indeterminable age dressed in filthy, torn rags, was asked to move to the centre of the room, was given an oil lamp and he began to read a letter he had written and intended to send to a national newspaper, the Morning Chronicle, to make the plight of the stocking weavers publicly known. He mentioned fifty families, three hundred-and-twenty-one and persons in all, each one engaged in stocking weaving, the man operating the frames, the wife and older children seaming the stockings and the little children winding the wool. They had a hundred-and-nine frames altogether and each frame yielded on average 5½ shillings per week, for each family a weekly average of 11s and 4d. After the expenses for house rent, frame rent, fuel, light, soap and needles were deducted, 1½d were left per day per person for food. For clothing there was nothing. The houses contained only a few sticks of furniture and there were no beds, only whatever straw they could lay their hands on. The children went barefoot and ragged. The man stopped to regain control of his voice when he spoke of his own children, though he made no effort to hide or restrain his tears.

"Everyday I hear them crying for bread. Readers, I am sure you have seen many things in your lives. But have you seen one of your own children die of hunger, and stood by, unable to help? Last Monday I got up at two, as soon as the Sabbath was over, in the dead of night and worked through till near midnight. On the other days I worked from six in the morning until eleven or twelve at night. But I shan't kill myself and leave my family in a worse condition than now. I shall sleep at ten and make up the lost time by working on Sunday."

He handed the lamp back and moved back from the centre of the room into shadows. There was a silence which acknowledged not only the family's suffering but also the man's courage in admitting publicly to what he saw as his humiliating inadequacy as a father and his desperate recourse to working on Sunday, something generally held in the greatest disrepute.

A slightly better dressed man, a clockmaker, then reported briefly on his attendance as the Hinckley delegate at the Chartist Convention. This was the first time that Will had heard of the planned demonstration which was to accompany the handing over of the Petition for the six points of the Charter to Parliament.

"Our aim is a half a million demonstrators and a million signatures on the Petition!"

At this point Will was asked to leave and he knew that there would be a debate about the Convention's decisions and other proposals, which would include physical force alternatives to the peaceful non-violent measures the leadership favoured. Those advocating illegal activities would understandably not welcome the presence of an unidentified witness so he wished them well and left without protest. Though it was almost midnight when he left the town, the clacking and rattling of the frames could still be heard from behind most doors and shutters, jagged, clashing, frictional noises, like the thoughts swirling in Will's head.

*

Mary and Will met often in the next two weeks. He asked her about Polly and Lizzie, but mostly he talked while they both drank tea. He told her about Manchester, about Betty and Hardcastle. He wanted to talk to her about politics, the Chartists and his visions of the future but there was something so real and immediate about her which stopped him, made him feel pompous and hollow as soon as he began to talk about how good life could be. And, while William thought about Mary constantly, not knowing whether she really listened to him or was interested in what he said, she began to wonder about him now and then too.

A few days after Haddon had visited her, she asked William.

"Were you there when Constable Haddon talked to Thomas and John?"

He looked suddenly worried but then relaxed when he realised what she meant.

"You mean about the trouble between you and Thomas? I wasn't there but I heard it – I hid in the scullery under the stairs."

"In the pantry?" She laughed, the first time he heard her laugh. "I know you're good at hiding. But spying? I thought you were the one who gets spied on!"

He watched her smile, pleased that she was smiling because of him.

"Be happy you didn't hide in my pantry. I'm sure there are no cockroaches in Jane's - mine's swarming with the little buggers. As well as mice."

If at that moment Mary had ordered him to catch all the cockroaches in her pantry, in the whole house in fact, he'd have been proud and happy to do so. She hadn't thought about the extent of his affection but she had already realized that William felt something for her. She'd seen it often enough, men keen, apparently desperate to be alone with her. Whatever Jane believed about her, and she seemed to believe that Mary herself was somehow responsible for the lust men had for her, she had never made love to anyone but Thomas since she had known him. She asked:

"Well, what did you hear?"

"He told the policeman what happened. That you hit him with the stone. That he fell, hit his head on the table and came round just as we all arrived."

"And Haddon? What did he ask?"

"First question was how many times you hit him. As if it matters …"

"And what did Thomas say?"

"Nothing. Before he had time to say anything, John said that Thomas had told him you hit him once. But hard. And then Thomas said that was right."

"And why? Did they say anything about why we were fighting?"

"Fighting?"

"I almost killed him. Isn't that fighting?"

"But before that you weren't fighting, Thomas said."

Mary felt both anger and disappointment rising up inside her.

"So you agree with Haddon that him trying to, to violate me, shaking his fist in my face wasn't fighting."

William paused before he told her.

"Thomas said you were angry with him because he, you know, was too quick. He disappointed you and you hit him. Because, well, because he couldn't give you what you wanted. He begged Haddon not to report it. Said he'd be a laughing stock and that you'd be punished just when you were hoping to have another baby."

"Did you believe that William?"

"The important thing is that Haddon believed it."

"No, he didn't believe it. Not all of it anyway. And what about you? Tell me."

"I half believed it. More than half, I suppose. I mean, remember how we saw him in the kitchen. And your hands. We all saw what was on your hands. It seemed natural to believe him."

Mary thought about the details William mentioned.

"For somebody who believes what Jane says about me. Natural perhaps for somebody who doesn't know me."

This was William's chance and he took it. Before, he had been somehow encouraged by the idea that Mary was such a passionate woman and now she seemed to confirm her alienation from her husband, which she had hinted at before, and this encouraged him too.

"I want to know you, Mary. Really know you. Nobody need know about us."

The scene seemed familiar to Mary and so she wasn't shocked. Hardly surprised even. Since she had been married, other men had propositioned her, usually married, respectable men.

"I like you, Will. If I had a lover - that's what you're saying isn't it? – it could be you."

She paused and looked straight at him.

"I have wishes and desires, too, William."

"Then what's to stop us?"

He gripped her hand and she didn't withdraw it. She continued:

"And I have one special wish. You can make it true."

He tried gently to pull her towards him but she held him away.

"That night, when I came to Jane's for help, you were holding a book. Can you read it?"

He just nodded, and she said almost passionately:

"That's my desire, my wish. Teach me to read. And then to write."

*

The spring had arrived early and by the end of March the weather was as warm as early summer. This didn't alter much in the yard behind the house or in the street in front of it, but where Mary had arranged to meet William, alongside the canal, the bushes were already green, some were already beginning to blossom and there were small, wild flowers amongst the grass. She knew the place well and had often come there to savour its profusion in Spring and Summer; the purple nightshade with its ruby berries, the raking, treacherously barbed blackberry branches, sometimes white with May; convolvulus and honeysuckle weaving, climbing entwining through the hedges, decorating them with the tiny white trumpets and surrounded them with fragrance. She had chosen the spot because of its seclusion, not because of its associations, its memories of Henry. Wearing a coarse grey dress, when William arrived she was sitting barefoot with her thighs pulled up to her chest, her hands clasped around her ankles and her chin resting on her knees, thinking about the past. He pushed her boots to one side and sat down beside her, laying the book between them.

"Is this the book you were reading that night?" she asked.

"No. It's Jane's."

"It's not the Bible, is it? Why didn't you bring yours?"

"The Bible's much bigger than this. My book is too, well, too hard to begin with. I don't know if it'll be possible anyway. Teaching you to read, I mean."

"You think I'm not clever enough to learn to read?"

"I don't know if I can teach you. I've never taught anyone before."

"Who taught you?"

"I taught myself. Before I went to school."

She sensed the slight trace of complacency in his voice.

"So you have taught someone!"

He was still trying to find an answer when he noticed she was making fun of him. She was smiling again, about him. Maybe today she'd agree to make love with him. The place was ideal. Perhaps that was why she had chosen to meet him here.

"Read me something. Out loud. Please."

He picked up the book, found the first page of the text and began to read aloud:

"As I walked through the wilderness of the world I lighted on a certain place, where was a den; and I laid me down in that place to sleep: and as I slept I dreamed a dream. I dreamed and behold I saw a man clothed with rags, standing in a certain place, with his face from his own home, a book in his hand and a great burden upon his back. I looked and saw him open the book and read therein; and as he read

*he wept and trembled: and not being able longer to
contain he broke out with a lamentable cry, saying:
What shall I do?"*

He stopped and looked at her. Now she was lying on her side,
her elbow on the grass and her head rested in the cup of her
hand.

She spoke first.

"It's a bit like here, isn't it? A den. A man with a book. But
I'm not dreaming. I stopped dreaming long ago."

"But is that what you're asking yourself, Mary: What shall I
do?"

"I was thinking more about what I've done."

"Think about the future too, Mary."

"A future? With Thomas?"

He placed his hand on hers and pressed it gently. She looked
down at what he was doing, deliberately.

"A future with you, William?"

"It's up to you to decide, Mary."

She picked up the book, rolled onto her back and opened it
at random. She glanced at a few of the illustrations and handed
it back to him.

"But, William, you promised to teach me to read today. And
next time bring your own book with you too. I don't think I'm
going to like Jane's."

Chapter 16

John Bacon felt good as he strode along the footpath towards the new stretch of railway one of his gangs was laying. He was about to be nominated for the first time as a sub-contractor, and would then be dealing directly with Mr Brassey, the line's main contractor. All he had to do now was to ensure that the current work he was carrying out was completed in an orderly way and in good time. He foresaw no problems. Both he himself and almost all his workers were experienced in the whole range of railway work – embankments, cuttings, bridges and even tunnelling. The track that John was working on with his gang of navvies was one of the easiest in the country. From Rugby to Stafford, it ran over rather than through 50 miles of agricultural land with only the slightest gradients and no significant natural obstacles. Though called the Trent Valley Line it only really met with the Trent in the last few miles and on the section John and his gang had worked, between Tamworth and Rugby, the line took, with slight meanderings, roughly parallel to the Watling Street, laid straight as a die by the Roman Julius Agricola almost two thousand years before.

North-west of Nuneaton, a town the Roman road wisely skirted past, the railway passed through the ancient settlements of Mancetter, Atherstone, Tamworth and Lichfied but it was the small, flat, anonymous market town the Romans had all but neglected that was to provide a hub of rail links that would transform the region. Apart from contributing to the main purpose of the line, to provide a more direct link between London, Liverpool and Manchester by avoiding Birmingham and relieving congestion there, Nuneaton would soon offer its own link to Birmingham as well as Coventry, Leicester and Ashby-de-la-Zouch and from there joining the Scotland lines.

This meant for John, if he remained in good health, well-paid work for at least another four years, probably for life as there were untold sidings and local connections to be laid. He knew it and he basked in that knowledge now. It gave him a wonderful confidence and sometimes even pride. It was his dream, some would have said vision, to set up a whole network of gangs with someone he could trust in charge of each gang and himself at the head of the whole operation. Maybe if his brother-in-law, Thomas could cut down a bit on his drinking and get things sorted out with his wife, he could take over one of these gangs. If he was to win and keep the respect of the navvies, Thomas couldn't afford to have any obvious weaknesses. A wayward wife and the inability to hold his drink would make him vulnerable.

John paused as he crossed the bridge over the canal, looked down at the placid water and spat with a boyish pleasure into it. From the bridge he could see the navvy camp about two hundred yards away on the left of the strip of dull water. The canal was a good two yards higher than the natural level of the field so it had been shored up with a deep bank which reached about ten yards into the meadow. The first row of dwellings were dug a couple of yards into this embankment which thus provided each of them with two sides and a back wall. Struts, posts and planks had been inserted to support the roof and keep out as much water as possible. Other dwellings were made of whatever materials the navvies could lay their hands on.

Although most of the men were already at work by now, there was smoke coming from many of the ramshackle huts and sheds. A few women were wandering about the camp. He could see dogs and a pig or two roped to pegs and rooting the soft soil. And there was something in the navvy way of life, an almost lawless, self-regulated day-to-day existence, accountable to no-one and with its ample supply of beef, bread and beer, that appealed to him. John was a brawny, usually amiable ganger who knew the business and was able to indulge in the randies and the drinking sessions in the camp as well as the next man and to settle disputes with his fists when words were insufficient. But he was also respected as competent and reliable by Craddock, Jermyn and Buchanan and the rest of the town's core of capital and respectability. In fact it was the lawyer, Buchanan, who had advised him to invest his small inheritance in purchasing the concession to work the first stretch of rail in 1846 and, as a member of the Nuneaton consortium with a major shareholder in the London and North West Railway, it was also Buchanan who had supported John's submission to become a sub-contractor.

Now, shortly after the opening of the line, it was not only a geographical mesh that the railways were bringing to the town. When the confidence-building publicity run was made from Euston, transferring to the new Trent Valley line at Rugby in June 1847, the cream of British political, economic and engineering life had been on that train: Sir Robert Peel, who had instigated the building of the line and across whose estate at Tamworth the line ran for several miles, Thomas Brassey and George Hudson, the railway magnates, and Robert Stephenson, whose already legendary father George had surveyed the original route, were amongst those on board. But as well, there were quiet, sleek, less celebrated men like Craddock and Buchanan, greasing their own wheels within wheels. And in a special compartment for the men, as opposed to the gentlemen, John sat together with other sub-contractors and gangers, enjoying the lavish quantities of cold meats, pies, cheese and beer.

And John was wily enough to know that he could count on this financial and political battalion provided he could guarantee them a fair return on their trust. But his real battle was with his wife, Jane, and in this very private contest of two wills the weaponry of social power didn't help him. With a genuine contempt for those John most revered, Jane could isolate him from the comfort of his dreams and have him stand naked and cold in the debilitating glare of God's disapproval. She could strip him of his pride and turn it against him to instil in him the fear of death. Jane wanted only two things from life; a child and to live among God-fearing, pious people. She could have neither in Back Lane. Her plan, which she could make sound like God's will, was for John to work as a ganger for some years, saving as much as they could and then to emigrate to a small Christian community in New England, America, which she had been told about at the Baptist meeting house she attended. Though they no doubt regarded themselves as Dissenters, Craddock, Buchanan, the flour mill owner, the surgeons, the ribbon manufacturers were, for Jane, little better than Papists. She saw them going to church, their wives and daughters competing with the vain trappings of fashion just as the men did with the luxury of their carriages and rigs. Her husband was still a sinner who had yet to recognise the true path but, in his uncouth honesty, he was still capable of salvation. In the right surroundings she was sure she could do it. But not here in Nuneaton, where the idea of self-improvement was to become as corrupt and as indulgent as those who called themselves devout and God-fearing. If they had a child, she knew she would be able to terminate her husband's wavering forever. He might just manage to justify staying in Nuneaton when there were only the two of them, but he could never defend seeing their child grow up surrounded by sin and filth. Even if they moved into better housing, which they could already easily afford, the sin around them would remain. Given the choice he would have to choose a place where righteousness, not evil and the flaunting of God's word, was the norm.

As John neared the cutting where some of his men were working, he forgot about all this and focussed on what he wanted to see when he got to where this gang was working. He approached it from the side and the cutting, though relatively shallow, was deep enough to conceal the men working at its base. There were horses on the rim of each side of the trough, pulling the ropes away from the edge. In the other direction, the ropes ran over a pulley then down at an angle parallel to the slope of the bank. That end of the ropes was attached both to the wheel barrows full of excavated soil and also, as a safety measure, to the waist of the navvy steadying the barrow up the gradient. There were wooden planks laid out as a runway from the bottom to the top of the slopes so the barrow had a surface as clean as possible to run on. When the barrow reached the raised platform at the top of the run, its contents were tipped into a wagon, the sides of which were at the same level as the platform. Another horse was harnessed to the wagon, which was on temporary rails so the horse could pull it to an embankment being formed to cross a slight hollow a few hundred yards away. John had gangs working on both the cutting and the embankment and, while he could see the wagons being tipped over the far edge of the ridge, there seemed little activity at the cutting. This made him nervous because, if the work slowed or stopped here, then sooner or later everything on the site would grind to a halt. As he got nearer, almost close enough to look down into the excavation, he could hear raised voices. One of them, he thought, was Thomas'.

The depth was only about 10 feet but the banks had been cut in a long slow slope to ensure enough soil was won to build the nearby embankment. He quickened his pace and half ran and half slid, steadying himself with one hand on the plank barrow-run. A large man with heavy sideburns and wavy hair was bellowing at Thomas in an Irish accent.

"If you can't pull your weight, go onto a different job. You'd better talk to your brother about it now."

Although his voice was raised, there was no aggression or anger in it and he turned towards his boss, hoping for support, but John wanted to hear more and said:

"I'm not his brother and since when hasn't Thomas been doing his share of the work?"

"We've had to speed things up if we're to make the sets. And he doesn't seem up to it. Not today at least."

The group of men formed a sub-gang, a butty and John had been given a fixed price by the sub-contractor for the next section of rail and had passed it on to the men. He'd calculated it at five shillings and sixpence a day over ten days. It was a fair price and even if they needed the ten days they'd still be making an extra five shillings altogether, a normal day's pay. But the weather was good, the ground was dry and the digging easy so they wanted to finish it in nine days. John, whose share would be a good twenty pounds if all went well over the ten days, had promised to pay them cash with no truck vouchers so most of them planned to take the tenth day off.

"If he can't stand the pressure you'd better get us somebody else and put him on the tipping," another man chipped in.

"And we're losing even more time standing around here talking about it."

John looked at Thomas for his version, expecting him to defend himself, but instead he admitted:

"It's perhaps right what they say. But it's only today."

He looked at the big Irishman, who nodded his agreement. Thomas rubbed the side of his head where Mary had clobbered him with the stone weeks before and stared at the ground. John knew he had to decide quickly without creating any more disagreement.

"Thomas, get yourself off for today. You'll be alright tomorrow. Nobody here is saying you're not worth your salt as a rule."

The other men mumbled their agreement but the big Irishman still wasn't quite satisfied.

"But if we're a man short …"

John took off his jacket and threw it on to the side of the bank where the navvies had placed their belongings. He rolled his shirt sleeves up, spat on his hands and took hold of Thomas' shovel and looked at the Irishman.

"Any objections, Curly?"

"None at all, John Bacon!"

The other men agreed good-humouredly and the work began.

Thomas sauntered towards the finished track. If he followed it for two hours it would take him into the town. He and a few of the men who didn't live in the navvy camp came into work on a light truck that ran effortlessly on the flat, straight line. But now the walk would perhaps clear the dull humming inside his head.

Almost out of sight of John and the others, he turned and glanced back once more before the track veered slightly to the right, taking him out of their view. Now the land was almost perfectly flat, no cuttings or embankments and for a few hundred yards the track ran alongside the canal. He thought about walking along the canal tow-path instead of the railway line. It would take him a bit longer but the going was easier than over the rough fill between the sleepers. He still hadn't decided when he reached the point where the canal curved away from the railway. Before he made up his mind which route to take, he walked up onto the small bridge that crossed the canal. He stuffed some tobacco into his pipe, lit it and climbed carefully astride the wall of the bridge. In one direction he could see a few hundred yards of canal but in the other, the direction of the town, it veered away in a long slow bend to the right, gradually taking the water and the tow-path out of view.

On the broad flat meadow which opened out between the canal and the railway track there was little to see except for two figures, a man and a woman. They were a good distance away from him, two, three hundred yards, walking away from the canal towards the lane which crossed both the railway and the canal and would take them into town. The man was carrying something under his arm and the woman was holding something, flowers or twigs perhaps. As they were walking diagonally away from him, he couldn't see their faces but suddenly Mary's thick black hair became clearly visible and unmistakable even from that distance and angle. The man turned his head to look at the woman and Thomas got a clear view of William's face.

After a few minutes, they reached the lane and disappeared behind the high hedgerows that lined it. He clambered down from the wall and leaned with his back to it, staring vacantly in the direction he had come from. He knocked out his pipe against the bridge wall and slumped down, his legs hunched up and his back against the wall. He had half a bottle of gin in his jacket pocket and he hardly moved until he had emptied it an hour or so later.

*

It was early evening and John had enjoyed the day. He'd shown Curly he could out-shovel him, he'd driven the barrow up the running without the horse's help and he'd consumed four quarts of beer, a pound of beef and a good deal of bread. On top of that he'd hardly stopped talking and his men were subdued into a sullen respect for him. The reluctant pride that they had the best and the fairest ganger on the line was marred somewhat by the fact that they knew they'd never be able to complain he worked them too hard or too long. Put to the test they knew he'd be able to prove it could be done day in and day out by doing it himself.

But he was one of the few gangers who made sure the beer wasn't watered down and who paid cash as often as he could. He hated the trucking system almost as much as they did. The men subjected to it would seethe and swear what they would do at the end of the month when they finally got the balance on their wages, but usually, as soon as they felt the feel of the coins, they were off out in the town drinking and brawling until they'd forgotten their grievances for another month.

Leaving a couple of men behind to guard the site and look after the horses, John was on a truck with ten navvies being pulled along the rails at a brisk trot by Rocket, as this horse was known.

"And what about Tommy, Mr Bacon? He's a good lad, a bit moody sometimes maybe, but if this line's too hard for him, it might be better to get someone else in."

"I was thinking along the same lines, Curly. I've got a small gang doing some sidings and I thought I'd give him a chance to look after them."

"Where's that work? Not around here?"

"It's twenty miles away. He'd be living in. Decent lodgings and it won't be forever. About six weeks I'd think."

"He'll need somebody to be looking after that wife of his then. That's a job I'd do unpaid any day. Somebody pointed her out to me once. A fine woman. And they say she'd sooner do without her dinner than without her pudding!"

John felt uncomfortable with the indecent talk about his sister-in-law but the men's laughter and their genuine good nature won him over. That and the drink loosened his tongue.

"Well, she's one reason why he maybe better off away for a while. Let him gather his strength a bit. If you only knew half."

They laughed as much to encourage him to tell more as from amusement and then went quiet, hoping he'd tell them what he knew.

"Don't breathe a word of this, but I'll tell you why Thomas has been out of sorts lately."

And, invigorated by the beer and the excitement of the day, he told them the story as Thomas had told it to him, and, carried away by his gang's crude merriment, even embellished it with bawdy colouring of his own: that Mary was keen for it and then, just when she wanted it inside her, he'd come before he could give it her. And that she was so furious she smacked him over the head with a brick! Knocked him out stone cold, so that she'd even thought she'd killed him. Came into their kitchen wiggling her sticky fingers and when they got next door there he was lying there, his cock shrivelled up like a dried turnip!

They were still laughing uncontrollably when they noticed the horse had stopped. Thomas came down from the bridge, round to the back of the truck, stumbled in and called out in a blurred voice: "Gid up, Rocket!"

He was vaguely aware of the raucous laughter but couldn't be bothered to find out what it was about. It was nothing to do with him and he just wanted to get back to the house, eat and sleep and forget.

Chapter 17

By the end of March Will had attended three Chartist meetings in Hinckley and, after the latest one, he met both the Astleys as usual the next day after their shop had been closed for the night to inform them of all that had happened. The previous night's meeting had been by far the most momentous and decisive. Will had difficulty containing his excitement as he reported to the two attentive listeners.

"Last night there were a lot there, more than before. About twenty men and a few women, most of them stocking weavers, frame workers and their wives. Only two or three traders or craftsmen. These Hinckley weavers, they're not just poorer than even the mill workers in Manchester. They have this look in their eyes. Something wild and unpredictable. Some of them supported the Convention delegate when he talked about the rally. Most of them scoffed at him though and called the leaders traitors, even Fergus O'Connor. The only national figure they seem to respect is Jones, the physical force advocate. And even he is mild compared to some of them. The alternative motion to taking part in the demonstration was to storm Leicester Prison, free the prisoners and form an army and move on to large city and stage an armed insurrection!"

He paused, expecting the father and son to express their incredulity but they just waited patiently for him to continue.

"After a lot of discussion the motion was finally passed to support the rally. There's to be collecting to pay for as many as possible to go to London on the 12th of April. Just the rail fare so they'll have to travel back the same day or sleep rough overnight."

Again he looked at them for some verbal reaction but there was none forthcoming.

"And you, Will? What are your feelings about it?" the elder of the two men asked.

Will stood up and began to pace around the room. It was a more than a minute before he tried to answer.

"I was torn. On the one hand I can't deny their suffering. And their courage, the way they bear it. I can understand their anger, their impatience with peaceful methods. But, and I'm ashamed to admit this, I cannot abide by their blind obstinacy, their refusal to see that this demonstration will open the way for all kinds of progress. Not just higher wages. They'll have the vote. They'll be able to send their own members to Parliament, with a majority and they will pass laws to solve all their problems. Why can't they see that? There's no government that can ignore the voice of the people when it's backed by half a millions demonstrators and a petition with over a million signatures!"

He sat down again and Johnnie poured beer from a large jug into three glasses. He sat across the table from Will.

"Are you going? To London?"

Will raised his eyebrows at the naivety of the question.

"They only let me in because of your father's letter and then grudgingly. You don't believe I'd be delegated, do you?"

"You're not poor, Will. You can pay your own way."

His glass stopped just before it reached his lips as Johnnie's suggestion sank in. Of course he could go. Why not? Amazingly he'd never even considered it. Before he found words to answer, the old Astley stood up slowly, bade Will a goodnight and made his way towards the stairs at the back of the shop.

"I'll just help my father up the stairs, Will and I'll be back. Help yourself to more beer."

Alone in the spacious gloom of the shop, Will thought about the possibility of going to London. Strangely he had another reason for visiting the capital as his family's bankers were situated in the City and he needed to make arrangements for an account in a locally based bank. With this excuse, he could certainly persuade his brother to lend him enough money for the travel and accommodation expenses. Ten pounds or so should suffice. Then he could not only witness but actually participate in perhaps the most significant day in England's history. Only one thing could equal that for him. If Mary were to agree to take him as her lover. Just as his thoughts began to centre around her, Johnnie returned.

"You don't look happy, Will. Not still brooding about the weavers, are you? Look forward to the great day."

On impulse he decided to confide in this new but trusted friend.

"It's not politics, Johnnie. It's a woman. You know my, what is she, not my sister-in-law. My neighbour."

Astley understood at once.

"You're in love with Mary Ball?"

The alcohol, his tiredness, the sudden release from the excitement and tension since the dramatic Chartist meeting all combined to swill away Will's caution. He nodded but didn't speak. The other man could see, despite his apparent reticence, that Will was dying to reveal something to him. With the instinct of a hunter on the trail of elusive knowledge, a shy and wary prey, Astley sensed that one thrust was needed to induce the trapped emotions to break cover.

"You mean, you're lovers?"

"Not yet. I mean, no. I've asked her, begged her but she ..."

They both searched for the word, Will not daring to utter the word *refuse* and tempt its real finality. In one lucid moment Astley knew how to complete the sentence that hung in the air, inevitable but unpronounced.

"She hasn't yet said *Yes* is what you want to say?"

They both laughed but the delicious tension remained in the air around them like the blue smoke of a cigar in a windless room.

"Johnnie, I'd give anything to be with her. We spend time together. Almost whenever we want to. There's no lack of opportunity. And her husband. It's not because of him that she resists. Or perhaps it is. Perhaps she thinks the brute in him is in all men."

Astley thought about this woman he'd known almost all her life, had known her as a pert girl, then as an unusually alert and independently minded young woman, eager to learn from her own experience of life. And then Polly's murder happened and it was as if the self had deserted her body and left only a residue of Mary, just enough to ensure survival. But Mary had survived. He knew from the neighbours' gossip of quarrels, even fights with Thomas, that her spirit was not extinguished. In recent weeks, since the winter had gone, he'd seen her in the shop, lively, bright, vigilant, almost like she had been before the shock of Polly's murder had enshrouded her. He realised that this time also coincided with Will's presence in the town and his sudden insights gave him the almost smug feeling he was playing cards against a far inferior opponent. And on top of that, he had all the aces. Strangely though, he was determined the other player should win. He opened with a clumsy question:

"Does she mean more to you than your vision of Chartism, Will?"

"I only try to imagine what it would be like to have both."

He made sure Will was both listening to him and looking into his face before he spoke again.

"Well, my friend. Isn't this the perfect chance to do just that?"

Will realised that he was being slowly reeled in, as an expert angler guides his fish to the net but he still didn't know what Johnnie meant.

"Take her to London with you. The least you can do is ask her."

Will thought for a few moments.

"But even if she agreed, she'd be away for two or three days. How would we explain it?"

Johnnie shrugged.

"From what I hear Tommy Ball is away with his ganger, John Bacon, most weeks. Take the chance, Will. It's the best you'll ever get. And if Mary really wants you, she'll agree."

"And Jane? She misses nothing, forever hovering and spying ..."

"Jane won't say a word. She'll curse inside and wish Mary in hell but she won't breath a word. I've known that family all my life. I probably know more of what goes on that whole street than Constable Haddon. And I know what plans your brother has for Thomas, Jane's little brother. He wants to make him a ganger but then he'll have to deal direct with the paymasters, Craddock, Buchanan and the like. They won't accept a man whose house is not in order. They won't accept a man who can't deal with alcohol and who can't discipline his wife. Jane won't spoil her brother's future. You can be sure of that, Will."

Suddenly stone, cold sober, Will thought hard about what his friend had said, remembered John saying almost the same about his plans for Thomas and what the men who backed him, the pious, unbending Dissenters, expected from those they patronised.

"But if she refuses, I won't come back. If she doesn't say yes, then I'll stay in London and try to forget her."

Astley simply shrugged as if it didn't concern him but as soon as Will had left, he took out the book he used as his diary and began to write. Still agitated and stimulated by the evening, Will was also restless and, in the quiet of his room, took out his diary in the hope it would calm him, at least keep him from pacing up and down like a caged animal. Before he began to write the short entry for that day, he re-read all of what he had written since his arrival in Back Lane, beginning two months back:

*

William Bacon's diary

> *5thFebruary,1848 Nuneaton: The town is impenetrably dull, muddy and badly lit. Only the main street and a few other roads have gas lighting and that is very poor, giving not much more than an uneven glow. As the weather is rainy and heavily overcast, it is already dark in the late afternoon. My sister-in-law Jane is very thrifty and a few cheap tallow candles are all I'm allowed for light. What a broomstick of a woman she is! The opposite of Mary, whom I've seldom seen and hardly spoken to since the morning I arrived.*

> *7th February: Spent today reading whenever I could. When Jane is not working at her loom she is cleaning. Caught a glimpse of Mary crossing the yard. Must find some excuse to talk to her. I have no diversions and can imagine nothing more delightful than her company.*

> *8th February: According to old John Astley, a shopkeeper with enormous local and political knowledge, the weavers and the miners of the*

locality are rowdy and disrespectful but incapable of organised political activity – unlike the mill workers in Manchester. Perhaps that's just as well, I need to avoid attracting attention to myself, especially not from the constable who lives a few doors away. Jane was out and I knocked at Mary's door but, because she was weaving, I think she didn't hear me. At any rate she didn't open the door.

9th February: Went into town again, despite the rain. What luck that the shopkeeper Astley seems to be a bit of a free spirit, even more than radical. Has some pamphlets and even a few books. At least I have something to read to take my mind off my inactivity and off Mary.

10th February: Brother John as good natured as ever. He is still a bit slow-witted and terrified of his shrewish wife but he is a determined capable man and I am sure he will achieve his goals. He hints at a grand plan but hasn't confided details. Not yet. I tried to tease out some information from him about Mary but he saw through me at once. Thomas, Mary's husband, is Jane's younger brother and seems to have some place in John's plans. John told me to keep my eyes and hands off her.

28th February: Fine, mild day. Spent morning digging around drains in yard. Everything seems to confirm Snow's theories about the causes of cholera. Spoke at last for a long time with Mary. Desire, affection, lust, infatuation, whatever it is I'm obsessed with the thought of her. Perhaps I'm in love with her. Things are bad between her and Thomas.

But she seems disinterested, resigned, numb. If only I can awake something inside her! Betty once told me that many women have the same strong, irrepressible desires as men. I hope that's true of Mary.

5th March: Weather much better and, when Jane is not around, meet often with Mary. She seems not to be averse to my company, though she doesn't seek it either. She listens to me when I talk about reform and Chartism. She knows a lot from experience, though she has not much schooling. Sometimes I feel her knowledge of life, real life, is superior to mine, despite all I have read. She is sharp-witted as well as handsome.

7th March: If M. doesn't give in to me soon I fear I will have to leave. It's unbearable to be so close to her, so often. Almost constantly during the daytime. We have ample opportunity and I'm sure she cares for me. There's nothing to stop us. She has no religious scruples and I'm positive now that she has no voluntary relations with her husband.

9th March: I can hardly believe it but I think Mary has decided to become my lover. She wants to meet me tomorrow outside the town. Described the spot in detail. I can't quite believe it yet but why else would she want us to go to such a secluded place?

10th March: I asked her again today, pleaded with her, begged her, to no avail. Except that she asked me to teach her to read better and to write. At least this gives her a reason for meeting with me. If only I could make her feel joy just once then I know she'd be mine.

28th March: There are at this moment two equal passions in my life – the cause of Chartism and Mary. My love for her is something I carry with me all the time. It follows me to bed and stops me sleeping. I sense its presence the moment I wake up. It requires an enormous conscious effort for me to stop thinking about her and there is nothing that would prevent me from sharing her company as much as possible. I know she cares for me and enjoys my company but we are still not lovers. All I can do is wait. Lately she has neglected her weaving very much because she is so intent on mastering the written word, at which she has made great progress. I wish she were as hungry for me as she is for the reading matter and the practice I give her, though the books are little to her liking. We have almost finished Pilgrim's Progress and have dipped into the Bible but the language is so antiquated that it has little more than mechanical value for us. She laughed at the bits of Corinthians and Revelations I picked out – said they reminded her of Jane. But we also read some of the Psalms and Genesis, which I think she liked. There is an amazing gap between her intelligence and her knowledge, or better said her ignorance. Tomorrow I must go again to H****** to obtain more information about the rally.

30th March: My excitement is so intense that I can hardly sit still long enough to write this down. Everything is planned. On the 12th April, in two weeks, England will witness the greatest manifestation of democracy in its history. At least half a million people from all walks of life will demonstrate for the Charter. All our leaders, including the great O'Connor, will speak. Most believe that if there is one man who can be relied on to lead us to our goal then it is perhaps the eloquent Fergus O'Connor. But if he were to falter then at least Ernest Jones will never compromise. I believe it is he who will really carry the day for us. The voice of the people will be so clear and will possess so much authority that Parliament will have to give way. The power of the masses united behind the demands of the Charter and confirmed by the signatures on the Petition – we are confident at least a million! – will make violence unnecessary. I think universal suffrage is only months away. And justice and a decent life for all, men and women, then only a matter of time. Among the twenty men and women at the meeting there was something wilder about the atmosphere than in Manchester, more prone to violence. Notable absence of skilled tradesmen and craftsmen. Except for one watchmaker and a printer, almost all present were hosiery weavers or from other low paid trades. From the looks of them they are in a bad way. One group opposed the rally and wanted to attack the local workhouses and the prison in Leicester and, with the men they free, move into a larger centre where something in the way of an armed insurrection appears to be planned. The other group talked about a rally to be held in London in April. In the end they agreed to collect as many signatures as possible for the Charter and enough money to pay for the train fare to London for at least twenty men. One or two of the most radical refused to consider anything but direct violence and they reminded me of the Socialist in Manchester who turned out to be an agent. I said nothing though, not wanting to draw attention to myself or to accuse anyone unjustly. Arrived home long after darkness fell. As I passed Mary's kitchen window I saw her, by the light of a few candles, washing herself. She was naked to the waist and although she had her back to me, the sight aroused me so intensely that the thought of her replaced all the excitement I had felt about the meeting. I resolved to confess the true depth of my feelings to her at the first chance.

31st March: I am to go to London and take part in the historic rally! Tonight I confided in young Astley, told him about my love for Mary, who he knows well, just as he seems to know everyone in this town! In the short time I've been here he's become a good, trusted friend, and he suggested I ask Mary to accompany me. At first I couldn't take his idea seriously but with luck and caution we could keep it from John and the husband, Thomas.

John will lend me fifteen pounds! I just told him I need to go to London to meet the bankers to arrange banking facilities here in Nuneaton. This is also true but I didn't tell him the full story of course. I also managed to entice from him that both he and Thomas will be working so far away that week that they will not be coming home to sleep. That makes things somewhat easier. I think I understand Jane well enough now to know that she, even when she knows the full truth, will think twice before telling

John, let alone Thomas. I will ask Mary as soon as I have the opportunity. If she refuses me, I think I will not return from London but dedicate my life solely to the cause of social progress and try to forget her. But I wish more than I have ever wished for anything that she will consent.

Chapter 18

When John travelled out to where Thomas and his group of men were working on the last day in March, he was nervous. He knew how much was at stake for him and he'd tried to make this clear to Thomas without frightening him with too much responsibility. He stopped the truck, unharnessed the pony and walked along the siding the gang was working on. It couldn't have been easier work – flat, straight and good solid ground. Mounds of rock-split as well the massive sleepers and rail sections had been placed at intervals alongside the track base. Each of the men knew his job and all Thomas had to do was keep the work going smoothly.

But as John got within fifty yards or so he could see that work had stopped. He stood still, half hiding himself instinctively behind a shed. Perhaps they were just having a break. It must have been around noon. But his intuition wouldn't let him relax. He could see some of the men lounging around on the ground, swigging beer and munching chunks of bread, one group of four crouched on their haunches playing thimblerig. But Thomas and another man were standing face to face. John heard faint laughter and saw the man standing opposite Thomas look at the others, obviously awaiting some kind of response to something he'd said. But before he could collect their appreciation Thomas struck him swiftly but with tremendous force across the side of the head with the thick pole handle of his shovel. The man, a big red-haired Irishman, was shocked and stunned but didn't go down. He just let his own shovel fall with a clatter onto the iron and stone. As he raised his hands to the side of his head as if protecting his ears from noise, Thomas bent down quickly and filled his right hand with a few of the stone chippings at his feet, clenched his fingers round them and slammed his fist into the Irishman's gut. As the big man jack-knifed down, Thomas struck him again, walloped his fist into his face with a resounding smack. He sank first onto his knees and then onto his side, clutching his stomach and gasping for air though hardly conscious.

Nobody moved. They could all see the man lying helpless at Thomas' heavily booted feet. Thomas only took a few steps back and said something to the men that John couldn't hear. A few of the men got up and walked to their barrows and began filling them with stone. Two others lifted the Irishman to his feet, poured water over his head and within a few minutes the work was underway.

John remained where he was for a few more minutes and then heard the footsteps of two men approaching the shed. He moved completely out of their sight and they entered the shed but he could hear them talking in their rich Irish accent.

"You'll not be doing anything of the sort."

"But he's from the same county as me, almost the same village. I can't stand by and watch him get laid out by an Englishman, and do nothing about it."

"But that's it. He only laid him out. And Porrock deserved it. Don't go saying he didn't. You can't talk about a man's wife like that, gaffer or no gaffer, English or Irish."

"Bu he only told him what his cousin Curly had said. He didn't say it was true."

"Now come off it, Michael. Porrock was trying to get a laugh out of him and the lad was within his rights to smack him. I'd have done the same myself. So would you."

A pause signified he was getting his point across.

"And a good job he did of it, too. Admit it. He could have booted Porrock in the taters as he lay there. Or stamped his head in. But he didn't. Gave him just enough and no more."

They had sorted out some shovels and a barrow they come for and emerged out of the shed.

"Now just let things be. He's not a bad gaffer at all and we can earn us a nice bob or two on this stretch if we all knuckle down to it."

John couldn't have been more delighted if the reference had been spoken by Lawyer Buchanan. He peered cautiously around the corner of the shed to catch a glimpse of the two men. He knew both of them well, he thought, but hadn't realised before that one of them might well be capable of taking over a small gang himself if things developed as John hoped.

After a good five minutes he walked loudly towards the men as if he had only just arrived, still elated by what he had seen and heard so his cheerfulness was genuine.

"Come over here, Thomas. There's a thing or two I want to discuss with you."

Out of sight of the others, John laid his arm over Thomas' shoulder.

"You're doing a good job here, brother. The men'll be coming into the depot tomorrow to pick up their money. All cash, no truck. And there'll be an extra bonus. For you as well."

He paused, searching for the right words.

"It's as good as done now. The sub-contract with Brassey. You know what that means? For all of us? Look, Thomas, there's place there for you. But these men, Buchanan and Bull and their like, they're Churchmen, Dissenters, Independents. They like things to look right. Not like Jane. For her things have really got to be right. They just want things to seem. That's enough for them."

He knew what he wanted to say but was aware he was not saying it, not in a way Thomas could understand.

"Look, get things sorted out with Mary. Buy her something. A bonnet. A dress. Something people can see. Put her in her place and let people see it. Show them she's your wife and that she respects you. That's what they like to see."

John still wasn't sure he'd got his meaning across to Thomas, but he'd talked enough and couldn't say it any better no matter how long he went on. Thomas couldn't have put it into words either but he understood what his brother-in-law meant. That's what he'd do, buy her a dress and a bonnet. He'd choose it and she'd wear it. She'd look like he wanted her to. She could be what she wanted to be, in secret. But nobody else would know that. They'd only know what they saw. He'd put her in her place and, in his inarticulate but stubborn way, he was determined she'd be as miserable as possible.

*

The kitchen was empty when Thomas got home. So was the small, hardly used and barely furnished front room on the street side of the house. Again, a few wild flowers lay untidily on the table as if they had been tossed there in haste. Perhaps they'd been out together in the meadow again. The sight of the two of them wading through the long grass of the meadow, careless of their surroundings, flashed vividly and he closed his eyes to obliterate it. He stood for a few seconds at the bottom of the stairs straining his ears for any sound from either of the two upstairs rooms. If she'd been weaving he'd hear the loom clacking without having to listen hard. He could even faintly hear a few weavers at work in other houses on the street. He tried to think of the various places she might be. At Jane's? She seldom went there without a pressing reason. When those two met it was usually his sister who found some excuse to come meddling and fussing in their kitchen. She wouldn't be in town so late in the day either. So where was she and what was she up to? Again he suddenly saw the mental picture of what he'd seen from the bridge. Her long black hair falling across her face and a bunch of wild flowers or twigs in the crook of one arm, a yard or so behind her Will Bacon, both of them moving without haste through the grass and high clover of the rough meadow. He closed his eyes involuntarily and in the same instant he heard something creak in one of the rooms upstairs. He was suddenly alert and concentrated despite the beer and the fatigue of the day's work. He moved as quietly as he could up a few steps then stopped again to listen. Again the scrape of some piece of furniture and now it was clearly coming from the dingy room over the kitchen where Mary should have been doing her weaving. He was now only three or four steps from the top of the stairs when he heard the low indistinct murmurs. He couldn't make out any words but it was unmistakably her voice. Though the sounds were without meaning he sensed the unnatural rhythm of what he heard. Almost like praying, though he knew his wife had never prayed and never would pray. He listened as intently as possible and kept so quiet that even his own breathing seemed loud. As the voice rose and fell almost like a hummed melody, everything became clear to him, although he tried to resist the realisation. They were making love. She's got him here in his house, brazen, shameless and disgusting. He listened closely again but the voice had stopped. What were they doing now? Was he undressing her? Feeling her? Enjoying his wife? Or was she doing things to him with her hands and her mouth, using her fingertips, her tongue and her moist lips, teasing and caressing his lust? He remembered the times before she went so cold towards him, and encouraged him despite his anger and inebriation, he visualised Mary and Will now doing the same on the other side of the closed door. He sat down on the steps, covered his head in his hands, blotting out any real sound but couldn't dismiss the imagined sights and sounds in his mind. Suddenly he stood up. His right fist clenched and his left hand moved towards the knob of the door but before he opened it he heard John's bawdy singing from next door, faint but unmistakably cheerful and boisterous. It distracted him for one moment and in that instant he was confused. What would happen if he burst in on them now? Of course, his violence and rage would be directed at her but what if John's younger, beloved brother took it into his head to defend the bitch? There could only be one response if Will attacked him or even tried to restrain him. He'd fight back with all the strength and aggression coiled in his wiry, muscular body. Will wouldn't have a chance against him and he wouldn't stop until the younger, bigger but gentler man had been battered to pulp. Then John would have heard the commotion and would appear on the scene. And what then? He took a silent step backwards, down a step or two. And leaned, careful not to make a sound, against the wall. And even if Will just stood by and did nothing while he slapped and kicked her, John would still hear it and find out. He couldn't think clearly any further but he resigned himself to inaction. He could do nothing. Not now at least. One day, sooner or later, it would be different. But for now he'd have to put up with it without even a word of protest, let alone giving her the thrashing she deserved, with knowing his wife was giving herself to another man in his own house. Not knowing what to do, what to think he was almost unable to move until the low voice started again, this time with subdued but unmistakable passion. It was humiliation now that seized him. Not moral disgust at his wife's sexual licence but a simple inability to digest his own powerlessness. Almost with a force as physical as real nausea, he revolted against the obscene freedom she was indulging in. Not more than three, four yards away, separated from him by only a flimsy board wall his fist could have smashed a hole in, she was behaving as if he didn't exist, as if their marriage didn't exist, as if his power over her were nothing. In that moment, in those circumstances it was indeed nothing. Not bothering or being able to conceal his presence any longer, he almost ran down the stairs like a reckless child, making a tremendous din as he went. He snatched his coat and slammed the kitchen door behind him. By the time he came home, the additional alcohol would have dimmed his senses enough for him to be able to contain his fury and bear what he knew.

Even John next door heard the clatter on the stairs and the bang as the door shook the house. But after a slight pause he resumed his song. In the room over the kitchen Mary was briefly alarmed by the noise on the staircase and physically jolted by the impact of the house door. She knew it must have been Thomas but made no effort to explain his behaviour to herself. Her indifference was diluted by her relief and satisfaction that he would be out of the house for a few more hours.

Looking across the room at the window she could see that dusk was falling. How long must she have been there practising her reading with Jane's Bible? Much of what she'd read, she couldn't understand and most of it she found tedious. But some passages she liked and she could only fully savour and experience them if she read them aloud. She thought of going downstairs but on second thoughts he'd be out drinking till late so she'd make use of the little daylight left. In her deep, soft voice she read slowly some her favourite verses:

> *Thou hast ravished my heart, my sister, my spouse;*
> *thou hast ravished my heart with one of thine eyes,*
> *with one chain of thy neck. How fair is thy love, my*
> *sister, my spouse! how much better is thy love than*
> *wine! and the smell of thine ointments than all*

spices! Thy lips, O my spouse, drop as the honeycomb: honey and milk are under thy tongue; and the smell of thy garments is like the smell of Lebanon. A garden enclosed is my sister, my spouse; a spring shut up, a fountain sealed. Thy plants are an orchard of pomegranates, with pleasant fruits; camphire, with spikenard, spikenard and saffron; calamus and cinnamon, with all trees of frankincense; myrrh and aloes, with all the chief spices: A fountain of gardens, a well of living waters, and streams from Lebanon. Awake, O north wind; and come, thou south; blow upon my garden, that the spices thereof may flow out. Let my beloved come into his garden, and eat his pleasant fruits.

Chapter 19

They both knew that John Astley had known Mary almost all her life, so he would have no problem advising Thomas and Jane about the size of dress. The process was all nicely divided – Mr Astley recommended, Jane was to choose and Thomas to pay. Strange that the woman who was to own the dress and the bonnet wasn't there, especially as the two women, the one selecting the dress and the one who was to wear it, couldn't have been more different.

He showed them a few pictures, informed them about the prices and Jane soon reached a decision. She knew that Mary possessed only two, almost identical dresses. Both plain, coarse cloth which she often wore unbuttoned at the throat, exposing part of her smooth, sloping shoulders and her chest almost down to the swell of her breasts. In winter she would wear undergarments, long vests, under the dress and a heavy shawl across her shoulders, but in warm weather the dress was all she would wear. When Mary bent forward Jane would turn her face away from the sight of this voluptuous woman's naked skin.

The dress Jane chose was dark, almost black, long-sleeved with no decoration except a plain white collar and similar trimming at the wrists. For the sake of decency not fashion, she also ordered a few petticoats and long, grey cloth-stockings. Dressed in this way, with the addition of the bonnet and the laced boots, all that would be visible of Mary's body would be her face and hands. Thomas would have to make her brush her hair up so even this would be hidden by the bonnet.

Jane looked again at the sketch of the woman in the dressmaker's catalogue.

"And gloves," she said. "Plain, white gloves."

Mr Astley nodded. All they needed now was a gauze veil to drape down from the peek of the bonnet and Mary would look like she was on her way to a funeral.

"You know, Mrs Bacon, the Indians and the Turks cover the faces of their womenfolk with a kind of veil. But I wouldn't recommend it. The material is often very bright and it would only show up Mary's dark eyes to even better advantage."

Astley's insight into the goings on of this market town and his light sarcasm were proverbial. It was lost on Thomas, and Jane chose to ignore it. Nothing could detract from her moment of triumph. Unable to destroy or alter Mary's wilfulness, at least she now had the chance to hide it, to shroud it in these heavy robes of respectability and plainness. She would see to it that her brother, for once, would master his wife, bring her to the meeting house, suitably clothed, where, if she continued to reject God's will, could at least be subject to His wrath. She could hear the words now of Brother Jacobs searing like flaming arrows into the breathlessly concentrated attention of the brethren. Who could hear his words and not rejoice or wilt under their piercing truth?

> There is good and evil at war in the world, in every town, in every house and in each and every person. God and the devil. We are fearfully and wonderfully made. God was just. He gave Himself no favours. We are all capable of doing good or evil. The one thing He did do was to grant us free will so we ourselves choose whether to do right or wrong. But we must answer for our choices. This battle goes on

in the mind, in our deeds in all our waking hours although we usually are not aware of it. We have a thought and it can be either right or wrong and we decide what to do with that thought - we are free to do so without let or hindrance. The devil attacks us through our minds with his wiles and insinuations, his darts and arrows.

More than once, she had watched her brother harness the pony, Rocket, to the wagon that took the men out of the town, along the light track to where they were working. The bridle, the halter, the reins, the shafts, the blinkers and the nosebag. And then the horse, with hardly a word of command being spoken, would trot nimbly between the track on which the wagon ran, straight, unswerving, without a glance either to the left or to the right. That's how she'd train Mary in these clothes, smothering her passion and taming her wilfulness.

William Bacon's Diary

1848 8th April

She has agreed to accompany me! I think it was an irony of fate that decided her. Jane and Thomas tried to coerce her into going to church, or rather to the meeting house where Jane goes to worship. They bought her a complete set of suitable clothes and wanted to force her into them. And now their efforts to constrain her to their, or at least Jane's purposes, have goaded her to rebel. She laughed when she told me that she would wear the clothes for our journey!

10th April

Thomas and John left early this morning and are not expected back for at least five days. I'm sure that Jane will say nothing. There's too much at stake for her. If John finds out about me and Mary, he will drop Thomas as a ganger and that will hurt Jane too to see her younger brother suffer. And if John's business friends find out there's scandal in the family, how might they react? And this will place Jane's dreams of a new life in America at risk. The only ones with nothing to lose are myself and my beloved Mary. Perhaps, after London, she will commit herself to me. Soon, everything will be different.

Chapter 20

Even if any of the other travellers had known Mary they probably wouldn't have recognised her. The elderly woman sitting opposite her in the ladies' waiting room wondered a little at this strictly dressed person, a veil hanging from the rim of her bonnet to just above the tip of her nose. In the warm mid-April weather, she would no doubt have her own very private reasons for concealing her face. Perhaps grief, mourning, distress had reddened her eyes. Perhaps she was ashamed of travelling unaccompanied by rail. Whoever she was, she was obviously a respectable, pious woman otherwise she would not have been wearing those heavy, gloomy garments, clearly new and not by any means the cheapest, on such a bright day.

The train arrived with a loud shriek, snorting steam and sparks high into the air. Men in uniforms appeared from every doorway of the small but spanking-new station, whistles blew, flags were waved, instructions were shouted. Hordes of workmen scrambled noisily into the open third-class carriages, some with their shovels, axes, hammers and even an occasional wheel barrow. The second class carriages were half filled up with commercial travellers, and in the first class the elderly lady occupied a window seat facing in the direction the train was travelling. She noticed that the young woman, who was probably on her way to a funeral, as she ascended the few steps decently into the first-class carriage in front of hers, lifted her dress slightly but did not reveal even a glimpse of her ankle. Typical new-fangled Dissenter, the elderly lady thought, who had herself grown up in less moralistic times. Perhaps one of these low-church chapel-going non-conformists or even a Baptist. What a waste! Out of idle curiosity she determined to note where the young woman would leave the train.

When they stopped at Rugby station, the elderly lady peered along the side of the train, wondering if Mary would get out. Through the open window of the carriage Mary had boarded, a head appeared, the head of a handsome woman with long black hair. She had taken off the bonnet and veil and, as she turned to face in the elderly woman's direction, that curious lady could see that she had unfastened a button or two of her dress. She was smiling broadly and waving. A tall, handsome young man, standing at the station book stall noticed her and waved back. He paid for the book and ran to the carriage, leapt up the steps and disappeared at the same time as Mary's head withdrew from sight.

They won't be getting off before we reach Euston, the elderly woman thought. She settled back in her seat, took a French novel out of her bag and, before she opened it, smiled to herself, pleased that the spirit of the old days had not yet been completely doused by the new prudery.

William had spent all of the previous few days organising the journey and the guard assured him that he and Mary would have the carriage to themselves. For the first time, William felt safe in her company. Privacy and anonymity encouraged him, relaxed him and for some minutes he sat opposite her, saying nothing, just enjoying the sight of her. Only when the train began to pull out of the station, hooting and heaving, did he lean forward and kiss her cheek.

"I bought you this. When we are in London I want to write our names in it. My first present to you." He handed her a book.

"First book, first present, my first train journey. The first day of my life."

She held the book as carefully as if it were a new born baby, noticing every detail about it. Bound in green cloth covers, with vivid gold lettering, it glowed with newness, unlike the worn copies of the other two books she had read from with their faded, dusty pages.

"Strange name, Currer Bell. Is that a man's name or a woman's?"

"It's a man's name but that doesn't mean the author is really a man. Maybe it's a woman who doesn't want people to know who she is."

"Like me. But Jane Eyre, that's a woman. Is it a true story?"

"A novel, invented, like the Pilgrim book."

"William, have you of all people bought me a book about God?"

"No, it's about a woman. She's on a kind of journey too, I think, like Pilgrim. But that's all the books have in common. I haven't read it yet. You read it and tell me about it."

Mary looked out of the window. The train was now travelling at full speed and she watched the scenery fly by. Hedges, broken fences, houses, crows startled by the train, cattle. She was full of sensations she had never felt before. The strong smell of soot and smoke mingled with that of leather in the newly built compartment. Images, impressions moving towards and then away from her as the train hurtled forwards. The rattle and hum of the iron wheels, in rhythm with the joints of the track and then suddenly the great gush of sound and vibration as another train rushed by in the opposite direction. Her hand moved over the grained cover of the book and her finger tips felt the contours of the inlaid lettering. She looked at William and he leaned forward and kissed her on the mouth. She returned his kiss with pleasure but not desire. All her senses were intensely excited but she didn't feel sexually aroused. It was the sensuousness of the moment, not the sensuality of William's kiss that made her feel as if she had begun to grow.

She pulled her head back slightly, her face still close to his and, although she spoke softly, he heard her clearly through the noise of the train.

"Whatever happens later, I thank you for this time Will. For what you've given me."

William had drawn the blinds on the corridor side of the compartment and tried to pull Mary towards him. She resisted and he looked surprised, pained. She laughed quietly.

"We will be lovers. Or I wouldn't be here, would I? Tonight, in London. But now I want to read my book."

She kissed him again and he leant back in his seat, watching her intently all the time.

She opened the book as if it were so fragile that it might break. First the stiff cover only and then a blank page or two until she arrived at the first printed page, an advertisement for other novels. She read the title page and turned at last to the first page of the novel. She read the first paragraph out loud in a slow but even voice.

> *There was no possibility of taking a walk that day. We had been wandering, indeed, in the leafless shrubbery an hour in the morning; but since dinner (Mrs Reed, when there was no company, dined early), the cold winter wind had brought with it clouds so sombre, and a rain so penetrating, that further outdoor exercise was now out of the question.*

By the time she had read ten pages or so, Mary had come across many unknown words, situations and social contexts which were foreign to her personal experience. But that didn't stop her grasping fully the sense and power of the story. She read, amazed and fascinated and knew then already that this book would help change her life.

It was only three hours later, when the train went into the long, slow decline into Euston Station, that Mary closed the book. The most people Mary had ever seen in one place before were the several hundred who came to the annual Wakes in Nuneaton. Now the station alone was packed with at least as many and when they emerged into the street she could hardly believe what she saw. The sidewalks milling with men, women, children, walking, running, standing, crouching, selling, buying and begging, even between the traffic on the wide road nimble pedestrians dodged between the carriages, gigs and horse-drawn omnibuses.

William seemed to know where they were going and he gripped her firmly by one arm while she held onto her book with the other. Inside a cab, jostled and bumped up and down and from side to side, Mary gradually regained a clear perception of her surroundings and became aware of her own feelings.

"You look happy, Mary my love."

"Am I really Mary? Mary Ball? Or am I someone else? I am happy. At least I think it's happiness. I don't know a better word for it."

She looked out of the cab at the scenes outside.

"Has all this been going on all the time? Are we in the same world?"

"Are you afraid?"

"I can't put a name to my feelings, Will. They're so new. And so strong. But I know fear and I am not afraid. This is wonderful."

It took the cab a good hour to reach the inn where William wanted to stay – the Chapter Coffee House in Paternoster Row. His father had had connections with the publishing business and had always stayed here when he was in London, sometimes with John and William. Apart from being the only inn William knew in London, it was convenient for their purposes, not far from Blackfriars Bridge and also near the banking house he wanted to visit. As they neared the inn the streets of the City became even more crowded and colourful. Flower sellers lined the street near Covent Garden, hawkers, peddlers and street traders stood every few yards. And then St Paul's came into view, Mary craning her neck out of the window so she could get a good look at the dome.

William had taken her bonnet and veil out of her linen bag and he handed them to her.

"You'd better put these back on, Mrs Bacon. Don't forget to thank the real Mrs Bacon for them when we get back to Nuneaton. Without her, none of this would have been possible."

They were both still laughing when William paid the cabby but as they entered the dull, subdued atmosphere of the inn, they composed themselves and Mary lowered the veil over her eyes. There was a room free and William signed them in as Mr and Mrs Bacon, Manchester and no-one doubted it.

Later Will wrote:

> *William Bacon's diary. 10 in the evening, 11th April 1848. London.*
>
> *This has been without doubt the happiest day of my life so far and I expect tomorrow to surpass it. I have had many, many women but today, with Mary, I discovered for the first time what it really means to make love. She told me she had decided weeks ago to become my lover and we loved without shame or restraint. If tomorrow were not destined to be such a*

momentous day in the history of this country, even of the world, there is nothing I would like more than to spend the next two days in this room with Mary. But tomorrow we will go to the rally and not only witness but also play a part in the dawning of a new era in the progress of mankind. Mary is lying on the bed, reading. She is naked and, in my eyes, beautiful beyond belief, not in a pretty way like Betty, but boldly handsome. Her face has little conventional beauty. It is more round than oval. Her lips are full and her mouth a little broader than a lady novelist would like it to be. Her nose has a slight bump in the middle of it. Her big round eyes are strained on the book and every now and then she has to push back wisps of her jet black hair when it falls across her face. The light is good in this room, very good. I have some reading too, and I suspect we will read and make love for most of the night, though we need to be up early.

Mary sensed he was looking at her and looked up: "What are you writing, Will?"

William read the diary entry to her.

"This has been an unusual day for me too. Perhaps I am not alone, perhaps I am not the only woman who thinks what I think and wants what I want. Listen."

And she read slowly but without faltering from her book, Jane Eyre.

> *It is vain to say that human beings ought to be satisfied with tranquillity: they must have action; and they will make it if they cannot find it. Millions are condemned to a stiller doom than mine; and millions are in silent revolt against their lot. Nobody*

knows how many rebellions besides political rebellions ferment in the masses of life which people the earth. Women are supposed to be very calm generally: but women feel just as men feel: they need exercise for their facilities, and a field for their efforts just as much as their brothers do; they suffer from too rigid a restraint, too absolute a stagnation, precisely as men would suffer; and it is narrow-minded in their more privileged fellow creatures to say they ought to confine themselves to making puddings and knitting stockings, to playing on the piano and embroidering bags. It is thoughtless to condemn them, or laugh at them, if they seek to do more or learn more than custom has pronounced necessary for their sex.

"I think I am one of those millions, what does she say about them? *Millions are condemned to a stiller doom than mine; and millions are in silent revolt against their lot.* And you, William? Does she mean you when she says: *Nobody knows how many rebellions besides political rebellions ferment in the masses of life which people earth.* I think she means both of us. It makes me feel strong when I read this. Stronger than Jane and Thomas. Even stronger than my friend Lizzie. She's strong enough to give strangers what they want from her and take their money for it, but I doubt it makes her happy. That's all I want –the chance to do what makes me happy."

"Don't I make you happy?"

Mary tried to put into words what she had been thinking about for hours.

"No, you don't make me happy, Will. To be honest, I can't believe you're the only man I could love. But it's you I'm here with and it's you who gives me the chance of happiness, of living. I can't say what I mean, not yet, but I'm learning to. Perhaps tomorrow I can see and say things clearer."

"After tomorrow everything will be different, Mary. That's the *political rebellion* your Jane Eyre talks about and tomorrow it will be victorious. Peaceful but triumphant. Parliament will have to grant us universal suffrage and then it's only a matter of time, a short time, before new laws are passed and everyone is free."

"You know what Constable Haddon told me? He came round the day after my fight with Thomas and I told him that Thomas had tried to have me against my will. That's his right, he said. And my duty. To obey my husband. Do you think a man like Thomas will ever give up that right of his own accord? He owns me. He owns my body. He owns my will. Why should he make me a present of my freedom? Do people give their slaves freedom?"

"The new laws will force him to."

"When?"

"One day."

"One day! I want to live now and if he won't give me the right to live my own life, then I'll take it."

"Mary, you don't have to. When the next Parliament is elected all men will have the vote and they'll sweep away the old order. The new Parliament will change things between husband and wife."

*

When Mary woke up she could hear a strange hum. She had dreamt about the rail journey and at first, in her semi-conscious confusion, thought that what she could hear was the drone of a distant train. William was already up and dressed.

"What's that noise, Will? Can you hear it?"

He laughed.

"That's the sound of life, my love, London life. The City is waking up and going about its business. Look out of the window if you don't believe me."

Instead of looking out of the window, she got out of bed and began to wash herself.

"I don't want to watch it. Come on, let's go out and be a part of it."

They breakfasted well on eggs, fresh white bread and coffee and it was ten o'clock by the time they left the inn. William's prediction had been correct and, though neither of them had slept more than a few hours, they were not tired. He was still savouring isolated, tender, ecstatic moments of the night with Mary, but at the same time exhilarated by the expectations of the events of the day to come. She was absorbed by her surroundings, trying to combine details into an overall impression and to find words for it.

Paternoster Row itself was a quiet alley no more than eight feet wide, too narrow for even a one-horse cab to pass through it, so there were only a few men scurrying up and down the street, in and out of doorways, some studiously ignoring the rest of the world's existence, others touching their hats briefly in momentary, anonymous greeting, their boots thudding and clacking on the rough flag stones and their coat-tails flying and flapping behind them. And all the time Mary could hear that buzz now growing into a subdued roar in the background. For some reason the Row was the centre of the publishing business and on either side of the street were four-storey, flat-fronted book warehouses, some with windows onto the street so that Mary could see in the dim interiors books from floor to ceiling, in rows on shelves, on tables, in boxes, in neat piles and chaotic heaps. Other houses were boarded up or closed from view by blinds or heavy curtains. They were walking towards St Paul's and the Row curved slightly so that the end was not visible. Left, right and straight ahead, all Mary could see were these dingy walls and, if she looked up vertically, a blue sky. Then they turned the corner into Ludgate Hill and the loud, blurred monotone of noise became a cacophony of individual sounds and a frantic kaleidoscope of visual impressions, like a sudden dawn breaking and exploding into a deafening, dazzling chorus. And behind it all, the massive, grey stone weight of St Paul's, like the fist of some absolute authority, thumped down into the midst of its subjects, demanding obedience, sacrifice and tribute. They stood still as if they had been hit by a great wave and had to adjust to the impact and regain their balance. From the cab the day before, Mary had only been able to glance at snippets of what she now saw, heard, and smelled in its entirety.

They moved away from the cathedral towards the river and there were fewer and fewer people and suddenly, as they emerged from a narrow street, the world changed from stone to water.

"Mary, look over there, on the bridge!"

To their left they could see masses of people stretching from the north side half way across Blackfriars Bridge, the first of the demonstrators.

"It's not yet noon and there are so many already!"

He grabbed Mary's arm and they almost ran the few hundred yards between them and the demonstration. The road was lined with spectators, some goading the procession, others just curious. Bands, jugglers, fire-eaters and acrobats performed at intervals where they could find space. The beggars, street hawkers and prostitutes weaved and paused their way through the crowds, hoping for some business or charity. Looking across towards the south side of the bridge Mary could just make out, at the forefront of the march, a horse-drawn omnibus, its upper deck uncovered. There were men standing up in it, waving banners, one of them trying to hold some kind of speech. As this vehicle moved off, the other demonstrators, including Mary and William, formed orderly files and one row after another the procession set into motion.

Though mainly men, there were a good many women, some with children, amongst them. With inward pleasure, Mary read some of the banners – *Camden Temperance League*, *Bradford Women for the People's Charter* and, right in front of her, holding the *League for the Abolition of Slavery* a large group including black men and women.

"Mary, stay close to this group. I'll be back soon."

William made his way as best he could towards the front of the procession. As she watched him moving along the edge of the column she noticed that the spectators possibly outnumbered the demonstrators. It was a good half an hour before he returned.

"Just as I thought. Most of them will be making their own way to Kennington Common. When we arrive there should be about half a million. Just imagine it Mary, half a million for the Charter, for the right to vote. This is the day that's going to change the world!"

Chapter 21

Already at an early hour, the various troops billeted around London left their temporary quarters and, long before sunrise, had been posted and concentrated at various points where it was expected their presence might be necessary. Demonstrators arrived by the earliest trains from Manchester, Birmingham, Rochdale, Liverpool, and other parts of Lancashire, and there were some from as far even as Edinburgh and Glasgow. These persons, delegated to attend the demonstration, brought with them large rolls of signatures to be added to the already monster petition.

The rallying points of the Chartists in various localities began to fill up at an early hour and at a few minutes before ten o'clock a narrow procession set off along Southampton Street, into Upper King Street, through Holborn, into Farringdon Street, from there towards Kennington Common. A large body of special constables, under the command of Lieut.-Col. Clarke, accompanied them.

Another rallying point for the Chartists was Stepney Green. Numerous banners, with the words, THE CHARTER, *and* NO SURRENDER; THE BETHNAL GREEN NATIONAL LAND COMPANY; LIVE AND LET LIVE. *Moving along Whitechapel Road, over London Bridge in the direction of Kennington Common, the men walked arm-in-arm, six abreast, with pink and white ribbons attached to their button-holes. Together with the many on-lookers they made up a sizable number.*

All the public buildings were occupied with soldiery, and the officials and clerks armed not only with staves, as were the special constables, but with fire-arms. Somerset House, the Admiralty, the Treasury, the British Museum and all other buildings of significance were packed with troops, fortified and guarded, their bullet-proof shutters let down or windows barricaded where advisable. The residences of the Duke of Northumberland at Charring Cross, of Sir Robert Peel and other noblemen and commoners in Whitehall Gardens, were securely protected.

About two hundred police surrounded Trafalgar Square. All parks were locked and ingress and egress were allowed only to persons issued with a pass by the authorities of Scotland Yard. Patrols of the household troops marched up and down the Mall, and officers maintained constant communication between all posts. A special force was ready to march to Buckingham Palace from Wellington Barracks at any moment. The officers' private servants, as well as the regular soldiery, were armed.

All bridges were manned by strong detachments of experienced and determined soldiers.

This twelfth day of April 1848

As the rally stuttered its way through the streets of Southwark, the atmosphere became increasingly festive. Singing broke out from various groups and although Mary couldn't make out all the texts she could understand enough to know that they were weavers' songs, one or two she had heard at home. People were taking off their jackets, unbuttoning their shirts. Even the stern policemen who formed a line at each side of the march began chatting with the demonstrators. Mary wanted to see as many of the banners as possible and, as they made their way towards the front, she read them all, some ornately woven and proudly held by members of craft guilds and unions, some simply consisting of gold or white lettering on red cloth, obviously made specifically for this great day. One of them said simply: *Hinckley Weavers* and seemed to belong to a group of about fifteen men and half a dozen women. William greeted them warmly but there was something reserved, even suspicious in their manner towards him. In contrast to the general cheerfulness and optimism around them they all made a sombre, almost depressed impression. The contrast with William suddenly struck her.

Stepping forwards between the ranks, she noticed other clusters of men and women similar to the weavers and each time she realised what they all had in common. A subdued, restless mood hung over them and they were all visibly poor. When they were located at the edge of the procession the police didn't exchange pleasantries with them. Their faces were tense, their voices guttural, their clothing simple, coarse and worn. They looked like Mary saw herself and suddenly she hated the dress she was wearing. These people, her people would think she was like Jane, or even like the better-off women in the march. They did! That's why the woman from Hinckley had averted her eyes when Mary was about to speak to her.

Agitated by this sudden perception she looked for William, intending to try to express it to him but she found him talking with a tall, very well-dressed, bearded gentleman.

"Oh, Mary, this is Frederick, who I met in Manchester. Did I tell you? He's German. Frederick, this is Mary, my, er, my sister-in-law."

Whether or not the hesitation, the apparently reluctant ambiguity in the introduction was deliberate or not, Mary couldn't say. But she did notice a swift, almost imperceptible exchange of knowing glances between William and this stately German. It reminded her of the way Constable Haddon had spoken to her about Thomas' assault. This time, however, it made her thoughtful rather than angry.

"Frederick has written a book about the conditions working people live in and how they can free themselves from exploitation."

The German nodded a polite greeting to Mary. She looked up at him and noticed how his eyes dropped and roamed all over her upper body. She returned his look brazenly and without flinching until Engels for a moment suspected that young William had hired some gay female company for his stay in London.

"His first name's Frederick, love. His second name's Engels. And I'm Mary, like you. Mary Burns."

It was a small, vivacious woman who spoke to Mary in a broad Manchester accent spiced with the occasional Irish vowel. She linked her arm affectionately through Engels' arm.

"Don't be too hard on Freddy here, my darling. He's only a man after all. And he wouldn't dare make eyes at another woman."

"Not when you're nearby, my love!"

Engels lowered his head and Mary Burns raised hers to allow him to kiss her on the mouth. Seeing this Mary felt a surge of affection for her namesake. She felt first a bit envious and then confident as she watched the willingness with which her new friend accepted the sign of her lover's affection, here on the streets of London, in full public view.

"And allow me to correct my good friend William, here. It's not I who has written the book. It's myself and Mary here."

"Oh, you liar, Frederick! You know I can hardly even write my own name! And even if I could, the book's in German!"

"My love, you have learnt to write far quicker than I did. If I were as good a teacher as you are a pupil you'd have mastered it even faster!"

She leaned forward to talk directly to Mary.

"Frederick's taught me to read and write!"

Mary and William exchanged glances. Engels continued:

"And you have shown me the truth about the England we live in. All I have to do is write it down!"

"Well, that's true. Except that at the moment we don't live in England, do we, Freddy? Though we will again soon, won't we my love?" She threw a teasing glance at the tall German. She leaned a little bit forward again to get eye contact with Mary. "I took him through the streets where the poor live. I showed him in flesh and blood what he'd only read about. Especially the women and infants." There was a pause while the two women took intuitive stock of each other. "You know what I mean, love. I know you do."

She let go of Engels' arm and came across to Mary, taking her arm in hers.

"Come, on. Let's go and see something apart from these backsides in front of us. The men can come to London whenever they like. I daresay it's the last time we'll be here!"

As the two Marys, arm in arm, made their way out of the procession, Mary Burns called back.

"We'll meet up where the march enters the Common if we lose each other!"

*

As the column of demonstrators approached the site of the mass gathering, Kennington Common, the people at the front of the column became perceptibly quieter. The bands had stopped playing and the men in the omnibus at the vanguard of the march were standing still, gazing in the direction of the Common, which William could not yet see.

"Seems like those ahead are dumbfounded by what they see. I doubt if anyone here has ever witnessed half a million and more souls gathered in one place."

The German, slightly taller than William, looked down at him.

"Prepare yourself for a shock, my friend, but whatever you do, don't lose heart."

At that moment the Common came into view, twelve feet or so lower than the road they were on so that they had a good view over its whole area. At first unable or unwilling to grasp what he saw, William stood still, as did a good many others. Disappointment, confusion, a kind of paralysis spread through the whole of the procession as it became obvious there were not, after all, half a million demonstrators assembled. Even with the several thousand in the march, it didn't amount to a fraction of that number, which would have filled the whole of the Common. In fact, in his heart of hearts, William guessed there were no more than twenty thousand. Only the top corner of the park was occupied and the police, strategically grouped around the demonstration and almost equal in numbers to the Chartists, could afford to leave fifty yards between themselves and the crowd.

"Maybe more will join us when we march to Whitehall. Surely the people on the streets will fall in and support us."

But he recalled how most of the bystanders so far had done little other than either jeer and catcall at them or try to take their money by foul means or fair. His companion was amazingly composed, showing no surprise or disappointment.

"This is only a skirmish in a long war, my friend, one lesson in a long learning process."

William slouched away towards the main stand in the faint hope that the speakers would somehow manage to revive his optimism.

*

Extract 2 from Home Office Report
The main speeches

> *After the Chairman had delivered a short, inconsequential speech, Mr. Fergus O'Connor appeared to prolonged cheers of the crowd, and spoke at some length. As usual self-laudation and vague rhetoric about Liberty, Rights of the People, &c. accounted for most of his address. To the audible and visible disappointment of many of his supporters, he concluded by urging the assembly to disperse peaceably and at once, as the Government had taken possession of each of the metropolitan bridges, where the Chartists could not therefore pass without a violent struggle they were bound to lose. He tried with limited success to console them with the assurance that the Executive of the Chartist Association would transport the petition to the House of Commons, and that he himself would present it that evening. He left the podium without*

applause and some even acquitted him with boos, jeers and cat-calls.

Mr. Ernest Jones next addressed the meeting. Though he is what is called a physical force Chartist, he argued at once that it was useless for them - peaceable men - to seek confrontation with vastly superior forces. He regretted that this meeting had not been held on the other side of the river Thames, as in that case the bridges would not have to have been passed. As it was, the assembly was a victory in itself. Under these circumstances, he exhorted those present to follow the advice given by their friend and leader, Mr O'Connor. In one final and futile attempt to raise the spirits of the Chartists, he assured them, to a deafening volley of discontent, that the Charter's eventual success was certain. Mr. F. O'Connor returned, and asked the meeting for authority now to bring the Petition in their name to Sir George Grey. He would tell the Home Secretary that the people would avoid collision with any armed force, police or military. They were, he concluded, resolved to keep the peace inviolate that day.

Though the meeting formally granted this request, from the moment Mr. O'Connor left impatience and uproar began to dominate the mood of both the mob and even the delegates.

When Jones had finished his speech, William's resignation and dejection were complete. If even Jones had decided that it was useless to oppose the police and military, then the cause was truly lost. Already the Common was emptying as small disconsolate groups left in dribs and drabs, their banners furled or dragging on the ground behind them. He was so lost in his thoughts that he didn't notice Mary Ball and Mary Burns approaching him, each talking, listening, hardly taking their eyes off each other, agitated and calmly concentrated at once.

Neither did he notice the middle-aged but fit looking man observing him from a distance of about ten yards. Hardcastle, the Home Office agent who had chased William out of Manchester, had no wish or need to conceal himself. He would write his report on the rally for the Earl of Newcastle, make his recommendations and, if they were approved, he would then travel north and make contact with William before his mood changed.

*

William Bacon's Diary: Nuneaton April 13th 1848

> *Mary must have told Mary Burns everything about herself, including about myself and her husband Thomas. She made love to me last night, our last in London, with a passion and abandon that even Betty never achieved. But I cannot pretend to myself that Mary's behaviour excites only positive emotions in me. I always felt a secret wonder for something in her spirit I can't define. Now my wonder contains an element of anxiety, almost fear. She spoke for the first time of leaving Thomas, of going to Manchester with me to live near Mary Burns. She says this journey we have made together has opened her eyes to life. She can see things clearly that she only perceived vaguely before. It is bitterly ironic that these last few days, yesterday in particular, have led to such an erosion of my optimism and simultaneously have opened such horizons of hope*

for my beloved Mary. It is as if we are together and she basks in blazing sunshine and for me the same sky is blackened with storm clouds.

Thomas and my brother John are still away. Jane scowls, her lips pursed even more tightly than usual. She, of course, knows that Mary and I have spent the last three days together but is bound by self-interest to silence. If John were to find out about me and Mary it would be the end of her own brother's hopes of advancement in John's services. He made it clear to Thomas that there is a place for him in his plans only if he can maintain a show of decency in his life, and that would include Mary. And Jane knows that if John finds out about us at some time in the future, then he will guess that she had hidden the truth from him for the sake of her brother's advantage. How he would react to that, good, honest and trusting soul that he is, not even Jane can know for sure. It would certainly place all her plans for emigration at great risk.

I must think hard and deeply about my position in all this. My love for Mary is absolute and sincere. But I cannot see how we can start a new life openly together. If we went to Manchester, what would Mary do if we ever parted? Now at least she has the semblance of a marriage and while that lasts she has a roof over her head. Alone in Manchester, there's only one way she could survive. Can I accept the responsibility of that risk?

As long as John and Thomas are away we will have some freedom to meet. When they return I must convince Mary that we are to be cautious. Her recklessness disturbs me. She says that she'd welcome Thomas finding out about us. Maybe he'd throw her out and then the decision would be made for us. We'd have to leave together. Then John would know, but why should she care about his plans for Thomas or about Jane's dream of emigration? I must persuade her to exercise discretion and restraint until I have clarified everything for myself.

April 14th

We had a lucky escape because John and Thomas returned yesterday. I had been with Mary until darkness fell and the two men arrived late at night, I think around midnight. I heard John clambering up the stairs last night and at dawn this morning I watched them both walk off down Back Lane to work. I must try to talk to Mary as soon as I can to urge her to be patient. I only hope that nothing that concerns us happened last night when Thomas returned.

Chapter 22

It was warm for the time of year and, when William left her only a few hours after their arrival home, Mary was still naked. Although the shutters were open, she had no need to dress as there were only open fields opposite her window and it was almost dark. She drank some water and poured some into a bowl, removed her contraceptive sponges and washed herself, thinking about the time with Will. In those three days in London, she had learnt so much and about many things but above all about herself. Everything she had experienced seemed to converge on one single, as yet inarticulate perception: that she could be free to live her own life. Now, satisfied and drowsy, she would lie down again on the bed for a short time before she dressed. She pulled the coarse blanket over her and fell asleep.

When she woke up she thought for a fleeting moment that it was William lying on her, his face pressed down hard beside hers, a hand on each breast and his penis rammed into her. As soon as she came to her senses she realised it had to be Thomas and before she could even begin to resist he came, heaving and grunting until his orgasm relaxed him, still on top of her.

Neither of them spoke and Thomas rolled compliantly off her when Mary pushed him to one side. She saw he was naked from the waist down and pulled the blanket over him, out of disgust not decency. Within seconds he was fast asleep and Mary got out of bed as quietly as she could. At first she wanted to go down the narrow stairs but remembered she was undressed. Not really knowing what to do she sat on the edge of the bed, her elbows on her knees and her head pressed into her hands. Now she was wide awake and tried to reconstruct what had happened. She recalled falling asleep in the serene but stupid belief she was free! So free that a man she hates could walk in, ravish her and then fall asleep as if nothing had happened. She tried to remember Constable Haddon's exact words about a husband's rights and a wife's duties.

She leaned a little further forward and her heels knocked against something hard under the bed. The box of stones. Without deliberation she pulled it out from under the bed. It scratched noisily on the wooden floor but Thomas didn't wake up. Still on the top of the heap was the smooth white stone she had cracked his head with. Even in the near darkness she recognised it and its smoothness brought the memories of that evening back to her. She stood up with the stone in her hand. Thomas had his back to her and she could easily make out the shape of his skull. There was room enough on the other side of the bed for her to stand and smash the rock down onto his temple. Then she could turn his head so that he would be facing upwards, maybe still slightly conscious but still unable to defend himself. Perhaps he would even realise in his brute instinct for survival that his wife was murdering him, beating his head to pulp with his favourite object.

But it wasn't vengeance she wanted. She knelt down, put the stone back onto the others and pushed the box back under the bed. This time it made so much noise that he woke up. She was still kneeling when he came round.

"What are you doing, woman?"

She stood up and the little light there was from the window fell onto her fine body. He gazed at her for almost a minute.

"Come back here and let me give it you again."

Without covering herself Mary bent down, picked up the stone and walked round the bed so that she was right next to him. She held the stone in his face.

"If you ever touch me again, Thomas Ball, it'll be the last thing you ever do before you die!"

*

By the end of May Mary was sure that she was pregnant and also knew when it must have happened. Since London she and William had made love on every possible occasion but she had used the crude contraceptive techniques Lizzie had taught her. Convinced as she was that she must have conceived either in London or very shortly after her return home, by the same token she was equally unsure about who the father was. If it had been in London, then William was the father. The other possibility was that the child was Thomas' – the fruit of rape done when she was hardly conscious.

There was still time to abort the foetus. And even a small town like Nuneaton offered enough possibilities to have this done in secrecy. She was positive that William would pay any costs the women who provided such services might demand. At first she tried to envisage how a child would affect her relationship to William and to Thomas but the more she considered it, the more the two men receded into the background of her thoughts and the child became increasingly prominent. She recalled her other children, all named after Lizzie and all dead within months of their birth. After the last death, less than half a year ago, she had vowed to herself she would never have another child. In fact she was determined never to make love with Thomas if she could avoid it. It was like a death sentence imposed on her own emotions. But now things had changed. She had begun to live again. She had not merely won back the life she had before things had turned so bad between her and Thomas. With either Thomas or Will, their life together would be simpler if there were no child. But now she began to wonder about her own life. For as long as she could remember she had longed for a healthy child; more particularly, for a daughter. Perhaps this time, whoever the father was, it would be different. Perhaps this time the child would live, would have a future. Without reason but with growing certainty, she felt it could be so; that she could make it so.

Chapter 23

John was resigned to the fact that none of the Irish would be at work the day of a major boxing contest, so he had willingly informed the contractor that there's be no work done that day. Of the residents on Back Lane only Haddon, his family and Jane stayed at home, the policeman because he preferred not to have any official cognisance of the boxing match, for which no permission had or would be granted by the magistrates, and Jane because she despised such congregations. John, Thomas, Will and Mary let Rocket pull them in a truck along a siding used only by John's gangs. The fight was to take place in some meadows flanked on one side by the canal and they left the truck where the siding, the one that took John and his gangs out to the main track they were still working on, ran close the waterway's edge. They pegged Rocket down with a long rope, not that she'd have dreamed of wandering off anyway, especially as there was an open sack of fodder on the rough planks of the truck floor, and walked together over the canal bridge. Thomas remembered what he had seen from that bridge a few months before and glanced at Will then at his wife who were keeping their distance from each other. From the hump-backed bridge, they had a good view over the meadows. A great fan-shaped crowd was flowing from the other side through the opening which had been made in the fence adjoining the lane. Once through the bottleneck and in the meadow, the mass of people spread out again like a shell, and finally encircled the ring that had been raised more or less in the middle of the field. Both the lane and canal perimeters were slightly higher than the centre of the shallow basin where the ring was placed so that the spectators had a good view, regardless of where they were standing. The inner ring, an area with seats about five yards deep surrounding the actual ring, was roped off and carefully guarded by the fight's organisers, who only allowed officials, the two boxing teams and the sponsors into the space around the ring. As the boxers with their ensembles were still to arrive, the enclosure was not yet full but many of the privileged spectators had arrived early to avoid having to make their way through the crowds.

The seating arrangements near the ringside reflected their loyalties. The far side of the ring from where Mary and others stood, was reserved for Bendigo's followers, mainly local traders, better-off weavers and clockmakers from Nuneaton and Coventry, publicans, even one or two of the dissenting manufacturers, who had left their higher principles at home for their wives to nurture in order to savour this rare collective excitement. Though they had their backs to Mary, the men on the near side of the ring were more clearly visible and their clothes showed that Bendigo's opponent, Gaunt, had the wealthier partisans. Mary saw John nudge Will.

"Look, there, right in the middle of the first row. That's Newdigate. And I think it's Jermyn, the lawyer, on his right. The big chap next to him though, I don't know him. If he'd put that damned eye-glass down I might recognise him! You know him Thomas?"

Thomas was as sullen as ever, his eyes slightly bleary from his early drinking, and his mood soured and his temper aggravated by his memories of what he'd seen from this spot not so long ago. He grunted something which John took to mean "*No!*" then Will chimed in.

"Can't place him but I have seen him somewhere before."

"You, brother? How would you know somebody from these parts who we don't know?"

At that moment the man stood up from his seat and began to scour the area behind him with the long telescopic eye-glass, starting from some point diagonally to his right then scanning slowly and systematically the whole broad space between the front of the crowd and the canal, moving his sights gradually towards the bridge.

"Why didn't you bring yours with you, John? Then we could gaze back!"

They all looked at the object Will meant and the man holding it.

"I'll be damned if he's not got his sights on us! What do you think, little brother?"

Before Will could answer, the man lowered the telescope and spoke to Jermyn, who in turn seemed to whisper something to the Earl sitting next to him. As the two seated men turned round as best the could, Hardcastle pointed in the direction of Will and John, who had moved a short distance away from Mary and Thomas.

"Are they looking at us?"

"Or at Mary! She's more worth looking at than you are, big brother!"

John knocked his brother's arm in alarm, looking round quickly to make sure Thomas hadn't heard.

"Hold your tongue, Will. He's already in drink. There'll be enough fighting down there without you getting him to start on you!"

Will grinned and couldn't resist goading his big brother a little more.

"Well she is. Look at her."

The two men turned and looked at Mary who was leaning over the bridge wall, looking down into the water. Noticing their attention, she turned her head and smiled questioningly.

Dressed in a simple, loose-fitting dress of coarse cloth to cope with the hot weather, her naked legs visible up to the middle of her calves, she did look handsome to John. To Will, who noticed the few top buttons of her dress were open, she looked beautiful and to distract himself and possibly John from the love for her that stirred up inside him, he asked her.

"Mary, you've lived here longer than both me and John. Do you recognise that fellow over there with the eye-glass?"

She knew Will well enough to sense what he felt at that moment and, as she pushed herself between him and his brother, she let her bare arm touch fleetingly against his hand.

"No, more to the right."

And he put his arm round Mary's shoulder as if intending to direct her in the right direction. She complied by tilting her head until wisps of her hair fluttered in his face. To everyone apart from Thomas, it was an innocent scene, a young man seeking advice from his neighbour, both eager to guess the identity of a mysterious stranger, apparently viewing them with an eye-glass. But had they been alone and hidden from sight, both Will and Mary would have lain down in the long dry grass and made love, and for a brief moment their thoughts, coinciding on the same emotion, entwined like naked bodies. Then Mary swayed away from him and it was gone except for one of her long black hair that had somehow remained across his face.

"Yes, I do know him!"

John had noticed nothing of the tense moment of intimacy that had lingered briefly and almost imperceptibly around Will and Mary, like a breath or the faint swirl of hair, and he bawled out:

"This one of your jokes, Mary?"

"I know him, or perhaps I don't. He reminds me of somebody."

Just then heads turned in the direction of the canal, people pointed and a slight buzz of excitement became audible. From the bridge, Mary and the others had a perfect view as three long, low barges slowly emerged, one after the other, from the bend in the canal, each towed by a massive shire horse decorated with brass and cockades and led by a boy in military uniform. The first barge came right up to the bridge before it moored, allowing the other two enough space behind it to drift to a halt alongside the bank. A few soldiers sprang from the ornately painted regimental boats and secured them the best they could with thick, whitewashed ropes and pegs they drove deep into the soft ground with massive wooden mallets. It was on the side of the canal without a toe-path so boards were laid out between the edge of the decks and the rough ground. Some people cheered and shouted *hurrah!* as the first splendidly dressed officers appeared. Others, the weavers and miners who had come to cheer their champion Bendigo hissed and booed. When the ladies appeared, whoops of admiration and appreciative whistling greeted them good-humouredly. Elaborate coiffeurs, expensive low-cut dresses and their excited, uninhibited manner made it impossible to mistake their profession and their status in it. One woman held a bottle of champagne in one hand and drank carelessly from it. Some of the officers nipped a shot from their silver hip flasks. The crowd hooted approval at the entertainment the scene provided, almost as if a pageant had been staged for their additional amusement. John and Will, Mary still between them, watched, all smiling broadly and clapping intermittently with others on the bridge as the last soldiers disembarked to join their whores in the inner circle. When it seemed that, apart from the youngsters guarding the boats and tending the horse, everyone had left the barges, Mary happened to glance back at the hatch they had all clambered out of. Perhaps she was the only person who was not looking in the direction of the ring and beyond because a great shout broke out as the carriages bringing the boxers appeared in the lane. But Mary's gaze remained fixed on the person visible from the waist up, the lower part of her body still hidden inside the boat. At first Mary wanted to cry out: "Lizzie!" But something in the woman's manner, something rigid, magisterial and cold stopped her, and then she was gone, returned to the inside of the boat. It was Lizzie. But she didn't look like a whore. The way she had examined everything around her, critically and decisively, reminded Mary somehow of how Brother Muscat had taken in everything of significance in his mill at one single glance. Seeing Lizzie triggered something in her memory and she looked away from the canal, towards the masses of spectators and then at the elite around the boxing ring, scouring the now bustling, gesticulating groups of individuals for the man with the telescope. When she caught sight of him again, she knew where she had seen him before. First, at the hustings, then in the hotel courtyard, so long ago. Suddenly it seemed vivid and not long ago. Poll and Lizzie then. Now it was Mary and Madam Elisabeth. For both of them, life had changed. Her thoughts drifted swiftly and erratically over moments in the past, like a bee over flowers. Polly's mutilated body; her mother's coffin in the deep cold grave; the image of her own pallid face in the void behind the kitchen window. But before she could muse any longer, John took her arm and they all four moved briskly towards the meadow to choose a good place to watch the contest.

By the time they had found somewhere good to stand, both boxers were in the ring. Gaunt, a six-foot-six former farm labourer, was bony, muscular in a stretched and irregular way, his muscles, created by the random influences of nature and physical labour, cropped up unpredictably and without design. He leant with his back in the corner, glaring at his opponent. A good eight inches shorter than Gaunt, Bendigo wallowed in his own beauty and symmetry. His oiled, dark skin gleamed almost like gold in the bright sunshine. Perfectly proportioned with a deep chest, sloping shoulders and an iron stomach ribbed with muscle, he flaunted his body shamelessly. Parading histrionically around the ring, he stuck one arm between his legs and erected it like a gigantic penis until the whores screeched with laughter and made obscene gestures in return. Born and bred in the Midlands, the local hero derived his popularity not only from his looks and outrageous antics but also from some instinctive affiliation with the miners, the weavers and the downtrodden. Even Thomas, his brain addled by drink and resentment, felt this empathic union with the brazen, almost debauched theatricals but which, combined with the pugilist's facial expressions and his verbal exchanges with the crowd, were transformed into a mime of irreverence, a flagrant disrespect for anybody's expectations. He turned to face Gaunt' backers, the gentry, lower gentry and landed yeomanry, grinning with a provocative, arrogant insolence. They looked to Gaunt today not only to bring home their wagers but to put this upstart scum in his place and trample on the aspirations he inspired in the rabble.

The fighters were both wearing half-breeches. Bendigo's were golden and tight-fitting and Gaunt's grey and baggy. Both sported the specially made high-laced leather boxing shoes and a few layers of cotton ribbon wrapped round their knuckles. Finally, after more of Bendigo's antics, they came to the scratch mark in the centre of the ring, the bell sounded and the contest began. At once the tactics of each man were plain to see. Bendigo, technically accomplished and professionally trained as an athlete, landed sharp, hard punches from short range mainly into Gaunt's body, whose rustic, weather-beaten features winced in pain with each blow. Gaunt's chance was to soak up the punishment and try to fall onto Bendigo and, as the fight progressed, gradually weaken him and slow him down until he could catch him with his slower but heavier punching. A pattern began to develop. The smaller man would hammer a burst of agonising jabs, prods and hooks into Gaunt's ribs, stomach and sides but then, when the bigger man threw a punch which hardly made contact, he'd drop down onto one knee as though he had been hit and took the allowed breather but was up and away before the count began. This not only frustrated Gaunt's counter-attack but infuriated him and he whined and complained at the grinning Bendigo for his unsporting behaviour. It was indeed sailing close to the wind, but Bendigo executed the tactic so skilfully that the umpire couldn't intervene. To the tremendous din of encouragement from his supporters the taller man occasionally managed to wrap his arms around his taunter and drag him to the ground, collapse onto him in an attempt to wind and even injure him. Rounds were frequent and untimed, being called whenever a man went to the ground and took a count.

At first, Mary had tried to get Will to explain the rules as the fight went on, but he became so involved that she could only get his attention briefly between rounds. Gradually she too became engrossed by the drama, violence and by Bendigo's grace and beauty. The few rules, clumsily applied, were soon clear to her and, after twenty minutes or so, she was consumed by the craving desire for Bendigo to win, to conquer, to be victorious. Her appreciation of all the various elements of the spectacle coalesced into a simple unconditional loyalty. Now, whenever Gaunt achieved one of his moments of triumph, either landing a blow or managing to flounder across his opponent's body, forcing him onto the hard wooden boards and letting his full body weight pound down onto his chest, Mary shook her fist in the air, raised herself onto the balls of her feet and screamed comfort and encouragement at Bendigo and derision at the dull, clumsy, bucolic Gaunt.

After an hour in the sweltering heat of the late afternoon, both men began to slow down and Bendigo changed his tactics slightly. As his adversary's arms grew heavier and his guard dropped, the lithe boxer began to crouch and weave his torso, the other's punches flailing wide of his head. Then he sprang up and aimed his blows now at Gaunt's face, the impact of his bare, protruding knuckles cracking into the skin and bone with loud thudding smacks. As soon as the former farmer backed away, Bendigo relented with the pressure, thus avoiding a break so that the rounds now lasted five, ten, even fifteen minutes. The long rounds took their toll on the gallantly battling Gaunt and when, at one point, both his arms fell to one side Bendigo hit him with the full concentrated force of his powerful torso, the blow targeted accurately at the big man's upper arm. He screamed out and went down, howling in pain, writhing around the ring floor. His seconds dragged him into the corner for the break. One of them picked up the castor, a low-crowned beaver hat, and was on the point of tossing it into the ring but another restrained him, looking across at Newdigate, Gaunt's main backer, who sat leant forward supporting himself on his stout wooden cane. Almost imperceptibly, the Earl closed his eyes and shook his head. They put the hat away and Gaunt went back into the ring, his left arm apparently useless. He was now fighting for his reputation as a game pugilist, a sporting and gallant loser. This is what Newdigate also now wanted, in fact what he demanded. Perhaps his man's chances of winning looked bleak, but he'd bet and he expected at least a moral if not financial return on his money. For many in the crowd the mood had changed. The loyalties hadn't shifted but there was a drift to a rising consensus that the fight should be stopped before Gaunt, whose blustering, desperate but fruitless charges and one-armed assaults garnered applause even from the opposite camp, suffered unnecessary injury. Some of the more seasoned spectators had seen men die from their injuries in the ring, victims of their own indomitable spirit dedicated to the futile service of an uncaring cause. But on each extreme of this nebulous collage of emotions, which included Will and John, who had both put money on Bendigo, there were those committed solely to seeing their favourite win, consumed and driven by a passion they couldn't explain. Mary didn't know what a boxer had to do to win a fight. Her own fists screwed tightly and tucked under her chin, she watched every movement, heard every punch land on the lumbering giant's face and wanted the contest to end, not out of pity for Gaunt but finally to witness Bendigo's triumph. Incomprehensibly to her, whenever it seemed that his antagonist was about to slump into unconsciousness, Bendigo would back off in order to prolong the match, perhaps to give the crowd more entertainment, perhaps to torture the man he seemed genuinely to despise.

After an especially severe flurry of punches to his head, Gaunt went down again, sitting bemused, almost childlike, Bendigo glowering over him, taunting and goading him. As the big man struggled to his feet, the other, assuming the round was over, turned and walked a few steps towards his corner. But Gaunt remained standing where he was, called out *"Nigger Boy!"* the nickname Bendigo's enemies used and, as his tormentor turned round, smashed a tremendous blow with the last ounce of energy he had into the smaller man's face, sending him reeling into his corner, where he slumped to the boards. Pandemonium broke out. Even the occupants of the inner circle were on their feet, some screaming and waving their arms as frantically as the great mass of spectators. Most believed with Gaunt that he had already won but when the gong for the end of the break sounded, Bendigo was amazingly back on his feet, staggering, shuffling hardly conscious close to the ropes.

Now everyone was standing, even the those in the inner ring, either urging Gaunt to corner his prey and finish him off or bolstering Bendigo's resolve to survive until he could fully regain his senses. Mary was screaming his name repeatedly, pleading with him to revive and retaliate. "Bendigo, fight back, Bendigo, please Bendigo!" A great *hurrah!* exploded when Gaunt landed a punch with his left arm, signalling that he'd recovered the use of it but Bendigo rode it with the instinctive skill of a master prize-fighter. Three short steps and it was he who was now in the ring and Gaunt was against the ropes, unable to ward off the stinging jabs and hooks that the smaller man whipped into his face and torso, pummelling his flesh and lacerating his already bruised ribs, each blow causing excruciating pain. Despite the screaming from his seconds that he should go down and forfeit the round, his pride kept him upright until he collapsed, crumbled to the floor, his arms hanging over the lowest rope. Half dragging and half carrying him to their corner, they had thirty seconds to get him back on his feet. While the assistant second used smelling salts to spark the boxer back to consciousness and sponged his battered face as gently as possible, Jem Ward, the senior second, unwrapped the cotton strips from the boxers' hands to reveal the broken, bleeding knuckles. He saw the swollen wrists, puffed and flabby like sponge, and massaged the boxer's joints at the elbow and shoulder gently with his expert fingertips. A glance at Bendigo, who hadn't even bothered to sit down and was blowing kisses and waving to his ecstatic supporters, and he knew his man had no chance, as much the victim of his own clumsy tactics as of the clinical punishment his opponent had dealt out to him. Without consulting anyone, he picked up the hat and thew it into the ring. Like a high wave breaking, Bendigo's supporters exploded, leaping up and pumping their arms ecstatically into the air, many waving their betting tickets, others, like Mary, simply beside themselves with relief and satisfaction. Even above the din, Mary heard the boxer's words clearly as he raised his hand high over his head in triumph and shouted across to Gaunt's corner:

"My name is Bendigo!"

And on one side of the ring the crowd roared:

"Bendigo! Bendigo!"

On the other side, there was a hardly a ripple of movement. In the anonymity of the crowd, Will turned to Mary and smiled at her unexpected, partisan enthrallment in the fight. He could see that she didn't share his mixed feelings of both pleasure in winning and pity for the gallant loser. Though he couldn't see Thomas, he resisted his sudden desire to embrace Mary. John was right, even if he didn't know how right he was: no point provoking a confrontation. Mary caught his glance but she didn't share his caution. Her senses and feelings heightened by the almost inebriating effect of the contest, she pushed and squeezed her way the few feet through the jam-packed crowd until she stood directly behind Will, who was now looking rigidly straight ahead, trying to look unconcerned as her arms fold around him, pulling him against her stomach and pressing her breasts hard against his back. After the brief, intense contact, she moved away, leaving him to cherish the tenderness of the moment but also to worry about her recklessness.

Chapter 24

April 1849. As soon as her baby daughter had survived her early birth and her first, harsh winter, Mary felt with deep certainty that she would live and grow and be healthy. Now, almost four months old, this Lizzie could already do what none of her other children had achieved. She smiled, even laughed in a gurgling way, ate heartily and often, and imparted to her mother not grief, remorse and dereliction but a joyous contentment. In the early months of the year, the ground had been frozen as hard as stone for weeks at a time so that Thomas had often stayed at home, wandering and returning irregularly to and from the beer houses so that she had only spent short, nervous times with Will. Although they had not made love since weeks before the birth, she had never felt closer to him, involving him in the mellow happiness that encompassed herself and the child. Now, Lizzie was sleeping, Thomas would not be home till long after dark and she wanted to be alone with Will again.

She stood in the doorway, allowing the mild sunshine of early Spring to warm her skin, watching her sister-in-law sweeping the back-yard the two families shared. Mary felt the familiar tension rise inside her. In the gentle warmth, Mary let her black hair fall loosely over the collar of the coarse grey dress. Jane, though hardly older than Mary, seemed almost from a different generation, with her hair pulled back tight into a bun and her dark, heavy dress flattening the layers of her petticoats. Her body remained rigid as she jabbed and lunged at whatever her broom was hunting.

Every so often Jane would brush a small heap of leaves and dust onto the broken shovel and toss them as far as she could onto the rough patch at the side of the yard. Half a dozen scrawny, clucking hens pocked and pecked at the litter, hoping for a few extra insects or seeds. And Jane would turn to glance very quickly in the direction of the open kitchen door where Mary stood leaning shamelessly against the frame, doing nothing but watch her sister-in-law sweep the yard and she waited for her lover.

Both of them knew that he would arrive soon and then Jane would be watching, as best she could. As she heard his booted steps clacking and scraping through the entry into the yard, Jane's movements slowed involuntarily, almost stopped and she raised her head to look at Mary. Without hurrying, Mary had kicked off her unlaced boots, picked up the large jug and walked barefoot without a hint of haste across the freshly-swept stones to the pump in the middle of the yard. As he stepped briskly out of the tunnel-like alley between the two houses, the first thing William saw was Mary, her back towards him, as she pushed and pulled the creaky pump handle. He didn't notice Jane, who was now standing as motionless and idle as Mary had been seconds before. Mary looked over her shoulder, away from Jane, at William, smiling and flicking her head backwards to warn him of Jane standing in the corner of the yard a few yards behind her.

He dropped his bag and, standing close up to Mary's back, laid his hand on the pump from behind her. Mary didn't let go of the handle, just moved her hand enough to make room for his hand, almost enough room for both their hands. She spoke to him over her shoulder, softly.

"I don't need your help, William. How do you think I get water when you're not here if I can't work the pump myself?"

She sensed he took this as a rebuff, but before he could take his hand away she looked over her shoulder at him and said in a capricious tone that surprised him pleasantly;

"I said I didn't need your help. Not that I don't want it."

William glanced at Jane but kept his hand on the pump handle. He pushed with Mary on the lever until the nozzle coughed out short gushes of water in jerky spasms. Jane's eyes bored downwards, scouring the ground, as if, like one of the hens, she hoped the barren indifference of the stones would yield her some morsel of reward, however small.

The pump stopped and Jane watched Mary carry the heavy jug towards the house. William followed her into the kitchen, closing the door behind him and placing his hands on her shoulders as soon as they were out of Jane's sight.

They kissed softly and stood still before they reached the lower steps of the stairs, both of them intuitively relaxing without resistance into each other's closeness. She leaned with her back against the closed door and pulled him nearer to her, not tightly but so that their bodies were touching. Though they knew Jane was not far away, they were completely and securely out of sight and he had already begun to undo the buttons of her dress, kissing her naked shoulder. She led him by the hand towards the stairs and they moved up a few steps, neither wishing to break contact, laughing at their clumsiness. Suddenly and without any reason he was aware of, she stopped then pushed him away gently but firmly so that there was a space between them. She spoke in a low voice, caressing his cheek as she moved past him towards the kitchen.

"It's Lizzie. I think she's awake."

The child, who was sleeping as usual in the draught-free corner diagonally opposite the foot of the stairs, had woken up and immediately began to assert her presence with a determined mixture of crying and babbling sounds. As soon as Mary hurried across the room to her she stopped and began to kick and stretch her body as vigorously as her strength and the heavy blanket would allow. Her mother knew what she wanted and, the four top buttons of her loose dress already unfastened, she sat down at the table and began to wean her. Will leaned against the wall of the dim staircase and waited until his excitement had gone. He hadn't heard the child but now he could hear Mary murmuring lovingly to her. She called him in a low voice.

"Will! Where are you? Come down!"

He walked down the few steps and then to the table, at first standing and watching the mother and her child. Then without a word he sat down at the table opposite them. She sensed his annoyance but left him alone with it, concentrating her attention on her daughter and feeling a real satisfaction, as she always did, at the amount of milk she could give her. Lizzie's robust health, almost constant good humour and her already strong, forceful personality occupied and delighted her. It was a minute or so before Mary seemed to become aware of Will again and at first she just looked at him and smiled, expressing at once resignation, amusement and perhaps a little disappointment at Lizzie's untimely interruption. He understood and tried to return the smile but it was his disappointment that was unmistakable. She spoke first, consolingly.

"I wish she were your child, Will."

He struggled to keep any petulance out of his voice, trying to sound light-hearted, even jovial.

"She might be. You said yourself that your bits of sponge don't always work."

She smiled again at the intimacy implied in his remark. Already feeling ashamed of his irritation, he noticed her reaction, and his resentment began to disappear. The fondness had returned to his voice when he spoke again.

"And anyway, what does it matter? I'll love her and I'll be her father."

She couldn't move towards him because of the child at her breast so she closed her eyes to acknowledge what he had said. He leaned across the table and kissed her head which was bowed slightly forwards over the child.

"I mean it Mary. I promise you that …"

She raised her head abruptly and interrupted him.

"Don't promise me anything Will. You might promise something you can't keep. Just tell me the truth."

He was a surprised, even shocked at what she said and at the unexpected, needless energy behind it.

"Why do you say that? You don't think I'd lie to you?"

"Not lie. But you know, you might say things you want to be true. Nice things you think I want to hear."

They both thought about his euphoria a year before, his optimistic expectations of the great demonstration.

"I know I've been wrong about some things. Important things. Important to me at least."

He looked at her for some sign of sympathy then continued.

"But I believed it all, Mary. I still do. One day …"

She stopped him.

"I know you've never told me anything you don't believe. You needn't explain anything to me."

He stared at her, hoping to find in her face, her eyes a clue to what she was thinking but her expression was too distant. It was very quiet in the shady room. Only the buzzing of insects and remote birdsong stitched pattern into the otherwise plain silence. At first remote and hardly audible but then emerging clearly though still subdued from the direction of the street, children's voices, laughing, whooping and then chanting a rhythmic, tuneless rhyme, pierced the stillness like rays of light. Mary turned her head as if to greet the sounds as they drifted into their presence and Will noticed them too and they both listened intensely as the skipping or hopping children repeated the single verse of their street song:

"John Danks
Played his pranks
Upon poor Polly Button.
He drew his knife
To please his wife
And cut her up like mutton!"

The distance between them threatened to widen into his alienation as he saw how susceptible she was to the intrusion of thoughts that excluded him. Afraid any words of his might widen the rift, he bit on his lower lip, physically forbidding himself speech. She smiled slightly as she understood his discomfort. Although she wanted to reassure him, to draw him closer to her again, she also knew ill-chosen words might sound almost like a reproach and make the gap between them more lasting, even permanent. She paused and he waited, sensing she had more to say.

"I'd prefer you told me unpleasant truths rather than say nice things that are ..." She glanced at him and saw how tense he was, watching her intently and hanging on every word. The risk of hurting him, just minutes after they had been about to make love, had arisen unexpectedly, unwanted, but she knew she had to speak to the end now. "... that are dreams. At the moment anyway. Will, my love, there's nothing more I want than to be somewhere else, with Lizzie and you. But let's not dream about it. Let's think and plan."

He relaxed and was now listening to her, suddenly confident of her love again. The fear of rejection was gone and he felt as secure as he had done when she had held him just minutes before. She spoke again.

"It won't be easy, will it? Perhaps not even possible. It reminds me of Jane."

He looked suddenly puzzled and she saw this.

"No, not that Jane. I mean in the book. Jane Eyre."

Will suddenly felt the familiar unease Mary often provoked in him. There was an irreverence in some of the things she said and, though he admired it, was amazed at it in some ways; in others he sensed something that alarmed him. It often struck him how sardonic it was that he, the active Chartist, should shy away from a stark radicalism in her awkward efforts to express her innermost thoughts. It was her uniqueness, something indefinable about her that he had never known in a woman before that he loved about her, that fascinated but at the same time sometimes disconcerted him. Now he listened closely with that faint but irritating anxiety, to what she said.

"It all seemed planned out for Jane too. That she would get what she wanted most. But then it all collapsed around her and she was suddenly alone again. You know the story, don't you, Will?"

Grateful for the chance to speak without having to interrupt her, he replied.

"You mean when she found out about his wife?"

There was something inadvertently sprightly and boyish in the way he spoke. She looked at him with mock suspicion.

"There's nothing you ought tell me, is there?"

Now, enjoying her gentle teasing, he laughed.

"No skeletons in my cupboards, my love!"

She laughed with him until he added:

"But in the end they were together."

Then her voice dropped, putting distance between them again, and her answer was quick, as though she had already thought about and prepared it.

"Yes, but terrible things had to happen to clear the way for them."

His nervousness started again and he tried to placate her.

"But neither of them was guilty. They didn't do anything wrong."

"That's right, Will. But that's the difference between a book and life. My life anyway. I sometimes have the feeling that whatever it needs to change my life I'll have to do myself. Right or wrong."

He wished she'd stop talking in this dispassionate, detached, almost fatalistic way. He often felt marginalized, sometimes so strongly that he was even jealous of the child then immediately hated himself for such petty, spiteful emotions. He'd often had those feelings but never really told her openly about them. Spontaneously, he decided this was the right time to say it.

"Mary, you frighten me a little when you talk like that."

She glanced at him, eyebrows raised and a slight smile, about to speak, but he spoke first.

"Not frighten exactly. It makes me uncertain, worried. I can't put it into words exactly."

There was a long pause and he watched as Mary pressed her face gently against Lizzie's head, kissing her with almost no pressure of her open lips. Without interrupting her meal, the child tried energetically but without success to make eye-contact with her mother but she could only by accident entangle her tiny hands in her mother's thick black hair that hung down on either side of her. He was hoping that when she spoke again it would be about something that would reconcile them. She looked up at him with more of a grin than a smile.

"You sure you haven't?"

"Haven't what?"

"Any secrets from me? What did you call them? Skeletons in the cupboard?"

He wasn't sure if she was teasing him or not and, while he hesitated, she went on, sounding more serious now.

"You know everything you want to know about me. But I only know about you what you've chosen to tell me. Perhaps you have got a mad wife locked away somewhere. Or even a child."

His spontaneous outrage, though he controlled it well, was genuine.

"Mary! Can you believe, even think that about me?"

Both his face and voice betrayed his agitation now but she remained calm as if talking and listening to her own voice at the same time, ignoring the effect of what she was saying had on him.

"It wouldn't be hard for you to marry and then just up and leave if the fancy took you. Men can do that."

He stood up, unable to bear the way she was speaking any longer and she relented a little.

"Will, don't be shocked. I'm just talking. You're a good, honest man. I know that and I love you."

At once he swung round and looked at her and she saw that at this moment he really was dependent on her, that she had the power to injure or soothe him.

"I do love you Will."

It was true, but she said it because she knew it was what he most wanted to hear. When she saw that the words brought tears to his eyes and that he was about to move to her she felt she had somehow deceived him with the conciliation of her words, and before he reached her she said:

"But it's true. You are a man and you are free to come and go as you please."

She was herself surprised that she was talking like this. She hadn't intended to but now each sentence came fluently of its own accord and was so ripe, begging to be spoken that she couldn't resist. There was no malice in her words, neither intended nor evident, but she knew that what she was saying was hurting Will and making him insecure. He struggled to contain his exasperation and keep quiet in the hope this conflict would just dissipate. But then, in spite of himself, he blurted out, showing his hurt and confusion caused by the continual to and fro of his feelings.

"And I love you. Do you doubt that? But sometimes I think, for you love is not the same as it is for me." She looked up at him, waiting, and he took this as implying she expected to hear more and he continued. "And sometimes I think … No. I'm sure. My feelings for you are stronger than yours for me."

Without hesitation, she retorted. "Well, of course they are Will. So are Thomas' I daresay!"

He was also angry and unguarded now and spoke rashly:

"The difference is that there's no-one to distract me from you. You're the centre of my life and there's no-one else in my life to rival you!"

Mary knew what he meant and she couldn't have denied it, even to comfort him. Her love for Lizzie was immoveable and there was no power on earth that could even question it. Although the child was hardly four months old, Mary felt the bond between them and it grew stronger every day, with every look and smile they exchanged and with every experience they shared. She asked him.

"You're not asking me to choose between you and Lizzie, are you Will? To tell you who I love more? What does that matter? What good would that do?"

She said it to help him realise how pointless his remark was, not to goad or provoke him. But he was already penitent himself, feeling now angry with himself for such a needless insinuation and he tried to make up for it.

"Mary, you know I didn't mean that. I want to love Lizzie as much as a man can love his child. I want her to be our child."

He paced towards the window, his back towards her, but felt calmer. No longer flaying aimlessly with his words, he chose them carefully now and spoke in a measured way as he turned to face her.

"It did sting me, what you said." He added hastily, afraid he might inflame their conversation again. "I know you said it without the wish to pain me. But it did. You spoke about me leaving you. I would never do that and it hurts me to hear you say it."

His obvious sincerity made her want to believe what he said. she wanted to console him but at the same time insist on the simple truth, which he seemed to be resisting.

"I know that. I know it because of who you are. But you could leave me if you wanted to. It would be easy." She pause again before she repeated. "Because you're a man."

She waited to make sure that he really accepted what she said, that he wouldn't feel attacked again and retaliate. Convinced he was no longer feeling vulnerable, she took her thoughts a step further.

"You'd stay with me because you love me, Will. But what if you no longer loved me? What would there be to make you stay then? It would be easy for you to go."

She paused but he didn't speak.

"But for me it's different. It just is. I don't love Thomas. I hate him. I almost killed him once. Perhaps I would have done if he had tried to take me again by force. Could hate be clearer than that? No, I don't love him. But it's hard, perhaps impossible for me to go. Unless he threw me out."

He wanted to ask her why he didn't do that but he hesitated to pose the question. She answered it anyway.

"He won't let me leave if he thinks I have somewhere better to go to, if it could make me happy. There's not much he understands but he knows letting or making me go would be like releasing me from prison. He'll never do that. It was a mistake to marry Thomas. My mistake. But I've paid for it. I didn't know there was anything better in life then." She looked at the child then raised her head and looked straight at him. "Who would it harm if we left all this? And started a new life together somewhere else? Why is that so difficult?"

Confused and distraught, he tried to understand how she had seemed to move so swiftly from desire to this despair he heard in her voice now. If the child had not woken up and distracted her, they would now be making love in the room above them, just as they done so often before Lizzie's birth. Looking at her now, seeing her face tilted again towards her baby's, no longer directed at him, he felt this moment was somehow crucial. What had seemed so strong some minutes ago had become brittle and fragile and now he was afraid of losing her. She had been right a minute or so before; he was tacitly asking her to choose between him and the child, and he felt shocked at the sudden, blunt realisation. The single overwhelming need to make sure she didn't drift further away from him forced out the guilt, vanity and indecision that were separating him from her. He sat down at the table opposite and leaned forwards so that his head was as close as possible to hers. Although she didn't look up, he knew she was waiting for him to speak now. After the volatile emotions of the minutes before, he was now settled, sure and determined. Remembering her warning not to make easy promises he chose his words carefully and excluded any enthusiasm or persuasion from his voice.

"Mary, you're right. It won't be easy. But let's do what you say. Think and plan."

Pushing the chair back impulsively he was on his feet again, pacing around the room. She watched him, hoping he could find the words to convince her that they had a future together, the three of them. But she knew she wouldn't, couldn't believe him merely out of love. Testing him but at the same time hoping he could give her answers she could really believe, she interrogated him.

"And what will Thomas do? He couldn't stop me leaving if I were alone. But he's Lizzie's father. Though he doesn't give a dam for her. She's his all the same. He could claim her, take her away from me if he found us."

"If he found us. A big *if*! Manchester is big city." He realised this wasn't enough to satisfy her. "And he'll soon accept it. I sometimes think he already knows about us but doesn't care. As you say, he has no feelings for Lizzie. And how could he look after her anyway?"

Mary said nothing but nodded towards the wall behind him which joined and divided her house and her sister-in-law's, the other Jane. He understood the gesture and answered her unspoken insinuation with genuine confidence.

"I could talk to John. Tell him about us. I know him. He'd be shocked and sad at first. But he's a practical man. And he loves me and cares for you. He's easy-going most of the time but when he feels there's wrong-doing, injustice then he can put his foot down. He won't let Thomas or Jane stop us."

His arguments were strong. She accepted that.

"Then let's leave soon, Will. I know the longer we stay the more difficult it will be."

She was at last glad that they'd talked, even though it had been so tense and at times even hostile. They might have simply gone into the bedroom , which she had been looking forward to. But now the talking of the last few minutes had made her feel strong and optimistic again, more than lovemaking could have done. She spoke softly to him.

"Come over here to me, my love."

He went to her and knelt on the hard floor beside her chair, one arm around her shoulder and the other laid gently across the child and he stroked the tiny, warm head tenderly. He leaned across her body and kissed her breast close to Lizzie's face. Mary let her head dip slightly forwards and kissed the top of his head. For a few moments the three of them formed a unit, a triangle of affection and belonging, so close and involved with each other that neither of them saw Jane linger for a few seconds at the kitchen window then move swiftly away in the direction of her own house.

*

Will Bacon's Diary, April 12th, 1849

> *Exactly a year has now passed since we became lovers and my feelings for Mary haven't changed. Though the child, Lizzie, is not my own and was conceived in loveless moments of violence, she has brought us even closer than before. But, though I try to deny it to myself, my world has changed. One year ago, I would have stepped with Mary and her child into a new life together just as we boarded that train. I knew then where our journey would take us: into a bright future, a better world. But now I sense that is no longer so. There is nothing I want more than to be with her, without the constant conspiracy and deceit of adultery, to share time and space with her, to travel in her company. But now I cannot see the destination. That journey one year ago took us straight to our mutual goal, on those undoubting tracks, without deviation or reserve. I wish it were still so.*

20th April.

> *For fear she will doubt my love, I cannot talk with Mary about my uncertainty about the future. She may mistake it for wavering, for a lack of loyalty to her. She told me that when we returned from London, it was if she had emerged from one of the*

long, deep tunnels John often speaks about, where, no matter in which direction you look, there is no light except the pale glow immediately around you. The tunnels are cold and sometimes the air is still and breathless. Water drips through the walls shored up with timber, a temporary and untrustworthy protection against a sudden collapse. That's exactly how she used to feel, she told me. And now she is outside, in the light and able to look forward. Unknown to her but all too obvious to myself, the events in London have had for each of us the opposite effect. For Mary a new day dawned. For me, the world has become a darker place.

28th April

A few days ago we had our first clash of opinions. Not a quarrel and we took the opportunity to prove to each other again how strong the bond between us is. But she is right. We need to act and drive ourselves forwards, not wait and let random currents decide where we go. Tomorrow I will travel to Manchester by train and make arrangements for Mary to follow me as soon as she can.

Chapter 25

Charles Hardcastle was as old as the century. At fifteen he had managed to join the army just before the end of the French wars but almost all his military service had been in England and since then his enemy had been his own people, some would say even his own class. By the time he left the army he already knew many ways to destroy a man. They ranged from being able to kill men with his bare hands to influencing and manipulating their behaviour without them even noticing it. Whether his victims were his physical or social superiors made little difference. All that mattered to Hardcastle were his legal immunity and his financial reward.

His first well-paid work after his military service had taken him to Nuneaton, several years before John Bacon went to live there and sixteen years before William arrived in 1848. It was in 1832, the year of the great Reform Election, when Hardcastle was hired by the Earl of Newdigate to manage the campaign of his candidate, Dugdale and prevent the Radical candidate from achieving an almost inevitable victory.

He recalled those events as the train slowed down on its approach to the station. It had been difficult, complex and extremely risky work but Hardcastle did it well. There was a lot at stake. The railway link between Rugby and Stafford was then little more than a dream and would require an Act of parliament before it could be really planned, let alone built. But Newdigate was determined that it would run across his land, bringing him even greater wealth both from the sale of land and the national distribution of his estate's produce. And to ensure this, the landowner, like all others involved in railway construction, needed a man in Parliament. That was Hardcastle's briefing, to ensure that Dugdale, Newdigate's man, was re-elected.

Dugdale had been re-elected and Hardcastle had left Nuneaton with a thousand guineas. Now he was returning again, more experienced and again looking for change. At fortynine he knew he could expect no advancement at the Home Office, unless he used his savings to purchase a position. And in any case, the civil service, despite his long years of service there, was not his natural habitat. Even minor clerks, though they feared something about him, looked down on this still athletic but vulgar employee who was known to control a large circle of informants and sometimes reported to the Home Secretary directly.

Now he had been invited back by Newdigate himself. Unlike in the previous summer, when he had stayed at the Earl's Arbury Hall, he had been told this time to book into the Castle Hotel and to wait until he was contacted by a *mutual acquaintance*. As the train drew to a long, grinding halt in the neat little station with its gas lighting and modest but elegant footbridge over the track, he wondered who this person would be. He expected Jermyn, the lawyer who had been his direct contact during the campaign of 1832. Before he left the station he enquired about the location of the Castle Hotel and decided to walk the half mile or so to the other side of the town centre where the hotel was situated. He asked the boy lighting his way through the only partly lit streets about the whereabouts of Back Lane and, hearing it was almost on the way, they made the slight detour. It was dusk and the street had lamps only on the corners so he took the very slight risk of being recognised and walked the length of the street, which formed a crescent off the main street then back onto it about three hundred yards further. On the left hand side of Back Lane there was a malting factory and some rough fields, all the houses being on the other side. At first he noticed the three-storey, detached houses, one of which would have to belong to the Constable who had informed the HO about Bacon's residence there and who would provide Hardcastle with more information about Will's movements and plans. Then came a short row of two-storey quite new but very simple houses. Strange to think that behind one of those windows would probably be the young man whom Hardcastle, on a moment's impulse just over a year ago, had allowed to run and fight another day. He hadn't know why he had done it at the time. It certainly wasn't lust for the young woman Will had been with when Hardcastle and his men burst in on them. He had long been immune to such cheap and facile corruption. But whatever flash of intuition had motivated him, he already knew that it had been absolutely right.

Soon after he left the dingy lane and returned to the main street, the hotel came into view and he remembered the brief meeting there with Newdigate seventeen years before. He tipped the lamp boy generously, gave his name to the clerk and went straight to his room on the first floor. At first sight, it was strange how events had led to his repeated encounters with people and places associated with this unremarkable, small town. But on second thoughts, there was a clear causative chain connecting the apparent coincidences and so he was surprised but not amazed when the woman, now in her thirties, well-dressed and still extremely attractive, approached his dinner table and asked if he objected to sharing the table with her: she didn't care to be seen dining alone. Years of experience in remembering and recognising faces, something his work always and occasionally his life depended on, enabled him to identify her at once. He had never known her name, not even after she had supplied the information which proved crucial in securing the election of the Earl's candidate and thus the success of his brief. But he recalled clearly how she had followed him with her slightly younger friend into the safety of the hotel yard where she visibly enjoyed the attention she drew from the officers at the window above them. And then, a few days later, he had caught another short but unforgettable glimpse of her lounging scantily dressed in a room which must have been only yards from where he was now accommodated.

After some polite small talk it emerged that they had both been present at the Bendigo-Gaunt boxing contest in the previous summer, both of them there on business, Hardcastle's with Newdigate, and Mrs Johnson providing a large number of military gentlemen with the services of her trade, the same business which now necessitated one of her very rare and always fleeting visits to the town. Normally she would have avoided staying overnight at all costs, she informed him frankly, but, having attended to her business in nearby barracks at Meridan, she wanted to catch the early train to Manchester tomorrow morning. Though she didn't recognise him, she immediately felt at ease in Hardcastle's company. Of course he would know what business she was in. There was no other one possible. But he continued to treat her courteously and refrained tactfully from any direct mention of her trade. In a way, he was also in the business of prostitution, selling his services to those he despised most and accepting gratification for loyalty that was both mercenary and feigned. As a young soldier he'd often heard from the veterans of Wellington's Iberian campaign how the respectable trades people of the towns they had taken often came out to meet the approaching troops, offering them their young wives and daughters, sometimes hardly more than children, in return for their promise not to pillage their businesses or even to persuade them to place orders for their supplies with them. And that was the kind he usually cow-towed to, whose orders he obeyed and whose dirty business he took care of.

They had almost finished their meal and she was sipping the last of her champagne and he his cognac, when he casually mentioned that he sincerely hoped that wouldn't be the last of their meetings, especially as their business interests might coincide more than she might at the moment suspect. She didn't reply but thought carefully about what he had told her about himself, his experience as a soldier and about something he called *discrete services to the nation*, his implied dissatisfaction with his present life, and not least his anxiousness to invest both his acquired abilities and his capital into something rewarding, whether it be within the scope of conventional morality or not.

Although he was one of the first guests to take breakfast the next morning, Mrs Johnson had already left when he entered the breakfast room. When the waiter brought him a sealed envelope as he drank his coffee he felt sure it would contain a message from the woman. As arranged, Newdigate's servant arrived at nine to collect him, settled his expenses with the hotel and then, in the privacy of the carriage, Hardcastle opened the envelope to find a note in a fine hand inviting him to visit Madam Elisabeth Johnson whenever he happened to be in Manchester. He was not prone to sudden emotion and he felt satisfaction rather than pleasure as he re-read the note. What he most valued was a sense of completion, of events taking final shape and solidifying into a bridge providing a sure access to something new. The cab made its way through the already busy little town towards the meeting with Newdigate's lawyer, Jermyn, with his limp hands like soft, damp fungus. Hardcastle was confident that once he had accomplished his present assignment, the slip of paper he held would, like a kind of ticket, transport him swiftly and unerringly to where he had been drifting for almost twenty years.

Chapter 26

When Will told Mary he was travelling to Manchester they both tacitly shared the same secure feeling that their lives were on the verge of change. He believed as firmly as she did that within weeks, even perhaps days, they would be living together somewhere in the vibrant spawn of industrial Lancashire. So, as the train drew to a slow stop only a few minutes after leaving Nuneaton he assumed, like most passengers, that it was just a normal delay. Perhaps the driver had seen something on the lines – a branch maybe or even deer as they seemed to passing though parkland and he had spotted a small herd a mile or so back. Will looked up from his book and saw a man on horseback suddenly appear alongside his carriage, moving towards him until the two men were only a yard or two away from each other, separated only by the carriage window. The rider then signalled towards the front of the train which jerked and chugged forward a few yards, then stopped clumsily. Will's carriage door was now adjacent to a sort of improvised wooden platform and the horseman dismounted, walked across the wooden planks, his riding boots clacking with each step and opened the door.

"Mr Bacon? William Bacon?"

He took Will's expression of amazement to mean assent.

"This is where you get off, Sir. No need to be alarmed. You know Mr Hardcastle I believe?"

A few yards away from the platform, on the narrow surfaced road leading through the park, Will suddenly recognised Hardcastle in the driver's seat of a small fly. A whip in one hand, he tipped his hat in Will's direction with the other.

"Please Sir. If you don't mind. We don't want to draw any more attention to ourselves than necessary."

*

Fifteen minutes later Will was standing, next to Hardcastle, in the spacious entrance of Arbury Hall, Newdigate's family home. A servant had taken his bag and was ascending one side of the magnificent Spanish staircase. Will looked around and despite himself felt overawed by the opulence and scale of the building. The soaring fan vaulting and plunging pendants drew his gaze to the domed ceiling of the entrance. The arched windows were all decorated with intricate filigree tracery. Around him there were a few pieces of Chippendale furniture and he recognised the Reynolds portraits hung at each landing of the staircase. He had been in the homes of successful businessmen in Manchester and had then wondered at the prosperity in which they lived. But this was another world. He guessed correctly there were few homes in England that could outdo or even match the slightly understated but still immense luxury of this newly refurbished house. He suddenly realised that Hardcastle had spoken to him.

"I said I regret the slight deception I used to bring you here, Mr Bacon. I doubt you'd have agreed to come had I extended a simple invitation."

An answer was superfluous and anyway there was no regret evident in Hardcastle's voice. He had spoken merely to gain Will's attention just in time for when a door to their left was opened and held ajar by another servant dressed in the Newdigate family livery. He beckoned them to enter a room about sixty feet square filled with portraits, some large some miniature, landscapes and paintings of dogs and horses. Small pieces of furniture and sculpture were placed around the edges of the room. In front of the enormous fireplace, where wood burned almost without a crackle, the elderly Early sat alert and upright in a leather armchair. Two large hounds lay at his feet, their eyes fixed on his as if hoping he might give them a sign to do what they were trained to do and set about the strangers.

Eventually he spoke.

"Welcome to Arbury Hall, Mr Bacon. I'm sure Hardcastle here has explained our regret for the circumstances of your arrival."

Will tried to gain some moral high ground and spoke curtly, almost impolitely.

"The real reason would be even more interesting than your apology."

Newdigate noticed the lack of an appropriate form of address but ignored it. "The reason is simple and I will not waste your time, Sir. I have a proposition to make to you."

Will raised his eyebrows in expectation.

"But not now. Please, let me first of all extend the hospitality that until now I have been forced by circumstances to deny you. We will talk later, I hope. But only when you have satisfied yourself that you are here as my welcome guest and in accordance with your wishes. One word and Hardcastle here will arrange for you to travel where and when you will. We can stop a train or my man can drive you back into town. If you do stay to hear my proposal, then voluntarily so."

The older man turned his head and looked straight at Will, who recognised that he was not dealing with a senile, degenerate aristocrat but a shrewd, determined man who had no qualms about bringing him here on false pretences and was not prepared to feel obliged to Will or anybody else. There was a long pause before Will spoke.

"I accept your kind offer, Sir. The down train tomorrow afternoon would be most convenient for me. I hope we can have done whatever business you intend by then."

Newdigate tapped a few times with his cane and his dogs immediately looked at him expectantly, then let their eyes fall again with their usual disappointment.

"So be it."

He struck the brass railing in front of the fireplace with the cane more sharply and the liveried servant immediately re-entered the room.

"We'll talk further over dinner."

The servant made a discrete gesture that Will and Hardcastle were to follow him.

As they climbed the stair together Hardcastle turned to Will.

"We have a few hours till dinner, Mr Bacon. I know the Earl has instructed one of his men to prepare a couple of guns and a dog for us. Do you shoot?"

Will thought for a few seconds.

"No, but I'll gladly accompany you. Let's meet in an hour then."

As soon as Will got to his room he made sure the door was closed and took out his diary. His room was on the first floor at the end of the front side of the house so that he had windows facing both to the front and, on the left, a window overlooking the yard at the side of the house where he was to meet to Hardcastle. At one of the spacious front windows there was a desk with quills and ink. He looked down to his right onto a broad terrace with statues and stone vases planted with bushes and shrubs. On the wall of the terrace there were smaller pots with richly coloured flowers. Peacocks strutted and squawked bad-temperedly around the terrace, some struggling up the three feet or so onto the wall. Stone steps led down into a symmetrically planted garden with broad gravel pathways, well-cut lawns and benches. Beyond that the discretely landscaped parkland swept down past two small ponds and on to a large man-made lake. Either side of the lake there were patches of rough vegetation, high grass, ferns and low bushes and, at the far side of them, copses designed with a deceptively casual elegance. A few deer were grazing nonchalantly in the ample space between the garden and the lake. On the lake Will could just make out water birds – swans, geese and ducks. He began to write:

"Arbury Hall, home of the Newdigate family.

Should I be ashamed to be here? How did he know I would be on that train? And why am I here at all? A proposition. But what? I can't begin to imagine what this Earl, obviously wealthy far beyond anything I have ever seen or even imagined for that matter, intends to propose. And if I'm honest, that is why I am here. Curiosity. If I had left I would never have know what intentions he has. And I want to know. I desperately want to know. Mary believes that I am now on my way to Manchester to prepare our flight. I hope that what the Earl has to say to me is of sufficient import to justify my postponement of the journey north. It may benefit both of us . If so she will understand."

Thinking of Mary he flipped back the pages of the diary until he reached the entries he had made when they were in London – the ecstatic passages about the wonderful night they spent together before the great demonstration and the few meagre words and sentences he had managed to scrape together to try to record the desolation he felt after the demonstration had failed, that his hopes and those of almost all the Chartists had been shattered. Though he had tried to channel all his future plans into a life with Mary and the child and to look forward to their future together with optimism, he couldn't rid himself of the persistent conviction that his life had changed for the worse. A hard, indestructible grain of insight had lodged itself in his mind. He tried to wash it out, to swill it away, to dissolve it in rationalisation, self-persuasion and even forgetfulness. When he was with Mary he could ignore it as if their involvement were strong enough to deny its intrusion. But when he was alone or the world around him was quiet and his thoughts went their own way and he had to chase wherever they led him, then the cold, irrefutable certainty asserted itself again.

There was a quiet knock at the door. A pretty servant girl stood at the door, her arms full of bed linen. After she had entered and begun her work, he stood with his back to the side window, watching her, something she was clearly enjoying. In the solemn propriety of the Hall visitors like this handsome man were a seldom but extremely welcome diversion for the young female servants, who had seen Will arrive and had been discussing him since then. Peggy had had the idea to change the bed linen, although it was already clean and fresh. And there she was now. Both knees on the wide bed, leaning forward and spreading out the fine sheet with both hands so that she couldn't prevent her loose fitting tunic, which had somehow become unbuttoned during her work, from falling open and revealing just a glimpse of her breasts. Will was staring at her when she stopped, raised her head to look at him, kneeling forwards on the bed with her hands supporting her. She smiled unashamedly at his gaze fixed on her cleavage.

"Perhaps Sir would be kind enough to come over here and help me get done?"

Despite his excitement, he hesitated, not because his desire for her caused him any sense of guilt – the situation was nothing new for him. In an effort to distract himself from the sight of the attractive face and half-exposed bosom, he thought of Mary and instantly his lust for the adventurous young servant girl, who had seized this opportunity to have some rare pleasure, was gone. A look of offended disappointment spread over her lovely face as she realised he was not going to join her on the bed.

"Another time and I would have gladly helped you but someone is waiting for me."

He glanced out of the window and indeed he could see Hardcastle inspecting the guns in the yard below. Treading quickly down the stairs, he wondered why he had really rejected the girl's advances. Hardcastle could have waited and Mary would never have known about the escapade. Perhaps he had just become more serious in the last year or so, more like his brother John whose life centred around his aims for the future. It was a strange, significant moment for Will, as he asked himself grimly what aims he himself had for the future since his faith in the Charter had collapsed. He fought that old sense of dread as it rose up in him by thinking of Mary and the child but it swaggered its way into his thoughts, leering at him, mocking him, ugly, impassive and implacable, like the smirking gargoyle on the guttering of the neo-Gothic mansion.

*

The servant Newdigate had sent to accompany the two men had never in his life seen anyone shoot like Hardcastle. In two hours they disturbed ten pigeons and a few rabbits and he killed them all. Most of the time he had dropped the birds even before Will had realised they were there. One of the birds kept low so that he had to wait for the shot but even then he hit it, to the gun-carrier's amazement and the dogs' delight. For a change their work rate and their competence was matched by the marksmanship of the man behind the gun. As the light began to fade, they returned past the lake, up the long slow slope towards the terrace. To the side of the house, where they were heading, there was a group of old cedars, slowly filling up with cawing rooks as dusk approached. The sun was low behind the tall, majestically dispassionate trees; the peacocks were almost all motionless and silent, some of them silhouetted like ornaments on the terrace wall. In spite of himself, Will felt strangely impressed, affectionate towards the sombre, dignified beauty of the scene. The harmony was so complete that the temptation to recognise its worth was fleetingly irresistible. He shuddered at himself for harbouring such feelings.

The dining room had been prepared so that the three men ate at quite a small table, the long mahogany one which normally stretched fifteen feet through the room having been set to one side. They still had ample space. Dozens of tall, white wax candles had been lit so that there was plenty of light in the room, although the heavy velvet curtains smothered any light there may have been from outside.

They ate simply, drank sparsely and Will waited. At last Newdigate signalled to the two servants to leave the room. His cane lay on the table and they knew its rap would summon them back in due course.

"Hardcastle here informs me you have connections in Manchester, Mr Bacon. That your activities over the last five years or so have earned you something of a reputation, some respect. Considerable respect in fact. Let's not for the moment dwell too long on where this respect is harboured. It is never good to dwell on the past Mr Bacon. Things change so quickly you know. Fifteen years ago, the word Radical, for example, was for many synonymous with Jacobin. And today? Today, some call my good friend Mr Peel a Radical! Just because he read the writing on the wall and repealed the Corn Laws. Things change, Mr Bacon, they become assimilated in the course of progress. Throw a handful of poison in a river and in the first five yards it'll kill a six pound trout. Let it flow a hundred yards downstream and it won't harm stickleback! Radicals." He paused. "Same with Chartists. Hardcastle tells me you're a Chartist, Sir. Or rather, were a Chartist. Chartism's dead, you see."

He sensed Will was about to protest and raised his hands slightly. "Don't misunderstand me. I'm not judging you or even Chartism for that matter. It's just a fact. Chartism is dead!"

He brushed his lips unnecessarily with the white napkin and took a tiny sip of wine.

"So what will the Chartists do now, now that Chartism is dead? I mean the ones who are still alive. Some are still in prison. Some have fled. But those who are still here, those who have talent, determination. Those who enjoy respect. What will they do, Mr Bacon?"

Will felt as if this tall, frail man was either very wise or could uncannily understand his own frame of mind, divining exactly how he felt.

"That must be a question you ask yourself quite often. A fine fish like you won't be happy in the backwaters forever."

The statement was as accurate as Hardcastle's aim. Will felt himself drop into the Earl's purpose like the pigeons had plummeted into the rough.

"Mr Bacon. Have you ever thought of going into Parliament?"

Before Will could recover from the question and even try to form an answer Newdigate continued.

"That's my proposal. That you become a Member of Parliament. Radical, of course. What do you think of it? Yes or no?"

Will blurted out the questions he was asking himself.

"How? Why?"

Newdigate rapped his cane on the polished tabletop and the two servants entered noiselessly, taking up their positions slightly behind his elbows.

"Gentlemen, my library is at your disposal for the rest of the evening. Jameson will give you any help you need. Mr Bacon, may I ask you to think only of the one question. If your answer to that question tomorrow is *yes*, then all the other questions can be answered in due course. I wish you a pleasant evening, Gentlemen."

*

Both Will and Hardcastle took brandy in the library. Will smoked a cigar that Jameson had prepared for him. The library was well lit with numerous oil lamps so that the uniformly bound red leather volumes glowed redolent in the yellowish light.

"So now the cat's out of the bag, are you allowed to speak, Hardcastle? Did you know about this *proposal*?"

Hardcastle loosened up for the first time that day. He swirled the brandy around the almost spherical glass, sniffed it appreciatively and took a long slow sip from it.

"It was no surprise to me Mr Bacon."

"Does he expect me to go into parliament on his behalf. To be his puppet. Like Dugdale, here in the borough?"

"If my ears didn't deceive me the Earl put it quite straight and blunt. Would you like to become a Radical Member of Parliament? That's the question. If yes, you can talk about puppets with his Lordship tomorrow."

When Will went to his room the curtains were not drawn. Standing at the front window he could make out some of the garden and the slivers and botches of silvery light reflected from the lakes. Opening the window wide, he heard the peacocks flurrying and shuffling restlessly on the terrace as well as owls hooting from the cedar copse. Strangely, the air was more restless, tenser than in the light of day. He breathed in deeply, hoping to calm himself. He had drunk too much brandy and the cigar hadn't suited him. He tried hard to order his confused thoughts. Pulling the window closed he looked down at the desk. Befuddled as he was, he noticed that his diary was closed. Strange. After he had hurried out of the room to get away from Peggy he had paused on the stairs and thought of returning to close the diary and put it away but decided against it, afraid that if he had returned to the room and she had extended her invitation to him again, he wasn't sure that he would have declined a second time. And what did it really matter anyway? But now it did seem to matter that the diary was closed. Or did it? He slumped into the chair and loosened his clothes. His thoughts slowed down, his head cleared as, slowly but irrepressibly, a sensation of pleasure and contentedness came over him as though something knotted and blocked had been freed. In the luxury of the crisp white linen he slept soundly through till morning.

After breakfast the three men drove out, Hardcastle keeping the horses at a brisk trot with his usual accomplishment, to the edge of the estate where the land rose a little, giving them a good view.

"You see this stretch of country," the Earl began. "The most barren, useless acres of the whole estate. A soil almost too heavy to plough, that gathers water in every dip and cranny, hardly letting a drop drain through, until it is little more than solid mud. No coal. That's all over there, to the south, between Griff and black Bedworth, that's where the coal deposits are."

The men turned in the direction he indicated. In the distance small clusters of dwellings of some sort were just visible. From the vantage point they could also see the canal network, mostly straight, short stretches from the shallow pits leading at angles into the main arterial canal that took the barges of coal and other goods to Coventry in the south and Birmingham to the west.

"Further to the east and behind us in the west, there are woods, pastures, cornfields. But here, nothing of any value will grow."

He turned to face Will directly.

"Yet these few miles of land are by far the richest assets I possess, Mr Bacon. The reason is known to you. In fact you can see it approaching us now."

Their eyes followed the iron tracks that ran in almost a straight line south-east to north-west until they saw the plume of smoke so dense that the swarms of red sparks enfolded within it were hardly visible. They waited in silence until the train had rattled past them.

"The Trent Valley Railway. Rugby to Stafford, via Tamworth, where it crosses part of my friend Sir Robert Peel's lands. The stretch, I believe, is about fifty miles and about five of these run across my land here. My family has been here over three hundred years. Farming, forestry, then coal and the canals. Food, fuel, transport. Good, permanent business, gentlemen, that does not disappear overnight. And we have done well from it. You have seen our Arbury Hall, Mr Bacon? Evidence enough of the estate's good management. But the railways. The railways will outdo them all. London to Manchester in six hours. Some say that by the end of the century, four hours will suffice. Four hours in comfort, gentlemen. A few years ago it was a terrible, cramped, wet, cold, dismal, dangerous and very long journey. The railways and the land they lie on are a treasure, a treasure that multiplies itself. But like all treasures it needs protection. The more wealth it yields, the more coveted it becomes. And that's your part, Mr Bacon. With Hardcastle's help, it was Dugdale who secured the railway for us by sitting in Parliament. He was just the right man then. But times change. And to keep and nurture this line and others, we need men like you in Parliament Mr Bacon. To protect our treasures."

All three men sensed that the critical moment had been reached as they walked back towards the rig in silence. When they were seated, Hardcastle at the reins and Will and Newdigate facing each other inside, the Earl asked.

"Will you do it, Sir?"

Hardcastle took his time on the ride back to the Hall. After a long pause Will asked.

"Your conditions?"

"Only one condition. Whatever else you do, whatever laws, policies and movements you support and cast your vote for, all that is a matter for your conscience, for your convictions. I have seen enough to know that we cannot stop the march of progress and merely to slow it down does not entice me. But on one point you will serve my interests without question: when it comes to the railways then you will follow and execute my instructions to the letter. Without reservation. How you justify your actions is your concern. But it will not be difficult to do so. There will be, I assure you, other men like you in the same position, sharing the same benches in the Lower House."

"Where is the seat?"

"Where else? Manchester, of course."

Will felt such a swift surge of enthusiasm that he didn't notice the Earl's eyes narrow slightly as he scrutinised Will's reaction. As if he had suddenly emerged from a thick fog to see his pathway like a bright ribbon laid out in front of him, Will closed his eyes and inwardly watched Mary rejoice as her told he they were going to Manchester! He thrust one hand into his pocket while his other hand clenched and relaxed involuntarily, compulsively as he struggled to remain calm, trying to conceal his elation from Newdigate, who watched him impassively.

The rig came smoothly to a halt as Hardcastle let the two horses walk the last hundred yards, stopping in front of the main entrance to allow the Earl and Will to get out and then athletically leaping down himself while the groom took over.

"We can meet in an hour for luncheon, gentlemen. I daresay you will give me my answer then, Mr Bacon. You'll have ample time to pick up the train. Will you be travelling up or down?"

"Up." He paused. "Back into the town I came from. Your lordship."

Only when he had his back to the other two men did Newdigate allow the look of satisfaction to cross his face.

Will was ecstatic as he entered the room, shaking his lightly clenched fists in front of him. The pall of depression and resignation that had cloaked him since the calamitous day in April 1848 fell from his shoulders like a heavy, drenched coat, liberating him into feeling light, clean and dry.

He wished he could tell Mary now, this second and instinctively he went to the desk where his diary still lay. Before he began to write he saw a slight reflection in the window and turned on his heels.

"I'm sorry Sir. I was just tidying and seeing everything is alright for you. I didn't mean to spy."

Will was in such good spirits that he neither knew nor cared why the girl was in the room. He just wanted her to leave so that he could write down his thoughts before his bliss dissipated.

"What's your name?"

"Peggy."

"Peggy, it doesn't matter but please leave now."

She walked away from him but instead of leaving she turned around and leaned her back against the closed door.

"Yesterday you said another time. There's no one waiting for you now is there?"

Will walked slowly across the room and she thought he was going to kiss her. He cupped her face in his hands, kissed her lightly on the forehead.

"There is someone waiting for me. Someone I love. Please, go now."

As soon as the door had closed he almost ran to the desk, sat down, opened the diary and dipped the quill in the ink pot. Before he could manage to write a single word, he put the quill down. He intended to read this entry to Mary when he returned to Nuneaton in a few hours. It had to be exactly how he felt, to express his sentiments powerfully and precisely. He leaned back in the leather-covered chair, his hands clasped behind his head and looked down the long perfectly landscaped vista sweeping down to the lakes. There was something amusingly ironical in the fact that Newdigate seemed to assume that he had somehow trapped Will, manipulated him into entering Parliament to serve his own interests. There was the single stipulation; unconditional support for the railway lobby. But this involved no compromise of principles for Will. Even if businessmen did make fortunes from them, he welcomed the railways. They had even made his first night in Mary's arms possible. He would leave the older man in the fond illusion that he, Will, was in a way his puppet, when in fact he would be realising all his own political ideals at the Earl's expense.

He mused for ten minutes or more until he noticed that the keen intensity of his joy was beginning to become lost in an all-pervasive feeling of contentment. He had to write now or the moment would be gone but before he could begin, there was a knock.He smiled grimly, expecting Peggy again but it was Hardcastle who stood facing him when he opened the door.

"Just a few minutes of your time, Mr Bacon. His Lordship has asked me to clear up one small detail before we make the agreement over luncheon."

They sat down at a small table.

"Agreement? You mean a contract?"

Hardcastle smiled.

"There's no need for anything in writing, Sir. You can trust his Lordship and, well, I'm sure you'll honour your side of the bargain."

Will thought he detected the faintest hint of a threat but Hardcastle continued.

"No, just a verbal statement of the rights and obligations, so to speak."

"You mean remuneration?"

"Oh, no. His Lordship's lawyer, Mr Jermyn will deal with that. No, Sir, it is, let us say, a matter concerning your private life. That's the kind of thing the Earl likes me to handle. Sensitive things that need to be settled between men, not by lawyers."

Will was curious about what Hardcastle meant but felt no apprehension. He suspected he was going to demand that he became a member of the Unitarian church. Well, that would be a small price to pay especially as Will regarded himself as a serious doubter rather than an outright non-believer.

"His Lordship mentioned the borough in question is in, or to more precise, near Manchester. Most voters, the men the Earl is co-operating with in your election, the whole liberal community in fact tend shall we say towards a low-church allegiance. Dissenters, Independents, Unitarians, Methodists, even some outright Calvinists. Puritans, respectable, moral folk."

This confirmed Will's feeling that he was one step ahead of these people and he smiled to himself and found himself strolling across the room towards a small table where there was a port decanter and glasses. A toast drunk together with this admittedly uncomplicated but efficient man would be appropriate, he thought to himself. Already slightly giddy with joy at the turn in his luck, he even felt a rush of affection for the fellow.

"No need to beat about the bush, Hardcastle. If his Lordship requires that I join one of those churches or chapels I'm quite prepared to make that small sacrifice and accommodate him."

Hardcastle paused for a moment and then walked across to the desk and picked up Will's diary.

"Will. Let me put it to you plainly. Man to man."

He paused and flipped casually through the pages of the heavy note book then suddenly stopped, as if he had discovered something of significance by chance. He looked up at Will and spoke in a flat tone that gave the sentence added finality:

"You can't take the woman with you."

Will stopped pouring the port, placed the glass and decanter on the table and turned to face Hardcastle, who continued in a level, slow voice.

"She'll have to stay where she is. From now on all your indulgences will have to be legitimate and proper in the eyes of your backers. You'll have to drop her."

Will felt as if Hardcastle had slapped him hard across the cheek. He watched in a state of shock as Hardcastle began to read from the diary; first, the entries he had written when he and Mary were in London, then more recent passages.

"Mary is a married woman with a child, Will. Perhaps by the laws of nature, it's yours. I don't know. But by the laws we live by, it's her husband's. You, a Member of Parliament, living with a fallen woman? You know as well as I do that respectable, God-fearing people won't stand for that." He sat down again, leaned forward and looked Will in the eye. "Now, my friend, I need an answer now. Do you go to Manchester without Mary and change the world? Or do you stay with her and fester in Back Lane, Nuneaton? Can we count on you? Yes or no?"

Will closed his eyes and his hands began to clench and relax obsessively. He thought of the weight he had been carrying around with him since the demonstration, of the shattered hopes that had been dragging him down. He thought of the offer Newdigate had made him and he forced himself not to think of Mary.

At last, he returned the other man's expectant but patient gaze. It was choice he had to make between the two most important things in his life, but it was a clear choice and so, without further hesitation, he nodded and spoke the word Hardcastle was waiting for.

"Yes."

His job done, Hardcastle walked across to the desk and laid the diary on it. Will asked him harshly:

"Hardcastle! It was Peggy, wasn't it?"

After brief consideration, the older man answered:

"Will, I don't like to talk about a campaign when it's finished. If it went well, sounds like boasting. Bad, sounds like whining." He went towards the door, paused and turned. "Let's just say, if you hadn't been such a fine chap, if you'd given Peggy what she wanted, she might not have come to me and the Earl might not have found out about you and Mary before it was too late."

*

Half an hour later, conversation over luncheon was confined almost exclusively to disjointed small talk.

"Just one point, Mr Bacon. My lawyer, Mr Jermyn, will be contacting you to finalise all the details – allowance, accommodation and such matters. You know the location of his chambers in Nuneaton I presume?"

"It'll have to be in Manchester, I'm afraid, your Lordship. You see, I've changed my mind."

Newdigate's cane clattered to the floor and both he and Hardcastle looked up sharply. Will noticed their sudden undisguised alarm but he took no pleasure in it.

"I've changed my mind about the train. I'll be taking the down train after all. To Manchester, not back into Nuneaton."

Early that afternoon Newdigate's servants flagged down the north-bound train and Will boarded a first-class carriage.

He passed through Nuneaton many times when, in the course of the next twenty-five years, he journeyed between his constituency and Parliament, but whenever the train stopped there he was so engrossed in his documents or a newspaper that he didn't notice the short halt.

Chapter 27

In the months since the Farnells, an Irish family with two children and a pig, had moved into the house next to Mary's, a slightly formal but close friendship had developed between Mary and Mrs Farnell. The younger child, William, was the same age as Lizzie and his brother Patrick was six but it was Barney, the pig, that Mary saw most of. The flimsy wooden palings between the two yards couldn't deter Barney for long, so when he was out of his small pen, which he usually was, he'd wander snuffling, grunting and rooting his way into the yard next door. Mrs Farnell perhaps hadn't appreciated Mary's remark that you'd have thought that John's surname would have been enough to keep Barney out of their patch, especially as they all knew that Barney would be slaughtered in the coming winter.

He was a real bacon pig, a hairy, brick-red Tamworth with a long, arched back. Mr Farnell had bought him as a piglet from another Irish family who had somehow managed to bring a sow over with them from Ireland, where Tamworths were called Irish Grazers and were said to produce the finest bacon and lean, firm ham. It was no-one less than Sir Robert Peel himself who was the first English breeder to take notice of these leggy, narrow hogs kept by the Irish migrant workers who camped for seasonal work on his estate at Tamworth. He liked their almost athletic build and their strangely long heads, their trim jowls and straight snouts.

Barney's indifference to the former Prime Minister's admiration of his species was typical of his whole attitude to life, especially its brevity, which he had already perhaps sensed. He was irreverent, rowdy, vulgar and would even brush past Jane and into her kitchen while she was brandishing her twig broomstick at him, like Gabriel at the gates of heaven, and calling him all kinds of Biblical names. Perhaps it was because she associated Barney with Satan that she feared him and was wary of getting too close to him, as if his insatiable indulgence in life's pleasures might be contagious. Much as it pained her, whenever Barney launched a raid on her kitchen she'd have to beg help from Mary, who simply grabbed Barney by the ears and hauled him out back onto the yard.

Though it hadn't prevented her ordering whatever the Farnells would be able to spare of Barney's carcase when his time came, Mary enjoyed his less determined visits when he would allow her to stroke his smooth, almost furry skin. Wistfully, she'd often envisaged Lizzie sitting astride him, just as Patrick did, though she knew it would never happen. By Christmas at the latest the relentlessly foraging, voracious, blithe and jaunty hog would be hanging in salted strips in the Farnell's larder under the stairs.

So, as Mary looked out of the kitchen window that sunny morning and saw Barney lying on his side enjoying the warming rays, she felt a little twinge of guilt that she had been so rough with him the evening before. Hearing Jane's screeching, she'd hurried next door to help, dragged Barney out of Jane's kitchen as usual, but in her haste had forgotten to close her own kitchen door. By the time she'd caught up with him again he'd not only trotted across the kitchen but had prised open the door of the small scullery under the stairs and was already rummaging, blissfully unconcerned by the chaos trailing in his wake.

In the confined, dingy space Barney twisted and turned, writhing away from Mary's attempts to collar him, but at the same time he managed to disturb and scoff whatever was edible on the lowest shelf. Both furious and in a panic, Mary used everything within her reach to get him out, kicking, shooing, pulling and pushing him, berating him with non-Biblical names that made Jane, listening from the other side of the kitchen wall, shake her head in disapproval, until he was finally out on the yard and she could slam the door on him. Licking his lips and shaking his head without any sign of resentment but with such energy that his ears flapped, he had ambled off perkily in search of more open doors.

Mary had watched him saunter off and by the time he was out of sight she began to see the humorous side of the fray, even though he had managed to disrupt everything on the lower shelves of the pantry and to devour it all before she'd grabbed him by the ears. Consequently, she felt a bit ashamed of herself at the way she had treated him. After all, he was just an animal and didn't know better. And the Farnells loved him as if he were a member of the family so she was glad that they hadn't seen how she'd manhandled him, scolded and even given him a few hard shoves with her booted foot.

Now he lay there, quite a beautiful animal in a way, contented and no doubt well-fed, though normally at this time of day, between his feeds, he'd be scavenging around for any grub he could find. Perhaps he was dreaming, Mary thought, as she went towards the pump. But his dreams had better be about the past and not the future.

"Good day to you Mrs Ball!"

Patrick came skipping out of the house and ran up to the sleeping pig and tapped him lightly with a long twig, the usual sign that his swill was on the way. Without waiting for a response, the boy turned, expecting his friend to jump and trot after him into the house. But Barney didn't move, not even twitch or raise his head. Patrick bent over him, his hand resting on the animal's motionless body and his face close to the pig's breathless snout.

"Ma! Ma! Barney's dead! He's dead!"

Hearing her son's frantic shouts, the mother came rushing out and knelt down at the side of the dead pig, stroking his belly with one hand and pulling the sobbing child close to her with the other.

Hours later Mrs Farnell was drinking tea in Mary's kitchen. Her grief had quickly made way for the practicalities caused by Barney's departure.

"Perhaps he's no good for bacon, nor lard neither. Not that Grazers yield much lard anyway, you know. But we don't know what killed him. The meat might be bad. He was a lovely pig and he'd have made some lovely bacon. But what can we do about it now?"

Mary and Jane listened intently, as much charmed by Mrs Farnell's lyrical Irish brogue as by what she was telling them.

"My ole man's out of himself. Blabbered like a babe. Since he was a boy he's always sent his own pig off. So looking forward to it an' all. But his fellows have been great. They've already had a whip round and they're off tomorrow to get us new pig. One of them has a cousin in Tam'orth that's got some dandy piglets."

The three women sipped their tea.

"Wonder what it was that killed him though. Something he ate, my ole man reckons."

Jane, who had been listening closely, went over to the sink and threw the slops of her tea into it. As she walked back towards Mary she looked over Mrs Farnell's shoulder, who sat with her back to her and gave her sister-in-law a hard, meaningful look. She sensed that Mary, not understanding, was about to ask her what the glower was supposed to mean, so she tightened her face and shook her head, making it clear to Mary that she should keep her question to herself.

*

The next day it was Patrick who called out the new name spontaneously as soon as he saw the young pig being carried into the yard.

"Barney Boy! Come here, Barney Boy!"

And it was indeed as if Barney, after a short holiday, had returned home a few sizes smaller. Mr Farnell opened the wooden crate and Barney Boy ran out towards Patrick, lifted his long snout briefly as if to signal his return then made straight for the Farnell's kitchen, Patrick in pursuit.

Mary stood in the doorway of her house holding Lizzie, alongside Mrs Farnell, who had William on her arm. Jane watched the scene from behind her kitchen window, throwing an instinctive glance at her broomstick, like a soldier checking his ammunition supply.

"To be sure, it'll be more like a christening than a wake we'll be having for Barney after all!"

Mary smiled and hugged Lizzie closer to her. Although Will had been away for five days now, Mary wasn't worried. In fact, she took this as a good sign that his search for work and accommodation was getting results, not allowing him to return to Nuneaton.

Mary knew it must have been more than a year ago now when she and Will became lovers because he'd mentioned the exact date of the demonstration so often – 12th April. Lizzie was strong, healthy and active despite being born, according to Mary's calculations, almost a month premature. She realised what the failure of the Charter had meant to Will. But she'd had disappointments enough in her life to know that any experience could be overcome. Almost any at least. Hardly daring to even think about it, she knew that she would not be able to bear losing Lizzie now. The deaths of each other child had hit her hard, slammed into her and left her dazed and numb but they had happened when she had few expectations of life. They had all been born so sickly that their early deaths were inevitable. She had loved each of them but without hope or joy. With Lizzie it was already different. She was alert, wilful, full of likes and dislikes with a vocabulary of noises, gestures and facial expressions, most of all her smile. Sometimes Mary and Mrs Farnell would lay their babies down on their bellies alongside and facing each other. William, bigger than Lizzie, phlegmatic but heedful and fully aware of Lizzie's constant animation, would only cry feebly when Mary lifted her baby out of his sight, whereas Lizzie would turn towards her companions, stretching her arms towards where he lay, making determined noises in his direction as if issuing him with impatient orders which he seemed to understand but was unable to obey.

As Mary and Will still kept their relationship as secret as possible, she couldn't really share these moments with him so she had quickly become very friendly with Mrs Farnell through this time their children shared. Jane never joined them in these moments, but hovered at a distance, observing them. Her scorn and disapproval were intensified by Mary's closeness to the Farnells because they were Irish and Roman Catholic. The family's arrival in Back Lane had even led to the occasional appearance of the Roman Catholic priest, who usually came to admonish Mr and Mrs Farnell for never attending church, though this didn't mitigate the effect of his visits on Jane, who regarded the Papist priest's visits as only slightly less calamitous than an outbreak of the cholera.

The mild, windless air, the excitement around Barney Boy's arrival, the awkward group of hulking, gentle-mannered Irish friends of the Farnells and the two babies, who invariably provided the centre of attention regardless of whatever else was going on in the yard, all this supported Mary's conviction that things had changed for the better – and permanently so. Materially, her life was much the same as a year ago. Hens clucked moronically around the rough ground, sometimes scurrying indignantly away from Barney Boy just as they steered clear of Barney; the wrought iron pump dripped relentlessly into the massive stone basin below its spout; from the street, the distorted sounds of children shouting, singing and laughing, dogs barking and sheep bleating. It wasn't happiness, just as soil, raked and seeded was not a garden. But for the first time since Polly had been murdered, or since her mother had died, Mary felt that she stood where happiness might yet grow.

Chapter 28

Darkness was falling when Thomas and John arrived home. She heard their heavy boots scuffing in the alley between their and the Farnells' house as well as John's garrulous voice booming into the evening air. Thomas slouched into the kitchen, sullen and tense as always, the smell of alcohol heavy on his breath. He had one of his stones with him which he slammed down onto the wooden table.

"Not inside for two minutes and you're waking Lizzie. Here."

She placed a bowl with gruel, a chunk of bread and jug of water from the pump in front of him.

"Salt!"

"You know where it is!"

She hadn't lit any candles yet and though the kitchen was still light enough, she could hear him groping around in the scullery after the salt.

"It's on the second shelf up."

At last he found the slip of paper and slid the salt into his gruel, expecting her to leave as she normally did. He looked up and caught her staring at the stone next his bowl. Tired and befuddled from work and drink, he glowered at her. There was an unusual softness about her expression which stopped him speaking. She lit the tallow candle on the table but not the one she normally used to light her way up the stairs. Something stirred inside him, confusing but at the same time encouraging him. Was she going to show him affection?

"Thomas."

She spoke steadily but softly. He couldn't remember the last time she had called him by his name. He glared at her inquisitively as if she were a wounded animal and he was trying to locate the exact point of weakness.

"We're leaving. Me and Lizzie. We're going. I can't tell you where and I can't tell you when. But we're going away, and soon."

He continued to slurp his gruel and spoke at the same time:

"You mean with him?" He cocked his head in the direction of Jane's house. "With the Chartist?" He stopped eating and scowled at her. "What are you telling me this for?"

Sensing confrontation, she tried to say something to stop him flaring out of control:

"We needn't part as enemies. Lizzie is your daughter."

He laughed so suddenly and spontaneously that he seemed to surprise himself.

"Yes. She is. Mine. And you are my wife. Mine. Just like this stone is mine." He picked it up and looked at it. "It's mine. It belongs to me. I can do what I like with it. I can throw in the box with the others. I can bury it in the garden. I can put it here on the table. And it stays where I put it. Or I can do this with it!"

Without warning he hurled the stone in the general direction of Mary's head, missing her by a yard but making it hammer with a loud thud against the wall.

Now he was shrieking uncontrollably with laughter so that could hardly make out what he said:

"The whore and the Chartist!"

Mary made for the stairs.

"The whore is leaving me, her husband!" He was shouting so loudly that Jane and John must have been able to hear him.

"You can't leave me any more than that stone can jump up and run back to the cutting where I found it!"

As she climbed the stairs without haste Mary thought that if she had thrown the stone from a distance of six feet she wouldn't have missed the target. He hadn't dared to aim too accurately at her head, she was certain of that and felt no fear of him. But she acknowledged his power over her and feared for Lizzie so she dragged the cot across the tiny space between the two upstairs rooms, out of the bedroom all three shared into the room she used for her weaving. There was a bolt on the inside of the door but she didn't use it. An iron rod, part of the weaving frame, lay on the floor and she placed it near the chair where she would now spend the night. She was sure he wouldn't disturb her but if he did try to enter it might even be to harm the child and she wouldn't hesitate to crack his head with the iron bar. The fact that he knew that made her feel safe.

She could hear him moving about and then the door opened and slammed shut. He'd be going down to the public house to buy a jug of beer or to drink there so she could leave the sleeping Lizzie alone and get all the things she needed for the night. And when he returned he'd be barely conscious from tiredness and drink and so even less of a threat. But what he had said about his hold over her, that she belonged to him, she couldn't discard this as easily as she had overcome any fear she may have had. She needed to know where Will was so that she could leave as soon as possible. It was six days now. Or was it seven?

The next morning she waited until she heard him and John leave before going downstairs with Lizzie on her arm. All morning she waited. Before Will had left they had practised reading his handwriting together so that when the letter came there'd be no mistakes. But now it was at least seven days since he'd left and surely he must have sent some message.

After lunchtime John came home alone, which he sometimes did if things were going smoothly at all the sites. She tapped on the window and beckoned him in for a cup of tea. They chatted for a few minutes and then, as casually as she could, she asked.

"By the way, John, have you heard from William since he left?"

Sincere and ingenuous as he was himself, John seldom felt suspicion of others without good reason and he sensed nothing ulterior in Mary's question.

"Didn't Thomas tell you? Got a letter two or three days ago. Message in it for you and Thomas – I made him promise to pass it on. Didn't he do it? Must have slipped his mind. It's his drinking, isn't it? We heard him last night …"

"And what was the message, John?"

He pulled a sheet of paper from his pocket and scanned through it till he found the passage he was looking for.

"Here is the bit meant for you and Tom:

> And this is very important, dear brother, though it may seem just a polite formality to you. Please tell Mary and Thomas that my biggest regret about this enormous and sudden change to my plans is that I will never see either of them again. It is in the nature of the choice I have had to make that my contact with Nuneaton and everyone who lives there (except for you, dear brother and your wife) must be severed completely and finally, for all time. The life I have chosen to lead dictates this as a painful necessity. Please pass this message on etc.

He says it's too early for him to give any details but it looks as if he has landed …"

John rambled on in his guileless way but Mary had stopped listening as the shock hit her. She bowed her head, letting her hair hang in front of her face like a curtain to hide her expression from John. Struggling to suppress any sight or sound of anguish, she sought distraction in recalling Thomas' apparently senseless laughter from the evening before. Even that witless husband had been able to detect the irony in her absurdly misplaced belief in her own future. He had seemed to feed and thrive on it, she recalled. Alone and dependent on him, she gave him power. She reiterated the words John had read from the letter: *It is in the nature of the choice I have had to make.* Choice! What choice did she have now? The workhouse. Or she could prostitute herself and choose between gin and opium to finish her and Lizzie. Or she could stay with Thomas, let his violence and spite seep into their existence like the vile overflow from the cess pit that had contaminated their drinking water. She didn't know and couldn't imagine why Will had deserted her but one thing was clear: he had not chosen between life and death but between two good ways of life, and had opted for what was better for him. There was no life in any of the directions she could take.

Even John sensed that his presence was unwanted now and was about make his way home, still ignorant of the reason for Mary's sudden distraction, when he heard Lizzie crying upstairs. He shook Mary's arm gently.

"Can't you hear her, Mary my love? Mary? Are you ill, sister?"

Seeing her reassuring look, John left and Mary went wearily up the steep, narrow stairs, her mind locked into focus on this point in time when so many crucial memories seemed to intersect. The baby had heard her mother's steps and, after a short pause for intense listening, the crying became intermittent and less urgent. Suddenly enervated, Mary sat down on the top step of the stairs and blanked out even the sound of Lizzie's occasional complaints. While John had still been there she'd tried to maintain some kind of façade but this crumbled now and she confronted herself mercilessly with the impact of Will's message, which he hadn't even had the stomach to address to her directly. The need for discretion was no excuse. He could have sent a letter to John Astley for her. She covered her face with her hands but didn't cry. Even when her babies had died she hadn't done so. But then her life had been more barren. Her sorrow then had involved no loss of hope and that was what now etched into her like vitriol. If only she had never met Will at all, there wouldn't be this pain now. And she tried to force herself to say the words aloud. *I wish I had never set eyes on him!* But it wasn't true. For a few seconds she emerged from her thoughts and heard Lizzie now chuckling, and she called to her.

"One minute my love."

It was as if the child had suddenly remembered her right to be annoyed at being kept waiting and, after another pause for thought, she reverted to her fretful lamentations, which by now lacked any real commitment. Despite everything, Mary smiled. No, it was not a misfortune to have met Will. Meeting him had given her the willpower to think hard about her life, to benefit as much as possible from the experiences of the last year and a half. He had taught her to read and write. The journey to London, a catastrophe for him, had given her the chance to think and feel even more strongly than before Polly's death. And most of all she had Lizzie. She was not Will's child but she wouldn't have been born, not even conceived without his presence in Mary's life. It was simple. She had to think of her and Lizzie's future. This desertion was a terrible blow, far more painful than Henry's callous self-interest, and she knew she would agonise over it in many quiet moments to come. But now, if she subsided into self-pity and grief, she would lose the chance to make use of the good things the last year had contained. And there were many. The truth was that she had something to lose, still far more than she had ever had before the day when she and Will had met in the secluded, canal-side bower and when she had inwardly decided this idealistic young man would become her lover. With total clarity, she saw it would be a stupid, destructive mistake to submerge herself in blaming or even hating Will. However justified, that would harm more than help her and her daughter. She couldn't tell herself that her desire for a better life was at an end, terminated by an act of brutal, inexplicable heartlessness. That would be a lie. She now had the strength to do something to keep that desire alive.

She stood up at last, brushed the dust off her dress and went into the room where Lizzie was lying.

As soon as Lizzie saw her mother approaching, she stopped crying and began kicking with her tiny legs and waving her hands excitedly in the air above her face which broke into a big, gummy smile. Mary stooped to lift her.

"And what about you, my little one? If I stay here and just give in to the brute? Will you one day have to do the same?"

She looked down at the gurgling, happy, tiny girl, as she opened her dress to breast feed her. With her daughter at her bosom she went slowly down the stairs, at each step taking care not to jolt her. By the time she reached the kitchen she knew that she would resist, that she would not simply abandon herself and Lizzie to endure Thomas' dominance. It was strange, even now, after all his threats and acts of violence, she knew he was not a cruel man by nature. Not especially cruel. Was Will less callous? It was the power imbedded in them both, their freedom to choose, which they enjoyed, whether rich or poor, ignorant or educated, enlightened or dull, just by sheer dint of their manhood. His was not the power the Newdigates and the Buchanans, or even the Muscats had. Nonetheless, Thomas had his domain too, small in scope but where he was the undisputed master. All he possessed was within the confines of the cramped house but everything there, including herself and Lizzie, was his chattel.

Mary's contempt for his barking insistence on his rights didn't alter the fact that she knew it was just as he had said it was. She had known it before Haddon had cautioned her after she had thumped Thomas with the stone and made the law plain to her a year or so ago. But it was more than law. It was nature, the world. She thought of the evening she had struck him twice, once in panic and once with full intent to split his skull and spill the little brain he had onto the kitchen floor. That evening was also the first time she had really become aware of Will, seeing him looking up from the book in the light of the oil lamp. Later he had taught her to read properly and to write enough. The first thing she would do when Lizzie was old enough would be to teach her to read. She'd seen children's books in Astley's shop, mainly silly Christian texts with pictures of God's creation, cherubs and angels. But she would keep her daughter away from the clutches of the chapel somehow, despite Jane. Perhaps Johnnie Astley could order other books for her and Lizzie. She smiled when she thought of him, her oldest friend, since Lizzie had run away so many years before, her only friend. He had been so happy when Mary told him her daughter was to be called Lizzie that she thought he was going to cry. She looked down at her darling, contented daughter and, as she did so, caught sight of the stone Thomas had hurled across the room the night before, still lying there in the angle of the wall and the floor. The night he raped her she really had meant what she said and he knew it. Would it have been better to try for the second time to hammer the side of his head in with a stone? With a slight, grim smile, she acknowledged that Haddon wouldn't have been so sympathetic a second time. Without disturbing the child, Mary bent down and picked up the stone, feeling its shape and weight, then placed it carefully on the table.

*

17th May

John must have told Thomas that afternoon about his conversation with Mary because when he walked through the kitchen door that evening he had a self-satisfied grin on his face.

"Still here, wife? Not joined your Chartist lover yet?"

As usual she placed the gruel, bread and the jug on the table. He was unusually good-tempered. He didn't appear to be drunk and he didn't complain about the gruel. Within a few minutes he'd gulped his food down, taken a key off a hook next to the door and was outside rummaging in the ramshackle shed at the back of the yard. After half an hour so he emerged with a battered basket and a fishing rod.

"If you hear stones against the window in the night it won't be one your fancy men. So don't get up. It'll be Joseph Petty. We're off fishing. Burton Canal."

He moved towards the stairs.

"I'm off at three in the morning and we've got a long walk to the cut. So don't let the brat wake me."

Although it was a warm at 10 o'clock, Lizzie was sound asleep. Thomas was in bed so Mary made herself a cup of tea and sat down and thought. After an hour so, before she went upstairs, she went into the scullery and brought out a metal box hidden in the corner under some rags. The letter from Mary Burns was still pressed inside her only book, Jane Eyre. Relieved that it was still there, she packed the few other objects back into the box, trying to fend off the memories they provoked and then spread the letter out on the table. With Will's help, Mary had written to her friend at an address in Manchester to inform her about Lizzie's birth and good health.

The letter she now held had been dictated to Engels by his lover somewhere abroad and was the only letter Mary had ever received, though it had been addressed to Will to prevent Thomas knowing about it. The thought occurred to her that Thomas might suddenly appear so she went upstairs to the room where Lizzie was sleeping, a lighted candle in one hand and the letter in the other.

*

18th May

She dozed but didn't sleep and, in the early hours of the morning, did in fact hear something tapping sharply on the window where Thomas slept. Immediately he was up and, after some rustling and the sound of the shutters opening and closing, his door opened and he almost ran noisily downstairs. From the creaking, subdued banging and scraping noises she knew he must be in the scullery, trying as best he could in the darkness to grab the bread and cheese he had laid out ready the night before. She heard him cursing loudly and even thought of going down with a candle to speed up his departure but then she heard the house door open, slam and shortly afterwards muffled voices and footsteps in the street in front of the house.

So he was gone and wouldn't be back before early evening so that Mary had a whole, long day alone, to think, plan and prepare. The first thing she did was to take Lizzie gently in her arms and go the bed Thomas had vacated, where they both slept the few hours until the usual early morning sounds of animals, birds and people woke her. Not wanting to wake Lizzie, she washed herself in the kitchen with cold, fresh water she had pumped into the tall jug. She had already laid a fire and as soon as it was burning, she had a kettle-full of water heating up so that she could wash Lizzie in warm water. It was another fine day, already warm although the sun was still low in the clear, pale blue sky. She expected Thomas would return home before it got dark. He'd be hungry, probably in drink and his temper would depend on the success of the day's angling.

Before she heard Lizzie's intermittent but determined voice, half crying, half calling, she had everything ready, hot water, the bowl and a rough but clean towel. Calm but in a way also impatient, she could already envisage how most of the day would unravel and she welcomed it expectantly.

Carrying Lizzie with the help of a kind of improvised sling made from an old sheet, Mary went into town with Mrs Farnell, who held the somewhat heavier but more placid William in the same fashion. She bought bread, milk, vegetables and a small piece of cheap but fresh, unsalted beef at Astley's store, where Johnnie made the usual fuss of Lizzie. And she bought two-penny worth of arsenic from Illife's chemist's shop as mice and bugs were thriving in the fertility of Spring.

By the time she arrived home it was really hot. On one side of the yard, Barney Boy lay listlessly in the shade of the elderberry tree and on the other side Jane sat, scraping vegetables, on a chair placed just outside the kitchen in order to escape the heat of the stove she'd had to light for hot water and cooking. Of course, she saw Mary and Mrs Farnell arrive but acknowledged them with only a barely perceptible nod and a further contraction of her already pursed lips that she may have imagined was a smile.

By the time Mary heard Thomas' footsteps in the alley, she felt poised and composed despite what she believed lay before her. He threw his tackle into the shed, locked it, came into the kitchen, hanging up the key without a word. At a glance she recognised from the morose tension about him that the day had not gone well and that, though he had been drinking, he was still almost sober. He saw the unusually large amount of bread on the table, smelled the appetising gruel, lifting the lid of the pot to examine the contents, and sat down at the table, grunted something incomprehensible and poured himself a cup of water. He noticed the letter that lay in front of Mary.

"For me? Fetch Jane to read it."

"It's not for you. And I can read it myself."

"Since when can you read?"

"Will taught me. Does it matter now?"

"Oh, Will taught you? And what did you teach him in return? A few of a whore's tricks? The ones your Lizzie, sorry, Elisabeth taught you?"

He knew he could hurt her with these references to their former intimacy, when his body had almost constantly ached for hers and when, for the sake of peace, she'd oblige him indifferently. But she didn't retaliate and his attention returned to the letter.

"Is it from him?"

"Thomas. It's from a friend of mine. You don't know her. "

He had never doubted that she was cleverer than him. In fact he took a pleasure in it, sensing dimly that it enhanced his possession of something that was naturally his superior, like an exotic pet he kept captive and dependent. But those words "friend of mine" suggested the beast was out of its cage and that was a thought he couldn't bear. And she'd called him Thomas again. He looked at her blankly, groping mentally, trying to fathom what was going on.

"What are you saying, woman?"

"I want to leave, Thomas. Go away forever. Not to Will." She lifted the letter. "To a friend, a woman."

"Where?"

She paused, then told him:

"Manchester. It's north of here, more than a hundred miles."

"I know what Manchester is!"

Vaguely he knew there was a town called Manchester. The Irish navvies in his gang had relatives there and they'd even visit them, travelling the hundred odd miles in the third class carriages. They told him of streets full of cheap whores, mills bigger than the whole of Nuneaton and machines that made more noise than ten trains together. He began to grasp what she meant. She preferred a life in that earthly hell to her life with him. Plans to emigrate with Will, he would have understood that, although he'd have done anything to prevent it. Even he would have had to admit that her lover would be offering her a better life. But to drift to a place where life was harder, more vicious and even less secure than Nuneaton, just for the sake of being from him, that filled him instinctively with rage and disgust. She was reading aloud from the letter.

> *"If it should ever come to that, dear Mary, then you know there is always a home awaiting you here. We'll be back in Manchester soon and until then you can stay with my sister Lydia. We don't live in luxury, but there's a room for you and Lizzie and you'll find good work here too. Freddy's a decent man even if he is a German and a mill-owner himself! You'd have companionship and some help with the child, who we'd spoil with love. I just want to tell you our offer's there, my love. It's your choice."*

She stopped.

"Let me go Thomas. What good is it doing either of us to live like this? Hating each other. Give up your claims on me and on …" She paused because she knew that they had reached the real crux. "… and on Lizzie."

His response was exactly what Mary had expected. He began to laugh, compulsive, guffaws of laughter that regenerated convulsively as even his debilitated wits detected new aspects of the exigency Mary was in. She listened to the waves of crowing hilarity that rose and broke and diminished only to return as loud and raucous as before. She had drifted into the marriage, allowing him out of lack of will to use her body in the hope that at least a child, a healthy, surviving child, would result from it. And then, when she had at last found the strength and motivation to oppose him, he had raped her while she was hardly conscious and this violent act of malice had produced Lizzie, the child she had craved and now loved above all else. And now, it was the existence of the child that bound her to him. The child, that gave her reason to live, gave him the simple power to block the light out of her life. She waited until he had calmed down.

"Why not, Thomas?"

He stared at her as if she were the stupid one, as if searching for signs of light in her open eyes.

"Because she's mine! You're mine! This house is mine! Just like this stone. After what you've done with your Chartist lover, your adultery in my house, in our marriage bed, I could throw you out. Just like I could throw this stone away." He picked up the stone that was still lying on the table from the previous night. "It's mine, just like you and the brat. Why should I give it away? I'd be mad to." He mustered additional concentration. "You know I don't want John to know about you and … him. That's why I can't just throw you out."

He began to talk as if she weren't there, as if he'd learnt the words and was now reciting them at the right moment. He remembered the night when he had shoved her out of the door, mindlessly assuming he'd seen the last of her. But she'd smashed open a window, climbed back into the house, into his house, and made him look a fool in front of the woman. Even thinking about it wounded and confused him. He closed his eyes in an attempt to blot it out of his memory, trying to concentrate on what he wanted to say to her, what Jane had tried to drill into him.

"Jane has explained it to me. It's better John doesn't know. If I throw you out, he'll find out about your filthy past. So, it's like this." He looked at her, licking his lips in appreciation of his own fleeting importance. "You can go if you want. You can leave in the dress you're wearing now and take nothing else. That would be thieving. Everything in here belongs to me and if you take any of it, you're a thief. But the child stays."

"How could you look after her?"

But she knew the answer before he spoke it.

"Jane is her aunt. She can have her."

It was the final, definitive fact. Mary knew she was in a trap - she had been thinking about it all morning. *But the child stays.* He was determined and prepared and, above all, he had Jane's support. She knew already that the door was bolted and locked. But with these last four words, the key was thrown away. But losing any faint, last gleam of hope brought light, not darkness. Instead of collapsing into the former habitual dull resignation, her mind focussed on what she had decided to do.

She took a large, deep bowl to the pot on the stove and filled it with the stew. She placed the bowl on the table, pushed it in front of him, then, wiping her hands unnecessarily on her dress, took the few steps towards the stove. He noticed there was, as usual, no salt on the table, tried a spoonful of the gruel then, pulling a face, went into the scullery, banging his head on an upper shelf and cursing. He returned with the salt he'd found on one of the shelves and tipped it into the bowl.

As he sat down, he suddenly looked flushed and he began to sweat.

"Think I've caught a chill. Must have been that swim. I don't know if I can eat anything."

She spoke with her back turned towards him, but clearly and a little louder than she needed to.

"There are some salts. On the mantle piece." She paused before lying: "Lizzie's a bit off colour. I put them ready for her but you can take them. She seems better now."

It was as if she was listening to herself speak and was amazed how natural and genuine her voice sounded. He looked towards her, slightly surprised by her offer of help and almost expecting her to fetch the salts for him but then, seeing she was apparently ignoring him, stood up more slowly than before and brought the slip of paper back to the table, sliding the generous portion into his bowl. She heard the paper rustle and his heavy spoon clunk against the bowl as he stirred the thick gruel.

Mary filled a bowl for herself and with some effort began to eat. He saw this and snapped at her:

"You can eat it without salt?"

Without raising her head, Mary muttered:

"What choice have I got? You've finished the rest of it."

She ate slowly and when she finished he was slumped with his head and his arms sprawled across the table. The stone lay next to his head. It was still light outside, a beautiful mild, dulcet evening. She rinsed the bowls thoroughly under the pump and as she turned to go back into the house she caught a glimpse of Jane's silhouette against the kitchen window and remembered Thomas' words: *Jane can have her.*

"Over my dead body," Mary muttered under her breath as she entered the kitchen.

Still trying to avoid looking at him, she was conscious of trying to behave normally when she spoke.

"Why don't you go to bed? I want to tidy here and feed Lizzie."

He was snoring but woke up when Mary spoke to him. Standing up abruptly, he really did not look well. His face was quite red and there were small beads of sweat on his forehead. Nevertheless, he pulled on his jacket and left without a word for the pub.

Chapter 29

19*th May*. Mary had been so deeply asleep that at first she couldn't decide whether the noises that woke her were real or not, let alone who or what was making them. Lizzie was breathing deeply and regularly in her peaceful slumber and Barney Boy couldn't be responsible for the weird, unearthly groans as they were obviously coming from the street side of the house. Suddenly wide awake, she knew it must be Thomas and she charged into the room to see him convulsed in pain, his stomach arched upwards, his face bright red and soaked in sweat. Between the terrible moaning, wailing and sobbing, she could just hear him utter between clenched teeth:

"Doctor. Fetch doctor!"

Barefooted she hurried down the stairs, found their own kitchen door unlocked as usual and banged frantically on Jane and John's back door. Jane appeared with a covered candle.

"It's Thomas. He's in pain. Please fetch Doctor Prouse, quick!"

Without a word, Jane pulled on her shoes and was gone with the candle towards the doctor's home. By the time Mary had lit a few candles in the kitchen and upstairs, John had arrived. Soon after him several neighbours, Mrs Farnell and others, were there, some outside, others inside the kitchen. Only John and Mary were upstairs with Thomas, Mary trying to sit him up and holding him bent slightly forwards and John trying to give him water to drink. He swallowed some but most ran out as the spasms shook his body. The commotion had wakened Lizzie and when Mary had picked her up, stroking her soothingly and murmuring to her softly, the Doctor had arrived and sent both Mary and John out of the room and they sat in silence with the neighbours. Jane made tea then fetched some milk out of the scullery and warmed it up for Lizzie.

After about half an hour Dr Prouse came into the kitchen, took the tea Jane offered him and sat down next to Mary and Lizzie at the table.

"It looks bad, Mary. I've given him something to still the pain but I think there's little else I can do to help him. Did you notice anything this evening? Any symptoms?"

"I only saw him for about an hour. He'd been fishing all day. Said he'd gone for a swim to cool off and that the water was cold so he thought he'd caught a chill. He was red in the face and sweating when he went to the pub. I didn't hear him come home."

"Just what I thought. Inflammation of the stomach. It all fits – the heat, the cold, dirty water and then the alcohol."

He drank his tea, playing and chattering with Lizzie who was wide awake and enjoying the unusual level of activity and the attention of the numerous visitors.

"He should be quiet for most of the day. Give him this powder when he's in pain and try to get him to drink as much water as he can. All we can do now is hope for the best and that his constitution is strong enough for him to recover."

The day passed much the same as usual except that Mary was the only person who knew for certain Thomas was dying. In the salts he'd taken from the mantle piece and the salt from the scullery, there'd been enough arsenic to kill a horse. But he'd taken it. She hadn't given it to him. She hadn't poisoned him. When she had begun to mix a little poison with the salt she was hesitant and really had intended to lay it out in the scullery to kill vermin. Then she remembered Barnie, storming through the kitchen and the pantry, finally becoming a victim of his insatiable appetite, his stubborn nature and his nimbleness. She'd struggled with the pig but before she'd managed to get him out of the pantry, he'd upturned and devoured everything on the lowest shelf. She'd felt some guilt about the pig's death. After all, she had laid out the poison and if she'd been faster and had taken the escapade more seriously perhaps she could have closed the pantry door and saved Barney's life. In any case she was happy that Mrs Farnell didn't suspect what had happened to their beloved Grazer. But now it was a man's life that was slowly fading in the room upstairs. Her husband, the father of her daughter. Of course she'd thought about all this a dozen times after she received Will's message. She'd gone through every detail of how to ensure that he would take the poison. Thinking he might be too lazy to fetch the salt from the pantry himself and that he'd find it strange if she did it for him, she had the idea of dividing the poison, mixing some of it with the medicinal salts they took for almost every minor ailment. She'd perhaps talk him into taking them. He might find her concern for his health unusual but he'd hardly suspect her of wanting to poison him. To kill him. But in the end it was much easier than she had hoped. He had taken both doses with almost no encouragement from her. If he hadn't taken the salts, perhaps she would have put them into his gruel herself without him noticing. She had intended to but she didn't know if she would have done it. That would have been murder, wilful murder. She'd read about that in a copy of the Coventry Herald. As it was, arranging for him to poison himself hadn't been difficult. The hard part would come after he died, she knew that. The article she read had been about the law and justice, about guilt, detection and punishment. Justice had been described as a pair of scales, weighing the evidence to decide of the scales would tilt to the side of guilt or innocence. But Mary had thought for a long time about it and concluded that this might well be how the law worked, how the courts reached their decisions. But she would not even go to court. She would have to be her own judge and jury because only she would know how Thomas had really died. So it wasn't evidence that she placed in the scales, but people, lives - on one side Thomas and, on the other, herself and Lizzie. And then she considered guilt. Unlike Barnie, Thomas could have averted his inevitable death. All he had to do was to relinquish something that was of no value to him anyway, less valuable to him than the stones he collected. She had given him the chance to do that, pleaded and reasoned with him though she'd known all the time he wouldn't comply, that he would insist on his ownership of his wife and daughter. And he had the right to do that. That was the law. But was it just? Was it right? And, merely because it was the law, did she have to accept it? She knew what her life would be like if she accepted what Thomas offered her. Even in the dank, idiotic fog that suffused his brain, there was enough fetid light, enough guile for him to know that she would never agree to part from Lizzie. In the balance she was faced with, which he had confronted her with, should she ascribe to his survival more value than to the life she could, without him, live with her daughter? She knew that the law, religion, domineering men and submissive women provided an unequivocal answer. For her, there was no provision for escape or protection. It was Thomas with his stubborn, senseless refusal to let her and Lizzie go, who had forced her to find a way of to this dilemma. And now, the life seeping out of him, he was paying the price. She had made her decision and had removed the weight of his worth from her scales of justice. Mary knew that if she did nothing rash or stupid then Thomas would soon be relieved of his suffering, the doctor would certify death by natural causes and she would then be free to start a difficult but new life with Lizzie, and possibly one day with Will too.

The only possible stumbling block was the arsenic. Buying the poison demanded no explanation. Like most of her neighbours, she did so several times a year. But how would she explain, if required to do so, that there was none in the house even though, a few days before together with Mrs Farnell, she had purchased and signed for enough of the stuff to last several months? The only person who might notice the absence of arsenic was Jane, who was constantly meddling, cleaning, tidying and ferreting around the house, even while she tended her dying brother. But she didn't know when Mary had last bought the powder. Only Maria Farnell had been with her when she bought it, but she would never know that it had all been used within three days, so the information, as long as it remained divided, like two halves of a torn letter, between Maria and Jane, was harmless. But Mary wanted to eliminate any risk. If by some remote chance Jane found out that so much of the poison had been used in such a short time, she'd have to say she'd mixed it all with salt and placed in the pantry to kill bugs and mice. Jane knew that her sister-in-law's house was infested at the moment. Then Mary would go into the pantry and have to act surprised that the poisoned salt was gone. She'd say: *He must have taken it by mistake without her knowledge!* She had confidence now in her ability to lie. With luck she might not even have to say it herself; perhaps Jane would voice the suspicion for her. She had been lucky so far. Why shouldn't that continue? If all this happened before Thomas died she would tell Dr Prouse about him taking the poison by mistake, and the doctor would simply, when death did occur, certify an accidental death rather than death by natural causes. Perhaps he would even see no reason to complicate the matter and stand by his original diagnosis. Certainly he would never dream of questioning Thomas, who was already too far gone to give a coherent answer. Once the death certificate had been issued and Thomas was buried, then the danger would be over. Again, she realised how luck had been on her side when her husband took the poison himself and, even when it began to work, had not suspected any involvement on her part. When it was all over, and that would be very soon now, she would not be proud or triumphant about what she had done but she knew it would not cause her to feel any lasting guilt either. Many men had been legally hanged for less than what Thomas had done to her. He'd had thirty years of a hard life but he'd lived it as he wanted. And who knows, perhaps Thomas really was dying of an inflammation of the stomach that had been brought on his drinking and then bathing in the cold May water. It was quite possible that the arsenic had only accelerated his already inevitable and imminent death.

Her one fear now was that she would inadvertently reveal, by some chance indiscrete remark, that she knew with certainty that Thomas was about to die. That would be her undoing. And she feared Jane's alert malice most of all. Although she had almost managed to avoid any contact with Jane, who every hour or so came in to look at Thomas, she had no option but to speak with her when her sister-in-law sat herself down at the kitchen table and watched as she fed her child. Jane spoke first.

"He seems a bit better. Calmer at least. What did the doctor say about his chances?"

Jane had heard that as well as she had, but Mary still thought carefully before answering.

"It depends on how strong his body is, how healthy."

She hesitated, then added.

"It would be a good sign if he passed water. But he hasn't, has he?"

"He's soaked but that's sweat," Jane said.

Mary suddenly thought of the possibility that Thomas had vomited and despite her deliberate caution, she asked as casually as she could.

"Has he fetched up?"

She could have bitten off her tongue as Jane gave her a sudden, puzzled look.

"Fetched up? The doctor didn't mention vomiting, did he? What do you ask that for?"

Reluctant to say anything more, she was relieved when a noise from upstairs distracted Jane.

"Was that him? I'd better take a look."

As soon as Jane was on the stairs Mary called after her.

"I have to get some things from Astley's. Can you stay till I'm back?"

Intent on getting out before Jane could return and repeat the question she'd managed to avoid answering, she wiped Lizzie's cheerful face, settled her in the sling she already had around her upper body and was off. It had been stupid of her to ask about the vomit but she'd been dwelling on the remote possibility that someone might suspect Thomas had taken poison. She believed that arsenic might be clearly visible in vomit and really there was, as Jane's surprise had shown, no reason why she should ask such a question. This indiscretion, though without any consequence, served as a warning and she determined to be even more careful, to avoid any situations where it might happen again. Instead of going to Astley's store she walked to where she always went when she felt the need to calm down.

*

When they arrived at the paddock, the first time Mary had been there for half a year, they found it empty. The wooden sheds that served as stables in the far corner had been demolished and workmen were skimming off the topsoil and carting it away in barrows and horse-drawn wagons. One of the workmen told her where Caroline's new paddock was but it was too far for them to walk now, so Mary perched her daughter on the wooden fence and watched for a half an hour or so then made her way back home. As she turned the corner into Back Lane she reckoned she'd been out for three hours or more so Lizzie would be peckish – she had, as Mrs Farnell put it, a healthy appetite – and would need cleaning but they were both now in good spirits again. Mary had overcome any anxiety she had about her ill-advised question, and the prolonged closeness to her mother had made the child audibly contented. Mary hummed deeply as she walked towards the house because she knew her daughter, whose face she was stroking gently with the palm of her hand, enjoyed the mellow, soothing sound. The bond between them had never been closer or stronger and, despite how precarious everything seemed, she felt a profound, pleasant single-mindedness, an irrational but irrepressible optimism, which she hoped Jane wouldn't detect as it was dangerously similar to happiness. Tending to the baby gave her a good excuse both to prevent Jane noticing her mood and from continuing their conversation.

"I'll take a look at him when Lizzie's in bed and call you if I need to."

She spoke without facing her sister-in-law and as soon she was sure she was gone, out of sight and hearing, she lifted the chuckling Lizzie high in the air, then pressed her face tenderly against hers and whispered softly.

"Lizzie, my love, my darling. It'll soon be over. He'll be gone soon and then we can begin to live!"

*

20th May

It was almost a repetition of the previous night. In the early hours Mary was wakened by his screams, ran to Jane who fetched the doctor. He went upstairs alone and after ten minutes or so returned, the expression on his face revealing to the expectant looks from Mary, Jane, John and a few neighbours that Thomas was dead. The low voices hushed completely and no-one moved. Dawn had not yet broken so there was no sound from outside the house. He mumbled a few hardly audible words of comfort to Mary, who was nestling her wide-awake daughter in the crook of her arm, and then the total silence was only interrupted by Lizzie's inarticulate but unambiguous low chortles and gurgles. Jane glanced sternly at Mary, as if blaming her for the child's inappropriate glee at the moment of her father's death.

The doctor wrote something on a piece of paper and handed it to Mary.

"This is the death certificate Mary. Not the first one I've given you, is it? But look after it well."

Before Mary could take it, Jane asked:

"Can I see it?"

The doctor hesitated.

"He is, was my brother, Dr Prouse."

She looked quickly at the document and saw the words *natural* and *inflammation* of the stomach and handed it to her dead brother's widow. As she took the certificate, Mary glanced at Jane but detected no trace of suspicion.

For fear of disease, especially in the hot weather, Thomas was buried in the afternoon of the same day. Only the four of them, Mary, Lizzie, Jane and John, attended. After the short funeral, they were returning in the small fly they had borrowed. John talked to Mary over his shoulder as they made their way slowly towards Back Lane.

"We've been talking, Mary, me and Jane. About you and the child. What are you going to do now? Have you thought about it?"

It was uncomfortable for this sincere, sentimental man to be so direct towards Mary so soon after her husband's death but Jane had pressed him to speak to her without delay. He let the whip float over the horse's neck, the knot swinging to and fro, as if he were angling and searching for the best spot to drop his bait.

"It won't be easy for you will it? Thomas had money coming to him from me – wages and bonuses. And I always docked a bit of his wage and saved it for him, without him knowing. Jane's idea. So you'll have something to tide you over. And you know you can stay in the house for nothing. After all, we're flesh and blood. At least, Jane and Lizzie are."

His speech, though well prepared and thoroughly rehearsed inwardly, needed time to be delivered in its entirety. The two women, watching Lizzie on the floor of the fly lying on a blanket folded over the narrow strip of board between them, let him ramble on, though they both already knew exactly what he was trying to say. In fact, Jane had instructed him precisely about what needed to be said. Nevertheless he struggled to string the gist of it together while the two women sat opposite each other, implacably avoiding each other's gaze.

In her mind, Mary turned over that innocuous but staggering question: *"What are you going to do now?"* She realised with crystal clarity that for the first time in her life she was presented with choice, real choice. A man was asking her what she intended to do. It was not lost on Jane either, though she saw it differently. God had given us free will, not choice. We were free to decide to take the path of righteousness, to do the Will of God, or to take the path of sin and damnation. There was only one true path, that of duty and obedience, but in His mercy and wisdom He had ordained that we should take it of our own accord, otherwise there was no virtue. Mary lifted Lizzie and held her close to her breast. She interrupted John in mid-sentence.

"I want to do what's best for Lizzie, John. I want her life to be different to mine. Better than mine."

"Then give her to me!" was Jane's spontaneous thought. *"You will only infect her with your sin, drag her away from the one chance she has to find salvation."*

"John, are you going to tell Will about Thomas' death?" Mary asked as blandly as she could.

Jane's hands began to fidget compulsively. She needed something to hold, to squeeze and twist as if the hatred and scorn she felt for this brazen harlot were a liquid secreted from the palms of her hands and she needed something to wipe it away on. She picked up the blanket and folded it repeatedly, unaware of what she was doing. This woman's husband barely twelve hours dead, the soil not yet settled on his grave and she was enquiring after another man, lusting already after fornication. Mary didn't see John turn round as she sat with her back to him but she noticed Jane cast a short, rigid nod in his direction.

"Yes, it wouldn't be decent not to tell him. You remember how he insisted I passed his news on to Thomas? Must have been some bond between them. I never noticed. But then I don't notice these things at all. Just like Rocket here, blinkered and set on one course. But we get there, don't we Rocket old friend. We plod on but we get there!" He let the knot of the whip dangle affectionately against the back of Rocket's ear. "You like that old girl, don't you?" He remembered Mary's question. "Yes, I'll write today and with luck he'll have it tomorrow. A miracle, this Penny post. It's the railway makes it possible, of course. To think how many miles of that track I've laid myself. My gangs I mean. Thomas as well. Don't suppose many people think about that when they're speeding up and down between London and Manchester or sending off ..."

Jane coughed loudly, stopping John's rambling in midstream. He gave Rocket a gentle dab with the reins then asked.

"But you didn't say Mary. What you plan to do."

"First, I have to write a letter, too. And then, when I've got the reply, I can tell you."

She directed what she said at Jane.

The two women left John to take the fly away and behind the house they met Mrs Farnell sitting in the afternoon sun with William sleeping peacefully on her arm. All three went into Mary's kitchen with the babies, Jane making tea while Mary and Mrs Farnell chatted. Emerging from the scullery with a small jug of milk, Jane spoke into the air in front of her, as usual without looking at anybody in particular as she spoke.

"If folk have to many cockroaches and mice in the scullery, the least they can do is put down poison."

Mary and Mrs Farnell exchanged looks. Jane went on.

"If I knew where the arsenic is kept in this house, I'd do it myself now."

She picked up a bag of salt, which she intended to mix with a pinch of arsenic in the usual way of pest control, and looked at Mary, expecting her to say where the poison could be found. "Thank you Jane. But I don't have any in the house at the moment. I can fetch some. "

But before she'd finished Mrs Farnell interrupted her.

"None in the house, Mary my love? But 'twas only t'uther day that you bought two penny worth at the chemist's. I had to sign too, remember?"

It was well-intended and spoken without the slightest hint of reproach so that Mrs Farnell was surprised at Mary's speechlessness, who needed a moment before she could compose herself and give an flustered answer. She looked at her almost innocently sweet-tempered neighbour and it was her feelings of guilt about Barney's untimely death that robbed her of any composure. Hoping to end the discussion about the missing poison, she spoke in an off-hand way.

"I put it in a cup and I threw the cup out by mistake. It was all in it."

"Oh, I see."

There was a short silence and Mary felt relieved but then the Irish woman added thoughtfully:

"Mary, dear, I hope you didn't leave it anywhere our Barney Boy can get it. You know what a forager he is. A real Grazer if ever there was one!"

"No. I thought about that. So I buried it somewhere. No, Barney Boy won't be able to get at it, I'm sure of that."

Jane brought the two cups of tea over, set them unceremoniously on the table and turned to leave, speaking straight ahead, as if to the door.

"Well, I've got something important to attend to, so I'll have to be going. Good day, Mrs Farnell."

Mary was happy to see her sister-in-law leave. The questions about the arsenic had made her invent an answer in moments of panic but the danger was gone now. The Irish woman waited until she heard Jane opening the door of her house before she spoke.

"What's got into her? And what right has she got to be nosing round other folks' pantries? Don't let her interferin' busy-body ways be getting you down, Mary my love. You've enough on your plate to be thinking about already!"

*

21st May

John was right about the letter. Will opened it just after he'd finished breakfast the next day. His hotel was next to the main railway station and near the post office, which had perhaps accelerated the delivery by a few hours. He read the few lines of John's plain but clear hand-writing.

> *My dear brother, just a few words to tell you the sad news that our – mine and Jane's, that is – brother-in-law Thomas Ball died last night. He took ill in the night before last and although his wife Mary sent for the doctor at once and all possible was done for him, he was dead at about two this morning. The weather being unseasonably hot, we buried him today. The cause of death was stomach inflammation, brought on so Dr Prouse thought by bathing in cold water, in the Burton Canal, on a hot day then heavy drinking in the evening. It's not the first such case he's seen, he said. But that won't be much comfort to poor Thomas. As you recall, he leaves behind his widow, Mary, and daughter Lizzie. The Lord knows what will become of them now. With sincere affection from me and Jane, your loving brother John.*

He re-read the letter, dwelling on the word *Mary*. With the letter hanging in one hand he stood at the large window of the fourth-floor room and scanned as far as he could see. The dismal weather only allowed him a view of a few hundred yards across the station and along the south-bound tracks. Drizzle occluded everything beyond the great signal gantries that heralded the exit from the railway station. Somewhere, beyond that great bank of opaque, damp space, was Mary, perhaps hoping he would come to her. He could understand if she refused to share her life with him now, but at least he could ask and now, a widow, she was free to decide. Within the hour he had boarded the London-bound train and was heading towards Nuneaton.

At about the same time that Will was reading the letter, but in bright, warm weather, Constable Haddon knocked on Mary's back door and let himself in, peering at first cautiously inside the kitchen where Mary sat at the table, writing. He accepted the predictable offer of tea, glancing around the room while Mary filled a cup from the sooty, metal tea-pot.

"Strange thing to have on the kitchen table, Mary!"

He lifted the stone, admiring its smoothness and its nigh perfect shape.

"Thomas collects, collected them. He brought that home a few days ago."

"Wouldn't fancy a wallop round the bonce with that!"

Mary ignored the remark and Haddon at once regretted it. He took a long, appreciative slurp from the tea, his eyes peering over the rim at the letter Mary had started to write, then at the quill and ink pot.

"I thought John took care of all the formalities for you?"

"He did. This is a private letter."

"And you're writing it yourself, as well. Didn't know you had such a fine hand. In fact I didn't know you can write at all."

"I learned last year."

"Taught yourself to write, eh? Well done!"

"Somebody helped me."

"That who you're writing to? That somebody?"

"No. It's nobody you know, Constable."

He didn't pursue the matter but just added inconsequentially:

"The Penny Post, all over the country. Amazing what progress does." He slaked off another skimming of tea and gulped it down. "Some things never change though."

Mary was becoming impatient.

"Constable, I'll have to go upstairs and wash and dress Lizzie soon in a minute or two. If you just dropped by to pass the time of day ..."

"Well, that and to make sure you're alright, Mary. And just one other thing. Jane told me you'd buried some poison, arsenic I think she said, somewhere in the garden."

He saw her eyebrows rise.

"Oh, I just bumped into her by chance yesterday afternoon. Just come back from the funeral she said. And we were chatting you know about this and that. And then she mentioned it. Asked if it might be dangerous if it got into the water somehow. Don't remember where you buried it, I suppose?"

"Not exactly. Somewhere behind the yard. It was in a cup. I buried it deep. So Barney Boy can't get at it. If you think it's dangerous, I'll look for it and throw it in the river, a bit every day. That shouldn't do any harm."

"No need for that Mary. Safer where it is. You just look after Lizzie and forget all about it. Thanks for tea."

As Mary went to the stairs she had her back to Constable Haddon so that she couldn't see him remove the shed door key carefully from its hook and slip it into his pocket as he left the house into the yard.

As soon as she had washed, dressed and fed Lizzie, she laid her down on a doubled blanket on the kitchen floor, she re-read what she had written so far.

My dear Will,

It was a shock for me to hear you are not coming back. I don't know why and John does not know why. Perhaps you met someone you love more, someone who is more like you than I am. Perhaps she has no child so you needn't share her love. But I think the main reason is that, if you have met another woman, she has no husband. Or perhaps, away from me for a few days, your feelings have changed. But I can't really believe that. I just want to tell you now that Thomas, my husband, is dead. Perhaps you know already, John said he wanted to write to you. I can't pretend, especially to you, that I am sad about his death. For me and Lizzie, it means we can still have a new life, a real life. I still believe and hope we can share it with you. I was almost dead when I met you. Then I had Lizzie. These two things made me want to live again and now I have the chance. Mary Burns offered to let me live with her and Frederick and I think that would be good. But most of all, I would like a life with you as my husband and the father of my daughter. Please write to me and tell me if you now want this too. If not, I must make other plans.

She scored a line the best she could across the width of the page under the last line of what she'd written and then wrote under it.

Will, since I wrote what is above this line, something has happened. I can't tell you now if it is important or not. But do not come to Nuneaton again or write to me yet. I will write again soon. Please wait.

Mary

She underscored a few words with the scratchy quill, folded the paper into an envelope and sealed it. She wrote William Bacon on the envelope, but the address? She had no choice, she'd have to ask John for it when he came home that evening. By then she would think of an excuse for needing it or, if necessary, she'd have to tell him that she and Will had been lovers and that she wanted to write to him. He might be shocked at first but what did it matter? But now she had to get away from the house and try to find some quietude, calm down and think. As she was cuddling Lizzie, holding her close and lifting her into the sling she carried her in, she decided they'd go to see Caroline, in her new paddock. It was a long walk with the child to carry but she could rest on the way and being with Lizzie alone would distract her from her troubled thoughts. By the time she'd fed Lizzie and got everything ready, it was almost two o'clock but they could be back home before John returned. As always, Jane was watching her from behind the kitchen window as she walked the few steps to the entry between the houses. Instead of turning right into the Lane, which would have taken her past Jane's front window and then into town, she went to the left, towards the railway station. Glancing over her shoulder as she left the entry, she noticed her sister-in-law's face, half-hidden by the decent lace curtains, at the window of her front room. She felt the warmth of the child nestled in the sling at her breast, now fast asleep and Mary kissed her head lightly and within a few minutes had reached the town's fine new station. She intended to go into the station, over the footbridge which crossed the four tracks and straight out the other side into the narrow lane which would take her out of town towards the fields where Caroline was now stabled. A train had just pulled in and passengers were getting on and off it. She stood still for a minute or two, fearing that if she got too close to the massive engine it would wake the child when it pulled out of the station. Whistles blew, flags were waved, doors closed, opened and slammed closed again and finally, with a great burst of steam and a whooping hoot, it drew away, a high white plume of smoke rising vertically in the windless air like a gigantic feather. When it had receded into the distance, she made her way along the full length of the platform towards the bridge and just as she was about to ascend the steps, a station employee touched her elbow.

"Excuse me, madam, would you care to follow me?"

Puzzled but unconcerned she thought he'd mistaken her for a passenger and wanted to check her ticket or deal with some railway business, but rather than argue with him she followed him without a word through the door of the waiting room he held open for her. She turned in surprise as the door closed behind her, leaving her alone with someone whose face was hidden behind a broadsheet newspaper. Even before he lowered the paper, she had guessed it was Will and so she was looking straight into his face when their eyes met. It was at least half a minute before she spoke.

"You've been to the house?"

He shook his head.

"I saw you from the train, just before I got off. For a moment I even thought you wanted to get on, go to London. So I stayed on as long as I could, just in case. I asked the guard to catch up with you and bring you here."

She could hear the question in his voice and knew he wanted some sign from her, some indication of her reaction to his appearance, how she felt towards him but she waited and he continued.

"John wrote to me about Thomas. I got the letter this morning and caught the first train."

Unable to explain her silence, he began to suspect she was punishing him, refusing to speak in order to make him suffer, though that would have been unlike her. Unlike how she had been before he left. Perhaps his own letter and her husband's death had changed things and had changed her. He stood up and moved a few steps towards her.

"Mary, I'm sorry. The letter. I can explain. But things are different now. Aren't they?"

"We can't talk here Will."

She took the envelope with his name on it from the pocket of her dress.

"I wrote this to you. No, don't open it now. Take it with you and read it. I'd better go."

"But we don't have to hide now Mary. Now that Thomas is, is gone. We can be together. If you want to."

"We can't be seen together, Will. Not yet. In a few days but not now."

She could see that he wanted an answer, to know why he couldn't come back to Back Lane with her and let the world know they were together.

"We can meet tomorrow. Here. I'll come as soon as I can but you'll have to wait for me. I'll explain everything then."

His body relaxed and he resigned himself to agree.

"But you can't stay at Jane's tonight."

He thought for a moment.

"I've got friends near here. I can stay there."

He moved impulsively towards her, his arms slightly outstretched as if he intended to embrace her but she moved away and he stopped.

"I'll be here at about eleven."

"I don't know when I can be here, Will. But wait for me."

She left and closed the door behind her. Through the window, he watched her cross the footbridge without looking back. After waiting a few minutes, he left through the main exit and waited for one of the horse-drawn cabs to amble up to him. As the weather was so fine, he clambered up beside the driver who took him to Arbury Hall.

*

It was after 7 pm when she opened the unlocked door to the kitchen and was startled to see Constable Haddon sitting at the table. He stood up as soon as she entered.

"Sorry to give you a start, Mary."

They crossed as he made his way to the door and she into the kitchen.

"I've been talking to Jane. She tells me that things were not so good between you and Thomas. Jane says that young Will, John's brother, might be waiting for you somewhere. If he is don't go. I don't want you leaving this house and yard till one or two matters have been cleared up. One way or the other."

He paused before adding:

"You do understand me, don't you Mary?"

Her confusion was genuine as she asked.

"Clear up? What matters?"

But she received no direct answer.

"Just do as I say, Mary. Please."

He waited for her to nod her affirmation. Reaching into his jacket pocket he took out the key and hung it back in its place near the door.

"I've had to borrow a few of Thomas' tools from the shed, a pick and a shovel to be precise. We've dug over most of the garden while you were out. There's no cup buried out there Mary. Never was, was there? A couple of John's men did the digging. They'll be at it again tomorrow when we exhume Thomas' body. He'll be dug up and they'll examine his stomach. If they find arsenic, it'll look bad for you Mary. So heed my words. Don't leave this house or yard. For nothing nor nobody."

The last sentences were spoken with a sternness she had never heard from him in all the years she had known him. In a softer tone he said:

"I'll be round again tomorrow, Mary. We'll perhaps know by then. You know it's my duty, this exhumation. But I hope, I pray and hope it's all a waste of time."

*

22nd May

The next morning the body was disinterred and taken to Dr Prouse's surgery, who opened it up and removed a sample of the stomach. While the corpse was already being re-buried, he was already on his way to the University Clinic in Birmingham, accompanied by Constable Haddon, where he met the Professor of Chemistry and a leading forensic specialist, Prof. George Shaw. Dr Prouse removed the large jar with the stomach sample from his leather bag and within three hours he and Constable Haddon were returning to Nuneaton with the report jointly prepared by the doctor and the Professor, and also signed by Haddon as a witness.

It was early evening when the cab set them down near Trent Valley Station where Jane Bacon was waiting for them. The three spoke together in low voices for a few minutes, then Jane rushed off in the direction of Back Lane, almost running the few hundred yards from the station.

Apart from caring for Lizzie, Mary had hardly moved that day. She had neither seen nor spoken to anyone except Lizzie, who now lay fast asleep in her arms. She heard scurrying footsteps in the entry, light, short steps that she instantly recognised as Jane's. At once she understood. Jane had come to tell her the results of the post mortem.

Without hesitation Jane burst into the room, the low sun behind her so that Mary could hardly make out her face as she stood in the doorway. Only when Jane had closed the door and had turned to face her did Mary see the triumphant, smug smirk spread over her sister-in-law's face.

"You're done for Mary Ball! They've found arsenic in my brother's stomach."

Remote and detached as she was, Mary registered how animated, buoyant Jane was, speaking fervently and profusely as she had never heard her before.

"He'll be here soon, Constable Haddon. And you know what for. Now they've buried my brother again. But he won't be returning to God's house, will he? You saw to that. You sent him off before he could see the light and save his own soul."

Mary broke in. "What have you come here for? To gloat?"

"Give me the child!"

Impulsively, Mary shrank back in her chair, pulling Lizzie closer to her.

"Give her to me or do I have to drag her away from you?"

The two women stood on either side of the table, staring into each other's eyes. They both knew these moments were crucial and as Jane exuded confidence, Mary felt terror taking hold of her.

"What are you going to do? Take her with you? You know what Haddon will do with her? Where he'll take her. Let him do it! There are women in the workhouse who can wean her. Poor women, but whose milk is untainted by sin."

The jubilant scorn in Jane's voice, her feigned and mocking indifference to Lizzie's fate, crowed her supremacy and Mary's resistance succumbed to the acceptance of what they both knew was, for the moment at least, inevitable. If Haddon arrested her, Jane would have to take care of Lizzie. There was no immediate alternative.

Despite everything going on around her, Lizzie was fast asleep and, as Mary held her a little away from her breast to be able to look at her, Jane leaned across the table as if to take the child but Mary moved away.

"I'll bring her to you. When I'm ready."

Without a word, Jane made for the door and was gone and Mary withdrew into utter loneliness so that when Haddon arrived some time later, when the room was dark, she acknowledged his presence but her feelings didn't change. They sat at either side of the rough table, with only his notebook, a lighted candle and the stone between them.

"It wasn't murder, Constable."

"There'll be an inquest tomorrow. It'll be for the jury to decide if you're to be tried for murder. You've lied once already, Mary so you'll have a hard job getting anyone to believe you now."

"The pig, Barney. It came in here a few weeks ago and must have eaten the salt and arsenic. The next day it died. You must have heard about it."

Haddon nodded.

"Mrs Farnell was here. I thought she'd realise what had happened. I just said the first thing that came into my head. That's why I lied. To stop her thinking about it."

"If that were so, you might have stopped Mrs Farnell thinking. But you started Jane off."

"I was stupid."

"Either too stupid or too clever, Mary. If you ask me, the outcome will be the same whatever."

"But not murder. They can't accuse me of murder. What would happen to Lizzie? They can't hang me!"

"Mary, you know I should arrest you now. You might try to escape now you know about the post mortem. If you give me word you won't leave the house I won't arrest you till we have the result of the inquest. That'll be tomorrow or the day after. At least you can spend that time with the child. Do you promise me that?"

*

He had left satisfied that she would keep her promise but, before he went home for the night, he visited the station master, gave him a description of Mary, who, he said, if she did try to take a train would certainly be carrying a small child. In the unlikely event of an attempted escape, the railway man was to prevent her leaving the station and send for either himself or Constable Vernon at once. Flattered and proud of the policeman's confidence, he promised to pass the information on to his assistants and bade Haddon a good night. On the way from the station master's room to the exit, the policeman passed the waiting room and, although it was reserved for ladies, he noticed that a gentleman was still sitting in the corner trying to read a newspaper in the dim, unlighted room. His instincts almost prompted him to open the door and either inform the gentleman that he had actually no right to be in that room or to offer to have someone come and light the gas lamp. On reflection he decided to do neither. After all, no ladies were in the room and the man's presence there was a station master's business not a policeman's. And he had more important things on his mind than to worry about an unknown traveller's eyesight.

*

Half an hour after Haddon had left, John arrived and Mary called him in to the kitchen. Her secretive, almost conspiratorial manner made even the uncomplicated John uncomfortable. Of course he'd heard the rumours about Mary, about Haddon's suspicions, although, in a rare moment of authority, he'd forbidden Jane to utter a single word of it to him but he held steadfastly onto the good in people until there was absolutely no choice but to discard it. They sat across the table from each other, his weather-beaten hand laid comfortingly on her forearm.

"It's Will," she said. "He's at the station."

"What station?"

Apart from laying most of its tracks, John had helped build the town's pride and joy of a station so he hardly needed telling where it was but he didn't seem to comprehend anything Mary said.

"He's waiting for me there."

"Waiting for you? You're not going away, are you?"

"I wanted to talk to him, explain what's happened. Why we can't go away."

"You want to go away with Will? Is it all true, Mary?"

"Some of it's true, not all. But he's there now and expects me to meet him there. But I can't."

"You want me to watch out for the little one while you go?"

"John, no. I can't leave the house. I promised Constable Haddon."

She paused and gave him time to try to arrange all the information he was getting into an order that made some kind of sense, preferably a pleasant kind of sense.

"Things look bad for me, John. They think I murdered Thomas, poisoned him."

"But why would you do that, my love?"

"Oh, I had reason enough, John."

He looked at her and thought before he spoke again and by then he had forced himself to realise what had happened.

"But if Haddon finds Will there, he might think he's involved! He must be mad to come here now," John said.

"He came after he got your letter. He only knew Thomas was dead, not that I, not about my trouble," she explained.

She gripped his hefty forearm.

"Can you go to the station, John? Tell him to go away as soon as he can? If Haddon finds out he's here … "

"I just saw Haddon going there, to the station. I'd just settled Rocket down in his stable in the sidings and as I came out of the side exit, there was Haddon going in the main entrance! I didn't think anything of it then, but now …"

He stood up and hurried to the door where he stopped and turned to Mary.

"Jane saw me come down the street. If she asks about me tell her I forgot to do something in Rocket's stable."

To reach the station, he had to pass Constable Haddon's largish house on the corner of Back Lane and the Hinckley

Road and couldn't resist a glance through the bay window into the well-lit front room as he went by, though he couldn't make out anything other than vague movements inside. Once he had reached the platform he made a conscious effort to look casual and unconcerned. The last of the mainline trains had already left and so there were only one or two members of the staff, many of whom John knew personally from his work at and around the depot, still there.

"Evening, John! What brings you here?" He turned and recognised the assistant station master. He answered evasively. "Nothing important. Somebody I thought I might meet here. Nobody about is there?"

"Well, Constable Haddon was here about twenty minutes ago. Spoke with the station master. Police work. Very secret. Sorry can't tell you about it."

He pulled the skin under his right eye downwards in a cabalistic sign of conspiracy.

"But they've both gone now." He sighed to emphasise the responsibility he bore. "They've left me to see to things."

"Nobody else about?"

"Bloke or wench?"

"Man."

"There was a chap. Strange sort. Had been here on and off all day. Sitting around the waiting room mainly. I almost mentioned him to Constable Haddon but then thought better of it. Then when Haddon had left, the down train came in and this chap jumped on it like his life depended on it. You know, like getting that train saved his skin! Anyway could that be him? Must be up past Atherstone by now."

John tried not to reveal the enormous relief he felt and paused before he spoke, pretending to be considering his answer.

"No, chap I'm after is a navvy. Came in off the site with me and I forgot to tell him something. Thought he might still be here."

"A navvy? No this one was a bit of a toff. Well-dressed. Maybe something a bit dodgy about him but a gentleman in any case."

*

23rd May

Although the coroner's inquest only had the simple task of deciding on the cause of death, it was making unexpectedly slow progress. According to the law, the evidence was presented by experts but committal proceedings could only be opened after a decision by a jury, and what was normally a formality was proving to be frustrating for those, especially the coroner and the police, who had anticipated the inquest lasting minutes rather than hours. The stomach sample had been identified as that of Thomas Ball, late of Back Lane Nuneaton; the post mortem had been carried out by competent persons and in accordance with medical practice and legal requirements, as testified by the witness Constable Haddon, also of Back Lane, Nuneaton. And no-one disputed that the silvery black substance presented to the inquest was in fact arsenic and had been detected in Thomas Ball's stomach. As the coroner was about to declare this the cause of death, he was interrupted by a jury member, John Astley.

"Mr Jackson, Sir, may I ask a question before the proposal is put to the jury?"

"You may indeed, Mr Astley. In fact, it would have surprised me if you hadn't wanted to ask something. Please, go ahead?"

Without hesitation Astley said. "My question is directed to Dr Prouse."

The doctor, who had known John Astley for decades, was delighted to return to the seat next to Jackson's and was relishing John's interrogation.

"Doctor, what we see in front of us, in the jar, is this the complete stomach of the deceased person?"

There was good-natured laughter throughout the small room at the back of the Castle Inn, which was being used for the inquest. Most of those present had had a few glasses of beer, had eaten well at the expense of the town, a small recognition of their otherwise voluntary and unpaid services as jurymen, so, despite the seriousness of the occasion, the mood was relaxed and familiar. They all knew John Astley and were sure that this apparently silly question was simply leading to a more sensible one.

"No, of course not. It is a small sample taken for examination purposes."

Astley pointed towards the small glass tube containing the arsenic and asked:

"And was this substance, all of it, found in this sample of the stomach?"

Dr Prouse thought carefully and answered teasingly: "Well, yes." He looked around the room with a knowing expression. "But then again, no."

Amused chattering started amongst the jurymen but Astley continued in a serious manner: "Would you perhaps explain what you mean by this?"

The doctor eagerly seized the rare opportunity to demonstrate his knowledge of the latest forensic developments and paused to order his thoughts before he began his answer.

"Until recently, about twelve years ago, it was impossible to detect the presence of arsenic in the body of a deceased person. This, of course, coupled with the fact that arsenic is both odourless and tasteless, accounts for its popularity as a poison.

So popular in fact that arsenic, or rather arsenic trioxide, is known in France as the *inheritance powder*."

He paused and smiled, expecting some kind of acknowledgement of his ability to present expert knowledge in such an entertaining way but, although the jury members were clearly absorbed by his evidence, there was no sign they were aware of any humour in it. The doctor persisted:

"*Inheritance powder* because so many impatient heirs used it ..."

The coroner interrupted him.

"That is fascinating, Doctor Prouse, but we do need to reach a conclusion soon. Could you answer Mr Astley's question somewhat more succinctly?"

The doctor resumed in a more matter-of-fact tone:

"We used the Marsh Test on fluids removed from the deceased person's stomach. I don't suppose I need explain the details of this testing procedure ..." He looked questioningly at Jackson, who simply shook his head emphatically, so Dr Prouse concluded. "The test produced this substance," he indicated the tube containing the arsenic, "from the sample examined. As has already been established, it is arsenic and was responsible for Thomas Ball's untimely death."

Astley nodded, as if to confirm that this was the answer he had expected and then, when he was sure he had the attention of everyone present, he asked.

"Does the amount of arsenic we see here provide scientific proof that the poison was the only possible cause of Thomas Ball's death?"

Some of the jurymen nodded their approval of the question as it sounded very pointed, though they had no idea of the actual point it had.

"No, I doubt it. It may have caused some discomfort such as vomiting, loosening of the bowels, but would probably be an insufficient quantity to result in fatality."

One of the jurymen whispered to the man beside him.

"He means it weren't enough to do for him."

"Ooh! That's a turn up for the book!" replied the suitably impressed neighbour.

"It ain't of no matter," the man on the other side of him said, "it's only a sample."

Astley waited for the chattering to cease before he put the next question.

"Could it kill, let's say, a cockroach? Or a rat?"

"I'd think so, yes," replied the doctor.

"And one last question: could this amount of arsenic enter the stomach by accident, by normal, everyday means?"

Prouse had realised by now that this was not just one of Astley's self-indulgent demonstrations of his loquacity and powers of logic or even of his occasional desire to embarrass and annoy anyone in authority, so he answered carefully.

"What do you mean exactly by *normal everyday means*?"

"Well, for example. Arsenic is often mixed with salt to kill rats. Some is bound to remain left over and find its way into food. Especially in kitchens not remarkable for their standards of cleanliness. As a doctor, I'm sure you are aware of many other ways arsenic can enter the body without it deliberately being induced into the stomach by an external party."

"He means poisoning," the academically inclined juryman explained to his neighbour, who nodded sagaciously.

Dr Prouse was now anxious to answer without any ambiguity and stated.

"I emphasise that we are talking about the actual quantity we extracted from this small sample from the stomach, when I answer your question in the affirmative. Yes, it is possible to find this quantity of arsenic in the stomach of a person who has died from natural causes. But that would be in the whole of the stomach not just in let us say, one tenth of it which we have here as a sample."

"But it is possible, is it not, that by some chance, the arsenic in the sample constituted the total amount of the substance in the stomach altogether? And if that were the case, then poisoning would not be the cause of death!"

The coroner, Mr Jackson, knew Astley well enough to know that once he had the bit between his teeth there would be no chance of him voluntarily relenting in his argumentations. Now in his mid-thirties, John still spent much of his time in the family store but, unlike his father who had always been on the fringe of town life, he had found an identity and role in the communal culture that satisfied both himself and even those citizens who regarded him as their opponent. Whereas his aged father was still a Jacobin, a fiercely contentious disciple of William Godwin, resolutely committed, at least verbally, to the ideals of the French Revolution and the principles of philosophical anarchism, John had managed to integrate himself into the community's political life without abandoning his unswerving loyalty to simple values of social justice and as much democracy as possible. He served on committees, took part in public meetings, wrote letters and gave evidence at enquiries. And the miners, weavers, the growing number of casual labourers who took work wherever it was going as well as the women mill-workers and domestic servants tacitly acknowledged, without praise or reverence, that he was their unequivocal champion, in deed as well as in word. Like all local professional people, Jackson was well acquainted with John's skills in situations like the one now emerging and so he sought at once to head off any confrontation by interrupting the proceedings.

"Gentlemen, I suggest you take a short break while I confer with Dr Prouse, Constable Haddon and Mr Astley. Refreshments are available in the hotel. Expenses will be borne by the court, of course."

The other jurymen gladly made for the public bar of the hotel, leaving the court official to negotiate with Astley.

"John," Jackson began, "let's not argue. On the one hand, we know that you are theoretically right. Of course, what you are suggesting is conceivably possible. On the other hand, you know that it is extremely unlikely. We have here a fraction of the stomach mass – as Dr Prouse said, perhaps a tenth of the stomach's content at the time of death. But even just double the quantity of arsenic would be enough to cause an adult's death and would exceed the amount that could enter the body by what you called, what was it, *normal, everyday means*. Now I appeal to your common sense. Are you going to give us a chance to reach a verdict or are you going to obstruct what you know is a fair hearing? You know as well as I do that if we can't reach a decision then I'll send you all home and form a new jury. Without you."

John Astley had a deserved reputation for being resourceful, stubborn and compassionate. Jackson knew that, and he also knew that he was not irresponsible enough to simply sabotage what was essentially a correctly administered inquest. And so he was not surprised when John Astley made his proposal.

"I take your point, Andrew. My proposal is this: that Constable Haddon or his deputy travels today to the University in Birmingham and requests of the Professor of Chemistry a signed declaration that the amount of arsenic in the sample indicates, beyond any reasonable doubt, that a sufficient quantity of the substance was present in the rest of the stomach to have caused the death of Thomas Ball. And that this quantity would only be present if in fact the deceased had swallowed an unusually, fatally large portion of arsenic, either by mistake or by design." He glanced at his friend Dr Prouse and said: "What the experts call an *acute* dosage, I believe?" The doctor nodded with an affectionate smile and let Astley continue: "I know this will involve an adjournment, but only of a day and there'll be no need to form a new jury."

The Coroner looked at the faces of the other two men, Dr Prouse and Constable Haddon, who both gave their assent to the compromise, and said:

"Of course, John, our only duty today is to decide if death was caused unnaturally by the intake of an unusually large quantity of arsenic. How that poison got there will be a matter for the jury at the Assizes to decide."

Once the others had reassembled on the cramped seats, Jackson adjourned the hearing until twelve the next day, much to the satisfaction of the jurymen who relished another day's indulgence in the Castle Hotel's cold collation and ales at the town's expense.

Haddon and Astley, who had known each other for nearly thirty years, left together and as they walked towards the town centre, the policeman said.

"You had that up your sleeve all the time, John. You know Vernon will be back tomorrow with the declaration. What was the point?"

Astley sighed and for a moment the policeman thought he was going to cry.

"I've known Mary all my life. For years she was like a sister to me. Now it's not for me to judge her. And if she's guilty the law will take its course. But before that declaration arrives, you can't arrest her. At least, you don't have to. So I've done all I can for her. Given her one more day with her daughter, one more day of freedom. That's all I could do and all I wanted to do."

They shared a long silence before Haddon spoke again.

"I'm not proud of my part in all this either. When I think about it as a man, a neighbour, it seems such a waste. If Jane Bacon hadn't come to see me that day and hadn't told me her suspicions concerning Mary. All as part of her civic and Christian duty, of course. We both know Jane, don't we?"

Astley, the diarist, the town's chronicler, didn't speak for fear of interrupting the constable's train of thought which exposed a rare insight into the inner thoughts of this inscrutable, dedicated police officer.

"If she hadn't told me about the strife between Thomas and Mary, just how bad it was, and about the arsenic, we wouldn't have dug him up. And if we hadn't, who'd be the worst for it now? Certainly not little Lizzie. God knows what will become of her."

He stopped and took Astley by the elbow so that the two men stood still, facing each other.

"But that's my job, John. To enforce the law. And that's what I did. I made sure the law as it is was observed. Let's hope the court will see that justice is done."

Chapter 30

When she opened the kitchen door early that afternoon, she expected to see Constable Haddon standing there. Although she'd been thinking about it all morning, somehow she was still unprepared to go with him. Above all else, Lizzie was sitting in the middle of kitchen, playing with brightly coloured wooden bricks her uncle John had made for her. If it had been Haddon, what would she have done with the child? So, despite her scattered and despondent state of mind, she felt a spontaneous, intense relief when she saw Mrs Farnell standing there with William on her arm. Hearing Lizzie's sounds of glee and self-congratulation at her achievements with the bricks, he strained his sturdy, stolid little body in an attempt to look over Mary's shoulder and catch sight of his beloved playmate. The women noticed his impatience and Mrs Farnell placed him on his belly a couple of yards away from Lizzie but facing her. Without being asked, she sat herself at the table while Mary poured tea.

"I met John Astley in town. He told me the inquest has been put off till tomorrow. They couldn't agree on something or other."

Mary turned swiftly to face her and asked:

"How did he look? I mean, was he cheerful?"

The Irish woman understood exactly what Mary meant and it hurt her to tell the truth.

"No, Mary my love. He looked, well, shattered. His eyes were red. I think he'd been crying."

They both looked at the children. William, on his belly with his arms splayed out in front of him like a large reptile, raised his head and growled with pleasure at the sight of Lizzie, and seemed to sense ungrudgingly that she was mentally and physically more developed than himself. His large head bobbed up and down and he kicked his legs of behind him as if he were swimming against a strong current.

"I wonder what they'd be saying if they could talk now."

It was Mrs Farnell who spoke but Mary was thinking the same. And their train of thought followed the same track but that was too painful to articulate. What would happen to Lizzie after Haddon had fetched her mother tomorrow afternoon at the latest? Would the two children be separated? Would Mary ever see Lizzie again?

The little girl, who already sat upright, leaving her free to use her hands to play and explore, held one of the wooden cubes and stretched it out towards the boy, whose frantic efforts didn't budge him an inch forwards but did tire him out for a moment and his head lay on its side on the floor while he regained his strength. But Lizzie couldn't wait and, for the first time in her life, she let herself fall gently onto her side, then rolled onto her stomach and half crawled, half dragged herself the few feet to where William lay. She still had the brick in her hand and, in her over-generous efforts to give it to her friend, she pushed it against the top of his head and he began to cry more in shock than pain. Lizzie immediately began to cry too, flabbergasted that her well-meant exertions should result in her friend's tears. Despite everything, the two mothers laughed as they picked up their children and seated them on their laps, facing each other, and the crying stopped as suddenly as it had begun.

"Did you see that, William? You lie there on your belly like a lizard with no back legs while Lizzie here can romp about like a little lamb. You ought to be ashamed of yourself, you big bag of lard, you!"

Mary was grinning at her neighbours loving castigation of her own son and exaggerated praise for Mary's child, but then as the thoughts about the future forced themselves back into her mind, the low laughter turned gradually to deep, body-wrenching sobbing.

"Stay with me today, please, Maria. Please don't leave me alone."

"I will do that Mary, my love. I'll not leave you till we put the little ones to bed. Now dry your eyes and we'll have something to eat."

Tears were streaming down her own face as she spoke and she made no attempt to hide them, but was thankful she had control over her voice.

She stayed until it was almost dark and the two children could hardly keep their eyes open. After she'd put William to bed she returned to Mary and they lay, silent and motionless on the same bed till dawn broke. Neither of the women slept that night and the intensity of their emotions and their tiredness gave their thoughts, erratic, harrowing and compulsive as they were, an unreal but blinding clarity. As soon as she heard the street drowsily waking up, Mrs Farnell kissed Mary on the cheek and left. The night had seemed to last an eternity but now she felt as if it had only been an instant ago that she had kissed Lizzie and laid herself onto the bed still fully dressed. Somehow, it hadn't surprised her the previous night when her neighbour had walked into the bedroom without a word and lay down beside her. Suddenly realising she'd gone, she said aloud:

"Thank you!"

But by that time the other woman was in her own kitchen, trying to control her emotions as another day broke.

*

A single-minded calmness had settled over Mary, not liberating or even soothing, but oppressive and heavy. She had decided what she would do, a terrible but ultimate decision that preoccupied her as she washed and dressed herself in fresh clothes. She could hear Jane and John moving about next door and as soon as she was ready she went into their kitchen without knocking or even greeting them.

"Jane, I want you to take her. Now, while she is still asleep. Just as she is. You can fetch the other things when I'm gone."

She wanted to say: *Talk well of me. Tell her how I loved her. Try to explain what happened.* But she knew that would be a waste of time and she could sense the triumph swelling up in her sister-in-law, though she couldn't bear to look at her.

The two women went back to Mary's house and Jane made straight for the stairs and within less than a minute, as if afraid Mary might change her mind, she came downstairs with the sleeping child wrapped in the blanket. Mary kept her back to the other woman but made sure she could hear her.

"If I ever do come back, you must return her to me. Do you promise me that?"

Jane stood still for a few seconds before she spoke.

"I promise." And was gone.

Haddon delayed it as long as possible but when he heard that the child was with her aunt he arrested Mary for the wilful murder of her husband Thomas. A few neighbours were in the street, some distraught, others just very quiet: others, like Jane, watched from behind half-drawn curtains as the policeman climbed into the police carriage with his female prisoner, knocking the window to signal to the driver to set off as soon as possible. The roads were bone dry and hard and the two horses had soon left anybody who may have tried, out of curiosity, to follow the carriage behind them and out of sight.

"Mary, I've got the coach for the whole day. I have to take you to Coventry jail."

It was his last good act towards her, to secure her the privacy of the coach. He thought for a moment and then stuck his head out of the side window and spoke with the driver who increased the pace with a flick of the whip. They'd already turned left into Bond End and after another few hundred yards the coach edged its way carefully to the right, over the low bridge crossing the River Anker and into the Market Place where they negotiated a complicated left turn through the square crowded with pedestrians and horse-drawn vehicles, and finally into Coventry Street. Soon the road was flanked with fields on either side. Then came the houses of Chilvers Coton with its small, beautiful church and the cemetery where five of her children were buried. She thought of Maria and William as they passed the small, new Catholic Church, though neither had seen the inside of it since the boy's christening. Then they drove out of the town, on the turn-pike road with its smooth, macadamised surface. The rhythmical movement of the well-built carriage with its sprung suspension and large wheels, the regular sound of the horses' hooves and the warmth all mingled with her lack of sleep and she became drowsy, even occasionally falling asleep for brief moments. The coachman used the brake to steady the horses as they descended into Griff Hollows, then, after they'd crossed the canal at the bottom, there was the slow, strenuous haul up the other side, and the jolting and noises from the horses and the driver kept her wake. Once they'd reached the top on the other side of the deeps, he allowed the horses to walk at their own pace and rested them on a grass verge outside Griff House, a large house to their right. With Haddon she got out and walked a few yards while the horses grazed and drank from a stone trough built for the post coaches which had used this road and resting point before the railway had made them superfluous. She could see groups of small houses huddled together under the smoky, grimy air a few miles ahead. She knew that they were the mining villages on the outskirts of the next town, Bedworth, which was, apart from her visit to London with Will, the furthest she had ever been from home. Haddon had noticed that she was fighting against sleep and when they got back inside, he took a large blanket from under his seat and handed it to her and she used it as a cushion and support between her head and the side of the coach. Within seconds she was in a deep sleep and when she woke up they'd arrived at the jail in the centre of Coventry and the policeman was handing her into the custody of Governor Stanley.

*

Mr Stanley was a Benthamite, without undue charity or warmth but not gratuitously unkind and, like him, the prison was disciplined and hygienic, but without excess. Efficient, orderly and unambiguously well organised, the prison reflected Stanley's uncompromising adherence to the regulations and standards his civic masters had prescribed. Though a religious man, he carried out his work according to his secular, utilitarian principles. It was not his job to inflict additional punishment or to make judgements, so Mary was treated well and was left alone. Stone, iron and heavy, polished wood, all resilient, forbidding and impenetrable surfaces, surrounded her, though she was hardly conscious of them. Those who saw her mistook her morose silence for remorse, even penitence, or her numb detachment for indifference. They asked themselves how she was able to conceal, to subdue her feelings but for much of the time she had none. Her single thought was for Lizzie and that grief consumed her like the material darkness that filled her cell and smothered even the weakest light. Mostly she paced around the tiny cell, hearing nothing, not seeing, hardly aware of whether her eyes were open or closed. She ate the meagre food they brought her and drank the water. Twice a day she found herself in the bright light of the prison compound, not knowing how she got to be there, walked around the perimeter until without any apparent transitional time or space she was back in her cell. A stool, a bunk, a closet with a lid that shut tight, a large jug and a bowl furnished the space within the three rough brick walls and the iron grid that was the cell door. Neither she nor anyone else had lit the candle that stood on a tiny shelf next to the bunk since she arrived and so the light only varied from dark to pitch black as little light seeped in through the tiny high window in the back wall until at last night fell and all internal light was doused. If she had wanted to keep track of time, she could have counted the meals someone brought or the times she exercised in the prison yard or the daily emptying of the closet but the divisions of time failed to interest her, failed even to exist. There could only be one finite measure of time: when she would see Lizzie again and hold her, stroke her face, kiss her, talk to her, feed, clean and love her. There was no other time except that between the now and that reunion, like the vacuity between herself and the remote moon she could sometimes see framed in the barred, glassless opening high up one wall, time uninterrupted by division, space unmitigated by degree of distance.

But there was a disruption when she was visited by her lawyer. Two burly women, Stanley would not allow men near the female prisoners, carried and dragged a table and two chairs down the stairs, through the wide iron gates at one end into the area flanked by the cells on the three other sides. One of them shouted at Mary and, when she didn't respond, rattled a metal mug along the bars of the cell door.

"Ball! Come to your senses woman! Your lawyer's here!"

Mary didn't even know she had the right to a defence counsel until the flustered, red-faced man who sat across the table from her explained who he was.

"Dennistoun is my name. My partner, Mr Miller, will also be in court on the day of the trial. The nature of the charge brought against you requires that you are provided with legal representation."

"Nature of the charge? And I have no money here."

He paused.

"Well, not so much the charge as the possible punishment. The death penalty. And the Parish rates," he checked some papers, "in your case, Nuneaton, will meet my costs."

Mary looked around her and took stock of her surroundings for the first time since her arrival there. There was a jug of water and one glass as well as a pile of papers on the table between her and this plump man whose head was bowed over his documents, his nose almost touching the top sheet of paper as he peered at her over the top of his spectacles. Looking beyond the top of his head to the back and then to each side of the room, she saw the inmates of the other cells squatting on their stools as close to the cell doors as possible, relishing this rare moment of diversion. Sensing their attention fixed on her, Mary gradually became aware of herself and her mind began to focus. The first thing she noticed was that he had a large mole right in the middle of his bald pate just behind his forehead. He took a small box out of his leather bag, removing from it his writing utensils, a quill, several nibs and an ink pot sealed with a bit of rag stuffed into the small opening. He set them out meticulously on the table, licked a nib generously and fixed it to the quill and dipped it repeatedly in the ink. He then laid the quill on the table, lifted his head upright, half closed his right eye as a sign of his seriousness and began to prepare the case. Some of the women prisoners were standing, gripping the bars of the cell doors.

"Mrs Ball. I have here Constable Haddon's report, including your statement and his account of the events. I also have various witness statements that the Constable later collected. It is clear to both myself and my colleague Mr Miller that things do not look good for you! It's clear the prosecution will argue that you murdered your husband Thomas in order to be free to join your lover, a Mr ...," again he referred to his papers, "... a Mr William Bacon, whose whereabouts are at present unknown. At any rate unknown to me, the police and the prosecution. They will argue that your marriage was unhappy, that your husband was violent towards you, and that you often quarrelled. They have witnesses to support all these claims. Furthermore they contend that you wilfully poisoned him, your husband, to allow you to escape and live with the said Mr Bacon. For the alleged crime no eye-witnesses are offered and, without wishing to raise any unfounded hopes, much of the circumstantial evidence is based on hearsay. We have been unofficially informed that Justice John Taylor Coleridge will probably preside over the Assizes. If the prosecution manages to convince the jury that you did indeed wilfully cause your husband's death in order to continue an already adulterous relationship, then there is no judge in the land who would be less likely to show mercy than Justice Coleridge. It is therefore absolutely imperative that the jury believes you had a happy, at least tolerably so, marriage, that there was nothing immoral in your acquaintanceship with Mr Bacon and that you therefore had no reason to poison your husband. If the success of my efforts to establish this seems to be in serious doubt and the court tends to believe you were somehow implicated in your husband's untimely death, I shall change my plea from innocent of murder to guilty of manslaughter."

Mary thought for some time without speaking. The inmates waited in silence, some biting their fingernails, some with hands clenched in anticipation against their mouths; one or two feigned disinterest but nonetheless not budging an inch from the door.

"The truth is he beat me, as well he could. He tried to take me against my will. At least he did until I cracked his head and threatened to kill him if he touched me again. I wanted nothing more than just to leave him and live with my daughter, without him."

Some of the women moved restlessly around the confinement of their cells, their bodies somehow emanating the sympathy with Mary that their minds couldn't articulate. Others remained pressed hard against the iron bars, seeking eye contact with Mary. One of them cried out:

"It was almost the same with me, Mr Lawyer! Mine brought hags home with him. And when I said a word he knocked my teeth out and beat me till I could hardly breath for the pain in my ribs. And then he threw me out and now I'm here for thieving. God knows where my little ones are."

She stood up and also began pacing around the small space she had, wringing her hands together, pressing them against her face and then turned abruptly, spreading her arms out above her head and grasping the cell door.

"I wish I'd killed the swine!"

Another woman in the same row of cells called out.

"And he'd have deserved it!"

From the cells opposite another shouted.

"Why didn't you do him in then?"

"Because I didn't have the stomach for it!"

"Your bairns wouldn't be any the better for it if you had!"

"No worse off neither. And he'd be rotting in hell where he belongs!"

Suddenly almost every prisoner in the three rows of cells had something to yell or say or screech. Some just made noises indicating support or protest at what the haggard, toothless woman had said. Others banged with anything they could lay their hands on against the bars of their cage. The lawyer turned and gestured to the turnkey at the entrance to intervene and the burly woman left her seat, walked into the middle of the room and blew a piercingly loud whistle several times. The shouting subsided immediately but the tension remained, the inmates listened intently as Mary and Dennistoun continued. He looked at his notes to refresh his train of thought.

"You cracked his head, you say. You threatened to kill him. Not very encouraging information."

A murmur went around the room but dissipated instantly when the guard raised her head.

The lawyer continued:

"Can anybody bear witness to this?"

"Constable Haddon knows I hit him with the stone. So do Jane and John. But only Haddon knows why."

She related the two versions of her attack on Thomas in a few words, interrupted by hoots of laughter and obscene comments from the women. The guard didn't interfere, keeping her head down because she didn't want the lawyer to see the effect the infectious hilarity was having on her. The lawyer appeared to be slightly consoled by Mary's account, fiddled with his quill, then asked.

"And this gentleman, Bacon, William Bacon. Where is he now?"

Mary looked straight at the lawyer, thought for a few moments, then spoke into the stony silence.

"Gone."

Something in the women's collective re-arrangement of posture, voice and facial expression signalled instant apprehension and empathy for the stark significance of the word. Like a bell's low sonority, the word's resonance filled and hushed the whole space, settling on the women and imposing an awkward, reluctant silence on them. The female guard sensed it and her eyes skirted the room. Only Dennistoun seemed oblivious and went on with his questions.

"Just as well perhaps. If the prosecution knows where he is they might call him as a witness. Is there anyone, anyone at all who might swear say, under oath, that you had an adulterous affair with this Mr Bacon?"

"Jane. Thomas' sister. She knew about us. Or thought she did."

"So she could give important evidence. Evidence that would count against you?"

"But she wouldn't."

"How can you know that?"

"I know."

Dennistoun was at last beginning to get the measure of th iswomanandsoletitgo.Hewasnowleaningback in his chair, absent-mindedly waving the quill around in small circles with his right hand while the first finger of his left hand moved rapidly up and down between the tip of his nose and his upper lip. The women watched him and one or two began to imitate him, a vertical finger of the right hand drawing imaginary circles above their heads and their left hand flapping in exaggerated mimicry of the lawyer.

"Enough of that. Let's recount the events that led up to your husband's death. He was already ill when he came home, you maintain?"

The women's renewed concentration doused all sound like a heavy blanket spread over burning grass.

"It was hot and he'd been swimming to cool off. He looked poorly. His face was red and he was sweating."

"But the coroner found arsenic in his stomach. How did it get there? Did you administer it?"

"I put some mixed with salt on a shelf in the pantry. On slips of paper. I often did that. Everybody does it."

Some of the women nodded vigorously and others voiced confirmation.

"That was on the bottom shelf, for cockroaches and mice. The salt was on a higher shelf. He went to the pantry to get the salt. He took the wrong paper."

The lawyer leaned forward, his elbows now placed on the table and his chin resting in his cupped hands. A young woman prisoner placed her elbows on the horizontal strut across the cell door, bending over to prop her chin and sticking her bum up to caricature and ridicule the rotund lawyer, who didn't notice the sniggers.

"Now," he spoke as if he were about to spring something of great import and guile on Mary, "where was the food," checking his papers, "the stew, when he inserted the salt? In the pantry? Between the pantry and the table? On the table? Think carefully before you answer."

"On the table, you fool!" a woman shouted from one side.

"On the table," Mary answered quietly.

It may have been the onerous significance of the answer or the lawyer's realisation of the total irrelevance of his question that made him pause before he spoke again:

"Why did you lie? Why did you say you had thrown the arsenic away?"

"Am I to be hanged for lying?"

Though her words were meant for Dennistoun only, they created an immediate uproar. Shouting, metal mugs rattling against the bars, wooden plates thudding on the floor jolted the guard out of her seat, gesticulating and whistling.

"They won't hang you Mary!"

"Hanged for lying? Hang the priests first then!"

"And then the lawyers!"

After the commotion had died down he repeated the question.

Mary thought about Barney, how Patrick had loved him, how the Farnells talked constantly about the feast he would provide them and their friends with; her struggle with the cheerful raider of her pantry; the sight of young Patrick discovering the pig's corpse; Jane's look when Mrs Farnell had said that what killed him *must have been something he ate*; and then her own predicament when Jane pointed out that all the arsenic was gone. Of course she had had no real reason to lie at that moment. She could have just said nothing and let the moment's tension dissipate; except for this embarrassment that Mrs Farnell might guess the fact that Barney had devoured the salt and poison just as Thomas had done later. Would this plump, complacent man, already glancing slyly at his pocket watch to determine the proximity of lunch, would he understand or even take such an explanation seriously?

"I realised in that moment that Thomas must have taken the arsenic for salts and thought it might look bad for me. But I thought nothing of telling the lie. I didn't know that they'd dig him up. It was just panic."

The collective voice was undecided. Though many muttered acceptance of Mary's story, their support lacked conviction. And the doubt about the explanation for the lie leaked into their belief in her innocence, tainting it as damp rots fruit. Others were over-strident in their protestations of loyalty, outbidding each other's allegiance until it was unsustainably bloated and threatened to explode. Some, a few, remained silent, their heads close to the cell bars, their eyes fixed on Mary. The toothless woman spoke for those, quietly but with a steady tenacity that cut through the babble until everyone was listening.

"What difference does it make? What does it matter if she lied? Or why she lied? What does it matter if he took the poison by mistake or if she heaped it into the stew herself? He deserved to die and she deserves to live. Let her go! She's risked enough to be free. If we were more like her, we'd all be free!"

*

The meeting with the lawyer and the involvement of the other prisoners had a catalysing effect on Mary. As soon as he left, she became acutely aware of her surroundings, actively seeking as much contact as was allowed with the other inmates. Some were awaiting trial and others were imprisoned on short sentences for relatively minor crimes so that conditions, though strictly adhered to, were not too prohibitive. As there was not the remotest possibility or even the thought of escape, the guard was allowed to leave the cell doors unlocked for limited times during the day, which enabled those of the inmates who wanted to mingle with each other to do so. Many sought Mary's company during these brief periods but she became closest to the toothless wench, Hetty. As she had always regarded herself as completely uneducated and lacking in knowledge, a conviction that her relationship with Will had confirmed and strengthened in her own eyes, she was amazed how often she was asked for advice, even to write or read letters for the few illiterate inmates. It became a tacitly observed ritual that towards the end of the open spell, Mary would help Hetty wash herself. In these quiet intimate moments of trust and dependence, as the lukewarm water and the tiny piece of smuggled soap eased the pain of the sores and chaps on the inside of Hetty's legs, the older woman told Mary about her brutal life, which she expected to end in the jail. In these moments Mary felt she could help not only Hetty but other women like her. In these moments of sympathy, emotions and thoughts that were new to her turned her briefly away from her own grief. She had learnt so much about her life in the past months, and now the growing certainty that she was about to lose her life awakened a sense, though fleeting and vague, of regret and waste which didn't comprise only herself and Lizzie.

Chapter 31

Dennistoun was right about the judge. The nephew of the poet and father of the later Lord Chief Justice, Justice Coleridge had indeed been assigned to preside over the Warwick Assizes. During the winter and spring of 1848 - 49 he had been recuperating from illness in the family home at Ottery St. Mary in Devon so he had spent much time reading, corresponding with his closest friend, John Keble, and meditating on the political events of 1848 in which he had been deeply involved. He knew how close the land had been to anarchy. He had read the unrepentant look of hatred in the eyes of those he had sentenced to transportation, to imprisonment with hard labour and even a few, the ringleaders of the Bristol and Newport insurrections, to death. Guilt could be tempered, even mitigated and redeemed by penitence. And he was convinced of his ability to detect the tiniest seeds of remorse that might achieve redemption for even the worst sinner, and spare the repentant criminal the harshest punishment. Indeed, he had read the attestations of contrition the Newport rebels had submitted and had pleaded for and attained their pardon, commuting the mandatory death penalty to fifteen years penal servitude. He was not a vindictive man and his God was the God of the New Testament. But he knew that there were bonds that were absolute and eternal, that could not be broken and reset, boundaries that could not be revoked or redefined. The power of God was infinite or not at all. Diluted, it was glorified humanism but not divine. And this applied equally to the law. The law defined the perimeters of social existence and outside of it there was the godless wilderness, a frozen wasteland inhabited only by the damned. Mercy was reserved for those delinquents who had voluntarily returned to within the confines of obedience. Since his appointment as a High Court judge he could not recall pronouncing anything less than the maximum sentence for a crime unless leniency was justified by the precepts of Christian mercy.

*

Refreshed and invigorated by his time in the country home, the angular, sharp-featured but somehow frail, mild man, looked out of the train window as it hauled itself out of Euston Station. Even when he had pulled down the blinds, the summer sun was bright enough to allow him to read the book a bishop, a close friend of his had sent him. He read the inscription:

> *My dear Coleridge, not only our Saviour but also his adversary is moving amongst us and his works find many agents, some willing and corrupt, others simply gullible. Your intelligence, learning and faith will make it easy for you to uncover Satan in whatever guise he assumes in the pages of this volume.*

The name and title on the frontispiece meant nothing to him so, noticing only the book was already in its third edition though the date of first publication was given as 1847, he turned the pages conscientiously to the opening and read. Slight unrest at the tone of narration gave way, after a few paragraphs, to a mild disapproval, then a stern displeasure with the narrator's reading habits - a child reading a natural history book, sensual poetry and disreputable novels! By the time he had finished the short first chapter he knew he had something seditious, something heretical in his hands. At every level of authority the child at the centre of the story had rebelled and tried to create a place for herself incompatible with custom and order. Admiring in spite of himself the swift, unerring delineation of the recalcitrant girl's nature, he read on, convinced that punishment, enlightenment and penitence would follow. But even within the next few pages it became clear to him that the author intended that words like *resistance, mutiny, rebel, wickedness, insurrection* – words he himself had used to justify the sternest sentences the law allowed – were intended to evoke sympathy not condemnation, that the young Jane Eyre's ungovernable dissidence was to be perceived by the reader as a praiseworthy attempt *to achieve escape from unsupportable oppression*, almost verbatim the phrase one of the most extreme Newport revolutionaries had used to justify his violence.

By the time the guard knocked respectfully at his compartment door and informed him of the train's arrival in Coventry, he had finished the four hundred pages or so of the book and sat pondering its implications. His lucid, active mind, his vast knowledge of the Classics, the Law and the Bible, mild-mannered but tenaciously committed character focussed relentlessly on the novel. He resolved to write down his conclusions and send them to the Bishop who had sent him the volume to him and to his friend, the reverend John Keble, as soon as he arrived at his hotel.

*

On the same day Dennistoun visited Mary to confirm that the judge had arrived and that the trial would begin as planned in the County Hall on the following day, the 28th July. As usual they sat in the area enclosed by the cells. There was total silence apart from their voices and faint sounds from outside. Then some of the women began to cry, others tried to dismiss the gloom by shouting encouragement that no judge in the land would have the heart to sentence her to death, even if the jury found her guilty; she was innocent, why be so downhearted?

Before she re-entered her own cell Mary went to the bars where Hetty stood, her arms outstretched. They embraced as well as they could without speaking.

*

A plain, flat-fronted red brick building, the County Hall adjoined the jail so when the two guards had unshackled Mary they only needed to escort her a short distance from her cell into the court room. She took an involuntary step backwards as the heavy doors opened to reveal the scene inside. An atmosphere more like a crude theatre than the decent solemnity she had expected rocked her back on her heels. All the windows had been draped with heavy velvet curtains so that the only light came from the hall's oil lamps and some candles spectators had brought with them. A great wave of noise, shouting, laughter, cutlery and glasses chinking and clanging, washed over her as the doors closed behind her, attracting the attention of the spectators who packed the great hall. The raucous din gave way to an indistinct but still loud murmur and everyone present turned to look at her. On each side of the long room there were six tiers of benches. Between them, in the centre, tables with more benches, divided only by a narrow aisle like a church, had been set up to accommodate around two hundred people. About five yards away from the far end of the hall, an ornate, sturdy wooden barrier separated the mass of people from the actual court area. Mary and the two guards walked along the gangway to the barrier where a policeman allowed them through the narrow gate. In front of her was the raised platform from where the judge would preside. To her right the twelve men of the jury had already taken their seats. The rest of the space in front of the judge's desk was occupied by the lawyers' and the clerk of court's tables and chairs. After pausing slightly in front of the elevated stage where the judge would soon be seated, Mary took her seat in the dock on the right of the judge and opposite the jury, a guard on either side of her.

The noise level rose gradually until it was at least as loud as before Mary arrived but it dropped instantly to almost total silence when the door opened loudly and Justice Coleridge, in his heavy long black robes and flowing wig, carrying two heavy leather-bound volumes, walked with long even strides between the crammed tables towards his bench at the end of the room. The policeman held the gate open already for the judge who mounted the few steps and stood behind his chair, without hesitating or glancing to either side of him. Someone called out:

"The court shall rise!" and everyone stood up in stunned deference. Coleridge sat down, the cry was: "The court be seated!" and all took their places again with the feeling they had taken part in a brief, mystic ritual.

The clerk read out the charge of wilful murder and asked Mary to enter her plea. For the first time the judge looked at her as she spoke, faintly but clearly:

"Not guilty!"

A murmur of relief rippled over the room: a guilty plea would have shortened the trial to a few minutes and the spectators would have been deprived of their spectacle, like a boxing match where one fighter throws in the towel after only one round!

For the first time Coleridge took a good look at the defendant. He wondered if this poor, probably uneducated woman understood the seriousness of her situation. Nothing in her bland, flat voice or implacable facial expression suggested she did. Was it calmness, resignation, cold-blooded indifference or innocent confidence? The judge whispered something only audible to the clerk, who then passed the question on to Mary.

"Do you understand the nature of the charges brought against you?"

Mary looked down at him from the dock and seemed about to say something which she thought better of and simply replied in the same expressionless tone as before:

"Yes, I do. Of course I do."

When Mary was standing and the judge seated, their eyes were at the same level. He spoke again to the clerk.

"The defendant may be seated."

She seemed not to hear and remained standing. The clerk nodded to the two guards and they applied gentle pressure on each of her shoulders till she acquiesced and took her seat between them. Unnoticed by most of those present, Coleridge raised his head slightly, as if interested by this apparently insignificant incident. His gaze hardened and the two lawyers both knew he had seen Mary's apparent wish to remain standing as an affront, however slight and transient. Observing this, the prosecution counsel, Mellor, smiled wryly across at where Dennistoun sat, and raised his eyebrows slightly as if demanding an answer to an unspoken question. Mary's lawyer caught Mellor's innuendo but pursed his lips and looked straight ahead, though he also now knew for certain what one component of contest this was going to entail. Nevertheless, he intended to do his job as well he could and scoured the faces of the jurymen for some indication of potential sympathy. By the looks of them they were all prosperous tradesmen, probably clockmakers, owners of small weaving businesses, merchants and members of craft guilds. These men were not prone to take their duties lightly, neither privately nor here in the service of the Crown, and Dennistoun knew that any hopes Mary had rested on their independence of character.

Haddon had done his work well. There was unreserved respect in court for his thorough professionalism, the jurymen exchanging looks and nods of approval and even Coleridge found a few words of thanks for the clarity and relevance of his evidence. Before stepping down, the policeman looked across at Mary and then at the jury, as if considering an amendment to his statement but finally merely shook his head and returned to his seat.

The prosecution established and developed its case as Dennistoun had expected. By calling Joseph Petty and Thomas Watts, the men who had been fishing with Thomas, then the Dr Proust and the Professor of Chemistry, Shaw, the uncontested course of events as outlined by Haddon was confirmed. Then Mrs Farnell, Mary's next door neighbour took the oath in her rich Irish brogue. The good-humoured amusement quickly gave way to a tense attentiveness in the court, where by now dust and smoke hung in the narrow beams of sunlight which sliced through the narrow slits between the curtains.

She was being questioned about the visit to the shops she had made with Mary a few days before Thomas' death.

"And can you remember any particular item that the defendant purchased on that day?"

The struggle between loyalty and truth which tugged and pulled at the good woman, her eyes darting towards Mary then back to her interrogator, transfixed the spectators.

"She bought arsenic."

"Are you sure you recall this accurately?"

"Yes."

"How can you be so sure?"

"I signed the book. Mr Iliffe said …"

The judge raised his head inquisitively.

"Mr Iliffe is a chemist, your Honour," Mellor hastily interjected.

"… he said someone had to sign. That's the law. So I signed."

"How much arsenic did she purchase?"

"Two penn'th worth. I remember because Mr Iliffe said …"

She stopped in mid-sentence.

"Please go on, Mrs Farnell. What did Mr Iliffe say?"

"He said it was enough to *kill a horse* let alone a few bugs!"

A gasp whirled through the room. Mrs Farnell bit on her bottom lip and wanted to cry out that she didn't mean that Mary had done anything wrong but Mellor continued with his questions before the impact of her answer could dissipate.

"So on the 16th of May the defendant bought enough arsenic to kill a horse, as the expert chemist put it. Now think about the afternoon of the 19th of May. It may refresh your memory to recall that this was the afternoon on which the deceased, the defendant's former husband, was buried. For the first time, that is."

While some spectators only smirked, others laughed quietly but Coleridge scowled. He detested histrionics in court, even the hint of anything theatrical. Mellor regretted his quip and tried to lend his voice additional solemnity to compensate for his indiscretion.

"On this afternoon, after the funeral, you had a conversation with the defendant and her sister-in-law, Jane Bacon, the sister of the deceased. Is that true?"

"How did you know that? Constable Haddon never asked me about that!"

"Answer the question!"

"Yes, it's true."

"Was arsenic mentioned during this conversation? If so, what was said?"

The woman's discomfort increased the import of her evidence, weighing it even more heavily against the neighbour she felt so much affection and respect for.

"Jane wanted to put some down for the vermin but Mary said there was none in the house. She said …"

"So although she had bought arsenic two days before, a quantity sufficient to kill a large animal," he looked at the judge to make sure he had registered his strenuous avoidance of irony, "nonetheless there was, the day after Thomas Ball died of arsenic poisoning, none in the house! Is that what was said?"

As if in the hope it would somehow invalidate her answer, she restricted it to the mono-syllabic: "Yes."

But she achieved the opposite effect. The judge demonstratively made a note on a piece of paper in front of him; Dennistoun turned glumly to his partner, Miller, who had just joined him at their desk, and blew out a long loud sigh of resignation; the prosecution lawyer paused for a moment to let the moment freeze in time for as long as possible, then sat down without a further word; the crowd reacted so loudly that Coleridge banged with his gavel for order.

No-one had forgotten how Haddon's report had laid great stress on Mary's initial lie about the poison, so Dennistoun decided to say nothing. When his turn came, he would try to win credibility for Mary's second version of what happened, or at least to glean a seed of doubt to sow in the jury's mind, a reasonable doubt about Mary's guilt of wilful murder so that he could change the plea to manslaughter.

The densely smoky air in the room was now stiflingly hot so Coleridge, on the advice of the clerk, allowed a short adjournment in which the windows were flung wide open and the curtains drawn back to allow fresh air and bright sunlight to gush into the hall. The hall half-emptied as people rushed out to refill their jugs with beer or stretch their legs. The lawyers, clerks and journalists mingled in the area in front of Coleridge's platform, sipping water and conversed. Mary had followed every syllable of the trial and she realised what the outcome now depended on. The prosecution would now call witnesses to convince the jury she had had a lover and thus establish her motive for murder – to rid herself of the husband who stood in the way of her and Will.

Although some who gave testimony wanted to help Mary, all their evidence counted against her. No-one in Back Lane had liked Thomas, the sinewy, taciturn labourer whose raised voice could be heard in the street spitting out its hardly articulate but unmistakable threats, curses and accusations. Now they were forced to repeat on oath what they had heard but the more they emphasised Thomas' wayward cruelty and Mary's determined independence, the closer they edged the woman they really wanted to save towards condemnation.

Mary feared that Jane might after all give evidence but as far as she could see she was not even present in court. Mary had no illusions about her sister-in-law. She knew her absence could not be intended to protect her. She wondered briefly why she wasn't there at least to witness and savour her ordeal. Perhaps she feared that if she let Lizzie out of her sight then she might lose her, return to Back Lane to find the child had been taken away by Mary's family or someone else. But then, Sellina Ryland, a former neighbour, took the witness stand and Mary's attention returned to the trial. For some reason she sensed this woman's evidence might sway the jury. The prosecution began with his questions.

"You knew the defendant and the deceased, did you not?"

"I was their next-door neighbour till recently, till the Farnell family moved in. A good three years we were neighbours. And I knew Thomas Ball since we were children."

"What would you say: was theirs a happy marriage?"

"I wouldn't say happy. I wouldn't say bad either."

"Did you ever here them quarrel?"

"I heard them quarrel. Not often. But, well, when they quarrelled, they quarrelled, if you understand me right."

"Perhaps you can give us an example?"

"He called her a whore. Swore at her. Threw things. Threatened to beat her."

"And you say that's not bad?"

"But he didn't beat her. Well, at first he did. Then it stopped. Strange, really."

"Strange that a man doesn't beat his wife?"

"He was afraid of her, that's what I think. That's why it stopped. She told him she'd do him in."

"You heard the accused threaten to kill her husband?"

"No. He told me. Said she was unnatural."

"What did he mean by that? Unnatural?"

"She wouldn't let him have his way with her, his natural rights. Wouldn't give in to him."

"When was this? Think carefully before you answer."

He glanced at the judge to assure himself of his attention, then at the jury but there was no need for him to doubt their concentration.

"Well it was soon after the baby died. The one before Lizzie."

The judge murmured something to the prosecution.

"Lizzie is the name of the accused's daughter, My Lord. How old is this child?"

"Mary said she came a bit early. That was in January, this year. So she's about seven months."

"Born in January, conceived in April. Four months after the deceased told you that his wife, the accused, was denying him his marital rights!"

He turned away from Sellina, who was trying desperately to work out the consequences of what she had just said, and faced

362

first the judge, then the jury, though his words were ostensibly addressed to the witness.

"So quite clearly, this child cannot have been the natural child of the husband of the defendant of the man she had sworn before God to love, honour and obey."

He looked directly at Justice Coleridge.

"I ask myself, My Lord, how many other of God's sacred commandments this woman has wantonly broken!"

As the lawyer walked back to his seat, the judge turned to the jury.

"I will refer to this point in my summing up, but the gentlemen of the jury should note now that it is conjecture on the part of the prosecution and not an established fact that the child is illegitimate."

Before Sellina stepped down, Dennistoun signalled his wish to cross-examine her.

"Mrs Ryland, how long did you know the deceased?"

"Nigh on all my life, Sir. We lived in the same street till I got married."

"And you have often seen the child in question, Lizzie Ball?"

"Of course."

"Now, think carefully. Did you at any time doubt that Lizzie was indeed the natural daughter, of the deceased, Thomas Ball, husband of the accused?"

"Never, Sir, not for one minute."

"And that, despite the fact that he had told you, months prior to the child's conception, that intercourse did not take place between him and his wife?"

"Yes, I knew anyway it was Thomas'."

"And how did you know this?"

"Because she's the spitting image of him. Like a pea from the same pod. As sure as Barney Boy is a Stafford pig, that's how sure I am Lizzie is a Ball!"

Almost as if in conscious imitation of the prosecutor, Dennistoun turned to face Coleridge and the jury.

"And so we can conclude beyond reasonable doubt that marital intercourse did in fact take place between the defendant and the deceased: that reports of strife, violence and distress in their marriage are based on gossip and should not be accepted as evidence by this court."

Coleridge looked hard at Mary. Until now apparently listless, uninvolved, her expression was, surprisingly, not one of agreement with her counsel's crucial assertion. Instead of relief and welcome, concern creased her forehead and tightened her lips, her face signalling to the judge as clearly as words could that she resisted Dennistoun's benevolent description of her marriage. He raised his hand, the palm turned towards the lawyer, who listened intensely to the judge's words:

"Gentlemen of the jury. Please take note that what our learned friend here has so confidently affirmed is essential, indeed decisive to the verdict you will soon have to reach. If it is indeed true that the defendant and the deceased enjoyed, as the counsel says, a happy and intact marriage, then it follows that the defendant had no motive to commit the crime of which she is here accused. To justify this conclusion you will have to dismiss the statements we have heard from neighbours and acquaintances as hearsay, as gossip. That is the import of the evaluation you are obliged to make. Do you understand that?"

The jurymen, seated in three rows of four, consulted as best they could without leaving their benches. After a minute or so, the foreman stood up.

"Your honour, we would like to hear what the defendant has to say."

The noisy, communal mumble that filled the hall was punctured by short but clearly audible calls:

"Let her speak!"

"Give her a chance!"

Coleridge rapped his mallet for order and the noise subsided into an expectant silence. He peered over his spectacles at the two opposing lawyers.

"My learned friends, please approach the bench."

Constable Haddon had taken his seat at the front of the courtroom, with his back to almost everyone present. But he knew that somewhere behind him John Astley would be sitting too, tense and expectant but without much real hope that the judge would bend the law on trial procedures and allow Mary take the stand and give evidence. But he also knew that John would be wondering the same as he was: what would she say if she were allowed to speak? The policeman was right. At this moment, while Coleridge was lecturing the two lawyers, the shopkeeper closed his eyes and, in an effort of imagination, tried to imagine the cross-examination he was sure the judge would not allow:

Judge Coleridge: In the interests of justice and because our learned friends both assent, I am taking the unprecedented step of allowing the defendant to give evidence on her own behalf.

Prosecution: I have no questions, Your Honour.

Defence: Mary Ball, were you in anyway involved in the untimely death of your husband, Thomas Ball?

Mary: Yes.

Defence: Tell the court the nature and extent of this involvement.

Mary: I mixed salts with arsenic and he put them into his gruel, ate it and died a short time later of arsenic poisoning.

Defence: Did you administer the poison?

Mary: What do you mean, administer?

Defence: Did you place the poisoned mixture in the gruel?

Mary: No. He did that himself.

Defence: Did you know the salts would kill him if he took them?

Mary: Yes.

Defence: Did you try to stop him mixing the poison with his gruel?

Mary: No. I didn't see him do it. I had my back to him.

Defence: Would you have stopped him?

Mary: No.

Judge Coleridge: Order in court!

Defence: Why didn't you prevent the death of your husband?

Mary: My life, our life, mine and Lizzie's, were unbearable with him. It was no life.

Defence: Why didn't you leave him?

Mary: He wouldn't allow me take the child. If I had left him, I would have had to leave my daughter behind.

Defence: Do you know this or do you simply suppose it?

Mary: I know it. I asked him and he laughed at me. He said he would give the child, his child, to his sister to look after.

Defence: If he had let you go with the child, where you have gone to? To a lover?

Mary: To friends in another town. I once had a lover, a man I admired and trusted but now he has disappeared and I have no-one except Lizzie.

Defence: Did the deceased love the child?

Mary: No. I think he thought it was not his natural child. But he had no love for any of the other children either, the ones that died.

Defence: If he didn't care for you or the child, why didn't he let you go?

Mary: Because we belonged to him. Though we had no value for him, we were his and he didn't want to part with what was his by law.

Defence: Do you know what divorce is?

Mary: Why do you ask me that?

Defence: It's of no matter as you have no right to it anyway. Many women are in the same situation as you were but they don't cause their husbands to take poison and die. Why didn't you accept your life as it was?

Mary: I don't know. There's something inside me that makes me rebel. I believe I have only one life, here on earth. I wanted that life for me and my child. But it belonged to him. I wanted him to give it to me but he wouldn't. It was a life for a life. I took his away from him but only to get my own.

Defence: You said you took his life away from him. So you do admit it was murder?

Mary: No. It was a crime perhaps but it wasn't murder. He took the poison. He took it by mistake.

Judge Coleridge: I think we have heard enough.

Had they been observing him, those sitting next to Astley may have thought he was inebriated as he sat there with his eyes closed and a wide smile on his face. They would have been absolutely certain when, completing his fantasy, he raised his clenched fists in jubilation, smiling but at the same time tears were streaming down his cheeks as he imagined the outcome of the scene.

Judge Coleridge: Gentlemen of the jury, have you reached a verdict?

Foreman: Yes, Your Honour. We unanimously find the defendant not guilty of murder, but guilty of manslaughter.

Then the banging of Coleridge's gavel startled Astley and the lawyers had already taken their seats when he heard the judge pronounce:

"The request to hear the defendant is refused. The prosecution and the defence may now sum up their case."

Everything Coleridge's intuition and experience had divined about Mary was confirmed by the evidence he had heard. Bold, brazen, unrepentant, she had the same shameless disdain for Christian decency he had so often seen in the insurgents and rioters he dealt with in the year before. He thought of the book he had read on the train, the headstrong defiance of its *heroine*, who insisted on marriage not as a holy union as laid down by the scriptures but as a social convenience to allow her to fulfil her selfish and carnal ambitions. Despite his learning and fastidious adherence to law, his perception of what was happening in the court melted inexorably into a vision of evil. Neither secular law nor the will of God provided for the freedom Mary craved. It simply did not exist. She had transversed the boundaries ordained by God and thus chosen her own destruction.

After both lawyers had summed up, Coleridge again emphasised for the jury the points on which their decision would hinge.

"The prisoner's version is that she made up the mixture of arsenic and salt which the deceased then consumed, mistaking it for a portion of salt. The counsel for the defence would have us believe that this, if it constitutes a crime at all, is a matter of culpable negligence and therefore at most manslaughter. The prosecution maintains that, in order to escape from a marriage which barred her way to her life with her lover, she wilfully placed the mixture of arsenic and salt in her husband's gruel, thus causing his death. That would clearly be murder. The question therefore is whether or not the accused actually administered the fatal dose. That she did so, for that there is no proof. No-one who intends to poison someone does so in the presence of a third party. That is, in essence, on which you, members of the jury must decide."

No-one, not even Mary, left the courtroom while the jury adjourned. Outwardly so calm that many spectators assumed she was either resigned or indifferent to the verdict, she tried to form a pattern out of the turmoil of the last few hours. She had lied about the cup, a seemingly inconsequential lie at that moment but it had provoked the first suspicions against her. No-one she knew, except perhaps some of the women prisoners, would deny she had done wrong. But it wasn't murder. She had done nothing to warrant death. Even the Law that blocked her every avenue to a life away from Thomas while he was alive, surely even such a Law would not condemn her now to execution, now that he was dead and the way was open to something better. Punishment, prison, a postponement of her freedom, even prolonged separation from her child – all that she could accept. She clasped her hands and closed her eyes but she wasn't praying. Her mute, impassioned plea for mercy was intended for the twelve men who were at that moment deciding on her fate. And so she wavered between a faint hope of survival and the dreadful, vivid prospect of the gallows.

After two hours they all returned and the judge spoke.

"Have you reached a decision?"

"We have, My Lord. We find the defendant guilty but we enter a plea for mercy."

He waited for the commotion to subside.

Coleridge looked at Mary who still sat with no sign of emotion, with an unnatural calmness about her. He knew she was guilty. There were no gestures, not even words to convey it but he recognised the flagrant defiance, the unbending refusal to subjugate her own will to that of the dictates of law, even to the Will of God. He had seen it in the grim, solemn recalcitrance of the ring-leaders of the Newport Uprising and of the most social conflicts of the thirties. And now he sensed it as distinctly as if evil had its own smell. But she had somehow deceived the decent gentlemen of the jury. Their gullibility was about to be the cause of the greatest of misdemeanours, to pervert not just the course of justice but the will of God. He could not let this happen without making the jury fully aware of their obligations to the law.

"What exactly are the grounds for this plea?"

The foreman's eyes were lowered as he spoke.

"We have, Your Honour, doubts about some of the evidence."

"Do you suspect any of the witnesses of lying under oath?"

"No, Your Honour. But much of their evidence could be mere gossip."

"Then if you have doubts, you must resolve these doubts and reach a clear verdict. You have consulted now for more than two hours. If you still have doubts about the defendant's guilt, then you must retire and reconsider until you reach a clear verdict."

The foreman felt the weight of the pressure on him, stifling him like a heavy blanket and in a moment of panic tried to discard it.

"But we plead for mercy, Your Honour!"

Coleridge allowed himself a long pause and spoke slowly.

"Gentlemen of the jury. The verdict is for you to decide. It is my duty to pronounce the sentence. If the defendant is guilty then the law allows only one possible punishment."

The jury members grouped themselves as closely as possible for a short discussion and then the foreman stood up:

"We find the defendant guilty of wilful murder!"

Amid the steady crescendo of shouting, screaming, crying and even some cheering, Justice Coleridge reached into the drawer again where the black cap lay like a sleeping cat. The din stopped instantly when people saw him place it on his head and turned towards Mary who only registered the final sentences of the verdict:

"… for the murder of the man whom you had sworn before God Almighty to love, honour and obey, and who stood in the way of your adulterous passion for another. In doing so you have not only committed a heinous crime but have also grievously offended the Saviour who died for our sins. Therefore you cannot expect mercy, neither in this life nor in the eternity thereafter. Mary Ball, you shall betaken to a convenient place and hanged by the neck until you are dead. Afterwards your body shall be buried in an unmarked grave in the grounds of the jail."

Although expected, the finality and merciless clarity of the sentence shocked the spectators, and, in the few silent moments that followed, many fixed their eyes on Mary, who showed no sign of emotion. Only one man hurried clumsily out of the hall before the din started again, as if trying to escape the reality of the scene he had witnessed.

Chapter 32

John Astley had followed every minute of the trial, his head resting for most of the time in his cupped hands, his elbows pressed down onto the rough table before him. His eyes, slightly squinted for concentration, were fixed either on Mary or Justice Coleridge whose words, gestures and facial expressions he had noted mentally. Moving only occasionally to waft away the billows of cigar and pipe smoke or to reject the waiters' offers of food and drink, he was inconspicuous and unnoticed even by those present who might have recognised him. When the jury had returned to give their verdict he had covered his face with his hands, pulling them away in a moment of gnarled hope when the foreman expressed the doubts about Mary's guilt. But he knew the plea for mercy would make no impact on Coleridge' adamance. The simple humanity of the jury, vaguely seeking a way to use their intuitive compassion for this young mother to move the massive, unyielding obduracy of the law, reminded Astley of his feelings about the great demonstration: The banners, the broadsheets, the speeches, the resolutions, the cheering and even the Petition, all this fluttering and foraging against the organised, armed resilience of the State, like a whirling mass of butterflies touching daintily against thick glass, fatuously imagining their wings' flimsy impact might shatter it.

"Why don't you do it?" he thought to himself, as the foreman stood up to read the verdict. "Find her Not Guilty!

Tell him she doesn't deserve to die. You have more power than this judge. There are twelve of you. You have the power to decide between guilt and innocence."

But he felt no conviction in his mute exhortations. It was as if he had incited the militia and the army, a year before in London, to turn their weapons on their masters.

He left the courtroom as soon as the general uproar, cheering and booing had started, mainly because of his revulsion at the proceedings and also to avoid the remote possibility of making eye-contact with Mary while she was being led out, shackled and handcuffed, down the central aisle towards the exit at the rear of the hall. He was out and making for the nearby row of cabs before hardly anyone else had left. The excitement, even some of the smoke and the inebriation, seemed to have seeped out of the hall into the narrow streets together with the news of the death sentence and they combined into some brew that intoxicated the masses outside. As if trying to shield himself from this invasive, infectious hysteria, he hunched his shoulders and scurried away from the din. The brief walk helped him relax a little and begin to try to order his thoughts. She had been found guilty. One of the most powerful and revered judges in the land had unequivocally pronounced the death sentence. He had resigned himself to the trial's almost inevitable outcome weeks before and he tried to avoid becoming obsessed again with its brutal finality. This would only incense him, paralyse him with grief.

Without really being aware of the intervening minutes, he suddenly found himself seated in the corner of a cab which was already moving through the crowds on the street. Slowly regaining his consciousness of his surroundings he glanced up but hardly noticed a heavily bearded man in the opposite corner. Their eyes made contact for a brief moment, nods were exchanged and Astley subsided back into his reveries. After a few seconds he realised that the man had not averted his eyes and he returned the look, this time recognising Will Bacon instantly, despite the heavy disguise. Astley's nimble mind collated and organised all the information in a flash and only asked:

"Were you in court when they called your name?"

Will closed his eyes and shook his head slightly in negation.

"I wanted to be as near as possible without going inside. I wanted to know at once."

"I would have written to you anyway."

"Even a day would have been too long to wait."

The two men who felt most love for Mary sat for minutes, sharing the same thoughts in silence. Finally Will spoke.

"There is one thing that we, you ..." He hesitated. "One thing that can be done."

For moment Astley imagined Will was going to say something wildly optimistic or, even worse, some fatuity about repentance, confession, absolution.

"A petition for a pardon."

Astley knew about this and he felt suddenly baffled that he hadn't considered it himself when he heard the jury wavering. Many years before, he recalled, a young Nuneaton woman had left her illegitimate baby to die in the local woods. A Royal Pardon had been granted and arrived on the day of the planned execution.

"What grounds could be given?"

"You were present throughout the trial, John. Was there anything mitigating? Anything to alleviate what she did?"

The use of his own name and the avoidance of Mary's struck Astley like a slap in the face and Will seemed to understand his startled look and admitted:

"I can't bear to say her name. Is that cowardice?"

Astley wanted to return the question: *"Why didn't you take the stand, give evidence?"* but he knew instinctively it would only waste the little time they had and divert them from the slim chance of saving Mary's life. Instead he replied factually:

"The jury asked for mercy. They said they had problems with some evidence. Probably the way things were between Mary and Thomas. But without strife in the marriage Mary would have had no motive. It was touch and go. The right word at the right time might have saved her. Like poisoning, adultery is seldom committed in front of witnesses."

He paused and let the remark sink home, watching Will wince slightly. It was vindictive and served no purpose, he knew that, but felt no remorse for it. The younger man came over and sat directly opposite him and he added:

"But Coleridge was having none of it. He demanded and got a clear verdict. Guilty of wilful murder."

Will heard the bitterness in his companion's voice and, by way of comfort not contradiction, pointed out:

"But that's mandatory, John. It's not in the power of the judge ..."

He was taken aback by the vehemence of Astley's immediate interruption.

"I know the law. But I also know those who administer it. You wouldn't know Polly Buttons, would you? Before you came here, fifteen years ago, she was murdered. And I was at the trial. I can hear the judge now as he instructed the jury: *If there arises any reasonable doubt in your minds as to the guilt of the defendant, then you are duty-bound to reach a verdict of Not Guilty.* That's what Coleridge should have said."

There was a long silence until Will spoke again.

"What about ... the child? Was she mentioned?"

"Lizzie. In the evidence, yes. There was some confusion about Lizzie's paternity."

Enough was enough, Astley suddenly thought, and this was serving no purpose. He was even about to apologise to Will, who was here at some risk. He might have been arrested and become implicated if Haddon had caught sight of him. Will's crude disguise wouldn't have got past the Constable. Before he could speak, Will did:

"If she, if Mary ..." he looked at his good friend as he spoke the name as if offering some kind of truce and his glance was answered with a slight nod, "... if Mary were to be executed, then Lizzie will be, would be an orphan. Surely that would be to punish an innocent child for the mother's crime. In the court's eyes I mean of course. That's an argument for a pardon surely."

Astley repeated it.

"For a pardon!"

They drank in the idea and it was like alcohol on an empty stomach. The intoxication was instantaneous. As if they had been searching for the way out of a locked room then a door had swung open without effort and of its own accord. It seemed so obvious and convincing that they hugged each other, laughing a hysterical, dizzy mixture of delight, pain and fear. As Astley threw himself backwards onto his own seat again he found Will's beard entwined around the buttons of his coat and held it up like a dead squirrel. The two men, one about to be elected as a Member of Parliament in a Manchester bye election, the other a respected local tradesman, exploded gleefully, caught up in a giddy spiral of giggles and snorts as they tried to regain their composure.

For some reason the cab had stopped and Astley moved back the drawn curtain of the coach window and looked out onto the centre of the small, bleak mining town which lay almost mid-way between Coventry and Nuneaton. He knew the place well, All Saints' Square, flanked on three sides by dismal rows of public houses and beer shops. The desolation outside, despite the still bright sunlight, had an icily sobering effect on his mood.

"God, will things never change for the better here?"

Will, surprised by his companion's sudden, unaccountably pessimistic tone, followed his line of vision and chuckled at what he saw; groups of men and a few women, some rowdy, some sullen, but all apparently the worse for drink.

"Look out of the other window, my friend. Isn't that your answer?"

He leaned over and drew back the curtain on the other side of the cab. Of course Astley knew, as he turned his head to the right, what would come into view: the magnificent Almshouses, a mock-Elizabethan building, hardly ten years old. He looked beyond the wrought iron railings, over the landscaped quadrangle with its pump house, at the red-brick façade with its dark roof and high chimney stacks. On either side, an equally long wing stretched towards the road where the coach was still stationary. Uniformed elderly inmates sat sunning themselves on the benches set alongside the parched lawn or pottered around the ample flower beds. The sight calmed him but, as the coach moved off slowly, his innate scepticism had taken hold and he assumed the role of devil's advocate.

"But is the case really strong? Mothers have been hanged before."

"You saw that monument to charity we just passed, John. Times are changing. Slowly perhaps. Far more slowly than I once dreamed. But compassion is sometimes stronger than retribution."

The conversation moved as hesitantly as the coach and they were passing, at a quicker pace, through in the small mining village of Collycroft before Astley spoke again.

"But we argue that the child's future, her life even will be at risk if she is orphaned. Is this really so?"

Neither of them liked Jane but both knew she had always coveted the child and she would provide a secure if loveless home. Astley broached the objection but he'd hardly spoken when Will interrupted him.

"John, this pardon will be granted, if it is granted, in London. Not in Nuneaton. Those who decide on it will know nothing of Back Lane, of Jane and John Bacon. They will know what we tell them."

"We must tell the truth, wherever it's heard."

"Of course. But not the whole truth." He noticed that, in spite of himself, the shopkeeper's cold reserve was beginning to rekindle into something like approval so he continued. "Apart from us, who knows the child is safe, apart from a dozen or so people in Back Lane, Nuneaton?"

Astley had to fight back an involuntary surge of local patriotism as he heard Will's scoffing pronunciation of the place names. Grudgingly his warmth for their original idea returned but he let Will speak further, whose voice dropped a little into slight concern.

"There is one possible problem though."

But Astley had anticipated this.

"Don't worry about Haddon, Will. He won't get involved of his own accord. He's got no axe to grind against Mary. If the law decides to spare her life, he'll have no quarrel with that."

The younger man didn't question Astley's opinion. He knew it rested firmly on reliable knowledge and insight. He listened, regaining his fervour as the older man spoke.

"Asked, he'll answer truthfully, of course. But why should anyone question him? No. The request for a pardon must be judged on the power of our plea alone. Then we, Mary has a chance. A real if small chance."

Neither of them spoke again until the cab finally reached the railway station. They shook hands, a long, firm handshake then Will hurried towards the platforms.

"I'll write to you soon …," Astley called after him, and checked himself wisely before using Will's name.

Within minutes of arriving home, Astley began drafting the petition. Succinct, forceful and without recrimination, the short text pleased him and for the first time his hopes began to feel a rational if still flimsy platform beneath them. Of course the petition would go to the Home Office who would pass it on to a group of high court judges. They would meet informally, probably in a London gentlemen's club and decide whether to recommend mercy or not. Then they would pass it back to the Home Office to either formally reject it or to obtain royal approval. It was hard for Astley to imagine that Justice Coleridge would not be involved somewhere in the process. And this disturbed him. Coleridge was no run-of-the-mill judge. In addition to being the nephew of the poet, he had been the friend of Thomas Arnold, founder of Rugby School, and also of one of the most controversial figures in the Anglican Church, John Keble. A man of immense erudition, with total faith in and commitment to Christianity and connections at the highest level, the judge's integrity and authority were beyond even the slightest doubt. Not even the slur of privileged birth could be used to detract from his achievements and his status. From humble yeoman stock he had risen by virtue of sheer application and ability to become the most respected assizes judge in the land. The shopkeeper knew all this. His involvement in the Chartist movement and his reading about trials and legislation had confronted him on more than one occasion with the judge's name. He knew that even if the appeal were to be referred to the appeals court then, of all English judges, Coleridge was the one whose initial judgement was least likely to be revised. He therefore based the text on purely humanitarian grounds, tacitly accepting the legal validity of the guilty verdict but pleading for a revised sentence of fifteen years transportation and allowing the child to remain with the mother. Perhaps after they had dined, if the brandy had been mellow, the oysters fresh and the waiters servile and attentive, the appeal judges might just possibly feel benign enough to let this woman live.

Astley knew, however, that the outcome of a petition to this court and the chances of it gaining the Royal Pardon, the only legal means of averting the execution, were also dependent on the influence and standing of those supporting the petition. The signature of John Astley, shopkeeper, former Chartist and son of a radical anarchist was not destined to carry much weight. He made up a list of local dignitaries, beginning with Newdigate, Chetwoode and Dugdale and ending with Craddock, Buchanan and Muscat. Within an hour he had scored out every one of the names. He knew they would either refuse their support or that their support might prove to be even detrimental to Mary's cause. He felt his precious but meagre optimism begin to disappear. It was now dark. He poured himself a brandy, lit a cigar from the candle on his desk and leaned back in his leather armchair. Closing his eyes he imagined himself visiting Mary in jail, telling her of the petition, giving her hope and then returning, Lizzie on his arm, to inform her that she had been granted a Royal Pardon. She would take Lizzie from him and hug and kiss her, knowing that they would at least be able to spend the punitive years, hard and arid as they would certainly be, together. He opened his eyes and all he could see was the bluish smoke swirling tantalisingly away from him, as elusive and as intangible as the dream he was chasing. He wanted desperately to visit her but he wouldn't, couldn't do so unless he thought the petition would have some chance of success. And that depended on the sponsor as much as on the persuasiveness of its argumentation.

It was only when Will's letter arrived a few days later informing Asley that he had indeed been elected as a Radical

Member of Parliament that Astley laughed at himself again for overlooking such a glaringly obvious solution to his problem.

Chapter 33

Unlike in the dream induced by a large brandy and a good cigar taken in the cosiness of his own shop, when Astley visited Mary it was not with Lizzie on his arm but with the lawyer Dennistoun a stride or two behind him, stopping every twenty yards or so to transfer his bulging briefcase from one hand to the other, checking the time on his pocket watch each time he did so as though time were out to trick him into missing his lunch. They were greeted personally by the Governor Mr Stanley and, after a few minutes, were led by a heavily-built female turnkey through the warren of tunnelled corridors, through iron doors and down rough stone steps to the cells. In the centre of the chamber flanked on three sides by the rows of cells Mary was already seated a the table used for visits when the cell was too small or the visitors too important. Apart from Dennistoun only her sisters had visited her since the trial and they had done nothing but weep and hug her and tell her how they wished she hadn't done such a wicked thing but they loved her all the same. As usual her thoughts were on Lizzie but she smiled slightly when she saw John. The two men sat down opposite her and it was almost a minute before Astley spoke in a deliberately low voice, almost a whisper.

"Mary, we want to try to obtain a Royal Pardon."

As soon as he spoke, some of the women moved from their bunks where they were lying or from the back of their cells where they were standing, and hugged themselves against the bars of the cell doors. They made no secret of their interest and one them shouted:

"Speak up, will you? We all want to hear. We don't get much to occupy our minds in here! Mary'll tell us about it later so you might as well let us hear what you've got to say. That's right, ain't it Mary love?"

She turned towards the woman and nodded.

"Let them hear you, John," Mary said. We've got few secrets from one another in here."

Dennistoun had taken out some papers and a quill and as usual was, to the delight of the prisoners, already twirling it above his head. He was expecting the customary shrieks of laughter though he still hadn't worked out what caused them.

"A Royal Pardon. We're asking them to change the sentence to transportation."

He didn't wait for her to ask. "And for Lizzie to be with you." He could see she turning the abruptly delivered message over in her mind. "You'd be in prison with hard labour and your work would pay for your and Lizzie's keep, first with you, then somewhere near."

"So at first I'd be with her then, close to her?"

Astley nodded.

"And we'd see each other every day?"

Astley looked at the lawyer who replied with what Astley suspected was a deceptively knowing air:

"I can't voucher for every day. But often. Yes, I'd say often. Frequently even."

He drew spirals in the air above his head as if to lend added subtlety to this distinction.

Oblivious to the delighted shrieks of the women, Mary pondered what Astley had said.

"But why should they? They sentenced me. Why should they change the sentence?"

The laughter stopped immediately. One or two of the inmate began to sob.

"For Lizzie's sake. To spare her …"

He stopped himself too late.

"You mean to spare her what I've done to her? Made her an orphan."

There was an unusual harshness in her voice that wounded him more than the words themselves. The prisoners heard the pain in Mary's voice and began jeering at Astley, which he tried to ignore but their sudden aggression intimidated him, despite the locked iron doors. The articulate, clear thinking man was suddenly lost for words.

"That's right, keep your big mouth shut, Half Pint!"

He raised his eyes as he caught this ferociously delivered reference to his tactlessness and lack of inches. Mary heard it too and, regretting her sharp tone, laid her hand on his.

"I know you won't judge me, John. But it's true. What I've done will cost me my life and Lizzie's too. What will become of her? When I'm not thinking of the times I spent with her I'm thinking about what's going to happen to her. When I'm dead."

Mary's conciliatory gesture and softer tone of voice silenced the women. They heard what she had said and grasped the feeling behind it.

"I was in court, Mary. I heard every word. I think I know what happened."

Again the women furthest away from where they were sitting shouted at Astley but without hostility.

"Speak up short-arse!"

"He said he was in court and knows what happened!" another women called out.

"Well, he's as short on brain as he is on legs then, because only Mary knows what really happened. That's right, Mary, love?"

385

"Careful what you say, Mary! I don't trust the pen-twizzler further than I can spit against the wind!"

Dennistoun suddenly realised the taunt was directed at him and he looked up abruptly. He stood up and whispered in Astley's ear.

"I think it would indeed give you both more freedom to express yourselves openly if I were not present."

As the door closed behind the lawyer, Mary spoke steadily, deliberately.

"I'm glad he's dead. And I had a hand in it. I won't deny that. But it wasn't murder."

She looked at her friend but he remained silent.

"Why did it have to come to this? Is there any good served in taking my life and ruining Lizzie's? He was making our life hell. His death gave us the chance to live. Does it matter so much now how it came about?"

"The judges think it matters, Mary. The jury found you guilty of murder. They believe you have to be punished for that, whatever the consequences. But if we can convince them that they'd be punishing Lizzie, an innocent child, at the same time, there might be a chance they'll change the sentence."

All the women were absolutely quiet. Most were standing at the doors of their cells, their arms holding the bars above their head, extended upwards like the bare branches of dead trees.

"And I'd be with her?"

Astley nodded towards the lawyer's empty chair.

"He says it's possible. For a time. The sentence might be for life but perhaps they'd pardon you after ten, fifteen years. Until then, you'd be little better than a slave."

"Slavery doesn't frighten me. My life with him was no better than slavery. At least my body would be my own. When he was alive, even that belonged to him and he thought he could do what he wanted with it. A husband's rights and a wife's duties,

Constable Haddon called it when I told him he'd tried to take me by force."

"I came here to give you a little hope, Mary. It's a faint hope. This might give you comfort."

He took a small, thick book from the side pocket of his jacket. As she slowly became aware that it was a Bible her eyes opened wide in astonishment. He kept his eyes fixed steadily on hers to stop her speaking and said firmly.

"The Governor has approved it. Read it when you are alone."

He wanted to hug her, to tell her that, whether it was murder or manslaughter or an accident, that he wanted her to live, that he wanted, like her, the death of her husband to be the cause of her freedom not of her death. But he knew that these were thoughts that he would carry with him to the grave because he would not live to see the day when he might express them. And so he contented himself with the simple truth.

"I'll do everything in my power for you, Mary my love."

The small, neat man turned and walked slowly down the middle of the gallery, cells on either side of him, towards the broad iron doors which the turnkey opened to let him out. The women, rowdy and uncouth while he was speaking, now kept silent, touched by his awkward but honest attempts to help Mary, and some even glanced at him grudgingly as he walked slightly self-consciously down the avenue between the cells. Only when the door closed with a loud clang and the heavy key was turned in the lock did the tension in women's limbs relax. Some of them slumped against the cell doors and others lay on their narrow beds, some stretched out on their backs, others curled up like sleeping children. The guard took Mary by the elbow and led her gently to her cell where she could try to nurture her tiny hope and at the same time steel herself for disappointment. When guard had gone, she opened the bible at the beginning of the New Testament, where Will's letter, a folded thin sheet of paper, had been placed. She read it slowly several times.

> *Mary, there are many things I could and want to say to you but this is not the right time. But there is something important I have to tell you. John has asked me to sign the plea for your Pardon. I am in two minds about his request and I want you to understand why. On the one hand, there is nothing I wouldn't do to help you escape the terrible situation you are in. But, though I am now a Member of Parliament, I am unknown, obscure. My name, in itself, carries no weight. I do, however, know persons who are more influential than myself and am determined to beg them for their support. I have great confidence that at least one of them will agree to give it. We are doing all we can. Please believe in my enduring love, yours, Will.*

So her first angry thought was that Will was putting his own security first as always. She fought against the resentment and contempt for him she felt returning. But, as she re-read the letter, she wondered if what he wrote was not in fact true. Perhaps it was better to win more influential signatures. And she herself had insisted he stayed away from Nuneaton when she was under suspicion. Perhaps she should have let him return. If he had lied on oath and said they hadn't been lovers, then there would have been no need for her to choose between the truth and another lie. But when she told him to stay away she hadn't really thought that Haddon would arrest her. Once they'd buried Thomas she would be free, she had thought. Now she was being told to hope again. A frail hope but one fixed on something real; a petition for mercy, instead of death by hanging, years of virtual slavery. A grim enough alternative but they would be years spent with contact to Lizzie and years that would one day be the past. It wasn't as strong as hope but something like comfort stirred inside her.

Chapter 34

It was the unbearable inactivity when so much needed to be done that made Astley visit Jane. The house was spotlessly clean, the child asleep and she was alone downstairs. She was as taut and tidy as ever, dressed in the customary decent black but there was something in her movements he had never noticed before. He might have called it joy if he hadn't known her so well. He decided it was a sense of triumph. After some tense moments John came to the point.

"Mrs Bacon, the last time I asked you to let Mary see her child, you refused. I've come to ask you to reconsider that answer."

"The child's entrusted to my care Mr Astley. I have the right to decide. After all there's no father to do so is there?"

"Yes, I know the magistrates put the child in your care. Otherwise goodness knows what would have become of her."

"The workhouse. She'd have gone to the workhouse. I've saved her from that at least. For the time being anyway."

Astley was puzzled.

"For the time being?"

"Yes, of course. I told the magistrate of my promise to, to her. That if she ever came back I'd return the child to her."

"If she ever came back?"

"Of course she won't come back. We all know that. But they said that must remain open until…" She left the sentence unfinished but Astley completed it.

"Until the execution?"

She gave no answer and no sign she had heard him.

She looked compulsively up at the ceiling separating her from the child. When she spoke she spat out the words like small sharp objects.

"She won't come back now or ever! God won't let that happen!"

He watched her stand up, pace around the kitchen, wipe the already pristine stove and sensed the pent-up energy in this sinewy figure. She sat down again and her thoughts seemed to have calmed, even softened her so he took his chance.

"Then let her see the child. Just once. Give her this one last memory she can take with her to the grave. Please! Why can't you grant her that?"

She stood up, but this time calmly, almost serenely, looking out of the window in the direction of the barren yard and the rough piece of land beyond it with its scruffy bushes and the clucking hens. Her face and voice though told him she must have been seeing something else something far beyond the confines of the garden. She turned her eyes directly on him and spoke slowly and steadily with the assurance of simple but ultimate knowledge.

"I always asked myself why the Lord gave her a child and denied me one even though that was what I most longed for. For years I couldn't understand and I thought He wanted to test my faith in Him and in His justice. But I could never understand why He did that by rewarding her. Now I understand. He gave her the child to punish her all the more when she lost it."

She turned so suddenly that Astley drew back instinctively in his chair.

"And by doing that, He made me a part of His plan. I won't betray or disappoint Him, Mr Astley. Not for the momentary pleasure of the harlot!"

He realised there was no point staying longer but anger mingled with his resignation. All he was asking for was a single act of charity and this woman was denying it in the name of God. And so he couldn't resist the one parting shot, almost a jibe.

"You know, Mrs Bacon, there's man's law too as well as God's in this land."

She didn't appear to be listening so he continued, wanting to ensure she felt some discomfort if not pain from his darts.

"And that's why we'll be appealing. For a Royal Pardon."

He was at the door now and she still didn't appear to have registered anything of what he had said and this stung him try once more to shake her placid smugness.

"So your sister-in-law may in fact return one day after all and hold you to your promise!"

He left and as he scurried along Back Lane towards the main street he knew he shouldn't have said what he'd said. It was unkind, whether she deserved it or not. And it was gratuitous. But he couldn't quite rid himself of a residue of satisfaction in his regret at having goaded her. He shrugged off any further thoughts of it. After all, even if she had taken in what he'd said, which he doubted, there was nothing any of them could do until the decision on the plea for mercy would be made, nothing except wait and hope.

*

Some days before the petition was to be presented, Astley received a letter from Will. He knew it would contain news about the support he had been trying to win for the pardon so he opened it gingerly, knowing that its contents might indicate that the plea either still had a chance or that all hope had already gone forever. He slit the envelope open with his fine brass paper knife and spread the letter open and flattened it out on his desk before beginning to read. Fraught with suspense and a desire to know at last if their efforts had even the slimmest chance of success, at the same time he wanted to postpone the finality of knowing in case the news was bad.

It wasn't. From the first words of the letter it was clear that Will was overjoyed at his success. He skipped over the first few lines, taking in only words like *enormous optimism, reason for hope* until two words stopped him and he returned to the beginning of that sentence and re-read it:

I have held back the great, astounding and staggering news until now, dear Astley, to allow your mind to prepare for its magnitude. It's simply this: Charles Dickens! Yes, my dear friend, none other than the great Charles Dickens has agreed not only to support with his signature but to help with the wording of the plea! There is not another name or person in the land who could lend our petition more weight than his! A chance meeting at the home of Mrs Elisabeth Gaskell the Manchester novelist, whose works I know you are acquainted with and admire, provided the unique almost unbelievably fortuitous opportunity to broach the subject. Dickens accepted immediately. His active opposition to public executions and to the death penalty in general meant he was already open to my requests for support and when he heard the proposed grounds for our plea he was positively enthusiastic. He even went so far as to express encouraging words about its possible success. He agreed that we should concentrate wholly on the fate of the child rather than reopen the question of guilt. Apart from the force of the case for mercy itself, this would also allow Justice Coleridge the chance to desist from opposing the granting of the pardon. This in itself would be tactically advantageous, as Coleridge's view will certainly be requested. Dickens, who knows him, assumes the eminent judge might well be present at the Home Office when the final decision is made.

Astley knew that by this time the written plea for a stay of execution and a commutation of the death into a term of imprisonment, even transportation, would now be in the hands of the Home Secretary, Sir George Grey. So there really was nothing he could do but, despite his natural aversion to undue optimism, he felt sprightly, as he walked aimlessly through the town. Suddenly finding himself at the railway station he went inside, crossed the footbridge and began to enjoy the cloudy but windless and warm early August weather. There were still few houses on this side of the railway track but there was a decent footpath between the open fields on the other side. A group of children caught his attention and he wandered towards them and, as he got nearer, saw they were feeding two large horses. A well-dressed man in his early thirties was in the paddock and there were gleaming leather harnesses draped over the sturdy wooden fencing.

"Good morning, John!"

Astley smiled by way of greeting as he recognised Henry Gilliver, now the Head Book-keeper at Muscat's thriving mill and the owner's nephew and his thoughts immediately returned to Mary. Of course, these must be the retired drays from the mill, still cared for by the company and loved by many of the town's inhabitants, especially the children. It was the animals' gentle strength the children loved. There was a power and size about them they seemed to bear almost with embarrassment, as they moved their beautiful, massive bodies delicately and precisely, painstakingly intent on avoiding inadvertent harm to anything smaller and weaker than themselves. Henry glanced several times at Astley while harnessing the two horses, until at last he thought it right to speak.

"This one here, our good lady Caroline. She's was always her favourite."

Astley glanced back at the slightly younger man but didn't feign surprise or incomprehension. Each of them knew they were both thinking about Mary although Henry hadn't used her name explicitly.

"When we kept them near the mill, I'd watch her from the office window talking to her and feeding her some scraps. Caroline always seemed to sense when Mary was there and would amble across the field to her as soon as she arrived. I don't know what it was. Maybe what Mary brought tasted better than what anybody else brought. Or maybe it was just because it was she who brought it."

The children had moved on and it was so quiet Astley could hear the insects buzzing and the low sound of a very distant train. He felt no need or urge to speak and observed Henry as he adjusted the straps, stroking, soothing and murmuring to horses as he did so. Suddenly he stopped and leaned his forehead against the side of Caroline's solid neck.

"You know, John, sometimes I was on the point of coming down. Talking to her. Even, you know, asking her for another chance. More than once. Perhaps the children here could have been ours if I had. That was before either of us was married. Now it's too late. Much too late."

The horses stood almost still as they waited with their habitual patience and the two men were equally motionless, each locked in his own thoughts of what might have been.

Chapter 35

As anticipated Justice Coleridge was asked to attend the hearing in the Home Secretary's palatial and sumptuously furnished office. There were only the four persons present, Will, Justice Coleridge, the Home Secretary and the senior civil servant who conducted the proceedings and he began at a brisk pace.

"Gentlemen, Sir George and I note with great interest that the petition is supported by none other than our greatest living novelist. We are of course not yet prepared to divulge the official decision but I can say we find both the presentation of the case and the grounds for the submission to be of considerable weight. I do not therefore anticipate a long discussion and would therefore ask Judge Coleridge if he knows of any irrefutable reason for denying the plea for a Royal Pardon."

For the first time, despite the illustrious and influential support, Will, felt an intuitive leap of hope, a physical sensation that sent blood rushing to his head.

"She's going to be spared!" he thought to himself.

"Gentlemen, Sir George. After deep and prolonged consideration I admit that the argument brought forward in the petition is a strong one. Namely, the question of what, in the event of the execution of the condemned mother, would happen to the orphaned child: if the purposes of justice would not be better served by punishing the mother severely for her crime but at the same time preventing the consequences of that from striking the child. In short might not the innocent child suffer more than the criminal parent. So strong is this argument that, had the jury proffered it as grounds for mercy during the trial itself, I might well have added my voice to the plea for mercy."

Sir George glanced surreptitiously at his pocket watch and then at his amanuensis who interrupted the judge.

"Am I therefore to assume that you have no objection to a recommendation to Her Majesty that she sign the Royal Pardon in the case of Mary Ball?"

Will rejoiced at the interjection and was almost on his feet. He could only think of taking a cab to Euston and then the train to Nuneaton. He thought it was fitting that Astley should be the one to break the news to Mary. They would travel together to the jail though. Perhaps they might even persuade Jane to accept the inevitable and allow them to take Lizzie, too.

Coleridge drew a sheet of paper from his deep pocket. "Allow me to read this letter, which came to me by special messenger two days ago. It will not take long and is of some bearing."

Grey in his capacity of Home Secretary nodded permission and the judge began to read in a precise, unemotional voice:

> *Dear Justice Coleridge, my name is Jane Bacon and I am the sister of the Thomas Ball whose wife, Mary Ball, was recently found guilty of his murder. If I am correctly informed, you, Sir, were the judge at that trial who sentenced my sister-in-law to death.*

Grey and his servant exchanged impatient glances. Why was the judge taking up so much of the Home Secretarys Time reading this letter when it was obviously going to be an additional plea for a cause already won? Will noticed the looks, but he had no objection to waiting what he was sure was only a matter of a few additional minutes. Coleridge continued:

She was sentenced to death but now I have heard by chance that friends of hers are seeking a Royal Pardon.

He emphasised just slightly the words *of hers* and it was not lost on the listeners.

Unlike my sister-in-law I am a God-fearing woman. We, myself and my husband John, are not rich but we are decent people and know our Christian duties. Now the time has come for us to fulfil those duties. I don't know what reason you can have for granting the woman a pardon but I must say this: if it is on account of the child, the daughter Elisabeth Ball, then she cannot be the reason to grant that pardon. Since her mother's arrest and imprisonment I have cared for the child. She was entrusted to me by the magistrates in this town. If the woman is hanged, as the court sentenced her after a fair trial, then I will continue to give the child, our niece, a secure home and a Christian upbringing. Fears about the child's future are not a reason for sparing the murderess' life. I write this in the sincere belief that it is God's will. Mrs Jane Bacon, Back Lane Nuneaton.

There was total silence in the room, palpable but as blank and featureless as the thick, blue velvet cloth spread over the table around which the four men were sitting. Coleridge was the first to speak.

"This letter humbles me. I bear witness to this simple woman's Christian faith and strict, uncompromising adherence to it, resisting the temptation to indulge in false notions of tenderness. She is indeed the felon's Nemesis, the instrument of God's Will and the upholder of justice."

He passed the letter to Will for him to examine. He looked at it but his eyes didn't focus on the writing and he hardly heard as the civil servant, after a brief exchange of whispers with the Home Secretary, announced that the plea for a Royal Pardon would not enjoy their support and therefore would not be endorsed by Her Majesty. The faces remained expressionless and, even when Will gathered his papers together and left the room without a word after a minute or so, no-one else had spoken. The train was well outside London by the time he could begin to order his thoughts consciously. He really had believed, was certain that Mary was going to be pardoned. At first he wondered how Jane had known about the plea for a pardon, but gradually the ruthless finality of the decision began to displace the curiosity he felt about how that decision had been reached. Now he sat alone in the carriage, moving on that two-dimensional track which knew only two diametrically opposed directions. So simple and unambiguous were his options in this form of transport which was determined not by the vehicle he sat in but by the invisible, inexorable metal parallels laid on massive wooden sleepers across a bed of stone and fixed to last forever with thick iron pins and bolts. He felt that something in his life had come to an end and that to dwell on it would only impair his progress now. The train had left Rugby and would soon be approaching Nuneaton. He could interrupt the journey there and speak with Astley personally, even visit John and try to see Lizzie for the last time. But he didn't. That would have refreshed connections, reasserted a link he now wanted to sever, this time for good. Even while the train was standing at least five minutes in the Trent Valley Station, his carriage almost adjacent to the waiting room where they met for the last time, he stared straight ahead at the backs of the empty seat in front of him, the landscape prints, and the sturdy wooden and string luggage rack above them. He would never look sideways let alone leave the train at this station again. As the train hauled itself into motion he began to write his letter to Astley, informing him in detail but without judgement of the failure of their petition. His attachment to Mary was dissolving into nothingness with each word, with every mile. After thinking for a long time he finally composed the last sentence of his letter. He wanted to be honest with Astley and he wanted to be honest with himself. And so there was no regret or emotion, no request for sympathy or confession of guilt when he wrote it.

"John, it is hard but it is an undeniable fact about the state of my mind now. I wish I had never met her."

Chapter 36

As a condemned female prisoner, Mary had been removed to a more isolated part of the prison with no contact to the other inmates. The isolation had numbed her so that when she read the lawyer's letter it was without emotion. It was almost as if the proper certainty of death had been re-established and that the tiny glimmer of hope had been an intrusive distraction which had now been dealt with. With the small but regular rations of food, the guard also sometimes brought verbal messages from the other prisoners. Apart from this brief communication she spent most of the day lying on her bunk, her open eyes fixed on the crudely bricked ceiling, trying to concentrate her thoughts on her daughter but involuntarily letting them wander haphazardly over her own past; faces, moments, feelings, all of them ending with regret, some with revulsion, except those involving Lizzie. In the sun on the yard behind the houses, gurgling her chuckles at the placid but alert William; the bossy demands for attention from this tiny, helpless creature and the way she kicked her legs and waved her arms as soon as Mary came into her sight. And then suddenly without warning, like the stoop of a hawk, an unwanted, menacing intrusion from somewhere deep in her consciousness would penetrate into her thoughts. Sometimes it was the horrific, silent vision of Polly, blood gushing from the deep gashes on each side of her throat. More frequent and even more painful, though, was the sudden memory of those piercing moments of insight, when first Henry and then Will retreated into their own territory of self-interest. Her isolation from Will didn't frighten her. She had already found the strength to deal with that. But she could not completely reconcile herself to the act of desertion, to the simple fact that he was capable of abandoning her and Lizzie to live, as far as he knew, the rest of their lives with Thomas. Without need of the word, she felt betrayal as an emotion, a sensation, as if something soft and reassuring had slid out of her, as a fire goes out, leaving a cold emptiness in her stomach. Thomas had never really betrayed her because she had never associated hope or aspiration with him. Those years between her marriage and meeting Will; how many? six? eight? Like nothing, like space, like the barren expanses of clay fields around the shallow coal mines near her home. All she could remember of those times was of herself and Jane standing over short, narrow graves. Perhaps it would have been better if all her life had been like that; barren and flat, without hope or love, and so no remorse. If she could only have found consolation somewhere else; in the Church, like Jane; in gin, opium or respectability; or in reckless luxury, like Elisabeth. But she knew that she'd really had no choices. She'd lived day in, day out until something good happened to her. At first she had believed that it had been Will but, after he had left her, without a word, to oil his skin, she knew it was Lizzie. Will's desertion had toppled her; but it was a no more than a great gust of wind compared with the crippling blow Thomas dealt her with when he refused to let her leave with the child. Will's withdrawal had shocked, numbed, and hampered her, but she had buffeted her way forwards. Thomas' power to divide her from her daughter had paralysed her, threatened her existence and devitalised her completely. Only his death had allowed her to move again, to feel that brief sensation of release from the tangle of forces dragging her into desperation.

The cell door clanged open and the female guard shook Mary by the arm.

"Mary, come on. Get up! The chaplain wants to see you. Make yourself decent."

She buttoned Mary's prison dress to the throat, tried to make her long black hair presentable by running her fingers through it and tapped her gently on the cheeks to encourage a little colour. They walked through long stony corridors, down slabs of steps, through iron doors and then up a winding staircase into the chapel, where the prison Chaplain, the Reverend Chapman, a tall heavily built man dressed in a long black frock coat, was waiting for them. At the top of the slightly angled steps, Mary supported herself on the stark iron railing, looking down at four rows of long, slightly curved stone benches, six-foot high trellised, wooden screens shielding the locutory from view and an Anglican altar with a few lighted candles, barely visible from where she stood. Though the prison director, Stanley, strictly forbade female prisoners being left alone with men, the guard obeyed the minister when he signalled her to leave them. He drew back the heavy curtain, expecting Mary to enter meekly and confess. Instead she sat down on the edge of the cold granite slab, as far from him as possible.

"Ball, it's my duty to prepare you spiritually for your execution. Do you understand that?"

The word *execution* shot through her like a flash of sharp pain and jolted Mary out of her indifference to where she was. As if her other senses had also been activated she felt the coldness of the windowless chapel and smelled the musty, dank air.

"You mean repent?"

He began to doubt the woman's mental faculties, even perhaps her sanity. He had heard from others that she still professed her innocence but he knew from experience that when execution was certain, all but the deranged would confess their crimes, in the hope of alleviating their sufferings in the eternity that awaited them.

"Child, you know that our Saviour died to free us from sin? Through repentance you achieve absolution. Please, sit down here."

He indicated the opening to the small, curtained area reserved for private rituals. As no response came from Mary, he sat down beside her on the stone bench and waited. Perhaps she still hadn't understood why she was there.

"You may confess here if you wish. Though you may be overheard."

He prompted her:

"Confess the sin you committed, beg the Lord for forgiveness and mercy and say that you repent."

He began again:

"If you wish, repeat the words …"

Without warning she interrupted him.

"What should I repent? That I am glad my husband died? Is my relief at his death the sin you mean? I can't think of any other."

The minister began vaguely to suspect that what he had at first mistaken for confusion and ignorance was in fact a stubborn resistance.

"You rejoice in the death of the man who took you as his wife? That indeed would be a sin in itself. But you are here to crave God's forgiveness for breaking one of the ten commandments. Though I suspect you have flaunted more of God's laws. Murder and adultery …"

"He was fool. A brute."

"God is his, our only judge! And in the name of God, you have been found guilty of murder!"

"If there is a God, then he was my witness. He must know I bear no guilt."

The chaplain sprang to his feet and began pacing from one side of the narrow chapel to the other, his heavy nailed boots thudding on the stone floor. The guard, who had seated herself in the corridor outside the chapel, sensed from the noise that something was going on and, fearing Stanley might admonish her for leaving Mary alone even with a minister, she carefully opened the door slightly.

"You, a common sinner, you dare to invoke the Lord God as your witness! Do you know what a blasphemy that is?" Instead of calming himself, he became more agitated and his vexation turned into outrage. Under his breath he repeated Mary's words to himself.

"*If there is a God!* You doubt His existence? You use his name in vain. You voice that doubt to me, His vicarious minister on earth?"

Mary watched the enraged priest dispassionately. He saw this and took it for insolence.

"Do you know, woman, do you know what will happen to you if you do not repent?"

"I'll never see my daughter again whether I repent or not. Nothing worse can happen to me."

"Hellfire. For eternity. Not the transitional flames of purgatory. There is no purging of unrepentant sinners. There is not forgiveness without contrition! No abatement. No relent."

Unable to comprehend her apparent immunity to the terrifying truth of his words, he wrung his hands and his eyes darted around the small, dimly lit chapel as if searching for some instrument to communicate his meaning. He had books with vivid illustrations depicting the tortures of hell. But they were not here in the chapel. He thought of reciting some passage of poetry or a Biblical text to convey to her the horrors of eternal damnation. Would she understand, even listen? Then he stopped abruptly and walked purposefully towards the altar and took one of the large, bright candles fixed into a brass holder. As he turned towards Mary, he didn't hear the rapid footsteps receding down the corridor as the matron hurried towards the staircase leading to where Stanley had his office.

Mary, in the loose-fitting grey flannel prison tunic, almost the same colour as the stone she sat on, didn't move when he sat down to her right, gripping the candle in his right hand. Without warning he pushed the sleeve of her dress up to her shoulder and wound his free arm around her left arm, gripping her wrist so that the whole underside of her forearm was exposed outwards. His massive body was pressed against hers so that she had to struggle and support herself to avoid toppling over under his weight. His face was so close she could smell his breath and see the bloodshot streaks in his eyes. He held the candle so that the flame was just a few inches from her nose.

"Just one little, white flame. You see it. Now you will feel it."

She thought he was going to push it into her face and she turned her head away but he ran it up and down her bare underarm so that she could just feel the heat.

"But when it stops and focuses its point on one spot, you feel that even just one flame can burn."

He contorted her arm so that the pale, tender underside was directly over the sharp tip of the flame. He held both her limb and the candle perfectly still so that the concentrated heat cut like a hot needle through the skin into the raw flesh. Mary closed her eyes as tightly as she could as the pain seared into her. Unable to move in any direction, she cried out then shrieked frenziedly as he moved the candle, its tip just touching her light skin, imperceptibly slowly along the length of her lower arm. At first she writhed and twisted furiously in an attempt to free herself but the pain sapped her strength. When he felt her body becoming limp he thought she would faint and stopped, setting the candle down on the bench beside him. Mary screamed again and again as the pain failed to abate, becoming more intense as she regained her senses.

He spoke, now with an almost manic intensity.

"Now, woman, imagine heat a million times as fierce. Forever. For all eternity. That's what is waiting for you if you refuse to confess your sins!"

Between the agonising spasms, she opened her eyes and saw her scorched skin and, Stanley and the matron entered, she retaliated.

"I'll see you in hell! Pig!"

She swung her legs over the bench so that she was standing behind the chaplain, grabbed the candlestick and raised it above her head. Her raw skin stretched and she felt the pain run even more intensely as if her blood in her injured arm were suddenly scalding hot until she almost lost her balance. But she tensed her body, her eyes clenched tightly shut as she tried to concentrate her will. The chaplain, shocked by her sudden determination didn't move away but only looked up at the candlestick trembling menacingly above his head. For a moment they both froze, the man seized by fear and Mary, her taut body poised to drive the weapon down as hard as she could into her tormentor's flabby pink face, like an axe into a soft log. Stanley and the guard both stood still at the door, too far away to intervene, expecting her to smash the heavy candlestick into the chaplain's upturned face. But Mary suddenly sank onto the cold stone floor, the weapon bouncing with dull thuds from the bench onto the slabs. The matron moved across and took hold of her as gently as she could, gasping with horror when she saw her wounds. They sat side by side, Mary sobbing uncontrollably, while Stanley escorted the mumbling minister out of the chapel in search of a doctor.

*

In her cell the doctor had dressed the burn and given her an opiate to allay the pain so she lay calm and composed when Stanley sat down next to her bunk on a stool he had brought. He thought a long time before he spoke.

"Mary, you know that was perhaps your last chance to repent. I've sent Chapman away. I can try to fetch the Reverend Bellairs, from St. Michael's cathedral."

"The judge condemned me in the name of God. And that pig of a priest wanted me damned in His name."

She moved her face sideways to look him in the eye.

"Can you bring my daughter here? Let me see her once before I die."

His head dropped, his gaze fixed on the floor between his feet.

"I've tried. Jane Bacon has legal custody of the child. She refused."

Mary sensed he hadn't said everything.

"What else did she say? Tell me, please. I'll be dead tomorrow. What difference can it make now?"

"She said she would give your daughter a Christian upbringing. And that the child will be told the truth about you. So that she'll hate your memory. She made me promise to tell you that."

He expected Mary to cry or break down when she heard that, and the steady resilience in her voice surprised him.

"She can't do that. There are others in the world, not just her sort. The Farnells. John Astley. Perhaps even Will. They know deep down that I'm not wicked. That I did what I did to make life better for me and Lizzie. That's the truth."

"And what did you do? What is the truth? Why don't you repent?"

"Mr Stanley, I'll not repent before a priest. If there is a God, then he already knows what happened. But I'll confess to you. I won't deny that I wanted him dead. I mixed arsenic, all I had in the house, with salts and put some of them on the mantle piece and some on the lowest shelf in the pantry. I told him where it was. When he fetched it I knew it was poison. I willed him to take it. I heard him scrape it into his gruel. I couldn't watch it but I heard it. And knew that he was killing himself. I didn't kill him. But I let him die. I thought if he took it himself I'd not be caught up. If Jane hadn't gone to Haddon I'd be with Lizzie now. And free from him forever."

"You let him die. But you could have let him live. You chose between life and death for him."

"He did the same for me. But he had the law to help him. If he'd let me live, he'd still be alive now."

"You didn't have to resist. You could have accepted your life as it was."

"Is that what I'm being hanged for, Mr Stanley? For not accepting my life as it was?"

He realised there was nothing more he could say to her.

"Is there anything you need, Ball? Anything I can do?"

Despite his stern and inflexible moral principles, his surprise at her strength had been infected with some admiration, though he chastised himself for harbouring such feelings for a murderess. She sat up on the side of the bed so their eyes were at the same level.

"Can you write down what I just said? And make it known the best you can?"

"Your confession? I can do that."

"Promise me please. Send it to Maria Farnell and John Astley. Perhaps they'll believe it. At least then Lizzie might know the truth."

She stopped and drew a sharp breath as she felt the pain from the burn returning.

"And can the doctor give me some more medicine? It stays the pain and calms me. Perhaps I'll sleep tonight. And dream of Lizzie as if she were really here."

Chapter 37

Astley hadn't slept more than a few hours since receiving Will's letter. The failure of the petition and his remorse at his part in it created a turmoil inside him that made it difficult for him to control his thoughts. Without much sleep, food or drink he felt a strange light-headedness and he knew he had to walk. After a time, as always, the rhythm of his motion regularised his breathing and his guilt and fear settled enough for him to think clearly. He had spoken recklessly to Jane. It was a fit of sheer malevolence that had made him do so. Perhaps understandable but wrong. Absolutely wrong. If only he had kept his mouth shut! But he resisted that line of thought, of what might have been. He knew that would only agitate the emotions that stopped him thinking. After he'd walked briskly for a mile or so, his pragmatism began to return to him and assume its usual role in his mind, like the calm, determined chairman of an unruly meeting. The last time he had seen her, Mary had had two wishes. He himself had incited one of them, the faint hope that the pardon might spare her life. That hope was now completely dead. But the other, Mary's desire to see Lizzie, to hold and caress her, was that really impossible to fulfil? And this strangely had seemed the stronger, the more substantial of Mary's two hopes. He began to think without emotion, factually and analytically. The execution was set to take place in three days' time. There was not even the remotest chance that he could apply for and be granted the right to visit her now, even if he could somehow get possession of Lizzie. He saw the grim truth without the embellishment of hope. The only real opportunity Mary would have to see her child again was from the scaffolding of the gallows, as one face in the sea of faces of those who would gather to watch her hang. Astley overcame the brutality of the idea, and forced himself to accept that more could not be done. But would it be so little for Mary? To die with her child's image imprinted in her mind, perhaps turning her final moments of consciousness into joy, the last emotion she would feel. The realist asked himself if anything better could occur between the last moment of fear and the nothingness of death. Totally calm now, he determined he would do it.

Back in his study he took a sheet of paper and wrote:

Possibility 1.

I beg Jane to relent and to grant me permission to take Lizzie to the execution in the hope Mary will see her.

Possibility 2.

I take Lizzie without Jane's permission.

Intuitively he knew at once that neither possibility would work. Thorough and practical as he was, he jotted down reasons why both ideas were both unfeasible and fraught with risks. And even if they could be present, what chance would there be that Mary would see her in the vast crowd expected? His resolution already began to disintegrate, to crumble and he felt desperation regaining its hold over his ability to think. If only he hadn't gone to Jane before. If only he had resisted the temptation to goad her! Now, although he knew it would lead him again into doubt and inaction, he felt himself moving step by step into guilt and regret, as if venturing against his better judgement into the hazardous darkness of an unlit lane. He had told Jane about the plea for a Royal Pardon. That had persuaded her to act swiftly and to write the letter to pre-empt any chance of mercy. Will had spelt it out with unmistakable clarity: if Jane hadn't written the letter then the Pardon would almost certainly have been granted. Astley would carry that knowledge with him to the grave. He tried to imagine Jane's letter. Where was it now? After the hearing, all the documents would have been returned to the interested parties but hadn't Will mentioned in his letter something about taking papers with him? Will's letter was still on his desk, four closely written pages. He re-read a part of it and confirmed to himself that the text of Jane's letter was quoted verbatim. Jane's letter! Will must have it! How else could he have quoted from it at such length? Astley stood up and strode around his study, lighting all the candles and all the oil lamps, turning them to their maximum power until the room was full of a yellowish but brilliant light.

*

As Astley had calculated, Will had wasted no time and the letter arrived from Manchester two days later, giving him just one day to try to achieve his aim. He had already spoken with Constable Haddon in strict confidence. He knew that John Bacon would be out all day and that Jane would be alone with the child so he left at once towards Back Lane. Deciding to use the back door, he walked briskly down the entry, turned towards Jane's house, glancing through the kitchen window of the unoccupied house where Mary and Thomas had lived, and knocked hard against Jane's door, so loudly that the hens jumped and squawked. He saw her at the table, reading a thick black book. She started when she saw him, closed the book and opened the door immediately.

He wasted no time with greetings, somehow fearing his resolve might weaken if he were even sociable. By no means a vindictive man, he had, however, no pity for the woman now. He saw her recoil involuntarily when he held up her letter. He took no pleasure in it but he saw her writhing in shame as he read it out loud. When he finished there was a long pause before she spoke.

"What do you want? There's nothing to gain from this."

"Nothing to gain. True. But tell me, Mrs Bacon, would you be pleased for everyone to know you wrote this?"

He held the letter, waving it slightly to emphasise his words. "Perhaps there are some in your chapel who would praise your sense of Christian duty." He spoke without sarcasm in his voice this time. "But many others would take a different view. Some might even see it as a cruel, a ruthless and selfish trick to send a young mother to her death so that you could get her child. To get the child you couldn't bear yourself. Isn't that coveting your neighbour's kin, Mrs Bacon?"

He had no intention of indulging in malice for its own sake but he wanted to be sure. He wanted her to feel she had no choice but to agree to his demand. "And your husband? The good-hearted John Bacon? He may lack your extreme sense of Christian duty but he has more charity in his heart than some whole congregations. How would he see it? What would he do if he knew you had written this?" He was not even sure that John didn't in fact already know about the letter and even perhaps shared the responsibility for it but her reaction, her eyes opening wider in spontaneous alarm and her hands cupping around her face, told him at once that his intuitive guess had been accurate. He was almost there, almost sure of her assent but he wanted to eliminate all doubt. He looked up towards where he knew Lizzie would be sleeping. Then he gazed, almost glowered straight at her before he spoke slowly, a little histrionically.

"And the child? Think about her in a few years time. What will she feel about you when she knows? Knows that it was you who decided her mother's fate."

She slumped, almost collapsed onto a chair and now he knew he had won. He glanced at the book, a Bible.

"I want the child for a day. Tomorrow."

"I know what you want."

"She'll be well looked after. Constable Haddon will have us driven there in his cab. One of his maids, who nursed his children, will accompany us. You needn't worry about Lizzie's welfare." He paused.

"Do you agree to it?"

She nodded.

"Then swear. On the book before you."

She did so and Astley's resolve, which he had with such effort concentrated on his singleness of purpose, relented and softened so that he inexplicably sensed a tiny grain of pity for the woman.

"And I swear to keep my silence. Not forever but for twenty years. The truth will have to be known one day."

It was a concession he didn't have to make but at the same time he was aware that she would live with the at first irksome then, as the years went by, menacing knowledge that, assuming they all lived so long, in twenty years' time her secret would be told. He was not a man to judge others but he did feel a fleeting satisfaction at that thought.

*

When they collected the child early the next day, Astley thanked Jane demonstrably in front of her husband for her act of charity and the benevolently gullible John laid his heavy arm around her shoulder in a gesture of acknowledgement, though some surprise was mixed with the pleasure he felt at his wife's uncharacteristic kindness. The driver waited until a sharp rap against the window indicated that Astley, Haddon, the maid and Lizzie were all settled inside the police cab then let it roll slowly out of Back Lane, the dark curtains half-drawn to keep out both the dawn light and the gaze of any passers by. He needed no further instructions and was confident they would arrive well within the three hours Haddon had generously allowed for the journey, despite the number of people on the roads making the same journey on foot and the crowds they could expect to fill the streets of the town centre when they neared the jail.

*

Mary had slept peacefully that night, her last. Hetty watched over her from the cell opposite as long as there was enough light and heard her murmur incoherent words. When she moved it was not the sudden writhing that accompanies disturbed and unpleasant sleep but the slow rolling movements of deep, placid slumber. In the morning she drank some tea and clergymen were there, praying but she was unaware of them taking her through heavy doors in gloomy corridors. In the Governor's office she was conscious of the drone of voices and, glancing out of the large window, could see the crowds already assembled in Pepper Lane. Then, as if it were a signal that events were to move forward faster and with more intent towards their conclusion, the guards pinioned her arms behind her back, tying them with a coarse rope at the elbows. She winced as the tightened rope stretched the skin under the bandage of her injured arm and the guard regretted his clumsiness but didn't speak. Then they strode without haste but with purposeful steps in an orderly, silent column. At first they moved deeper into the gloom of the County Hall then out of a side doorway and into a narrow alley, enclosed on all four sides by high brick walls. As they turned toward Cuckoo Lane, one prison wall was on their left and another directly behind them. Flanked on the right by the side wall of the building they had just left, Mary could see the high wall to the street looming in front of them with the Lodge Gate placed exactly in its centre. Mary stopped before they reached the gate and the procession halted, too. The matron in a coarse black dress next to her became nervous, fearing all the solemn and important men might blame her for the delay her charge was causing and was about to speak to her. Mary looked up at the patch of blue sky above her, breathed in deeply and the guard heard her say quietly, as if to herself:

"Let her be there! At least that. Please!"

Later the guard told Astley that she thought that Mary had meant in heaven when she looked up and said *Let her be there!* but later realised what she really meant.

And then they moved on, through the massive arched gate. As they emerged onto Cuckoo Lane, the matron tugged at Mary's shoulder to turn her sharply to the left and follow the others who, after a few yards stopped and stood in a row with their backs to the prison yard wall. She walked past them and now, directly in front of her, were the steps of the scaffolding, mounted against the wall that faced St Michael's Cathedral. Almost within touching distance, the front row of the crowd was prevented by a waist-high, stable railing from getting closer. Beyond this enclosure that had been erected all around the scaffolding and draped in heavy black cloth, the area was packed, the heads of the spectators forming a surface as dense as the cobbles embedded in the ground they stood on. The churchyard wall, the graveyard behind it, even the battlements and roof of the cathedral were all occupied by faces straining for a view of Mary as she slowly but without hesitation ascended the wooden stairs. As she reached the top platform of the gallows the already low murmur of the vast crowd ceased completely and there was total silence. The woman guarding her remained at the top of the steps and Mary walked the few yards to where the hangman stood alone. As she turned, her back towards the prison wall, looking over the upturned faces which filled the thirty yards between the barriers and the churchyard wall, many saw her large, round eyes open as wide as possible. They perhaps thought it was her fear of death intensifying her final perceptions of life. The guard saw it too, but only later did she realise that this was Mary's one last, futile effort to make out her daughter's face in the blurred mass of people below. George Smith, the executioner, dressed as usual in his long white coat and black top hat, moved her forwards, politely, almost apologetically, until she was only one step away from the trap door. She looked across at the cathedral. Then her face turned upwards so that she was looking along its soaring spire then into the cloudless sky above. It was exactly ten o'clock and the church bells began to peel, shattering the silence with their fragmentary, almost dissonant ringing clatter of sound. The executioner placed the rough noose around her neck, at first avoiding as much contact with her pale skin as possible, then adjusted it, gently ushering her short distance forwards onto the square trap. He checked with a glance that her head was directly below the cross beam of the gallows to ensure a swift, perpendicular and merciful descent. Proud of his craft, he had already made arrangements to ensure the time between Mary's fall and her death would be as short as possible. He glanced at the Sheriff who nodded almost imperceptibly his assent and then things occurred that seemed to many to be simultaneous, but to the few involved in their sequence, each was distinct and each separate moment was caught in its brief entirety. The hangman raised the black hood above her head and was about to lower it over her face when there was a flurry of movements and some restrained shouts at the front of the crowd directly in front of Mary. A shrill voice cried out the single word: "Mary!" Both she and the hangman looked down to where Haddon with all his strength, determination and the authority of his uniform had caused the commotion, bustling people out of the way to form a narrow space around Astley, who was holding Lizzie as high as his diminutive build allowed. His stomach was pressed against the straight barrier in front of him and there was an almost perfect semi-circle of free space more than a foot wide around him so that he was as clearly visible as if a beam of light had been pointed exactly at him and the child he held in outstretched hands in front of him. Mary looked straight into her child's face for the few seconds the hangman needed to recover his concentration. With her arms bound tightly behind her back and the loop of rope already around her neck, she was unable to move but Astley and others closest to the scaffold saw her face, until then set hard in an expressionless stare, relax into something like a smile just before the hangman pulled down the hood. And it was at this moment that the woman guard understood. A second later the trap door banged open and she fell with a dull, loud thud. The executioner knew he had done his work well and that she had lost consciousness forever. Astley hugged the child to his chest and despite the tears he felt a deeply comforting, impregnable certainty that Mary's had an instant before her death recognised her beloved daughter and that her last emotion had been one of joy. There had been no more time for fear.

In the prison some of the women had heard the trap door slam open, then almost instantaneously the tremendous thud as Mary fell like a heavy sack, the force of her arrested fall making even the sturdy scaffolding shudder momentarily. Most of them were already crying desperately; others sat on the edge of their bunks, feeling confused and slightly guilty at the exhilaration they got from the morning's excitement. Only Hettie stood leaning against her cell door, looking strangely resolute in the helplessness of her captivity.

Epilogue

It was almost a year before Lizzie Farnell returned to Coventry. With her daughter sleeping on her arm she entered the station and was relieved that Constable Robinson was still there and seemed to be alone. He recognised her immediately and came towards the door to meet her. She handed him the death mask, wrapped carefully in heavy brown paper even before either of them spoke.

"Relieved to see it again after so much time Constable?"

He smiled, taking her elbow and leading her to a chair while he spoke:

"I don't know if it would have been missed, you know. But anyway I'd have got it back if need be. He might be retired but Constable Haddon still knows pretty much everything that happens in his old patch."

She drank the water he'd given her.

"I suppose I'd better be off."

"It's good of you to make the journey, Mrs Farnell. Especially with the child to carry. Couldn't you have left ..."

He paused while he tried to guess the baby's gender.

"A girl. Elisabeth Jane Farnell. We call her Lizzie though," Lizzie said to help him.

"Couldn't you have left her at home?"

As if sensing she was the subject of their conversation the child stirred drowsily and as soon as she became aware of her mother's closeness she smiled.

"Yes, William, my husband, is at home. He wanted to come with us, but I wanted my daughter to be here with me. Just the two of us."

The policeman knew immediately that this woman had made the strenuous journey only to return.

"Do you mind if I come with you?"

He locked the door of the station behind them and in silence they walked the few hundred yards to the space between The Holy Trinity Church and the County Hall where the prison yard had been. Lizzie stood with her back to the church, facing the side wall of the red-brick building. The outside wall, where the scaffolding had been erected, had also been demolished but it didn't matter.

"Look, Lizzie. This is where it was." She moved a few yards away from the imaginary wall in the direction of the cathedral. "And this is where John held me up, so that she could catch one last glimpse of me before she died. Like this." She turned to face where the wall had been and help her child as high as she could. Suddenly she noticed Robinson watching her.

"I bet you think I'm daft as a brush, don't you constable? But I know she doesn't understand. I just wanted her to be here. At least be here once. You know. She's healthy now. But who knows?"

"Mrs Farnell ..."

She interrupted him.

"Please, call me Lizzie. You've been so helpful about this. Though it must make you wonder if I'm a little bit silly."

She knew he didn't but she looked at him quizzically. He just smiled and she felt a strange warmth about his understanding and support. He took her elbow and they walked diagonally across the space in front of them and then turned to face the side of County Hall, about thirty yards away.

"Lizzie, you're right. This space in front of us would have been the prison yard and here. Over there, the outside wall with the scaffolding and, well, the rope and the trap door."

It may have been a flurry of pigeons or the constable's hand stretching out in the direction of the wall, but at that moment the child jerked her head around so that she too was looking in the same direction as her mother and this stranger. They both noticed but neither of them commented.

"And where we're standing …" He looked down at the paved street under their feet. "This very spot, that's where she is."

The child was now wide awake and gurgling happily and her hands were in her mother's long black hair. Lizzie looked down too and though she understood exactly what he meant, she asked:

"What do you mean – *where she is*?"

"This is where she was buried. Ten feet directly below us. The unmarked, unconsecrated grave Judge Coleridge ordered."

The tiny daughter felt the slight, sudden tension in her mother's body, sensed perhaps the sombreness that surrounded her, as if a cloud had passed in front of the bright sun and cast a faint but perceptible shadow over her. It was exactly ten o'clock. Lizzie had planned that carefully but even so was startled when without warning the peeling of the bells tumbled into a rapid cascade of orchestrated chimes. The child was silent, puzzled, almost frightened for a few moments but then began to chuckle and babble merrily again as her mother kissed her gently and lovingly stroked her head.

It was a minute before Lizzie spoke and Constable Robinson watched her attentively all the time, trying to anticipate her reaction. Finally she said:

"I wish I could plant a tree here. So that its roots could go down and touch her bones. And so that people could see that something important happened here and not forget it." She suddenly became embarrassed at the emotion in her voice. "Sorry, Constable, we have to be catching the train."

She shook his hand and was walking away from him before he could speak. He remained where he was, watching her, knowing he would never forget that moment. His last glimpse of her was from behind as she hurried across the square towards the railway station. Before she disappeared he had one final sight of half of little Lizzie's face, her bright inquisitive eyes and her stubby nose, as she pushed her head up indomitably, impertinently to get a good view over her mother's shoulder in the direction where the flock of pigeons was resettling.

*

Will Bacon, one of Manchester's Members of Parliament, first made a name for himself in the debate around the Divorce Bill in 1857. Though it shifted the administration of divorce from Parliament to the courts, the Act did not significantly alter the grounds for divorce or the law governing property rights of husband and wife. Nonetheless, many public figures, including Justice Coleridge, saw it as a severe infringement on the sanctity of matrimonial bondage and feared it would lead to widespread promiscuity. Essentially he shared the view of the Ecclesiastical Commission of 1847 which he had advised on legal issues and which stated that whenever conflict arose in a marriage ...

> ... it is the duty of a wife to conform to the tastes and duties of her husband, to sacrifice much of her own comfort and convenience to his whims and caprices, to submit to his commands and to endeavour, if she can, by prudent resistance and remonstrance, to induce a change and alteration in

that behaviour of his which she finds distasteful or even injurious.

Will voted for the Bill but in a maiden speech which increased his standing and reputation as a promising Radical, he attacked it relentlessly for redefining the wife as part of the husband's chattel and reaffirming the virtual impossibility for a woman to obtain divorce. Even Conservatives, many opposed to the legal provision of any kind of divorce, attacked the dual standards of the Bill which granted the husband the right to divorce on the grounds of his wife's adultery but denied the same right to women. In his scathing and ironical verbal onslaught against the Bill, Will quoted Dr Samuel Johnson's assessment of the respective rights of husband and wife regarding adultery:

> *Between a man and his wife, a husband's infidelity is nothing. Wise married women do not trouble themselves about the infidelity of their husbands. The difference between the two cases is boundless. The man imposes no bastards on his wife. A man, to be sure, is criminal in the sight of God, but he does not do his wife any very material injury if he does not insult her; if, for instance, he steals privately to her chambermaid; Sir, a wife ought not greatly to resent this.*

Though greatly applauded, the quotation's barbs were blunted somewhat by the fact that the majority in both Houses almost certainly agreed with the Doctor's opinion.

Another question he approached was the care of children. The law, as laid down both by Equity and Common Law Judges was, that a man, however wicked, had a right to the custody of his children, and the Courts could not give them to an innocent woman. But on this point also, his amendment was defeated. His final parting shot in the debate was to quote the great legal expert and architect of the modern constitution, Blackstone:

> *By marriage, the husband and wife are one person in law; that is, the very being of legal existence of the woman is suspended during the marriage, or at least is incorporated and consolidated into that of the husband: ... So great a 'favourite' is the female sex of the laws of England.*

Despite being lost on many members of the House, who saw nothing so objectionable in the idea that, legally speaking, a woman in many respects ceased to exist on marriage, the speech established Will as an informed and eloquent speaker. Subsequently, women's rights became one of the banners which heralded and promoted his political career. In Manchester he had already become friends with many the leading Unitarians in his constituency, especially the novelist Mrs Elisabeth Gaskell. When attending parliament in the capital, he was a popular guest at the dinner parties of the liberal, reforming movement within the social life of the city. At the home of the flamboyant publisher Chapman he was seated next to Marianne Evans, herself living in a scandalous relationship with a married man, George Lewes, who, as a consequence of the divorce laws, was both unable to obtain divorce from his extravagant wife and was financially crippled by the payments he was obliged to make to her and his four children.

Although Evans, or Mrs Lewes as she insisted on being inaccurately addressed, had already by 1858 successfully published Scenes of Clerical Life, much of which was based on real events in the Nuneaton of the early 1830s, under the name of George Eliot, the true identity of the author was still not public knowledge. Only when she mentioned in passing that her home town was Nuneaton did Will remember that he had seen her in Astley's shop but, as she obviously did not recognise him, he chose not to disclose that to her. Though they talked most of the evening mainly on the rights of women and the North-South divide that occupied many intellectuals, neither of them, of course, mentioned Mary. Almost ten years had passed since that obscure, almost anonymous provincial woman had died on the scaffold. Evans had read the reports of the trial and execution in the Coventry Herald, which belonged to her close Coventry friends the Brays, but her recollection of the case had retreated deep into the archives of her memories. Will had not yet managed to suppress his memories of Mary, let alone forget her and it often caused him discomfort when some chance word or event recalled those times. However, he saw no point in mentioning her to Mrs Lewes, especially as it may have risked embarrassing, even annoying this respected and influential woman. Later in the evening Will was introduced to Barbara Leigh-Smith, the daughter of the wealthy Radical MP for Norwich. Unlike Evans, Leigh-Smith, better known as Mme Bodichon, was directly involved in the movements for the rights of women and helped publish a monthly journal devoted to this cause, its main demands being the right for women to enter certain professions and to personally own their earnings as well the vote for the wives of enfranchised men. In 1859 she introduced Will to a fellow feminist, the daughter of a rich Birmingham businessman, and they married in 1860.

For Mary's childhood friend, Lizzie Johnson, the day of the execution was, although she was not even present, an enormously important event. With her newly-wedded husband, Charles Hardcastle, she had provided entertainment for the sizable number of well-heeled spectators who had arrived in Coventry to witness and be a part of the festivities arising from the hanging. Lizzie, or Madam Elisabeth as she was known, and Hardcastle had met at what was for both of them the perfect moment. Operating on the edge or even beyond the law, she needed protection which did not incur dependence. Hardcastle had some money to invest as well as the expertise Elisabeth required. Not only could he recruit men to dissuade competitors' incursions into his wife's business interests, but his ability to manipulate by means of persuasion if possible and by means of intimidation if necessary, and, even more important, his vast network of contacts, both secured and expanded their business. In Coventry they had provided only the gentry and the upper echelons of the Church with the services they desired. They had done it with such discretion and to such a high degree of satisfaction that they instantly became the first address whenever the most demanding and financially powerful clients sought the ideal provider. Their ability to offer regular, well-paid assignments attracted the cream of the profession, mainly female but also, if required, male.

Neither Hardcastle nor Elisabeth knew who the woman was whose execution had attracted such masses of people to the town. The name had only been briefly known to him and, even if he had retained it, there were many of the same name. Elisabeth had known and forgotten so many girls and young women in the last sixteen years or so that it was unlikely she remembered her childhood friend, whom she had only known by her maiden name, Polly Wright. Either way, the immensely popular desire to witness the death by hanging was a windfall for their already lucrative trade. Amoral, commercially unassailable, they conducted themselves through their unconsummated marriage of convenience, feeling neither anxiety nor hope, neither sorrow nor joy.

In the 1851 census Lizzie Ball is listed as the niece of Jane and John Bacon of Back Lane Nuneaton. The Farnells, with their growing brood of children, lived next door. Though Jane never missed an opportunity to chide and goad the child with taunts about her mother's wickedness and how she would follow her to hell if she didn't show less headstrong waywardness, if not out of fear of God then out of gratitude to her aunt and uncle, Lizzie remained wilful. Hours spent locked in the darkness of the pantry under the stairs, occasional lashes with willow whips, even threats of being manacled to hell's furnaces for eternity alongside her murderous mother, couldn't undo the knot within her spirit. Her instinctive defiance grew strong and confident, and her pride became dignity by the time she was a handsome young woman of sixteen. Though she recognised the debt she owed her aunt and sometimes cried for shame at her own recalcitrance, still she denied that woman that ultimate sacrifice – to dissolve the tiny but stubborn loyalty she preserved to her mother's memory.

When William Farnell, who had adored her unconditionally all their lives, pleaded with her to become his wife, he found an unexpected ally in Aunt Jane. The Farnell family had lost all contact to their Papal origins and were, in Jane's estimation, decent folk, if lacking in piety. Most of all, however, she feared where her niece's unfettered will might lead her without the harness of marriage. Besides, what other respectable man would take the daughter of a murderess? So for some time, Lizzie smothered that germinal bond with her mother. As if it were a small plant, she denied it light and the chance to grow. But her private, silent thoughts were sustenance enough to preserve its life. She complied and married William when she was eighteen.

The first child, Elisabeth Jane, was born on the 29th August, 1869 – exactly one year after William and Lizzie had married.

Though neither said it outright, Jane knew that Lizzie considered christening her Mary but in the end she deferred to her aunt's pressure and chose the conventional combination Elisabeth Jane. The second was a son. The silent bargain she had struck with her aunt on naming the daughter gave Lizzie the right now to choose as she wished. She chose William, without as expected the paternal Thomas as second name as if to say: *"If I can't call my daughter after my mother, then I won't name my son after his grandfather!"* Everyone called the child William, or Bill, except sometimes, when only Jane was with her and the children, Lizzie called him Will.

In 1884 her Aunt Jane died, and Lizzie was glad that she had already acquiesced to her aunt's express wish and had named her sixth son, born in 1879, Thomas. A few days after her aunt's death, she received an envelope from solicitors acting on behalf of John Astley. In it was the only document concerning her mother's life that Astley had withheld almost ten years before; the letter Jane had written to Justice Coleridge. Now she knew everything and this knowledge intensified and complicated the struggle she had always had with her Aunt Jane but now it was a conflict that existed only within herself. Now that her antagonist had died, it was something only she could resolve for herself. And she knew that in the end it was not contention and strife with her aunt that she sought, but peace and understanding with her mother. When her next child, a girl, was born, months after Jane's death, she was given the names Grace Mary.

After more than twenty years of marriage her husband William died in1889 and she remarried Joseph Tonks less than a year afterwards. It had caused a sensation in Nuneaton and some disbelief in her new family when she announced first the wedding, and then that it would take place in church, and not only that but in St. Michael's in Coventry, within fifty yards of where her mother had been hanged some forty years before.

She had tried to have the ceremony on the 9th of August, the date of the execution but this was not possible so they had to settle for the nearest available date. It meant considerable expense, travelling, organisation and effort to have the event take place in a city almost ten miles away, where not one single wedding guest lived. Only one person present at the ceremony, a small, grey-haired, but still dapper man in his late seventies, really understood why she had gone to such lengths to do this and why she laid her bouquet of wild flowers on the pavement some twenty yards from the churchyard wall.

In 1923, a widow again since 1914, after living through the upheavals of the War and the massive social changes that followed it, she witnessed the passing of the Divorce Law which for the first time gave women the same rights to divorce as men. An alert, single-minded woman of seventy-five who had voted Labour in 1923 to see the first Labour Government hesitantly formed at the beginning of the next year, she took out the papers Astley had allowed her to keep, the report of the trial and the penny broadsheet sold in the streets of Coventry on the day of her mother's hanging. She recalled the agonising decision her mother had made and how she had paid for it with her life. She looked at the current newspaper article announcing the new Divorce Law and thought how her life might have been different had Mary been allowed to do then what had now become at least legally possible, though still hard to put into practice. Of course Lizzie knew the stigma and discrimination women strong enough to assert their rights encountered; she had experienced some of that when she, widowed with children, had married her second husband. But her mother had proved she could have faced that and much more too. And then the question she'd asked herself so many times when reading Astley's papers for the first time: why didn't he let her go? Why did Thomas insist on his right to subject, to coerce, to own her? As a child and as a young girl,

Lizzie had spoken at every opportunity about her mother with those who knew her, especially with her mother-in-law, Mrs Farnell, who loved the woman though she had only known her for such a short time.

And now, with only a few years left to her, she confronted herself again with the hardest question of all: why didn't Mary submit? Had she thrown her life away? Would it not have been better for everybody if she had accepted her lot and stayed with her husband as her marriage oaths demanded? Would her own life have been better if her mother had lived as the law, custom and religion dictated? True, in the 1920s, her own measure of independence did have some support from the law – though little from custom or religion. But would she even have known that spirit of resistance if her mother had not flaunted the law; if she had bowed her head and said nothing; or taken refuge in the church or gin or even opium like so many had done? Lizzie imagined all kinds of outcomes to her own question but never one answer that remained permanent or complete. But of one thing she was sure. Her mother did not die for nothing. She did leave a legacy that was now entrusted to Lizzie to pass on as best she could. Thinking of how she had caressed her mother's death mask more than fifty years before, she thought of how much she had always missed the mother she had never really known and how often she had longed, ached for the lost possibility of sharing at least some part of their lives. But she refused to regret. A few years before she died in 1927, she reassembled all the papers and all the memories and, with a firm, unhesitating hand, she began to write her mother's story.

THE END